PENGUIN BOOKS

THE KISS THIEF

AN ARRANGED MARRIAGE NOVEL

L.J. Shen is a *Wall Street Journal, USA Today, Washington Post*, and #1 Amazon bestselling author of contemporary, new adult and young adult romance. Her books have been translated in over twenty different countries, and she hopes to visit all of them.

She lives in Florida with her husband, three rowdy sons and even rowdier pets. She enjoys good wine, bad reality TV shows and reading to her heart's content.

T0322258

ALSO BY
L.J. SHEN

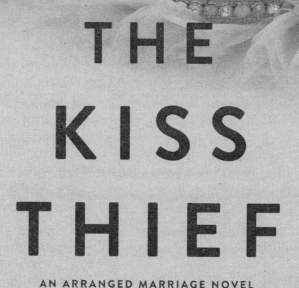

THE
KISS
THIEF

AN ARRANGED MARRIAGE NOVEL

L.J. SHEN

PENGUIN BOOKS

PENGUIN BOOKS

UK | USA | Canada | Ireland | Australia
India | New Zealand | South Africa

Penguin Books is part of the Penguin Random House group of companies
whose addresses can be found at global.penguinrandomhouse.com

First published in the United States of America by L.J. Shen 2019
First published in Great Britain by Penguin Books 2023

007

Cover design by Letitia Hasser, RBA Designs
Interior formatting by Stacey Blake, Champagne Book Design

Printed and bound in Great Britain by Clays Ltd, Elcograf S.p.A.

The authorized representative in the EEA is Penguin Random House Ireland,
Morrison Chambers, 32 Nassau Street, Dublin D02 YH68

A CIP catalogue record for this book is available from the British Library

ISBN: 978-1-405-95958-2

www.greenpenguin.co.uk

MIX
Paper | Supporting
responsible forestry
FSC® C018179

Penguin Random House is committed to a
sustainable future for our business, our readers
and our planet. This book is made from Forest
Stewardship Council® certified paper.

"It is amazing how complete is the delusion that beauty is goodness."

—Leo Tolstoy, *The Kreutzer Sonata*

SOUNDTRACK

"Young And Beautiful"—Lana Del Rey

"Take Me To Church"—Hozier

"Young God"—Halsey

"Can't Truss It"—Public Enemy

"Back To Black"—Amy Winehouse

"Nothing Compares 2 U"—Sinéad O'Connor

"Everybody Wants To Rule The World"—Tears for Fears

"I'm Shipping Up To Boston"—Dropkick Murphys

To Brittany Danielle Christina and Jacquie Czech
Martin, and to strong women everywhere.
May we be them, may we raise them, may we support them.

PROLOGUE

W HAT SUCKED THE MOST WAS THAT I, FRANCESCA
Rossi, had my entire future locked inside an
unremarkable old wooden box.

Since the day I'd been made aware of it—at six years old—I
knew that whatever waited for me inside was going to either kill
or save me. So it was no wonder that yesterday at dawn, when
the sun kissed the sky, I decided to rush fate and open it.

I wasn't supposed to know where my mother kept the key.

I wasn't supposed to know where my father kept the box.

But the thing about sitting at home all day and grooming
yourself to death so you could meet your parents' next-to-im-
possible standards? You have time—in spades.

"Hold still, Francesca, or I'll prick you with the needle,"
Veronica whined underneath me.

My eyes ran across the yellow note for the hundredth time
as my mother's stylist helped me get into my dress as if I was an
invalid. I inked the words to memory, locking them in a drawer in my brain no one else had access to.

Excitement blasted through my veins like a jazzy tune, my
eyes zinging with determination in the mirror in front of me. I
folded the piece of paper with shaky fingers and shoved it into
the cleavage under my unlaced corset.

I started pacing in the room again, too animated to stand still, making Mama's hairdresser and stylist bark at me as they chased me around the dressing room comically.

I am Groucho Marx in Duck Soup. *Catch me if you can.*

Veronica tugged at the end of my corset, pulling me back to the mirror as if I were on a leash.

"Hey, ouch." I winced.

"Stand still, I said!"

It was not uncommon for my parents' employees to treat me like a glorified, well-bred poodle. Not that it mattered. I was going to kiss Angelo Bandini tonight. More specifically—I was going to let *him* kiss *me*.

I'd be lying if I said I hadn't thought about kissing Angelo every night since I returned a year ago from the Swiss boarding school my parents threw me in. At nineteen, Arthur and Sofia Rossi had officially decided to introduce me to the Chicagoan society and let me have my pick of a future husband from the hundreds of eligible Italian-American men who were affiliated with The Outfit. Tonight was going to kick-start a chain of events and social calls, but I already knew whom I wanted to marry.

Papa and Mama had informed me that college wasn't in the cards for me. I needed to attend to the task of finding the perfect husband, seeing as I was an only child and the sole heir to the Rossi businesses. Being the first woman in my family to ever earn a degree had been a dream of mine, but I was nowhere near dumb enough to defy them. Our maid, Clara, often said, "You don't need to meet a husband, Frankie. You need to meet your parents' expectations."

She wasn't wrong. I was born into a gilded cage. It was spacious, but locked, nonetheless. Trying to escape it was risking death. I didn't like being a prisoner, but I imagined I'd like it much less than being six feet under. And so I'd never even dared to peek through the bars of my prison and see what was on the other side.

My father, Arthur Rossi, was the head of The Outfit.

The title sounded painfully merciless for a man who'd braided my hair, taught me how to play the piano, and even shed a fierce tear at my London recital when I played the piano in front of an audience of thousands.

Angelo—you guessed it—was the perfect husband in the eyes of my parents. Attractive, well-heeled, and thoroughly moneyed. His family owned every second building on University Village, and most of the properties were used by my father for his many illicit projects.

I'd known Angelo since birth. We watched each other grow the way flowers blossom. Slowly, yet fast at the same time. During luxurious summer vacations and under the strict supervision of our relatives, Made Men—men who had been formally induced as full members of the mafia—and bodyguards.

Angelo had four siblings, two dogs, and a smile that would melt the Italian ice cream in your palm. His father ran the accounting firm that worked with my family, and we both took the same annual Sicilian vacations in Syracuse.

Over the years, I'd watched as Angelo's soft blond curls darkened and were tamed with a trim. How his glittering, ocean-blue eyes became less playful and broodier, hardened by the things his father no doubt had shown and taught him. How his voice had deepened, his Italian accent sharpened, and he began to fill his slender boy-frame with muscles and height and confidence. He became more mysterious and less impulsive, spoke less often, but when he did, his words liquefied my insides.

Falling in love was so tragic. No wonder it made people so sad.

And while I looked at Angelo as if he could melt ice cream, I wasn't the only girl who melted from his constant frown whenever he looked at me.

It made me sick to think that when I went back to my all-girls' Catholic school, he'd gone back to Chicago to hang out and talk and *kiss* other girls. But he'd always made me feel like I was The Girl. He sneaked flowers into my hair, let me sip some of his wine when no one was looking, and laughed with his eyes whenever I spoke. When his younger brothers taunted me, he flicked their ears and warned them off. And every summer, he found a way to steal a moment with me and kiss the tip of my nose.

"*Francesca Rossi, you're even prettier than you were last summer.*"

"*You always say that.*"

"*And I always mean it. I'm not in the habit of wasting words.*"

"*Tell me something important, then.*"

"*You, my goddess, will one day be my wife.*"

I tended to every memory from each summer like it was a sacred garden, guarded it with fenced affection, and watered it until it grew to a fairy-tale-like recollection.

More than anything, I remembered how, each summer, I'd hold my breath until he snuck into my room, or the shop I'd visit, or the tree I'd read a book under. How he began to prolong our "moments" as the years ticked by and we entered adolescence, watching me with open amusement as I tried—and failed—to act like one of the boys when I was so painfully and brutally a girl.

I tucked the note deeper into my bra just as Veronica dug her meaty fingers into my ivory flesh, gathering the corset behind me from both ends and tightening it around my waist.

"To be nineteen and gorgeous again," she bellowed rather dramatically. The silky cream strings strained against one another, and I gasped. Only the royal crust of the Italian Outfit still used stylists and maids to get ready for an event. But as far as my parents were concerned—we were the Windsors. "Remember the days, Alma?"

The hairdresser snorted, pinning my bangs sideways as she completed my wavy chignon updo. "Honey, get off your high horse. You were pretty like a Hallmark card when you were nineteen. Francesca, here, is *The Creation of Adam*. Not the same league. Not even the same ball game."

I felt my skin flare with embarrassment. I had a sense that people enjoyed what they saw when they looked at me, but I was mortified by the idea of beauty. It was powerful yet slippery. A beautifully wrapped gift I was bound to lose one day. I didn't want to open it or ravish in its perks. It would only make parting ways with it more difficult.

The only person I wanted to notice my appearance tonight at the Art Institute of Chicago masquerade was Angelo. The theme of the gala was Gods and Goddesses through the Greek and Roman mythologies. I knew most women would show up as Aphrodite or Venus. Maybe Hera or Rhea, if originality struck them. Not me. I was Nemesis, the goddess of retribution. Angelo had always called me a deity, and tonight, I was going to justify my pet name by showing up as the most powerful goddess of them all.

It may have been silly in the 21st century to want to get married at nineteen in an arranged marriage, but in The Outfit, we all bowed to tradition. Ours happened to belong firmly in the 1800s.

"What was in the note?" Veronica clipped a set of velvety black wings to my back after sliding my dress over my body. It was a strapless gown the color of the clear summer sky with magnificent organza blue scallops. The tulle trailed two feet behind me, pooling like an ocean at my maids' feet. "You know, the one you stuck in your corset for safekeeping." She snickered, sliding golden feather-wing earrings into my ears.

"That"—I smiled dramatically, meeting her gaze in the mirror in front of us, my hand fluttering over my chest where the note rested—"is the beginning of the rest of my life."

CHAPTER ONE

Francesca

"I DIDN'T KNOW VENUS HAD WINGS."

Angelo kissed the back of my hand at the doors to the Art Institute of Chicago. My heart sank before I pushed the silly disappointment aside. He was only baiting me. Besides, he looked so dazzlingly handsome in his tux tonight, I could forgive any mistake he made, short of coldhearted murder.

The men, unlike the women at the gala, wore a uniform of tuxedos and demi-masks. Angelo complemented his suit with a golden-leafed Venetian masquerade mask that took over most of his face. Our parents exchanged pleasantries while we stood in front of each other, drinking in every freckle and inch of flesh on one another. I didn't explain my Nemesis costume to him. We'd have time—an entire lifetime—to discuss mythology. I just needed to make sure that tonight we'd have another fleeting summer moment. Only this time, when he kissed my nose, I'd look up and lock our lips, and fate, together.

I am Cupid, shooting an arrow of love straight into Angelo's heart.

"You look more beautiful than the last time I saw you." Angelo clutched the fabric of his suit over where his heart beat, feigning surrender. Everyone around us had gone quiet, and I noticed our fathers staring at one another conspiratorially.

Two powerful, wealthy Italian-American families with strong mutual ties.

Don Vito Corleone would be proud.

"You saw me a week ago at Gianna's wedding." I fought the urge to lick my lips as Angelo stared me straight in the eyes.

"Weddings suit you, but having you all to myself suits you more," he said simply, throwing my heart into fifth gear, before twisting toward my father. "Mr. Rossi, may I escort your daughter to the table?"

My father clasped my shoulder from behind. I was only vaguely aware of his presence as a thick fog of euphoria engulfed me. "Keep your hands where I can see them."

"Always, sir."

Angelo and I entwined our arms together as one of the dozens of waiters showed us to our seats at the table clothed in gold and graced with fine black china. Angelo leaned and whispered in my ear, "Or at least until you're officially mine."

The Rossis and Bandinis had been placed a few seats away from each other—much to my disappointment, but not to my surprise. My father was always at the heart of every party and paid a pretty penny to have the best seats everywhere he went. Across from me, the governor of Illinois, Preston Bishop, and his wife fretted over the wine list. Next to them was a man I didn't know. He wore a simple all-black demi-mask and a tux that must've cost a fortune by its rich fabric and impeccable cut. He was seated next to a boisterous blonde in a white French tulle camisole gown. One of dozens of Venuses who arrived in the same number.

The man looked bored to death, swirling the whiskey in his glass as he ignored the beautiful woman by his side. When she tried to lean in and speak to him, he turned the other way and checked his phone, before completely losing interest in all things combined and staring at the wall behind me.

A pang of sorrow sliced through me. She deserved better than what he was offering. Better than a cold, foreboding man who sent chills down your spine without even looking at you.

I bet he could keep ice cream chilled for days on end.

"You and Angelo seem to be taken with one another," Papa remarked conversationally, glancing at my elbows, which were propped on the table. I withdrew them immediately, smiling politely.

"He's nice." I'd say 'super nice', but my father absolutely detested modern slang.

"He fits the puzzle," Papa snipped. "He asked if he could take you out next week, and I said yes. With Mario's supervision, of course."

Of course. Mario was one of Dad's dozens of musclemen. He had the shape and IQ of a brick. I had a feeling Papa wasn't going to let me sneak anywhere he couldn't see me tonight, precisely because he knew Angelo and I got along a little too well. Papa was overall supportive, but he wanted things to be done a certain way. A way most people my age would find backward or maybe even borderline barbaric. I wasn't stupid. I knew I was digging myself a hole by not fighting for my right for education and gainful employment. I knew that *I* should be the one to decide whom I wanted to marry.

But I also knew that it was his way or the highway. Breaking free came with the price of leaving my family behind—and my family was my entire world.

Other than tradition, The Chicagoan Outfit was vastly different from the version they portrayed in the movies. No gritty alleyways, slimy drug addicts, and bloody combats with the law. Nowadays, it was all about money laundering, acquisition, and recycling. My father openly courted the police, mingled with top-tier politicians, and even helped the FBI nail high-profile suspects.

In fact, that was precisely why we were here tonight. Papa had agreed to donate a staggering amount of money to a new charity foundation designed to help at-risk youth acquire a higher education.

Oh, irony, my loyal friend.

I sipped champagne and stared across the table at Angelo, making conversation with a girl named Emily whose father owned the biggest baseball stadium in Illinois. Angelo told her he was about to enroll into a master's program at Northwestern, while simultaneously joining his father's accounting firm. The truth was, he was going to launder money for my father and serve The Outfit until the rest of his days. I was getting lost in their conversation when Governor Bishop turned his attention to me.

"And what about you, Little Rossi? Are you attending college?"

Everyone around us was conversing and laughing, other than the man in front of me. He still ignored his date in favor of downing his drink and disregarding his phone, which flashed with a hundred messages a minute. Now that he looked at me, he also looked *through* me. I vaguely wondered how old he was. He looked older than me, but not quite Papa's age.

"Me?" I smiled courteously, my spine stiffening. I smoothed my napkin over my lap. My manners were flawless, and I was well versed in mindless conversations. I'd learned Latin, etiquette, and general knowledge at school. I could entertain anyone, from world leaders to a piece of chewed gum. "Oh, I just graduated a year ago. I'm now working toward expanding my social repertoire and forming connections here in Chicago."

"In other words, you neither work nor study," the man in front of me commented flatly, knocking his drink back and shooting my father a vicious grin. I felt my ears pinking as I blinked at my father for help. He mustn't have heard because he seemed to let the remark brush him by.

"Jesus Christ," the blond woman next to the rude man growled, reddening. He waved her off.

"We're among friends. No one would leak this."

Leak this? Who the hell was he?

I perked up, taking a sip of my drink. "There are other things I do, of course."

"Do share," he taunted in mock fascination. Our side of the table fell silent. It was a grim kind of silence. The type that hinted a cringeworthy moment was upon us.

"I love charities…"

"That's not an actual activity. What do you *do?*"

Verbs, Francesca. Think verbs.

"I ride horses and enjoy gardening. I play the piano. I…ah, shop for all the things I need." I was making it worse, and I knew it. But he wouldn't let me divert the conversation elsewhere, and no one else stepped in to my rescue.

"Those are hobbies and luxuries. What's your contribution to society, Miss Rossi, other than supporting the US economy by buying enough clothes to cover North America?"

Utensils cluttered on fine china. A woman gasped. The leftovers of chatter stopped completely.

"That's enough," my father hissed, his voice frosty, his eyes dead. I flinched, but the man in the mask remained composed, straight-spined and, if anything, gaily amused at the turn the conversation had taken.

"I tend to agree, Arthur. I think I've learned everything there is to know about your daughter. And in a minute, no less."

"Have you forgotten your political and public duties at home, along with your manners?" my father remarked, forever well mannered.

The man grinned wolfishly. "On the contrary, Mr. Rossi.

I think I remember them quite clearly, much to your future disappointment."

Preston Bishop and his wife extinguished the social disaster by asking me more questions about my upbringing in Europe, my recitals, and what I wanted to study (botany, though I wasn't stupid enough to point out that college was not in my cards). My parents smiled at my flawless conduct, and even the woman next to the rude stranger tentatively joined the conversation, talking about her European trip during her gap year. She was a journalist and had traveled all over the world. But no matter how nice everyone was, I couldn't shake the terrible humiliation I'd suffered under the sharp tongue of her date, who—by the way—got back to staring at the bottom of his freshly poured tumbler with an expression that oozed boredom.

I contemplated telling him he didn't need another drink but professional help could work wonders.

After dinner came the dancing. Each woman in attendance had a dance card filled with names of those who made an undisclosed bid. All the profits went to charity.

I went to check my card on the long table containing the names of the women who'd attended. My heart beat faster as I scanned it, spotting Angelo's name. My exhilaration was quickly replaced with dread when I realized my card was full to the brim with Italian-sounding names, much longer than the others scattered around it, and I would likely spend the rest of the night dancing until my feet were numb. Sneaking a kiss with Angelo was going to be tricky.

My first dance was with a federal judge. Then a raging Italian-American playboy from New York, who told me he'd come here just to see if the rumors about my looks were true. He kissed the hem of my skirt like a medieval duke before his friends dragged his drunken butt back to their table. *Please don't ask my father for a date*, I groaned inwardly. He seemed like the kind of rich tool who'd make my life some variation of *The*

Godfather. The third was Governor Bishop, and the fourth was Angelo. It was a relatively short waltz, but I tried not to let it dampen my mood.

"There she is." Angelo's face lit up when he approached me and the governor for our dance.

Chandeliers seeped from the ceiling, and the marble floor sang with the clinking heels of the dancers. Angelo dipped his head to mine, taking my hand in his, and placing his other hand on my waist.

"You look beautiful. Even more so than two hours ago," he breathed, sending warm air to my face. Tiny, velvety butterfly wings tickled at my heart.

"Good to know, because I can't breathe in this thing." I laughed, my eyes wildly searching his. I knew he couldn't kiss me now, and a dash of panic washed over the butterflies, drowning them in dread. What if we couldn't catch each other at all? Then the note would be useless.

This wooden box will save me or kill me.

"I'd love to give you mouth-to-mouth whenever you're out of breath." He skimmed my face, his throat bobbing with a swallow. "But I would start with a simple date next week, if you are interested."

"I'm interested," I said much too quickly. He laughed, his forehead falling to mine.

"Would you like to know when?"

"When we're going out?" I asked dumbly.

"That, too. Friday, by the way. But I meant when was the point in which I knew you were going to be my wife?" he asked without missing a beat. I could barely bring myself to nod. I wanted to cry. I felt his hand tightening around my waist and realized I was losing my balance.

"It was the summer you turned sixteen. I was twenty. Cradle snatcher." He laughed. "We arrived at our Sicilian cabin late. I was rolling my suitcase by the river next to our adjoined cabins when I spotted you threading flowers into a crown on the dock. You were smiling at the flowers, so pretty and elusive, and I didn't want to break the spell by talking to you. Then the wind swiped the flowers everywhere. You didn't even hesitate. You jumped headfirst into the river and retrieved every single flower that had drifted from the crown, even though you knew it wouldn't survive. Why did you do that?"

"It was my mother's birthday," I admitted. "Failure was not an option. The birthday crown turned out pretty, by the way."

My eyes drifted to the useless space between our chests.

"Failure is not an option," Angelo repeated thoughtfully.

"You kissed my nose in the restroom of that restaurant that day," I pointed out.

"I remember."

"Are you going to steal a nose-kiss tonight?" I asked.

"I would never steal from you, Frankie. I'd buy my kiss from you at full price, down to the penny," he sparred good-naturedly, winking at me, "but I'm afraid that between your shockingly full card and my obligations to mingle with every Made Man who was lucky enough to snatch an invitation to this thing, a raincheck may be required. Don't worry, I've already told Mario I'd tip him generously for taking his time fetching our car from the valet on Friday."

The trickle of panic was now a full-blown downpour of terror. If he wasn't going to kiss me tonight, the note's prediction would go to waste.

"Please?" I tried to smile brighter, masking my terror with eagerness. "My legs could use the break."

He bit his fist and laughed. "So many sexual innuendos, Francesca."

I didn't know if I wanted to cry with despair or scream with frustration. Probably both. The song hadn't ended yet, and we were still swaying in each other's arms, lulled inside a dark spell, when I felt a firm, strong hand plastered on the bare part of my upper back.

"I believe it's my turn." I heard the low voice booming behind me. I turned around with a scowl to find the rude man in the black demi-mask staring back at me.

He was tall—six-foot-three or four—with tousled ink-black hair smoothed back to tantalizing perfection. His sinewy, hard physique was slim yet broad. His eyes were pebble gray, slanted, and menacing, and his too-square jaw framed his bowed lips perfectly, giving his otherwise too-handsome appearance a gritty edge. A scornful, impersonal smirk graced his lips and I wanted to slap it off his face. He was obviously still amused with what he thought was a bunch of nonsense I spat out at the dinner table. And we clearly had an audience as I noticed half the room was now glaring at us with open interest. The women looked at him like hungry sharks in a fishbowl. The men had half-curved grins of hilarity.

"Mind your hands," Angelo snarled when the song changed, and he could no longer keep me in his arms.

"Mind your business," the man deadpanned.

"Are you sure you're on my card?" I turned to the man with a polite yet distant smile. I was still disoriented from the exchange with Angelo when the stranger pulled me against his hard body and pressed a possessive hand lower than socially acceptable on my back, a second from groping my butt.

"Answer me," I hissed.

"My bid on your card was the highest," he replied dryly.

"The bids are anonymous. You don't know how much other people have paid," I kept my lips pursed to keep myself from yelling.

"I know it's nowhere near the realm of what this dance is worth."

Un-freaking-believable.

We began to waltz around the room as other couples were

not only spinning and mingling but also stealing envious glances at us. Naked, raw ogles that told me that whomever the blonde he'd come to the masquerade with was, she wasn't his wife. And that I might have been all the rage in The Outfit, but the rude man was in high demand, too.

I was stiff and cold in his arms, but he didn't seem to notice—or mind. He knew how to waltz better than most men, but he was technical, and lacked warmth and Angelo's playfulness.

"Nemesis." He took me by surprise, his rapacious gaze stripping me bare. "Distributing glee and dealing misery. Seems at odds with the submissive girl who entertained Bishop and his horsey wife at the table."

I choked on my own saliva. Did he just call the governor's wife horsey? And *me* submissive? I looked away, ignoring the addictive scent of his cologne, and the way his marble body felt against mine.

"Nemesis is my spirit animal. She was the one to lure Narcissus to a pool where he saw his own reflection and died of vanity. Pride is a terrible illness." I flashed him a taunting smirk.

"Some of us could use catching it." He bared his straight white teeth.

"Arrogance is a disease. Compassion is the cure. Most gods didn't like Nemesis, but that's because she had a backbone."

"Do you?" He arched a dark eyebrow.

"Do I…?" I blinked, the courteous grin on my face crumpling. He was even ruder when we were alone.

"Have a backbone," he provided. He stared at me so boldly and intimately, it felt like he breathed fire into my soul. I wanted to step out of his touch and jump into a pool full of ice.

"Of course, I do," I responded, my spine stiffening. "What's with the manners? Were you raised by wild coyotes?"

"Give me an example," he said, ignoring my quip. I was beginning to draw away from him, but he jerked me back into his arms. The glitzy ballroom distorted into a backdrop, and even though I was starting to notice that the man behind the demi-mask was unusually beautiful, the ugliness of his behavior was the only thing that stood out.

I am a warrior and a lady...and a sane person who can deal with this horrid man.

"I really like Angelo Bandini." I dropped my voice, slicing my gaze from his eyes and toward the table where Angelo's family had been seated. My father was sitting a few seats away, staring at us coldly, surrounded by Made Men who chatted away.

"And see, in my family, we have a tradition dating back ten generations. Prior to her wedding, a Rossi bride is to open a wooden chest—carved and made by a witch who lived in my ancestors' Italian village—and read three notes written to her by the last Rossi girl to marry. It's kind of a good luck charm mixed with a talisman and a bit of fortunetelling. I stole the chest tonight and opened one of the notes, all so I could rush fate. It said that tonight I was going to be kissed by the love of my life, and well..." I drew my lower lip into my mouth and sucked it, peering under my eyelashes at Angelo's empty seat. The man stared at me stoically, as though I was a foreign film he couldn't understand. "I'm going to kiss him tonight."

"That's your backbone?"

"When I have an ambition, I go for it."

A conceited frown crinkled his mask, as if to say I was a complete and utter moron. I looked him straight in the eye. My father taught me that the best way to deal with men like him was to confront, not run. Because, this man? He'd chase.

Yes, I believe in that tradition.

No, I don't care what you think.

Then it occurred to me that over the course of the evening, I'd offered him my entire life story and didn't even ask for his name. I didn't want to know, but etiquette demanded that I at least pretend.

"I forgot to ask who you are."

"That's because you didn't care," he quipped.

He regarded me with the same taciturnity. It was an oxymoron of fierce boredom. I said nothing because it was true.

"Senator Wolfe Keaton." The words rolled off his tongue sharply.

"Aren't you a little young to be a senator?" I complimented him on principal to see if I could defrost the thick layer of asshole he'd built around himself. Some people just needed a tight hug. Around the neck. Wait, I was actually thinking about choking him. Not the same thing.

"Thirty. Celebrated in September. Got elected this November."

"Congratulations." *I couldn't care less.* "You must be thrilled."

"Over the goddamn moon." He drew me even closer, pulling my body flush against his.

"Can I ask you a personal question?" I cleared my throat.

"Only if I can do the same," he shot.

I considered it.

"You can."

He dipped his chin down, giving me permission to continue.

"Why did you ask to dance with me, not to mention paid good money for the dubious pleasure, if you obviously think everything I stand for is shallow and distasteful?"

For the first time tonight, something that resembled a smile crossed his face. It looked unnatural, almost illusory. I decided he was not in the habit of laughing often. Or at all.

"I wanted to see for myself if the rumors about your beauty were true."

That again. I resisted the urge to stomp on his foot. Men were such simple creatures. But, I reminded myself, Angelo thought I was pretty even *before*. When I still had braces, a blanket of freckles covering my nose and cheeks, and unruly, mousybrown hair I had yet to learn how to tame.

"My turn," he said, without voicing his verdict on my looks.

"Have you picked out names for your children with your Bangini yet?"

It was an odd question, one that was no doubt designed to make fun of me. I wanted to turn around and walk away from him right there and then. But the music was fading, and it was stupid to throw in the towel on an encounter that would end shortly. Besides, everything that came out of my mouth seemed to bother him. Why ruin a perfect strike?

"*Bandini*. And yes, I have, as a matter of fact. Christian, Joshua, and Emmaline."

Okay, I might've picked the sexes, too. That was what happened when you had too much time on your hands.

Now the stranger in the demi-mask was grinning fully, and if my anger didn't make it feel as though pure venom ran through my veins, I could appreciate his commercial-worthy dental hygiene. Instead of bowing his head and kissing my hand, as the brochure for the masquerade had indicated was compulsory, he took a step back and saluted me in mockery. "Thank you, Francesca Rossi."

"For the dance?"

"For the insight."

The night became progressively worse after the cursed dance with Senator Keaton. Angelo was sitting at a table with a group of men, locked in a heated argument, as I was tossed from one pair of arms to the other, mingling and smiling and losing my hope and sanity, one song at a time. I couldn't believe the absurdity of my situation. I stole my mother's wooden box—the one and only thing I'd ever stolen—to read my note and get the courage to show Angelo how I felt. If he wasn't going to kiss me tonight—if *no one* was going to kiss me tonight—did that mean I was doomed to live a loveless life?

Three hours into the masquerade, I managed to slip out the entrance of the museum and stood on the wide concrete steps, breathing in the crisp spring night. My last dance had to leave early. Thankfully, his wife had gone into labor.

I hugged my own arms, braving the Chicago wind and laughing sadly at nothing in particular. One yellow cab zipped by the tall buildings, and a couple huddled together were zig-zagging giddily to their destination.

Click.

It sounded like someone shut down the universe. The lamp-posts along the street turned off unexpectedly, and all the light faded from view.

It was morbidly beautiful; the only light visible was the shimmering lonely crescent above my head. I felt an arm wrap around my waist from behind. The touch was confident and strong, curving around my body like the man it belonged to had studied it for a while.

For years.

I turned around. Angelo's gold and black masquerade mask stared back at me. All the air left my lungs, my body turning into goo, slacking in his arms with relief.

"You came," I whispered.

His thumb brushed my cheeks. A soft, wordless nod.

Yes.

He leaned down and pressed his lips to mine. My heart squealed inside my chest.

Shut the front door. This is happening.

I grabbed the edges of his suit, pulling him closer. I'd imagined our kiss countless times before, but I'd never expected it to feel like this. Like home. Like oxygen. Like forever. His full lips fluttered over mine, sending hot air into my mouth, and he explored, and nipped, and bit my lower lip before claiming my mouth with his, slanting his head sideways and dipping down for a ferocious caress. He opened his mouth, his tongue peeking out and swiping mine. I returned the favor. He drew me close, devouring me slowly and passionately, pressing his hand to the small of my back and groaning into my mouth like I was water in the desert. I moaned into his lips and licked every corner of his mouth with zero expertise, feeling embarrassed, aroused, and more importantly, free.

Free. In his arms. Was there anything more liberating than feeling loved?

I swayed in the security of his arms, kissing him for a good three minutes before my senses crawled back into my foggy brain. He tasted of whiskey and not the wine Angelo had been drinking all night. He was significantly taller than me—taller than Angelo—even if not by much. Then his aftershave drifted into my nose, and I remembered the icy pebble eyes, raw power, and dark sensuality that licked flames of anger inside my guts. I took a slow breath and felt the burn inside me.

No.

I tore my lips from his and stumbled back, tripping over a stair. He grabbed my wrist and yanked me back to prevent my fall but made no effort to resume our kiss.

"You!" I cried out, my voice shaking. With perfect timing, the streetlamps came back to life, illuminating the sharp curves of his face.

Angelo had soft curves over a defined jaw. This man was all harsh streaks and cut edges. He looked nothing like my crush, even with a demi-mask on.

How did he do that? *Why* did he do that? Tears pooled in my eyes, but I held them back. I didn't want to give this complete stranger the satisfaction of seeing me crumple.

"How dare you," I said quietly, biting my cheeks until the taste of warm blood filled my mouth to keep from screaming.

He took a step back, sliding Angelo's mask off—God knows how he got his hands on it—and tossing it on the stairs like it was contaminated. His unmasked face was unveiled like a piece of art. Brutal and intimidating, it demanded my attention. I took a step sideways, putting more space between us.

"How? Easily." He was so dismissive; he was flirting with open disdain. "A smart girl, however, would have asked for the *why*."

"The why?" I scoffed, refusing to let the last five minutes register. I'd been kissed by someone else. Angelo—according to my family tradition—was not going to be the love of my life. This jerk, however…

Now it was his turn to take a step sideways. His broad back had been blocking the entrance to the museum, so I failed to see who was standing there, his shoulders slack, his mouth agape, his face gloriously unmasked, drinking in the scene.

Angelo took one look at my swollen lips, turned around, and stalked back in with Emily running after him.

The Wolfe was no longer in sheep's clothing as he made his way up the stairs, giving me his back. When he reached the doors, his date poured out as if on cue. Wolfe took her arm in his and led her downstairs, not sparing me a look as I wilted on the cement stairs. I could hear his date murmuring something, his dry response to her, and her laughter ringing in the air like a wind chime.

When the door to their limo slammed shut, my lips stung so bad I had to touch them to make sure he didn't set them on fire. The power outage wasn't coincidental. He did it.

He took the power. *My* power.

I yanked the note out of my corset and threw it against the stair, stomping over it like a tantrum-prone kid.

Wolfe Keaton was a kiss thief.

CHAPTER TWO

Francesca

A WAR RAGED INSIDE ME AS I STUDIED EVERY COBWEB and imperfection on my bedroom ceiling that night, puffing on a cigarette.

It was just a stupid, fun tradition. Hardly a scientific fact. Surely, not all the predictions written in the notes turned out to be true. I probably wouldn't even see Wolfe Keaton ever again.

However, I was bound to see Angelo soon. Even if he canceled our date next Friday, there were many weddings, holidays, and community functions we were both attending this month.

I could explain everything, face to face. One stupid kiss wasn't going to erase years of verbal foreplay. I'd even gone so far as imagining his remorse once he found out that I only kissed Senator Keaton because I thought it was him.

I put out my cigarette and lit another one. I didn't touch my phone, resisting the urge to send Angelo an over-apologetic, hysterical message. I needed to talk to my cousin Andrea about this. She lived across town and, since she was in her early twenties, was my sole, albeit reluctant, advisor when it came to the opposite sex.

A curtain of pinks and yellows fell over the sky as the

morning rolled in. Birds sang outside our limestone manor, perched on my window ledge.

I flung an arm over my eyes and winced, my mouth tasting of ash and disappointment. It was Saturday, and I needed to leave the house before my mother got any ideas. Ideas like taking me shopping for expensive dresses and grilling me about Angelo Bandini. For all the tacky clothes and shoes in my wardrobe, I was a pretty simple gal by Italian-American royalty standards. I played my part because I had to, but I absolutely hated being treated like an invalid, airhead princess. I wore little to no makeup and liked my hair the best when it was wild. I preferred horseback riding and gardening to shopping and getting my nails done. Playing the piano was my favorite outlet. Spending hours standing in a dressing room and being assessed by my mother and her friends was my personal definition of hell.

I washed my face and slipped into my black breeches, riding boots, and a white pullover jacket. I went down to the kitchen and took out my pack of Vogues, lighting one up as I nursed a cappuccino and two Advils. A plume of blue smoke rose from my mouth as I tapped my chewed-up fingernails over the dining table. I inwardly cursed Senator Keaton again. Yesterday, at the dinner table, he had the audacity to assume that not only did I choose my way of life, but I loved it, too. He never once contemplated that maybe I merely made peace with it, choosing instead to pick my battles where I would emerge the victor over those that were already lost.

I knew I wasn't allowed to have a career. I'd come to terms with that heartbreaking reality, so why, then, couldn't I have the only thing I still wanted? A life with Angelo, the only man in The Outfit I actually liked.

I could hear my mother's heels clanking upstairs as she fussed about, and the whiny old door of my father's office pushing open. Then I heard Papa barking at someone in Italian on the phone, and my mother bursting into tears. My mother wasn't a spontaneous crier, and my father wasn't in the habit of raising his voice, so both of these reactions piqued my interest.

I scanned the first floor with the open-plan kitchen and large living room bleeding into an immense balcony and spotted Mario and Stefano whisper-shouting between themselves in Italian. They stopped when they saw me looking.

I checked the overhead clock. It wasn't quite eleven.

Know that feeling of an impending calamity? The first shake of the ground beneath you, the first rattle of the coffee mug on the table before the brutal storm? That was what this moment felt like.

"Frankie!" Mama called out, her voice pitching high, "we're expecting guests. Don't go anywhere."

As if I could just up and leave. This was a warning. My skin began to crawl.

"Who's coming?" I hollered back.

The answer to my question presented itself not a second after I asked, when the doorbell rang just as I was about to climb upstairs and ask them what was going on.

I flung the door open to find my new archenemy, Wolfe Keaton, standing on the other side, wearing a spiteful sneer on his face. I recognized him without the mask even though he'd worn one for most of the evening yesterday. As much as I hated the man, he was born with an unforgettable face.

Decidedly aloof and infuriatingly elegant, he bulldozed into the landing in a Regent fit plaid suit and a tailored blazer. He immediately shook the morning dew from his loafers as his bodyguards trailed in after him.

"*Nemesis.*" He spat out the word as if *I* was the one to wrong *him*. "How are you feeling this morning?"

Shitty, thanks to you. Of course, he didn't need to know that he had any impact on my mood. It was bad enough that he deprived me of my first kiss with Angelo.

I closed the door behind him without sparing him a look, welcoming him as much as I would the Grim Reaper.

"I'm doing fantastic, Senator Keaton. In fact, I wanted to thank you for yesterday," I mentioned as I slapped my grossly polite smile on.

"You did?" He arched a skeptical eyebrow, getting rid of his jacket and handing it to one of his bodyguards since I hadn't offered to take it.

"Yes. You showed me how a real man *shouldn't* behave, proving Angelo Bandini is the man for me." His security guy hung Wolfe's jacket on one of our hangers, ignoring my presence. Keaton's bodyguards were different than Dad's. They wore actual uniforms and most likely had a military background.

"As a gentleman, you have failed me. As a con, however, I give you an A plus. Highly impressive." I gave him two thumbs-up.

"You are funny." His lips were pulled tight in a flat line.

"And you are…?" I started, but he cut me off sharply.

"An attorney at law, and therefore extremely impatient when it comes to irrelevant chatter. As much as I would love to stand here and talk to you about our lackluster first base, Francesca, I have some business to attend to. I would advise you wait until I'm done because our little banter today was just the preview."

"That was a pretty bad preview. I wouldn't be surprised if the movie tanked."

He leaned forward, entering my personal space, and chucked me under the chin, his silver eyes lighting up like Christmas.

"Sarcasm is an unbecoming trait on well-bred girls, Miss Rossi."

"Kiss-thieving wouldn't go on my list of gentlemanly things to do, either."

"You kissed me very willingly, Nemesis."

"Before I knew who you were, *Villain*."

"There will be other kisses and all of them you'll give

without my asking, so I wouldn't go around making promises that are destined to be broken."

I opened my mouth to tell him that he needed to get his head checked, but he saw himself upstairs before I could speak, leaving me on the landing, blinking away my shock. How did he even know where to go? But the answer was clear.

He'd been here before.

He knew my father.

And he didn't like him one bit.

I spent the next two hours chain-smoking in the kitchen, pacing back and forth, and making myself cappuccinos only to throw them away after one sip. Smoking was the only bad habit I was permitted to maintain. My mother said it helped with curbing my appetite, and my father was still of a generation where it was seen as sophisticated and worldly. It made me feel grown-up, when otherwise, I knew I was being babied and sheltered.

Two of my father's lawyers, and two other people who also looked like attorneys, entered our house twenty minutes after Wolfe went up the stairs.

Mama was behaving strangely, too.

For the first time since I was born, she entered Dad's office during a business meeting. She came out twice. Once to provide refreshments—a task our housekeeper Clara was normally assigned to do. The second time, she got out to the hallway upstairs, mumbling hysterically to herself and accidentally knocking down a vase.

When the office door finally clicked open after what felt like days, Wolfe was the only one who came downstairs. I stood, as if awaiting some life-threatening medical verdict. His last remark had put snakes in my stomach, and their bites were lethal and full of venom. He thought I'd kiss him again. If he asked my father for a date, though, he was going to be sorely disappointed. He wasn't Italian, wasn't from an Outfit family, and I didn't like him one bit. Three things my father ought to have taken into consideration.

Wolfe stopped at the curve of our stairs, still on the last step, silently stressing how tall and imperial he was. How small and insignificant *I* was.

"Are you ready for the verdict, *Nem*?" The corner of his lips curved sinfully.

The hairs on my arms stood on end, and I felt like I was on a roller coaster the second before it dipped. I had to take a shuddering breath and brave the waves of fear crashing against my ribcage.

"Dying for it." I rolled my eyes.

"Follow me out," he ordered.

"No, thank you."

"I'm not asking," he clipped.

"Good because I'm not accepting." The harsh words felt violent on my lips. I'd never been so rude to anyone. But Wolfe Keaton earned my wrath, fair and square.

"Pack a suitcase, Francesca."

"Excuse me?"

"Pack. A. Suitcase," he repeated slowly as though my deciphering his words was the issue, and not their irrational content. "As of fifteen minutes ago, you're officially betrothed to yours truly. The wedding is at the end of the month, which means your silly box tradition—thanks for the story, it was a nice touch in my proposal—is intact," he delivered the news coldly as the floor beneath my feet quaked and shattered, sending me spiraling into an oblivion of anger and shock.

"My dad would never do that to me." My feet seemed to glue to the ground, too scared to go upstairs and test my own words. "He wouldn't sell me to the highest bidder."

A slow smirk spread across his face. He feasted on my rage with open hunger.

"Who said my bid was the highest?"

I launched at him with everything I had.

I'd never hit anyone—was taught that as a woman, making a scene was the most common form of the lower class. So, the slap on his cheek didn't come quite with the force I was hoping for. It was more of a swat, almost friendly, that feathered his square jaw. He didn't flinch. Pity and disinterest swirled in his bottomless, sterling eyes.

"I'm giving you a couple of hours to get your things in order. Whatever's left here will stay here. Do not test me on the issue of punctuality, Miss Rossi." He entered my personal space and clasped a golden watch over my wrist.

"How could you do this?" In a heartbeat, I moved from defying him to sobbing, pushing at his chest now. I wasn't thinking. I wasn't even entirely sure I was breathing. "How did you convince my parents to give you their approval?"

I was an only child. My mother was prone to miscarriages. She called me her priceless jewel—but here I was, marked with a Gucci wristwatch by a stranger, the watch obviously a small portion of a much larger dowry that had been promised. My parents cherry-picked every admirer who approached me at public functions and were notoriously protective when it came to my friends. So much so, in fact, that I didn't have *any* friends of my own, only females who shared the Rossi name.

Every time I met girls my age, they deemed them too provocative or not sophisticated enough. This seemed surreal. But for some reason, I didn't doubt for one moment that it was also the truth.

For the first time ever, I considered my father less than a deity. He had weaknesses, too. And Wolfe Keaton had just found every one of them and exploited them to his benefit.

He shrugged into his blazer and strolled through the door, his bodyguards at his feet like loyal Labrador puppies.

I shot up to the second floor, my legs on fire, adrenaline coursing through them.

"How could you!" The first person I aimed my anger at was Mama, who promised to have my back on the subject of marriage. I sprinted toward her, but my dad held me down and Mario grabbed my other arm. It was the first time his men were physical with me—the first time *he* was physical with me.

I kicked and screamed as they pulled me out of Dad's office while my mom stood there with unshed tears brewing in her eyes. The lawyers were all hunched in a corner of the room, staring at papers and pretending that nothing unusual had happened. I wanted to scream until the entire house crumbled and buried all of us under its ruins. To shame them, to fight them.

I'm nineteen. I can run away.

But run away to what? I was completely isolated. I knew no one and nothing other than my parents. Besides, what resources would I have?

"Francesca," Papa said with a tone etched with stony determination. "Not that it matters, but it is not your mother's fault. I chose Wolfe Keaton because he's the better choice. Angelo is nice but almost a commoner. His father's father was a simple butcher. Keaton is the most eligible bachelor in Chicago, and possibly the future president of the United States. He is also considerably wealthier, older, and more beneficial to The Outfit in the long run."

"I'm not The Outfit!" I could feel my vocal cords shaking as the words tore from my mouth. "I'm a person."

"You're both," he retorted. "And as the daughter of the man who rebuilt the Chicago Outfit from scratch, you are to make sacrifices, whether you want to or not."

They carried me toward my room at the end of the hall. Mama trailed behind us, mumbling apologies I was too freaked out to decipher. I didn't, for one second, believe that my father *chose* Keaton without consulting me first. But I also knew he was too proud to ever admit it. Keaton held the power here, and I had no idea why.

"I don't want the most eligible bachelor in Chicago, the president of the United States, or the Vatican pope. I want Angelo!" I barked, but no one was listening.

I am air. Invisible and insignificant, but vital all the same.

They stopped in front of my room, their grip on my wrists tightening. My body went slack when I realized they were no longer moving, and I ventured to peer inside. Clara was stuffing my clothes and shoes into open suitcases on my bed, wiping away her tears. Mama grabbed my shoulders and turned me around to face her.

"The note said whoever kissed you would be the love of your life, didn't it?" Her red, puffy eyes danced in their sockets. She was grasping at straws. "*He* kissed you, Frankie."

"He *tricked* me!"

"You don't even really know Angelo, vita mia."

"I know Senator Keaton even less." And what I did know of him, I hated.

"He's wealthy, good looking, and has a bright future ahead of him," Mom explained. "You don't know each other, but you will. I didn't know your father before we wed. Vita mia, what is love without a little risk?"

Comfort, I thought and knew, no matter what, that Wolfe Keaton would make it his mission to make my life very uncomfortable.

Two hours later, I rolled through the black, wrought-iron gates of Keaton's estate in a black Cadillac DTS.

Throughout the drive, I had begged the young, pimply driver in the cheap suit to take me to the nearest police station, but he pretended not to hear me. I rummaged through my bag for my phone, but it wasn't there.

"Shoot!" I sighed.

A man in the passenger's seat sneered, and I noticed, for the first time, that there was also a security guard in the vehicle.

Where my parents lived in Little Italy, you could find Catholic churches galore, quaint restaurants, and busy parks overflowing with kids and students. Wolfe Keaton, however, resided on the clinical and prestigious Burling Street. His was a stark white, hulking mansion, which, even among other huge houses, looked comically big. By its size, I guessed that it had required the demolition of the properties next to it. Running over others to get his way seemed to be a pattern.

Manicured lawns and elaborative medieval-styled windows greeted me, ivy and ferns crawling through the colossal structure like a woman's possessive fingers over a man's body.

Wolfe Keaton might have been a senator, but his money did *not* come from politics.

After we rolled past the entrance, two servants opened the trunk and pulled out my numerous suitcases. A woman who looked like an older and scrawnier version of Clara appeared at the door in a stern, all-black dress and pinned silver do.

She raised her chin, scanning me with a sneer.

"Miss Rossi?"

I got out of the car, hugging my bag to my chest. The jerk wasn't even present to welcome me.

She strolled toward me, her spine ramrod straight and her hands linked behind her back as she tossed an open palm in my direction.

"I'm Ms. Sterling."

I stared at her hand without taking it. She was helping Wolfe Keaton with kidnapping and forcing me into marriage. The fact that I wasn't clubbing her with my Louboutin bag stretched my extent of civility.

"Let me show you to your wing."

"My wing?" I followed her on autopilot, telling myself—no, *promising* myself—that this was all temporary. I just needed to gather my wits and formulate a plan. This was the twenty-first century. I would be next to a cell phone and a laptop and a *police station* soon enough, and this nightmare would be over before it could even begin.

And then what? You'll defy your father and risk death?

"Yes, dear, wing. I was pleasantly surprised by how old-fashioned Mr. Keaton was in regards to his new bride. No sharing a bed before marriage." A ghost of a smile passed her lips. She was obviously a fan of the idea. That made the two of us. I'd rather scratch my own eyeballs out than share a bed with the devil.

The marbled white landing presented two separate stairways leading left and right. The portrait-adorned mint-green walls of former presidents, high, elaborate ceilings, fireplaces, and lavish courtyards peeking through the tall windows all blurred together.

I gasped when we passed by open double doors with a constructed Steinway piano surrounded by floor-to-ceiling bookshelves and what looked like thousands of books. The entire room was accented in cream and black.

"You seem young."

"That's an observation, not a question…your point?" I said unkindly.

"I was under the impression he liked his female companion older."

"Perhaps he should start by liking his female companion willing."

Jesus. I actually said that. I slapped a hand over my mouth.

"Senator Keaton never had an issue attracting women. Quite the contrary," Ms. Sterling blabbed as we made our way to the eastern side of the house. "Too many women and too much variety made him jaded. I was beginning to worry." She shook her head, a reminiscing smile on her thin lips.

So on top of everything else, he was a playboy. I cringed. Angelo, for all his life experience and ruthless upbringing, was a true gentleman. Not a virginal one—I knew—but not a skirt chaser, either.

"Then, perhaps, I should be the one worried now since I'm expected to share a bed with him," I bit out. I'd apparently checked my manners at the door, along with my freedom.

When we got to my room, I didn't stop to appreciate the canopy four-poster bed, rich velvet purple curtains, vast walk-in closet, large vanity, or even the carved oak desk and leather chair overlooking the garden. It was pushed against the window, and I had no doubt the view was mesmerizing. But I didn't care for the best view in Chicago. I wanted to be back in my child-hood home, dreaming of my wedding to Angelo.

"Make yourself comfortable. Mr. Keaton had to fly out to Springfield. He's on his way home now." She smoothed the hem of her dress. So he was a US senator. And I didn't have to ask—I knew he had purchased a private jet prior to his political gig. I knew the Members' Representational Allowance by heart be-cause my father talked about rules often. He said that in order to break them, you had to know them by heart, too. Father had paid off a lot of political figures in his lifetime.

For some reason, his having a private jet made me even more bitter. Going to work alone left a carbon footprint that would require planting a medium-sized forest to rectify. What kind of world did he want to leave for his children and grand-children when, at a moment's notice, he was on a jet headed to Springfield or DC?

It occurred to me that I hadn't tried to lure her into helping me. In fact, she might not even know I was in trouble. I caught her cold, fragile hand in mine and pulled her back as she made her way to the door.

"Please," I urged. "I know it sounds crazy, but your boss just bought me from my parents. I need to get out of here."

She stared at me and blinked.

"Oh, dear, I think I forgot to turn off the oven." She rushed outside, the door closing behind her.

I ran after her, yanking at the door handle. She *locked* me in. Shoot!

I paced back and forth, then grabbed the curtain and tore it from its rails. I didn't know why I did it. I wanted to ruin something in his house the way *he* ruined *me*. I flung myself over the bed, a scream tearing at my lungs.

I cried myself to sleep that day. In my dream, I imagined Angelo dropping in for a visit at my parents', finding out what happened with Wolfe, and then looking for me all over town. In my dream, he drove here, unable to bear the thought of me being with another man, and confronted Wolfe. In my dream, he took me away, somewhere far and tropic. Somewhere safe. This was the part where I knew it was a fantasy—if my father couldn't stop Wolfe, no man could.

When I stirred awake, the last rays of the sun lazily filtered through the tall, bare windows. My throat felt groggy and dry, and my eyes were so puffy I couldn't even open them all the way. I would kill for a glass of water, but I would die before asking for one.

The bed was dipped to one side. When I cracked my eyes open, I found out why.

Wolfe was sitting on the edge of the queen-size mattress. He stared at me with his piercing gaze and seemed to burn past skin and bones and hearts, turning them all to ash.

I narrowed my eyes, then opened my mouth to give him a piece of my mind.

"Before you say anything," he warned, pushing the sleeves of his crisp white shirt up his elbows to expose veiny, muscular, and tan forearms, "I believe an apology is in order."

"You think an apology is going to fix this?" I snapped acidly, tugging at the blanket to cover more of my body even though I was fully dressed.

He smirked, and I realized he liked our exchanges very much.

"It'd be a nice start. You said I was not being a gentleman, and I beg to differ. I honored your tradition and demanded your hand after kissing you."

Unbelievable.

Now I was fully awake, my back pressing against the headboard.

"You want *me* to apologize to *you*?"

He smoothed the soft fabric of the pressed linen, taking his time to answer me.

"Shame your parents are set in their wish to keep you an obedient little housewife. You have a natural, fast grip on things."

"You're a fool if you think I'm just going to accept you as a husband." I folded my arms over my chest.

Wolfe considered my words gravely, his fingers traveling near my ankle but not quite touching it. I'd kick him if I didn't think he'd enjoy my anger even more.

"The notion that you can touch me or what's mine in any way, other than sucking my cock whenever I'm generous enough to allow it, amuses me. Why don't we get to know each other over dinner tonight before you make any more declarations you can't back up? There are some house rules you need to obey."

Lord, I wanted to hurt him so badly it burned at my fingertips.

"Why? Because I'd rather eat rotten fruit and drink sewer water than have a meal with you," I snarled.

"Very well." He produced something from behind his back. A simple white calendar. He reached over and placed it on the nightstand next to me. It was a nice touch, after giving me the watch that felt more like a shackle than a gift.

When he spoke, he looked at the calendar, not me.

"It takes twenty-one days to form a habit. I recommend you make me a pattern of sorts. Because come August twenty-second," he announced, rising up from the bed, "you will be standing at the altar, promising me the rest of your days. A promise I intend to take seriously. You're a collected debt, a retaliation, and, quite frankly, pretty decent arm candy. Good night, Miss Rossi." He turned around and sauntered toward the door, kicking aside the curtain on his way out.

A short hour later, Ms. Sterling arrived with a silver tray containing squashed, rotten-looking fruit, and a glass of water that was freakishly gray. She stared at me with crushing misery that made her already wrinkled face appear even older.

There was an apology in those eyes.

I didn't accept it or the food.

CHAPTER THREE

Wolfe

FUCK.
    Shit.
    Cocksucker.
Asshole.
Clusterfuck.
Nutsackdouchebagbuttfuck.

Those were just some of the words I could no longer allow myself to utter, in public or otherwise, as a senator representing the state of Illinois. Serving my state—my *country*—was my only real passion. The problem was, my real upbringing was quite different from the one portrayed in the media. In my mind, I cussed. A lot.

And I especially wanted to swear right now when my bride had exasperated me to no end.

Eyes the color of crushed wildflowers and glossy, chestnut tresses so soft they were practically begging for a fist to wrap around them and pull.

Chicago's elite fell to their knees at Francesca Rossi's beauty from the moment she set foot in Chicago a year ago, and for once in their miserable lives, the hype they created wasn't completely unwarranted.

Unfortunately for me, my bride-to-be was also a spoiled, naïve, overpampered kid with an ego the size of Connecticut and zero desire to do anything that did not include horseback riding, sulking, and—this one's a wild, albeit educated, guess—popping out fair-eyed, just-as-entitled kids.

Fortunately for *her*, my bride-to-be was going to get exactly the kind of cushioned life she'd been designed to lead by her parents. Right after the wedding, I intended to shove her into a glitzy mansion on the other side of town, pad her wallet with credit cards and cash, and check in on her only when I'd need her to attend a public function with me or when I needed to tug on her father's leash. Offspring were out of the question, although, depending on her level of cooperation, which, right now, could use much improvement, she was welcome to have some through a sperm donor.

Not me.

Sterling reported back that Francesca hadn't touched her dirty water and crushed fruit and made no move to eat the breakfast that had been ushered to her room this morning. I wasn't worried. The teenybopper would eat when her discomfort turned into pain.

I leaned against the Theodore Alexander executive desk in my study, hands shoved deep inside my pockets, and watched as Governor Bishop and the police commissioner of Chicago's Police Department, Felix White, verbally sparred for twenty mind-numbing minutes.

The weekend I'd found myself engaged to Francesca Rossi on a whim also marked the bloodiest weekend on the streets of Chicago since the mid-eighties. Another reason my marriage was essential for the survival of this city. Bishop and veteran cop White both circled around the fact that Arthur Rossi was to blame, directly and indirectly, for each of the twenty-three murders between Friday and Sunday. Though neither of them said his name.

"A penny for your thoughts, Senator." White sat back in his leather chair, tossing a penny between his thumb and index toward me. I let it drop on the floor, my gaze fixed on him.

"Funny you should mention money. That's exactly what you need to fight the rising crime rate."

"Meaning?"

"Arthur Rossi."

Bishop and White swapped uneasy expressions, their faces turning a nice shade of gray. I released a chuckle. I'd take care of Arthur myself, but I needed to do it gradually. I'd just taken his most prized possession. Easing him into the new situation was essential in order to crush him in the long run.

The decision to marry Francesca Rossi—unlike the takedown of her father, which I'd planned since age thirteen—was spontaneous. First, she showed up as Nemesis, an ironic twist that put a grin on my face. Then I noticed the twinkle in Arthur's eyes as he followed her at the masquerade. He looked proud and watching him happy grated on my nerves. She was obviously his Achilles' heel. *Then* she caused a stir. Her beauty and good manners hadn't gone unnoticed. I therefore deduced that Francesca would be useful both for hanging our marriage over Arthur's head as an ongoing threat and as a way to clean up my Lothario reputation.

Bonus points: she and I were going to be the sole inheritors of the Rossi Empire. Rossi would practically sign over his business to me whether he wanted to or not.

"Sins of the father shall not be visited upon his children." *Arthur's lips trembled when I showed up at his house the morning after the masquerade. I'd texted him that same night as my date unzipped my dress pants in the limo, getting ready to suck my cock. I advised Arthur to rise early. Now, he was so pale, I thought he was going to have heart failure. Wishful thinking on my part.*

Bastard was still on both feet, staring right back at me, his gaze asking me for a solid.

"Paraphrasing from the Bible, are we?" I offered a provocative yawn. "Pretty sure there were a few commandments written there you have broken once or a thousand times."

"Leave her out of this, Keaton."

"Beg for her, Arthur. On your knees. I want to see you stripped of your pride and dignity over your silver-spooned daughter who has never known hardship. The apple of your eye, the belle of every ball in Chicago, and, quite frankly, the runner-up to be my lawful wife."

He knew exactly what I was asking—and why I was asking it.

"She is nineteen; you are thirty." He tried to reason with me. Big mistake. Once upon a time, when I tried to reason with him, it didn't work. At all.

"Still legal. A wholesome, well-mannered beauty on my arm is exactly what the doctor ordered to clean up my rather dirty reputation."

"She's no arm candy, and unless you want your first term as senator to be your last…" He balled his fists so tight, I knew they'd draw blood from his palms. I cut him off midsentence.

"You will do nothing to harm my career, seeing as we both know what I have on you. On your knees, Arthur. If you're convincing enough, I might let you keep her."

"Name your price."

"Your daughter. Next question."

"Three million dollars." The tic of his jaw matched the rhythm of his pulsing heart.

"Oh, Arthur." I cocked my head, chuckling.

"Five." His lips thinned, and I could practically hear his teeth grinding against one another. He was a powerful man—too powerful to yield—and for the first time in his life, he had to. Because what I had on him could jeopardize not only the entire Outfit, but

also his precious wife and daughter, who'd be left penniless once I threw him in the slammer for the rest of his days.

I rolled my eyes. "I thought love was priceless. How about you give me what I really want, Rossi? Your pride."

Slowly, the man in front of me—the smug mob lord whom I hated with ferocious passion—lowered himself to his knees, his face a cool mask of hatred. His wife and our respective attorneys looked down at their feet, their deafening silence ringing in the air.

He was beneath me now, humble and lost and undignified.

Through gritted teeth, he said. "I am begging you to spare my daughter. Go after me in any way you want. Drag me through court. Strip me of my properties. You want war? I will fight you clean and honorably. But do not touch Francesca."

I rolled my mint gum inside my mouth, resisting the urge to lock my jaw. I could unleash the secret I'd been holding over his head and get it over with, but the anguish Rossi had put me through stretched just like the thing in my mouth. A gum that dragged achingly slow across the years. An eye for an eye and all that bullshit. No?

"Request denied. Sign the papers, Rossi," I pushed the NDA in his direction. "I'm taking the brat with me."

Back in the present, Bishop and White had somehow managed to raise their voices to heights that would deafen whales, bickering like two schoolgirls who showed up at prom wearing the same Forever 21 dress.

"…should have been alerted months ago!"

"If I had more staff to work *with*…"

"Shut up, both of you." I cut their stream of words with a snap of my fingers. "We need more police presence in the areas prone to trouble, end of story."

"And with what budget, pray tell, should I fund your suggestion?" Felix rubbed his wobbly chin, sleek with sweat. His face was scarred, the result of bad acne, and the top of his head was shiny, his graying hair peppered around the temples.

I pinned him with a look that wiped the smug off his face. He had some extra cash lying around, and we both knew where it came from.

"You have extras," I shot dryly.

"Brilliant." Preston Bishop flung himself back on the headrest. "Captain Ethic's here to save the day."

"I'd settle for ruining yours. Which reminds me—*you* have extras, too," I deadpanned, just as the door to the study flew open.

Kristen, my masquerade date, world-class BJ giver, and a royal pain in the ass, stormed in, her eyes as wild as her hair. Since I carefully chose my female companions with zero flair for dramatics, I knew she was privy to what the gentlemen in the room hadn't found out yet. Nothing else would get her so worked up, and she did, after all, work in finding out important information.

"Really, Wolfe?" She wiped blond strands of hair from her forehead, her eyes dancing in their sockets. Her shabby appearance explained why Sterling came rushing through the door behind her, muttering redundant apologies. I shooed my housekeeper away, focusing on Kristen.

"Let's take this outside before you burst an artery on my marble floors," I suggested cordially.

"Don't be so sure I'll be the one shedding blood in this exchange," she said, wiggling her finger at me. Poor form. That was the thing about girls who came to the big city from a small Kansas town and became successful career women. That girl from Kansas? She'd always live inside her.

My office was on the west wing of my mansion, next to my bedroom and a handful of guestrooms. I led Kristen into my bedroom, leaving the door open on the off-chance she was in the mood for more than talking. She paced, hands parked on her hips. My king-size bed stood out as a reminder of the place I never had her in. I quite liked fucking women in compromising positions. Sharing a bed with someone else was not an idea I'd ever entertained seriously. I'd learned people come and go out of your life frequently and without notice. Solitude was more than a life choice. It was a virtue. A vow of sorts.

"You screw me the night of the masquerade and then get engaged the next day? Are you fucking kidding me?" Kristen finally burst, the words gushing from her mouth as she pushed my chest, giving it her all. She did a better job than Francesca, but her wrath still left me unimpressed—and more importantly, unmoved.

I shot her a pitiful stare. She knew as well as I did that we were about as far from monogamy as humanly possible. I promised her nothing. Not even orgasms. They required minor work on my part and, therefore, were a terrible waste of my time.

"Your point, Miss Rhys?" I asked.

"Why her?"

"Why not?"

"She's nineteen!" Kristen roared again, kicking the leg of my bed. Her wince told me she'd just found out that, like my conviction, it was made of steel. I had quite the taste for expensive, unlikely furniture, something she'd know if she'd ever been invited to my house.

"May I ask how you became privy to my personal business?" I wiped at the speckles of saliva she'd left on my dress shirt. Humans, as a concept, were not among my ten favorite things in the world. Hysterical women were not even in the top thousand. Kristen was being highly emotional, considering the circumstances. She was therefore a liability in my way to the presidency and serving my country.

"My agency retrieved images of your young bride moving into your mansion, complete with pictures of her watching like a princess as your staff carried her many, many bags. I'm guessing she's a soon-to-be trophy wife. Speaks five languages, looks like an angel, and probably fucks like a siren." Kristen continued pacing, pushing the sleeves of her smart suit up her elbows.

Francesca, despite her many shortcomings, was not unpleasant on the eye. And she probably *did* have extensive sexual experience, considering her very strict daddy had been a continent away for most of her youth, leaving her to her frivolous ways. Which reminded me, I needed to arrange for her to get drug tested and checked for STDs. Slipups were not an option, and public disgrace would earn her a spot on my shit list, a place her father could confirm was less than picturesque.

"Are you here to ask questions and answer them yourself?" I shoved her shoulder lightly, and she fell to an upholstered cream seat below me. She growled, darting back up. So much for trying to calm her down.

"I'm here to tell you that I want an exclusive Bishop piece, or I will tell everyone who is willing to listen that your new blushing *extremely* young bride is also the daughter of the number-one mobster in Chicago. I'd hate for it to be tomorrow's leading headline, but—as you must agree—gossip sells copies, right?"

I rubbed my chin.

"Do what you gotta do, Miss Rhys."

"Are you serious?"

"As serious as someone can be without filing a restraining order against you for attempting to blackmail a member of the senate. Let me show you to the door."

I had to give her some credit—Kristen wasn't here to grieve the untimely death of our fling. She was all business. She wanted me to compromise the governor in order to save my own ass and give her a scoop that would likely get her an offer from CNN— or TMZ—the next day. Unfortunately for Kristen, I wasn't much of a diplomat. I did not negotiate with terrorists—or worse, journalists. In fact, I would not even negotiate with the president himself. Francesca had pointed out at the masquerade that Nemesis had slayed Narcissus, teaching him a lesson about arrogance. She was about to find out that no one stomped on her husband-to-be's pride.

The irony, of course, was that Francesca's father was the very person to teach me that lesson.

"Huh?" Kristen huffed.

"Tell the world. I'll just spin it as I'm saving my fiancée from the big, bad wolf."

I was the big, bad wolf, but only Francesca and I needed to know that.

"You didn't even like each other at the masquerade." Kristen threw her arms in the air, trying another tactic. I carefully placed my fingers on the small of her back and led her to the doorway.

"Affection has nothing to do with a good marriage. We're done here."

As I rounded the corner to the entrance, I caught a glimpse of brown curls tossing in the hallway. Francesca had been roaming, and she most likely heard the conversation. I wasn't worried. As I said before—she was as harmless as a declawed kitten. Whether I'd make her purr or not was entirely up to her. I wasn't especially keen on her affection and had other places to find it in.

"So, just to be clear, this is over?" Kristen stumbled next to me as I led her downstairs and out of my premises.

"Sharp as a fucking spoon," I muttered. I wasn't against taking mistresses, but I could no longer risk a high-profile affair. And as Kristen was a hungry journalist, everything about her screamed scandal.

"You know, Wolfe, you think you're so untouchable because you had a lucky streak. I've been in this business long enough to know you're too conceited to get much further than you are today. You're a real piece of work, and you think you can get away with even more." She stopped in front of the door to my house. We both knew this was her last visit here.

I smirked, shooing her away with my hand.

"Write the piece, sweetheart."

"This is bad publicity, Keaton."

"A good Catholic summer wedding of two young, high-profile people? I'll take my chances."

"You're not that young."

"You're not that smart, Kristen. Goodbye."

After I got rid of Miss Rhys, I went back to my study to dismiss Bishop and White, before I made my way to the east wing to check on Francesca.

Earlier this morning, her mother showed up at the gate holding some of her daughter's possessions, screaming she wouldn't leave until she saw her daughter was okay. Although I told Francesca that whatever she didn't have time to pack would be left behind, pacifying her parents trumped teaching her a valuable lesson about life. Her mother was blameless in the situation. So was Francesca herself.

I pushed my bride's bedroom door open and found that she had not returned from her wanderings. Stuffing my fists in my cigar pants' pockets, I sauntered across her room to look out her window. I found her in the garden, crouching in a yellow summer dress, muttering to herself as she stabbed a trowel into a flowerpot, her small hands swimming inside a pair of oversized, green gardening gloves. I cracked the window open, half-interested in the nonsense she was spewing. Her voice seeped through the crack of the window. Her ramblings were throaty and feminine, not at all hysterical and teenager-y as I'd expected someone in her situation to be.

"Who does he think he is? He will pay for this. I'm not a pawn. I'm not the idiot he thinks I am. I'll starve until I break him or die trying. Wouldn't that be a fun headline to try to explain," she huffed, shaking her head. "But what's he gonna do—force-feed me? I *will* get out of here. Oh, P.S. Senator Keaton—you're not even that good looking. Just tall. Angelo? Now he's a gorgeous specimen, inside and out. He will forgive me for that silly kiss. Of course, he will. I'm going to make him…"

I closed the window. She was going on a hunger strike. Good. Her first lesson would be about my apathy. The blabbing about Bandini did not concern me, either. Puppy love could never threaten a wolf. I made my way back to her door when a carved wooden box sitting on her nightstand caught my attention. I ambled over to it, the echo of her words from the masquerade bouncing in my head. The box was locked, but I instinctively knew she'd taken out another note, desperate to change her fate. I flipped her pillows on a whim and found the note underneath them. My beautiful, predictable, *stupid* bride.

I unfolded it.

The next man to feed you chocolate will be the love of your life.

I felt the sneer carving on my face and wondered, briefly, when was the last time I smiled. It was about something silly Francesca had briefly told me on the landing at her house before I bent her father's arm into giving her to me.

"Sterling!" I barked from my spot by my bride's bed. The old maid rushed into the room, the frantic wandering of her erratic pupils telling me she expected the worst.

"Send Francesca the biggest Godiva chocolate basket available with a note from me. Leave it blank."

"That's a wonderful idea," she squealed, slapping her knees. "She hasn't eaten in almost twenty-four hours, so I will do that right away." She dashed downstairs to the kitchen where she kept a *Yellow Pages* bigger than her frame.

I pushed the note back into place, rearranging the pillows in the same, messy heap I'd found them.

I cared more about fucking with Francesca Rossi's head than I did her body.

Now that was my idea of foreplay.

CHAPTER FOUR

Francesca

T WO DAYS OF NOTHINGNESS TICKED BY, SOAKING LIKE
blood on the walls of my room.

I refused to communicate with anyone. Even the in-desperate-need-for-love garden was left unattended, including the plants and vegetables I'd potted after Mama paid me a visit the day after Wolfe took me. She snuck seeds of begonias in the wooden box. *"The most resilient flowers, Francesca. Just like you."* Then Ms. Sterling caught up with my hobby and brought me some radishes, carrot, and cherry tomato seeds, trying to lift my mood and perhaps encourage me to expend some energy and consume something more than tap water.

Sleep was short, tormented, and interrupted with a night-mare: a monster prowling in the shadows behind my bedroom door, baring his teeth in a wolfish grin every time I looked its way. The monster's eyes were mesmerizing, but his smile was frightening. And when I tried to wake up, to unchain myself from the dream, my body was paralyzed to the mattress.

There were two things I wanted desperately—for Wolfe to understand we couldn't get married and for Angelo to realize that the kiss was a misunderstanding.

Ms. Sterling brought food, water, and coffee to my bed every few hours, leaving silver trays filled with goodness on my nightstand. I drank the water to keep myself from fainting, but the rest remained untouched.

I especially ignored the huge basket of chocolate my future husband had sent to me. It sat in the corner of the room on the fancy desk, collecting dust. Even though the low sugar in my blood made white dots explode in my vision every time I made a sudden move, I still somehow knew that the expensive chocolate would taste of my own surrender. A flavor so bitter, no sugar could sweeten it.

Then there were the notes. The cursed, exasperating notes.

I'd opened two out of the three, and both pointed at Wolfe as the love of my life.

I tried to tell myself that it was clearly coincidental. Keaton might have had a change of heart. Perhaps he decided to worm his way into my good graces with gifts. Though something told me that man had not taken one uncalculated step in his life from the moment he took his first breath.

Wolfe demanded my presence at dinner every day. Never in person, though, but through Ms. Sterling. I continuously refused. When he sent one of his bodyguards for me, I locked myself in the bathroom and refused to come out until Ms. Sterling physically kicked the burly man away. When Wolfe stopped sending food—something that made Ms. Sterling raise her voice to piercing levels in the kitchen even though he didn't budge—I laughed maniacally because I wasn't eating anyway. Finally, on the third day, Keaton graced me with his regal presence, standing at my doorway with his eyes narrowed to slits of cold menace.

Wolfe looked taller and gruffer than I remembered. Clad in a sharp bright navy suit, he was armed with a sardonic smirk that showed no trace of happiness. Light amusement danced across his otherwise dark eyes. Couldn't blame him. I was starving to death here, trying to prove a point he couldn't care less about. But I had no choice. I didn't have my cell phone, and though Mama had called the landline each day to make sure I was okay, I knew by the shallow and even breaths in my ear that Ms. Sterling was listening to our conversations. Even though she cared about my physical well-being, my guess was she was still Team Wolfe all the way.

The pleas, the plans, and the promises to be good—to be the greatest daughter in Chicago—if my parents demanded I return sat on the tip of my tongue. I wanted to ask about Angelo and if Dad was doing anything to try to get me back, but all I did was answer her worried questions with yes and no.

I pretended to smooth the fabric of my blanket over me and stare at my legs as I ignored him.

"Nemesis," he drawled with lazy cynicism that somehow—somehow—still managed to stab somewhere deep inside me. "Care to wrap your bones in something a little more dignified than pajamas? We're going out tonight."

"You are going out tonight. Unless you're taking me back to my parents', I'm staying here," I corrected.

"Whatever possesses you to think this outing is optional?" He braced the top of the doorframe with his arms, his dress shirt riding up and revealing muscular abs, dusted with dark hair.

He was such a man, and that threw me off. I was still in that tattered seam between a woman and a teenager, neither here nor there. I hated all the leverage he had on me.

"I'll run away," I threatened idly. Where would I go? I knew my father would send me right back to Wolfe's arms. He knew that, too. This was my glorified prison. Silky sheets and a senator as my future husband. Pretty lies and devastating truths.

"With what energy, exactly? You can barely crawl, let alone run. Wear the dark green dress. The one with the slit."

"So I can impress your perverted old politician friends?" I huffed, tossing my hair behind my shoulder.

"So you can impress your dramatically underwhelmed future husband."

"Not interested, thank you."

"Your parents will be there."

That made me perk up in an instant—another thing I hated. He had all the power. All the information. The bigger picture.

"Where are you going?"

"Preston Bishop's son is getting married. A pony-looking thing with a pair of nice legs." He pushed off the doorframe and walked over to the foot of my bed.

I remembered how he'd referred to Bishop's wife as 'horsey'. He was conceited and rude, arrogant and vulgar beyond belief, but only indoors. I'd seen him at the masquerade. And while standoffish and rude to my father and me, he was an impeccable gentleman to everyone else.

"It would be a good opportunity to introduce you as the future Mrs. Keaton. Which reminds me…" He produced something from his front pocket, tossing the square, black, and velvety thing across the length of the room. I caught it in my hands and snapped it open. An engagement ring with a Winston Blue diamond the size of my head twinkled inside it, catching every ray of sunshine slipping through the bare windows. I knew every minute in this house brought me closer to marriage with Wolfe Keaton, and escaping wasn't possible. The only man to save me from my future husband was, quite frankly, my future husband. Begging him to give me up wasn't an option. Maybe making him see that he didn't want to marry me was a tactic I needed to explore.

"When are we leaving?" I asked. The "you" turned into a "we," but he still didn't look pleased.

I will embarrass you beyond belief.

"Couple of hours. It is my understanding that you're used to being pampered and catered to, so Sterling will get you ready."

You will regret the day your filthy eyes met mine across the table.

"Take that back," I said.

"Excuse you?"

"Take that dig back. Stop holding my upbringing and the way I've been brought up against me," I demanded.

He smirked, then turned to leave.

"I'm not going." I tossed the engagement ring across the room. Though he could have caught it in his hand, he chose not to, letting it drop on the floor. Fighting for something—least of all for me—was beneath him.

"You are unless you want your phone privileges taken. The landline could be cut off. Not to mention, I'd hate to be forced to pierce your pretty veins to hook you up to a feeding tube," he said, drifting out of the room before pausing at the door. His back was still to me when it began to vibrate with soft laughter.

"You will also have your engagement ring on at all times."

"Or what?" I challenged, my voice shaking.

"Or I'm taking you to elope in Vegas, setting off a chain reaction of pregnancy rumors that will not do your family any good."

I sucked in a breath, realizing for the first time what we were.

A story of a Nemesis and a Villain with no chance at a happy ending.

Where the prince doesn't save the princess.

He tortures her.

And the beauty doesn't sleep.

She's stuck.

In a nightmare.

Three hours later, we walked through the doors of a ballroom situated at the Madison, one of the glitziest hotels in Chicago. With a cool wind, the twinkling buildings of the Magnificent

Mile and the red Michigan Avenue Bridge reminded me that I was still in my favorite city, breathing hope into my body.

I wore an off-the-shoulder blue Armani gown that highlighted my eyes and had my hair twisted in a Dutch braid.

Ms. Sterling practically squeaked when she did my hair and makeup, reminding me just how much I missed Clara. Home was just across town, but it felt like oceans away. Things I loved and lived for—my parents, my garden, horseback riding—were untouchable. A distant memory that grew an inch farther away every second of the day.

With his dazzling all-black suit, my fiancé put a possessive hand on the small of my back and led me through the entrance of the reception area. Crystal chandeliers and curved stairways greeted us. The room was hued milk and honey, the marble floor a checked black and white. We hadn't been invited to the ceremony at the Bishop's local church and spent the drive here in a silence that shredded my nerves. Senator Keaton hardly shared the sentiment. In fact, he answered emails on his phone, barked orders to his young driver, Smithy, and pretended I wasn't there.

The only attention he did give me was when he noted, "That's not the dress I told you to wear."

"Would you be surprised to hear I have a mind of my own?" I stared out my window as the vehicle slowed through Chicago's downtown traffic. "After all, I'm nothing but a sheltered teenager."

"And a disobedient one, too," he said.

"A terrible bride," I concluded.

"I can tame a dozen of you before breakfast."

The minute we sauntered through the glitzy wide doors, people began to swarm around Wolfe as though he was the groom himself. He drew me close to him by the waist, making a jolt of heat travel down my belly as he smiled and made polite conversation with his admirers. His personality outside the walls of his house or his car was completely different, his charm turned up to an eleven. With his two bodyguards huddling behind us, he oozed wide grins and polite conversation. A far cry from the formidable man I lived with.

The first people to set us apart and corner us into a private tête-à-tête was a fifty-something politician couple who came all the way from DC. Wolfe introduced me as his future bride, then chided me with a good-natured sneer. "Don't be shy. Show them the ring."

I stood frozen, my heart pushing through my throat and ready to jump out of my mouth before Wolfe pried my hand from the side of my body and showed them the huge engagement band. The woman grasped my hand, examined it, then slapped her chest.

"Oh, it is so perfect. How'd he propose?" She batted her eyelashes at me, the suspense obviously killing her. That was my chance to ruin all of Wolfe's hard work. I grinned, moving my hand slowly, letting the diamond catch the lights in the room and blind everyone in our vicinity.

"On the steps of the Art Institute. My poor fiancé made a spectacle of himself. Tore his dress pants from behind as he went down on one knee. His entire butt was on full display." I sighed, not daring to look up at his reaction.

"You did not!" The man burst out laughing, clapping Wolfe's shoulder. The woman snorted and flashed Wolfe a smile open with both admiration and lust. I chanced a look at Wolfe and saw his lips thinning in irritation. Unlike them, he did not find my story entertaining.

Their reaction put me in my element, though, and I couldn't wait to pull this trick again. For a moment, I considered he might tell them I was lying. But that wasn't Wolfe's style. It was an easy way out, and he looked like the kind of man to take the long, winding road to victory.

"It was worth the hassle." He grinned down at me, pulling me so close to him, I thought his body was going to swallow mine whole. "Besides," he hissed only for me to hear, his warm, minty breath tickling the side of my neck, "if my bride knew me even a little, she'd know I never kneel."

For a while, all we did was break the news of our engagement as more and more people came to congratulate us, thereby ignoring the newly wedded couple. Bishop Junior and his bride didn't seem to care the attention wasn't directed at them. In fact, they looked so happy, their eyes twinkling with love, that I couldn't help but feel even more angry toward Wolfe for depriving me of being with my true love. Senator Wolfe Keaton paraded me like a royal horse around the room, showing me off as though I was an asset. My stomach churned and whined in hunger, and it took everything in me not to sway by his side like a shaking leaf. To make matters worse, Wolfe nudged me when I needed to smile, dragged me into his embrace when I drifted away, and volunteered me to servitude on three different charity events in the upcoming months.

Attractive women giggled and slipped their numbers into his hand as they came to congratulate us on separate occasions, thinking I wouldn't notice. One of them, a UN ambassador, even reminded him about their marvelous time in Brussels two years ago and hinted at staying in town for a while.

"We should grab a drink. Catch up," the mahogany-haired beauty suggested in her syrupy-sweet French accent. He flashed her an Angelo smile. The kind that rearranged the molecules in the air and made your heart flutter.

"I'll have my secretary get in touch with yours tomorrow morning."

Bastard.

People praised our engagement and seemed to be comfortable with our age gap. In fact, other than Preston Bishop himself, who was at our table the night of the masquerade and witnessed the verbal bashing Wolfe Keaton had offered me, no one challenged our sudden engagement. Even Bishop settled for a raised eyebrow.

"This is a pleasant surprise," he said.

"It is, isn't it?" Wolfe retorted. "Life seems to be full of them."

His words were casual but held a deeper meaning I wasn't privy to.

Each time I'd been introduced to Wolfe's peers, I came up with a different story for our engagement.

"He forgot his words, then developed a sudden lisp. He had to write them down, and even that had a few grammatical errors. It was so endearing."

"The proposal was so romantic. He asked my father for my hand, the old-fashioned way, and I was so touched when he started crying when I said yes. He was bawling, actually, weren't you, Wolfey? Nothing a Xanax and a piña colada couldn't fix. Of course, I'd never have dreamt that this was my future husband's favorite cocktail."

"I'm so excited to be marrying a senator. I've always wanted to visit DC. Did you know that Nirvana was from Washington? Oh, wait, honey, that's not the same Washington, now, is it?"

I was relentless. Even when Wolfe turned from mildly annoyed to positively furious, the tic of his jaw suggesting he was going to snap at me the minute we were alone, I kept spewing nonsense I knew would embarrass him. And he—the perfect gentleman in public—kept chuckling softly and backing me up, all while redirecting the conversation to work and the upcoming elections.

Being introduced to half of Chicago's high society proved to be a time sucker. So much so that I didn't have time to look for my parents. After what seemed like hours, Wolfe and I finally made our way to our table. I slid into my chair, swallowing hard and trying not to swoon from lack of food. Keaton draped his arm across the back of my chair, brushing my bare shoulder with his fingers. The freshly married couple was at their central table, making a toast. We were seated next to another senator, two diplomats, and the former secretary of state. My eyes began to drift among the tables, searching for my family. I knew I would find them after dessert was served and when the dancing started, but I longed for a glimpse of Mama.

I found my parents seated at the table across the room. Papa looked his usual formidable, cutthroat self; the only signs of wariness were the dark circles framing his eyes. Mama looked put together as always, but I noticed the small things no one else would. The way her chin wobbled as she spoke with the woman sitting across from her, or the way her hand shook when she reached for her glass of wine. Next to them sat Angelo's parents, and next to them…

My heart stilled, swelling behind my ribcage like a balloon about to burst.

Angelo brought a date. Not just any date, but *the* date. The one everyone had been expecting him to bring.

Her name was Emily Bianchi. Her father, Emmanuel Bianchi, was a well-known businessman and an undeclared member of The Outfit. Emily was twenty-three with silky blond hair and glorious cheekbones. Tall and busty, she could fit my slender, tiny frame in her palm. She was the closest thing to Italian-American royalty after me, but since she was Angelo's age, their connection was expected—almost prayed for—among the families of The Outfit.

I'd met her plenty of times before, and she always treated me with a blend of boredom and dismissal. Not exactly rude but impolite enough to let me know that she didn't like the amount of attention I was getting. It didn't help that Emily went to school with Angelo, and that she absolutely despised me for spending my summers with him.

She wore a skintight black maxi dress with a deep slit that ran along her right thigh and was adorned with enough gold around her neck and through her ears to open a pawn shop. She had her hand clasped above Angelo's as she made conversation with the people around her. A small, possessive gesture he did not reject. Not even when his eyes wandered across the room and landed on mine, locking us together in a weird battle in which no one would win.

I stiffened in my chair, my heart jackhammering against my sternum.

Air. I needed more air. More space. More *hope*. Because what I saw in his eyes frightened me more than my soon-to-be husband. It was complete and utter acceptance of the situation.

They were both in their twenties.

They were both beautiful, single, and from the same social circle.

They were both ready for marriage. *Game over for me.*

"Francesca?" One of the diplomats whose name I didn't catch chuckled into his napkin, trying to draw my attention back to the conversation at the table. I broke away from Angelo's gaze and blinked, looking back and forth between the old man and my future husband. I could see Wolfe's jaw tensing with frustration that had built throughout the evening and knew he hadn't missed the moment I'd shared with my childhood friend.

I smiled apologetically, smoothing my dress.

"Could you repeat the question, please?"

"Care to tell us how Senator Keaton popped the question? I have to say, he never struck me as the over-romantic type," he chortled, stroking his beard like a *Harry Potter* character. I didn't even have it in me to taunt Wolfe. I was too caught up in the fact that my life was officially over, and Angelo was going to marry Emily, therefore fulfilling my worst nightmare.

"Yeah, of course. He…he…proposed to me on the…"

"Staircase to the museum," Wolfe clipped, chucking my chin in faux affection that made my skin crawl. "I don't know what I did to deserve her passionate kiss. You stole my breath." He turned to me, his grays on my blues, two pools of beautiful lies. People gasped around us, enchanted by the magnetic power of his expression as he stared at me. "I stole your heart."

You stole my first kiss.
Then my happiness.
And finally, my life.

"T-that's right." I dabbed my neck with a linen napkin, suddenly too nauseous and weak to fight back. My body was finally crumpling under the strain of not eating for days. "I will never forget that night," I said.

"Me neither."

"You make a beautiful couple," someone remarked. I was too dizzy to even tell if they were male or female.

Wolfe smirked, raising his tumbler of whiskey to his lips.

Defying him purposely—and undoubtedly stupidly—I allowed my eyes to drift back to the table where I longed to sit. Emily was now grazing her French-manicured fingernails along Angelo's blazered arm. Angelo looked down at her face, his mouth breaking into a grin. I could see how she defrosted him to the idea of them. How she lowered his guard, one touch at a time.

She leaned toward him, whispering something in his ear and giggling, and his eyes shot to me again. Were they talking about me? Was I making a complete fool of myself by staring at them so openly? I grabbed a glass of champagne, about to knock it down in one go.

Wolfe wrapped his fingers around my wrist, stilling my hand before it reached my mouth. It was a gentle, firm touch. Callous and hairy. A man's touch.

"Sweetheart, we've been through this. This is *real* champagne. The grownup kind," he said with a hint of exasperated sympathy in his voice, causing the entire table to roar with wild laughter.

"The trouble of marrying a youngster," the other senator snorted out.

Wolfe raised a thick, condescending eyebrow. "Marriage is a tricky business. Which reminds me…" He leaned forward, his blank expression turning into a sympathetic frown. "How are you handling the divorce from Edna?"

Now my furious blush became almost unbearable. I wanted to kill him. Kill him for this stupid stunt, for forcing me into marrying him, and for the fact that, by proxy, he just threw Angelo into Emily's arms.

I put the champagne glass back on the table, biting my tongue from pointing out that I'd drank plenty at the gala where we'd met, and he didn't seem to care much then. Actually, he took advantage of my tipsiness when he tricked me into kissing him.

"May I be excused?" I cleared my throat and, without waiting for an answer, stood and charged toward the bathroom, aware of the fact that my nemesis' eyes, as well as Angelo's and my parents', were all on my back, pointed like loaded guns.

The restrooms were at the end of the ballroom, Gentlemen and Ladies facing one another, under a massive wrought-iron, curved stairway. I slipped inside, sagging against the wall, closing my eyes, and taking the deepest breath my corseted bodice would allow.

Breathe.

Just breathe.

A hand clasped my shoulder. Small, warm fingers curling around my collarbone. I cracked my eyes open and yelped, jumping backward, my head hitting the tiles behind me.

"Sweet Jesus!"

It was Mama. Up close, her face looked too wary, too old, and too unfamiliar. It looked like she'd aged a decade overnight, and all the anger I'd harbored toward her in the past three days flew out the window. Her eyes were bloodshot and swollen from crying. Her normally proud, brown mane was littered with gray hair.

"How are you holding up, Vita Mia?"

Instead of answering, I flung myself into her arms, releasing a sob I'd been holding since Wolfe ushered me into his sleek black Escalade tonight. How could I not cut her some slack? She looked as miserable as I was.

"I hate it there. I don't eat. I barely sleep. And to make matters worse…" I sniffed, disconnecting from her so I could hold her gaze for emphasis. "Angelo is dating Emily now." I felt my eyes bulging out of their sockets with urgency.

"It's only their first date," Mama assured me, patting my back and drawing me into another hug. I shook my head in the crook of her shoulder.

"I don't even know why it matters. I'm getting married. It's done."

"Sweetie…"

"Why, Mama?" I stepped out of her embrace again, dragging myself toward the imperial sinks to pluck some tissue before my makeup was completely ruined. "What possessed Papa to do something like this?"

I watched her in the reflection of the mirror behind me. The way her shoulders wilted in her slightly oversized black dress. I realized she hadn't been eating much, either.

"Your father doesn't share many things with me, but trust me when I tell you this was not an easy decision for him to make. We are still shaken by what happened. We just want you to give Senator Keaton an honest chance. He is handsome, rich, and has a good job. You're not marrying beneath you."

"I am marrying a monster," I drawled.

"You could be happy, amore."

I shook my head, before throwing it backward and laughing. She didn't have to spell it out for me. Her hands were tied. I harbored many bad feelings toward my father but thinking them openly—not to mention uttering them aloud—was like pouring cyanide onto an open wound. Mama looked back and forth between the door and me, and I knew what she was thinking. We couldn't stay here much longer. People would start asking questions. Especially when they saw that I'd been crying. Keeping up appearances was vital in The Outfit, and if people suspected Papa's arm had been twisted by a young, ambitious senator who was new on the scene, it could kill his reputation.

Mama opened her purse and produced something, shoving it into my hand.

"I found this buried under a pile of dirty laundry in your room. Use it, Vita Mia. Start easing into your new life because it's not going to be a bad one. And for the love of God, start eating!"

She dashed out, leaving me to open my hand and inspect the recovered item. It was my cell phone. My precious cell phone. Fully charged and stocked with messages and missed calls. I wanted to inspect them all—privately, and when time allowed for it. I knew that my assumption that Senator Keaton had taken my phone privileges without asking him was a little extreme. Then again, blackmailing my father into giving him my hand was not exactly subtle courting, so no one could blame me for jumping to conclusions.

I threw the used tissue in the trash can and stormed out to the dim alcove under the staircase, my five-inch Louboutins slapping against the marble floor. I made two steps outside before I was cornered against the mirror overlooking the back of the stairway by a tall, delicate-boned frame. I groaned, slowly opening my eyes as my spine recovered from the collision with the mirror.

Angelo was boxing me in with his arms on either side of my head, his body flush against mine. His chest brushed the exposed, tender flesh of my cleavage, and our hearts crashed against each other in unison, our breaths mingling together.

He sought me out. He came after me. He still *wanted* me.

"Goddess," he whispered, cupping the side of my face and pressing his forehead to mine.

His voice was so drenched with emotion, my hands quivered their way to his face, holding his cheeks for the first time. He pressed his thumb to the center of my lips.

I held onto the lapels of his jacket, knowing what I was asking for, and asking for it anyway. The need to be held by him was stronger than the need to do the right thing by us. I longed for him to tell me that Emily meant nothing to him, even though it wasn't fair to her. Or him. Not even to me.

"I've been worried sick." He nuzzled his nose against mine brazenly. This was more physical contact than we'd had since we were born, and that—combined with my hunger strike—sent my head spinning in a dozen different directions.

I nodded but didn't say anything.

"You haven't been good at picking up the phone." He clutched my hand that held my phone, squeezing it for emphasis.

"I've just recovered it for the first time since the masquerade," I breathed.

"Why'd you do that?" Angelo asked, his body practically grinding over mine. Panic licked at my conscience. What if Angelo was touching me the way he'd never dared before because he had nothing to lose anymore? My father would never frown upon him for taking it too far—because he would never have to stand in front of Arthur Rossi and ask him for my hand.

I desperately wanted to explain everything about my sudden engagement. But I also knew that if my father couldn't do anything about it, Angelo sure wouldn't be able to help me, either. I didn't want us to be star-crossed lovers, stealing moments and sneaking kisses. Drowning in forbidden love. I didn't know much about my future husband, but I did know this—if I caused him a scandal, he'd retaliate and hurt those I loved. I didn't mind taking his wrath, but Angelo didn't deserve to be punished.

"Angelo." I raked my hands over his chest. I'd never touched a man like this before. So openly. His pecs flexed under my fingertips, and he felt hot, even through the fabric of his suit.

"Tell me," he probed.

I shook my head. "We fit."

"*We* fit," he countered. "*He* sucks."

I laughed through the tears lodging in my throat.

"I want to kiss you so bad, goddess." He grabbed the back of my neck—no longer nice and understanding and teasing— leaning down for the kill. He was trying to prove a point. A point I was already sold on.

"Then I suggest you do it right away because eighteen days from now, she will be a married woman, and I will have every right to break your fingers for touching her," a dry, menacing voice grumbled behind Angelo.

Stunned, I slipped my hands from Angelo's chest, my legs giving in from surprise. Angelo caught me by the waist, righting me. He snapped out of the dark lust blazing in his eyes, twisting to look at Wolfe. My future husband casually made his way to the men's restroom, his swagger completely unperturbed by the affectionate display in front of him. He was much taller, broader, and darker than Angelo, not to mention nearly a decade older, dripping with the air and power of a force you shouldn't cross. The authority he possessed was almost tangible. I had to bite the inside of my cheek to stop from apologizing for the scene unfolding in front of him. I looked up instead of down, refusing to declare defeat.

Angelo looked straight at him.

"Senator Keaton," he bit out.

Wolfe halted between the two entrances of the restrooms. I could feel his imperial body as he looked back and forth between us, assessing the situation with cool disinterest.

"I meant every word, Bandini," Wolfe said huskily. "If you'd like to kiss my fiancée goodbye, tonight's your chance to do it. In private. Next time I see you, I will not be so forgiving."

With that, he brushed his fingertips over my engagement ring, a not-so-subtle reminder of whom I belonged to, sending a shockwave through my body. He disappeared behind the restroom door before I could catch my breath. I thought Angelo would run away the minute Wolfe gave him his back, but he didn't.

Instead, he caged me against the mirror with his arms again, shaking his head.

"Why?" he asked.

"Why Emily?" I countered, raising my chin.

"You're the only woman I know who'd bring Emily up right now." He balled his fist, slamming it beside my head. I swallowed a gasp.

"I came with Bianchi because you are engaged to be married." Angelo licked his lips, trying to gain control over his emotions. "And also because you made me look like an idiot. Everyone was expecting an engagement announcement would be made any month now. *Every single asshole in The Outfit*. And here you are, sitting across the room at the table with the secretary of state, in the arms of Wolfe Keaton, playing the dutiful fiancée. I needed to save face. A face you walked all over with your pretty, seductive heels. Worst part, Francesca? You aren't even telling me *why*."

Because my father is weak and is being blackmailed.

But I knew I couldn't say it. It would ruin my family, and as much as I despised my father right now, I couldn't betray him.

Without realizing what I was doing, I held his cheeks in my hands, smiling through the tears that were running down my cheeks, chasing one another.

"You will always be my first love, Angelo. Always."

His harsh breath came down on my face, warm and laced with sweet, musky wine.

"Kiss me *right*." My voice shook around my request because the last time I'd been kissed—the *only* time I'd been kissed—was all wrong.

"I'll kiss you the only way I can without giving you my heart, Francesca Rossi. The only way you deserve to be kissed."

He leaned down, his lips pressing on the tip of my nose. I

felt his body shuddering against mine with a sob that threatened to rip through his bones. All those years. All those tears. All the sleepless nights of anticipation. The countdowns of the weeks, and days, and minutes until we saw each other every summer. Playing too close to each other in the river. Fingers knotting under the table at restaurants. All those moments were wrapped inside that innocent kiss, and I wanted so badly to execute my masquerade plan that night. To slope my head up. To meet his lips with my own. But I also knew that I would not forgive myself for ruining this for him with Emily. I couldn't tarnish the beginning of their relationship just because mine was doomed.

"Angelo."

He covered my forehead with his. We both closed our eyes, savoring the bittersweet moment. Finally together, breathing the same air. Only to be forever torn apart.

"Maybe in the next life," I said.

"No, *goddess,* definitely in this one."

With that, he turned around and glided down the darkened hallway, allowing me a few more calming breaths before I stepped out of the alcove and faced the music. When my shaking subsided, I cleared my throat and marched toward my table.

With every step I took, I tried to convey more confidence. My smile was a little wider. My back a little straighter. When I spotted my table, I noticed Wolfe wasn't there. My eyes began to search for him, a concoction of irritation and dread twirling in my stomach. We left things so awkwardly, I wasn't sure what to expect. Part of me hoped—prayed—that he'd finally had enough of me, and that he called things off with my father.

The more I searched for his tall figure, the faster my heart thrust against my sternum.

Then I found him.

My future husband, Senator Wolfe Keaton, was skating past tables elegantly. Three feet behind him, Emily Bianchi ambled, tall and provocative, her hips swaying like a dangled, forbidden apple. Her hair blond and shiny—just like his date from the masquerade. No one had noticed how her cheeks were stained pink. How they put some distance between their footsteps but headed in the same direction.

Emily was the first to disappear behind the massive, silky black draperies, slipping from the ballroom without notice.

Wolfe stopped, shook hands with an old, wealthy-looking man, and struck easy conversation with him for at least ten minutes before taking a sidestep and resuming his journey to the back of the ballroom.

As if sensing my gaze on him, Wolfe turned his head toward mine, amidst the hundreds of people around us, and locked our eyes together. He winked, his lips unflinching, as his legs carried him to his destination.

My blood bubbled in my veins. When I was busy restraining my passion toward her date, Emily had been snagging my future husband for a quickie.

I stood there, fists balling beside my thighs. My heart pounded so loud, I thought it was going to burst across the floor and flip like a fish out of water.

Wolfe and Emily had betrayed us.

Disloyalty had a taste.

It was bitter.

It was sour.

It was even a little sweet.

Most of all, it taught me an important lesson—whatever the four of us had, it wasn't sacred anymore. Our hearts were tarnished. Stained. And guilty.

Unpredictable to a fault.

And bound to break.

CHAPTER FIVE

Francesca

T HE NEXT MORNING, I THREW THE GODIVA CHOCOLATE IN the kitchen's trash where he would hopefully see it. I dragged my famished body out of bed voluntarily, driven by the one thing stronger than the pain of hunger—revenge.

The text messages I'd found on my phone were enough to fuel me. They were dated the night of the masquerade, the same night I'd avoided taking out my phone out of fear I'd beg Angelo and make a fool of myself.

Angelo: Care to explain that kiss?

Angelo: On my way to your house.

Angelo: Your father just told me that I can't come there anymore because you're soon to be engaged.

Angelo: ENGAGED.

Angelo: And not to me.

Angelo: Know what? Fuck you, Francesca.

Angelo: WHY?

Angelo: Is that because I've waited a year? Your father had asked me to do it. I came in every week to ask for a date.

Angelo: It was always you, goddess.

There weren't any new ones since then.

Eating was still firmly not on my daily agenda—something I'd heard Ms. Sterling complaining to Wolfe about on the phone as I breezed past her, a flowery chiffon wrap dress clinging to my ever-shrinking body. At this point, my stomach had given up and stopped growling altogether. Yesterday, I'd forced myself to steal a few bites of bread when Wolfe was busy making his point with Emily, but it wasn't nearly enough to appease my shrinking gut. Somewhere in the back of my mind, I had hoped I'd faint or cause enough damage to be rushed to the hospital where perhaps my father would finally put an end to this ongoing nightmare. Alas, hoping for a miracle was not only dangerous but crushing altogether. The more time I spent in this house, the more the rumors made sense—Senator Wolfe Keaton was destined for greatness. I would be a first lady and probably before I hit thirty. Wolfe rose up nice and early today to get to the regional airport on time and even made plans to go to DC over the weekend for some important meetings.

He didn't include me in his plans, and I very much doubted he cared if I died, other than the unwanted headline it would likely create.

Under my ivy-laced window, tucked in the heart of the mansion's garden, I tended to my new plants and vegetables, surprised by how they'd managed to survive without any water for a couple of days. Summer had been cruel so far, scorching hotter than the typical Chicago Augusts. Then again, everything about the past couple of weeks had been crazy. The weather seemed to fall in line with the rest of my frayed life. But my new garden was resilient, and I realized as I crouched down to weed the new vine tomatoes, so was I.

I carried two bags of fertilizer to the spot underneath my window and rummaged through the small shed located on the corner of the yard to find some more old seeds and empty pots. Whoever was assigned with the task of taking care of this garden had obviously been given the instructions to make it look manicured and pleasant but only minimally so. It was green, but reserved. Beautiful, yet unbearably sad. Not unlike its owner. Unlike its owner, though, I craved to cultivate the garden with my green thumb. I had plenty of attention and devotion, and nothing and no one to give it to.

After I placed all the material in a neat line, I examined the shears in my hand. I grabbed them from the shed, explaining to Ms. Sterling that I needed to cut the fertilizer bag open, waiting for the tiny elderly woman to turn her back to me. Now, as the blades of the clippers twinkled under the sun, and the unsuspecting Ms. Sterling was in the kitchen, berating the poor cook for buying the wrong type of fish for dinner (still hoping I'd grace Senator Keaton with my presence at dinner tonight, no doubt) my opportunity had finally arrived.

I crept my way back into the house, passing through the sleek chrome kitchen. I took the stairs two at a time, slipping into the west wing to Keaton's bedroom. I'd been there once before, when I eavesdropped on him and the pretty journalist. I hurried into his bedroom, knowing that Wolfe had at least another hour before he got home. Even with his jet-setting lifestyle, he still wasn't above escaping the Chicago traffic.

Whereas my room had been decorated with glitz, oozing of Hollywood's regency era, Wolfe's room was elegant, reserved, and plainly furnished. Dramatic black and white curtains dripped across the wide windows, a black channel-quilted leather headboard and coal-hued nightstands stood out from each side of the bed. The walls were painted a deep gray, the color of his eyes, and a sole crystal chandelier dripped from the center of the ceiling, seemingly bowing down to the powerful man who occupied the room.

He had no TV, no chests of drawers, and no mirrors. He did have a bar cabinet, not to my surprise, considering he'd marry booze if it were legal in the state of Illinois.

I trudged to his walk-in closet, snapping the shears chirpily in my hand with newfound energy as I swung the doors open. The black oak shelves stood out against the cool white marble of the floor. Dozens of suits sorted by colors, cuts, and designs hung in neat, dense lines, perfectly ironed and ready to be worn.

He had hundreds of scarves folded in precision, enough shoes to open a Bottega Veneta store, and blazers and pea coats galore. I knew what I was looking for first. His tie rack contained over a hundred ties. Once I found it, I serenely began to snip his upmarket ties in half, taking a somewhat bizarre liking to watching their fabric drop at my feet like orange and rust-colored leaves in the fall.

Snip, snip, snip, snip, snip.

The sound was comforting. So much so, that I forgot how hungry I was. Wolfe Keaton had screwed Angelo's date. I couldn't—and wouldn't—avenge his indiscretions by cheating on *him*, but I damn well could make sure that he didn't have anything to wear tomorrow morning except for his stupid smug expression.

After I finished the task of cutting all his ties, I moved on to his crisp dress shirts. *He had some nerve to assume I would ever touch him*, I thought bitterly as I tore through rich, smooth fabrics in crème, swan white, and baby blue. Consummating our marriage was expected. But despite Wolfe's good looks, I detested his playboy way of life, awful reputation, and the fact he had slept with so many women already. Especially as I was embarrassingly inexperienced.

And by inexperienced, I meant a virgin.

Not that being a virgin was a crime, but I regarded it as such, knowing Wolfe would use this piece of information against me, highlighting how unworldly and ingenuous I was. Not being a virgin was not really an option in the world I lived in. My parents expected me to stay celibate until my wedding, and I had no problem fulfilling their wish, seeing as I didn't particularly believe in having sex with someone I didn't love.

I decided to deal with the issue of my virginity when it was time. *If* it would ever be time.

I was so focused on my mission—ruining clothes and ties worth many tens of thousands of dollars—that I didn't even notice the *click-click* of his loafers as he made his way into his room. In fact, I only detected his arrival when he stopped outside his bedroom door and answered his phone.

"Keaton."

Pause.

"He did what?"

Pause.

"I'll make sure he can't move an inch in this town without getting raided by the CPD."

Then he killed the call.

Shit, I inwardly cussed, throwing the shears on the floor and scrambling to run outside. I slammed an open drawer which contained his watches, knocking something to the floor and running out of the walk-in closet, flinging the double doors of his bedroom open just as he stepped in, still frowning at his phone.

It was the first time I'd seen him since the wedding yesterday. After he'd disappeared with Emily, he came back twenty minutes later to inform me that we were leaving. The ride back home was silent. I openly texted my cousin Andrea on my phone, something he didn't seem to care about. When we got home (*this is not your home, Frankie*), I retired straight to my room, banging my door shut and locking it for good measure. I didn't give him the pleasure of asking him about Emily. In fact, I didn't show him that I cared. At all.

Now, as he stood in front of me, I realized that my reaction toward his fling with Emily didn't matter or earn me any extra points in our battle. He *did* hold all the cards. I instinctively took a step back, swallowing hard.

His tyrannical cold eyes ran along my body as if I was naked and offering myself to him readily, his lips still pressed in a hard line. He wore casual mouse gray dress pants today, neglecting the blazer in favor of a white shirt rolled to the elbows.

"Miss me?" he asked flatly, brushing past me and moseying deeper into the room. I let out a shaky laugh of dread when I realized he might notice the broken facedown framed picture I'd knocked over in my bid to escape and the ruined clothes waiting for him in his closet. The second his back was to me, I began to tiptoe out of his room.

"Don't even think about it," he warned, his back still to me as he poured himself a generous drink at the bar by the window, overlooking the main street. "Scotch?"

"Thought you said I couldn't drink," I mocked, surprised at the sarcasm that dripped freely from my voice. This mansion was changing me. I was hardening, inside and out. My soft skin clung to rigid bones, my attitude turned from bright to cynical, and my heart frosted over.

"You can't outside these walls. You're about to marry a senator and have yet to hit twenty-one. Have you any idea how bad that would look for me?"

"How is it fair that you can marry at eighteen but not drink until twenty-one? One life choice is significantly more monumental than the other," I blabbed nervously, rooted in place and watching his broad back. He worked out regularly, and it showed. I heard his personal trainer singing songs from the eighties as he walked into the foyer at five o'clock every morning. Wolfe exercised in his basement for an hour every day, and when time permitted it, he went for quick runs before dinner.

He twisted toward me, two tumblers of scotch in one palm. He handed me a glass. I ignored his peace offering, folding my arms.

"Are you here to discuss the legal age of alcohol consumption, Nem?"

There went that stupid pet name again. It was ironic he'd called me Nemesis. Because he was vain as hell, and just like

Narcissus, there was nothing I'd love more than to throttle him to his eternal slumber.

"Why not?" I continued talking in a bid to distract him from his walk-in closet and the mountain of destroyed ties and clothes at the center of it. "You can change things around, right?"

"You want me to change the law so you can legally drink in public?"

"After yesterday, I think I earned the right to a stiff drink anywhere you'd be."

Something glimmered in his eyes before he turned it off completely. A hint of a pleasant feeling, though I couldn't detect what it was. He slammed the glass he'd poured for me on the bar behind him, leaning a hip against it and examining me. Swirling the amber liquid in his tumbler, he crossed his legs at the ankles.

"Was it to your satisfaction?" he croaked.

"What?"

"My walk-in closet."

I felt myself reddening and hated my body for its betrayal. Wolfe slept with someone else yesterday, for goodness' sake. And had quite a bit of fun rubbing it in my face. I should be yelling at him, hitting him, throwing things at him. But I was physically exhausted from the lack of food and mentally beat from the news of our engagement. Throwing a fit, appealing as it might be, was something I did not have the energy to do.

I shrugged. "Seen better, bigger, and nicer walk-ins in my life."

"I'm glad you're underwhelmed since you will not be moving to this bedroom after the wedding," he delivered the news wryly.

"But I suppose you do expect me to warm your bed when you're in the mood for some domestic bliss?" I stroked my chin thoughtfully, giving him the same sardonic sass he dished at me. I enjoyed a moment of triumph when his eyes skimmed my fingers, only to find that his engagement ring wasn't there.

"I take it back. You do have a bit of a spine. Granted, I could snap it like a wishbone." He smiled proudly. "Nonetheless, it's there."

"Why, thank you for the recognition. As you know, there is nothing I value more than your opinion of me. Other than, maybe, the dirt under my fingernails."

"Francesca." My name slid from his mouth smoothly as if he'd said it a trillion times before. Maybe he had. Maybe I'd been his plan since before I came back to Chicago. "Go into my walk-in closet and wait until I finish my drink. We have much to discuss."

"I don't take orders from you," I said, elevating my head.

"I have an offer for you. One you'd be a fool not to accept. And since I do not negotiate, it will be the one and *only* offer I make to you."

My mind began to reel. Was he letting me go? He slept with someone else. He saw me nearly making out with my childhood sweetheart. And surely, after he'd seen the mess I'd made in his closet, his feelings toward me would only take a nosedive, if that were even possible. I made my way to the walk-in closet, crouching down and grabbing the shears for protection, just in case. I plastered my back against a row of drawers and tried to regulate my breathing.

I heard the clink of his tumbler as it hit the glass bar, then his approaching steps. My pulse kicked up a notch. He stopped on the threshold and stared at me emotionlessly, his jaw granite, his eyes steel. The pile underneath me mounted up to my lower thighs. There was no mistaking how I'd spent the better half of my afternoon.

"Do you know how much money you just destroyed?" he asked, his tenor reserved and detached as ever. He didn't care that I ruined his clothes, and that made me feel hopeless and lost. He felt completely untouchable and out of reach, a lonely star hanging in the sky, twinkling bright, galaxies away from my violent hands that demanded retaliation.

"Not enough to cost me my pride," I snipped the air with the shears, feeling my nostrils flaring.

He stuffed his hands in his pockets, leaning a shoulder against the doorframe.

"What's eating you, Nemesis? The fact that your boyfriend had a date yesterday, or the part where I *fucked* said date?"

So now I got an admission out of him. For whatever reason, part of me wanted to give Senator Keaton the benefit of the doubt about what happened with Emily behind closed doors. But now it was real, and it hurt. God, it shouldn't hurt as much as it did. Like a punch to my empty stomach. Betrayal, no matter by whom, cracks something deep inside you. Then you have to live with the pieces rattling in the pit of your stomach.

Senator Keaton was nothing to me.

No. That wasn't true, either.

He was everything bad that'd ever happened to me.

"Angelo, of course," I huffed incredulously, my fingers tightening around the shears. His eyes darted to my white-knuckled grip over my weapon. He shot me a smirk that said he could disarm me with only a blink, let alone his entire body.

"Liar," he said tonelessly. "And a lousy one at that."

"Why would I be jealous of you being with Emily when you were hardly jealous when Angelo cornered me?" I fought the tears that clogged my throat.

"For one thing, because she was a fantastic lay, and Angelo is a very lucky guy to have her sweet, expert mouth at his disposal," he taunted, unbuttoning the first button of his dress shirt. Heat slashed through my veins, making my body hit temperatures more fitting for a furnace. He'd never spoken any sexual words to me, and until now, our marriage felt more like a punishment than a real thing. When the second button released, a hint of dark chest hair peeked back at me.

"Second, because I was not, in fact, happy with your little display of affection. I gave you a chance at a proper goodbye. Which, judging by the way you two held each other when I left the restroom, you took in both hands. Did you enjoy it?"

I blinked, trying to untangle the meaning of his words. Did he think that Angelo and I…? Christ, he did. His passive expression did nothing to hide the earlier emotion I caught in his eyes. He thought I'd slept with Angelo at the wedding, and he was reacting against a crime he did not even try me for.

Fury gripped every bone in my malnourished body. Walking into this room today, I couldn't believe I'd ever hate him more than I did. But I stood corrected.

Now this? *This* was real hatred.

I didn't correct his assumption. It made the humiliation of being cheated on a tad less painful. The balance between our sins now more even. I squared my shoulders, owning up to this for no other reason than wanting him to hurt as much as I did.

"Oh, I'd slept with Angelo plenty of times," I lied. "He's the best lover in The Outfit, and *of course,* I personally checked." I laid it on thick. Maybe if he thought he'd gotten himself a rotten deal with an easy woman, he'd let me leave.

Wolfe cocked his head, his stare stripping me of whatever leftover confidence I'd had in me.

"How peculiar. I could have sworn you said that you wanted to kiss him at the masquerade and nothing more."

I swallowed, trying to think fast. I could count on one hand the amount of times I'd lied in my life.

"*As per the note.* I was only following tradition. I'd kissed him a thousand times before," I quipped. "But that night was about fate."

"Fate brought you to me."

"You *stole* my fate."

"Perhaps, yet it doesn't make it any less mine. Consider yesterday a one-off. I let you get the little menace out of your system. An engagement gift from yours truly, if you will. From here on out, I'm your only option. Take it or leave it."

"I suppose the rules do not apply to you," I arched an eyebrow, snapping the shears again. He glanced at them with an expression dripping of boredom.

"Quite clever, Miss Rossi."

"Then, Senator Keaton, I'll have you know they do not apply *at all*. I will sleep with whomever I want, whenever I want, as long as you continue to do so."

I was arguing my freedom to sleep around, when in practice, I was more virginal than a nun. He was the only man I'd ever even kissed. This, however, wasn't about my right to sleep my way through Chicago's elite—but merely a principle. Equality mattered to me. Maybe because for the first time, I thought I might be able to achieve it.

"Let me be clear." He stepped into the walk-in closet, erasing some of the distance between us. Though he was not close enough to touch me, sharing a space with him still sent a bullet of excitement and fear down my spine.

"You're not eating, and I'm not going to back down from this arrangement, even at the cost of burying your pretty little corpse when your body finally gives in. But I can make your life comfortable. My problem is with your father, not you, and you'd be wise to keep it that way. So, Nemesis—what could I give you that your parents wouldn't?"

"Are you trying to buy me?" I snorted.

He shrugged. "I already have you. I'm giving you a chance to make your life bearable. Take it."

Hysterical laughter bubbled up my throat. I felt my sanity evaporating from my body like sweat. The man was unbelievable.

"The only thing I want back is my freedom."

"You were never free with your parents to begin with. Don't insult both our intelligence by pretending so." His flatlined tenor whiplashed on my face. He took a step deeper into the room.

I cemented my back to the drawers, their bronze handles digging into my spine.

"*Think*," he enunciated. "What can I give you that your parents never will?"

"I don't want any dresses. I don't want a new car. I don't even want a new horse," I cried out, waving the shears in my hand desperately. Papa said whoever decided to marry me could buy me a horse to show his good faith. And to think I was devastated *then*.

"Stop pretending to care about materialistic things," he snapped, and I twisted around and threw an Oxford shoe at him to stop him from getting any closer, but he just dodged it and laughed.

"*Think*."

"I don't have any wants!"

"We all have wants."

"What's yours?" I was stalling.

"Serving my country. Seeking justice and punishing those who deserve to be brought to justice. You do, too. Think back to the masquerade."

"College!" I yelled, finally cracking. "I want to go to college. They'd never let me get a higher education and make something of myself." It surprised me that Wolfe caught the fraction of the moment in which I had to school my face from being both embarrassed and disappointed when Bishop asked me about college. My grades were great, and my SAT scores were glorious. But my parents thought I was wasting my energy when I should be focusing on getting married, planning a wedding, and continuing the Rossi legacy by producing heirs.

He stopped his stride.

"It's yours."

His words shocked me into silence. My quiet inspired him to resume his steps. He smirked, and I had to admit, albeit begrudgingly, that he was always raggedly stunning—his face all sharp edges like an Origami figure—but especially when his lips were curled in an Adonis-like grin. I wondered what he looked like with a full-blown smile. I hoped I'd never stick around to find out.

"Your father has explicitly asked me not to send you to college when we get married to maintain The Outfit's status quo in regard to women, but your father can also go fuck himself." His words stabbed me like knives. He spoke completely different than he did in public. As if he was another person with another vocabulary. I could never imagine him dropping the F-bomb anywhere but here. "You can go to college. You can go horseback riding, visit friends, and go on shopping sprees in Paris. Hell if I care. You could live your life separately from mine, play your part and, when enough years go by, even take on a discreet lover."

Who was this guy, and what made him so ice-cold? In all my years on Earth, and all my time spent with the ruthless men of The Outfit, I'd never met anyone quite so cynical. Even the most horrid men wanted love, and loyalty, and marriage. Even they wanted children.

"And what do I give you in return?" I elevated my chin, pursing my lips.

"You *eat*," he bit out.

I could do that, I thought grimly.

"You play the dutiful wife role." He took another step. I instinctively pressed myself harder against his drawers, but there was no escape and nowhere else to go. In two steps, he was going to be flush against me just like Angelo had been last night, and I'd have to meet the inferno of his body and the frost of his eyes.

He lifted the tips of a ruined, maroon-hued tie, eating the entire distance between us in one, purposeful stride, "I was planning a trip to DC, but seeing as your father is up to all sorts of trouble, I decided to stay in town. That means that on Friday, we'll have guests from DC. You will dress impeccably, you will cut the engagement tales bullshit in favor of a proper, decent version, and you will entertain them flawlessly as you were brought up to do. After dinner, you will play the piano for them, and after that, you will retire to the west wing with *me*, seeing as they will be spending the night in the east wing."

"Sleeping in your bed?" I barked out a laugh. Wasn't that convenient.

"You'll sleep in the next room." His body was now hovering over mine, and he was touching me without really touching me. He poured heat my own curves drank thirstily, and even though I hated him, I didn't want him to step away.

I opened my mouth to answer, but nothing came out. I wanted to refuse, but also knew that by agreeing to his deal, I'd have the chance to actually live a decent life. But I couldn't surrender to him willingly and completely. Not so fast. He laid down his rules, his expectations, and his price for his messed-up version of my freedom. We were striking a verbal deal, and the need to put a clause or two of my own was primal.

"I have one condition," I said.

He curved one inquisitive eyebrow, the tip of the tie in his hand gliding its way to my neck. I raised the shears in a knee-jerk reaction, ready to stab his black heart if he touched me in-appropriately. But not only did he not recoil, he actually awarded me with that smile I'd been wondering about. He had dimples. Two. The right one deeper than the left. The tie fluttered across my shoulder blade, making my nipples pucker inside my bra, and I prayed to God it was padded enough for him not to notice. I clenched from the inside, my stomach tumbling and dipping. A delicious ache spread in my womb like warm goo.

"Speak now, or forever hold your peace, Nemesis." His lips fluttered so close to mine for a split second, I wouldn't object if he kissed me.

Jesus. What was wrong with my body? I loathed him. But I also craved him. Terribly.

I looked up, tensing my jaw. "I will not be made a fool. If I'm expected to be faithful, so will you."

He moved the tie from my shoulder blade, dipping it down into the slit of my cleavage before moving it back up to my neck. I shuddered, fighting to keep my eyes open. A pool of wetness gathered in my cotton underwear. His eyes were dead and serious when he asked, "That's your one condition?"

"And the notes," I added as an afterthought. "I know you know about them because you ruined my kiss with Angelo. Do not read my notes. The wooden chest is mine to open, read, and explore whenever I'm ready."

He looked so blasé, there was no way I could detect whether he tampered with the box or not. And by now, I knew my future husband would never willingly volunteer any information to me.

My future husband. It was happening.

"I take verbal contracts quite seriously." He brushed the tie over my cheek, his smile still intact.

"So do I." I gulped, feeling his hand prying my fingers open. The shears dropped to the floor beside us, and he squeezed my palm in his, his version of a handshake.

Our hearts were pounding together in a completely different way from when Angelo and I were tangled in the darkened alcove like two messy teenagers fumbling for their first kiss yesterday. This felt dangerous and feral. It felt exhilarating, somehow. Like he could tear me apart, no matter how many shears I arm myself with. I forced myself to remember that he'd slept with Emily yesterday while being engaged to me. To keep in mind his cruel words when he thought I'd slept with Angelo on the same night I presented my engagement ring to Chicago's highest society.

He was not my playmate. He was my monster.

Wolfe picked up our entwined hands and brought them level with my chin. I watched in fascination as his dark, big hand enclosed my ivory, small one. Little, black hairs peppered each finger above his knuckles, and his arms were veiny, tan, and thick. Yet somehow, our size difference didn't look ridiculous.

My heart stammered in my chest as Senator Keaton bent his head down, his lips brushing my ear.

"Now clean the mess you've created. By evening, you will be given a new laptop connected to WiFi and a Northwestern brochure. By night, you *will* have your dinner and a snack. And tomorrow morning, after breakfast, you will practice the piano and shop for a dress that will make our guests foam at the mouth. Am I understood?"

He was crystal clear. But I chose to pull away, bat my eyelashes, and answer him with one of the taunting smirks he was so fond of. I lacked real power in the situation between us, so sarcasm didn't cost me a thing, and I found I had it in spades.

I brushed past him and strode away, leaving him alone in his walk-in closet.

"For someone who doesn't negotiate, you just went pretty far."

He chuckled behind me, shaking his head.

"I'm going to bury you, *Nemesis*."

CHAPTER SIX

Wolfe

I TUGGED AT THE NEW YELLOW TIE, TOSSING IT ON THE FLOOR.

Too calm.

I slid a green one from the rack, wrapping it over my neck before thinking better of it.

Too chirpy.

I plucked out a silky black velvet one and pressed it against my white shirt.

Perfect.

My sexual frustration was getting the best of me. I could barely walk straight without thinking of dipping my cock into the nearest open mouth in my vicinity. It'd been days since the last time I sank my dick in a wet pussy, and the last encounter with the fairer sex was lackluster, to say the least.

Emily, of course, was a magnificent bore to fuck. Just a tad more responsive than a corpse and possessing around the same amount of charm. Although, in her defense, I was more invested in fucking the rage out of my system than making it bearable for either of us. She was pathetic enough to fake an orgasm, and I was screwed-up enough to pretend I didn't notice.

It took me one second from the moment I laid eyes on

Francesca and the blue-eyed Bandini at the wedding to realize that they were already halfway into their foreplay, whether they knew it or not. Her eyes, even in the darkened niche, zinged with such intensity, the thought of dragging her across the ballroom and fucking her on the royal couple's table as punishment crossed my mind. But acting jealous and possessive was 1.) Not in my nature and, 2.) Unconstructive to my final goal. Besides, since when was I into teenagers? It was therefore counterproductive to let them have one last rodeo. If I tainted it, I couldn't get attached to it.

So, I let Bandini stain it for me.

Thoroughly.

Now Nemesis surprised me by wanting exclusivity. I supposed she would figure out, after weeks of being fucked rough and ruthlessly, that the arrangement was not in her interest and send me on my way to the nearest available mistress. Kristen, of course, was no longer an option, since she tried to run the piece about my engagement to Rossi. Consequently, Kristen got demoted from senior reporter to researcher. I called her editor and informed him that the lovely blonde he'd hired fresh out of Yale a decade ago was getting in bed with the wrong type of people.

The people whose lives she was covering.

Mine.

It was Friday night, and time for the big charade. Secretary of Energy Bryan Hatch was coming over with his wife to discuss his support in my future campaign. I had nearly six full years to serve as a senator, but the objective was clear: Presidency. It was, admittedly, part of the reason Miss Rossi was now the proud owner of one of the most expensive engagement rings in the state. Adjusting my image from someone who shoved his cock into enough mouths to silence the better half of the nation to the savior of a mob princess would earn me some much-needed points. Her noble upbringing was a nice touch as a first lady, too.

Not to mention, I'd mercilessly kill her father's business in the process, despite my so-called affection toward my wife.

They'd call me a martyr, and she'd never be able to call me on my bullshit.

I tied my newly bought black tie and scowled at the mirror in front of me. The walk-in closet had been thoroughly cleaned and the ruined items replaced. I patted the depth of my drawer for the framed picture I'd been looking at every time I needed to remember where I came from, and where I wanted to go.

It wasn't there.

Slowly, I pulled the drawer all the way out until it was fully opened. The photo *still* wasn't there. Francesca either destroyed it or took it with her. My money was on the former since she was positively certified after finding out I'd fucked her boyfriend's latest toy. Was she expecting me to watch her publicly grind over another man's cock and hand her a condom? Either way, she'd taken it too far.

I stormed out of my room, stalking my way to the east wing. Sterling jumped in my way down the hall just as she exited her own room. She flung her arms in the air, cackling like a happy hen.

"Your fiancée is looking ravishing, Senator Keaton! I cannot wait for you to see how beaut…" She did not complete the sentence. I bulldozed past her wordlessly, straight to Francesca's room. Sterling stumbled after me before I barked, "Don't you even dream about it, you old hag."

I threw the door to Nemesis's room open without knocking. This time, she really did it. The clothes and ties were just money, and meaningless in the grand scheme of things. The picture, however, was priceless.

I found my bride sitting in front of her vanity mirror, wearing a tight black velvet dress—it looked like we coordinated something other than trying to stab each other—a lit cigarette dangling from the corner of her luscious lips. She was shoving mud into a pot, gardening in the middle of her bedroom, in a Chanel evening dress.

She was crazy.

And she was *my* crazy.

What in the fresh hell did I get myself into?

I waltzed to her briskly, plucking the cigarette from her mouth and snapping it in half in one hand. She looked up, batting her eyelashes. She was a smoker. Another thing I loathed about her, and people, in general. At this rate, I was seriously contemplating getting to know this girl just so I could destroy her more thoroughly. Even though I decided upon requesting her hand that I didn't want to be privy to anything about her—other than, maybe, how her warm, sleek cunt felt as I pummeled into it.

"Do not smoke inside my house," I growled. My voice leaked fury, and that pissed me off even more. I was never angry, never affected, and above all—never one to give one single fuck about anything other than myself.

She rose to her feet, slanting her head slightly with an amused smile.

"You mean *our* house."

"Don't play games with me, Nemesis."

"Then don't act like a toy, Narcissus."

She was in rare form today. That was what I got for sitting at the negotiation table. Served me right. I pushed her against the wall with one, swift movement, snarling in her face.

"Where is the picture?"

Her expression switched from glee to dread, the smirk falling from her puffy lips. I looked down at her curly black eyelashes. Her eyes were marbles. Too brutally blue to look real, and I wanted her skin to match them in color as I choked her for being so stubborn. If only I'd known how much of a headache she'd be, I'd have probably resisted the temptation to take her away from her old man. But she was my problem now, and I wasn't one to admit defeat, let alone be dominated by a teenybopper.

I thought she was going to play dumb—any other weak woman would—but Francesca was in a mood to reinforce the fact she was not a pushover. Since our deal, I'd almost been lured to believe she was contained. She went horseback riding every day and toured Northwestern, accompanied by Smithy, my driver, her pain-in-the-ass housekeeper, Clara, and her cousin, Andrea. They all arrived at my mansion as though they were about to take a tour of the White House. Cousin Andrea looked like a lost member of the Kardashians with her hair extensions, fake tan, and tight clothes. She was in the habit of snapping her gum as a method of completing a sentence. I swore, she used it as a period.

"*Nice vase.*" Pop.

"*Are you guys legit in a relationship? Because he's a little old.*" Pop.

"*Do you think you should have a bachelorette party in Cabo? I've never been.*" Pop.

Sterling told me Francesca practiced the piano in the mornings, ate three meals a day, and gardened in her spare time.

I thought she was coming around.

I thought *wrong*.

"I broke it," she said, raising her chin defiantly. She was full of surprises, this one, and today, I was particularly in the mood for an eventless evening. "By accident," she added. "I'm not one for mindless vandalism."

"But I am?" I took the bait, grinning. I was more concerned about the fact that the cleaners had probably tossed away the picture *in* the broken frame than anything else. It was the last picture I'd had of us together. It was my entire world encased in cheap glass. My bride was lucky I wasn't above the law just yet. I could mar her beautiful neck in that moment.

She offered me a polite, cold smile. "But, of course, you are."

"Tell me, Nemesis, what did I break of yours?" I challenged her through gritted teeth, getting farther in her face and crushing her small body with my large one.

"Why, my dear fiancé, you broke my heart and then my spirit."

I was about to say something when Sterling knocked on the wooden doorframe softly, shoving her cotton-haired head between the crack. It was only then that I realized I had my knee between Francesca's thighs, and that both women were looking at my knee with eyes wide in shock. One from the doorway, the other with parted lips, her eyelids heavy. I took a step back.

Sterling swallowed. "Sir, Mr. Secretary and his wife are here to see you. Should I…should I tell them you're busy?"

Snorting, I shook my head, scanning Francesca with disdain one last time.

"Never been more bored in my life."

I supposed dinner went well, considering Francesca and I used our utensils strictly on our poached pears and herbed lamb as opposed to on each other.

Bryan and I sat across from one another, discussing my future plans before we even got to the main course, while my striking, entrancing fiancée—Bryan's words, *not* mine—asked his bland wife all about her mind-numbing charity foundations, including her Adopt-a-Clown aid for hospitalized children, and Bros for Hose—hose being literal fire hose—organization. Bryan was never going to live down the last title his wife chose. Francesca, however, nodded and smiled even though I knew, without a shadow of a doubt, that she was bored to tears. All she needed was a customary wave to rival Kate Middleton in the etiquette department. I was strangely—and annoyingly—pleased with her. Especially considering the fact she just managed to ruin the only thing I truly cared about in this whole, expensive, and pointless mansion. *The picture.*

I was dismembering my main course now, a lobster, imagining it was my future wife's limbs, when Galia Hatch perked up from her dish and shot another enthusiastic, borderline-deranged glance at Francesca. Her hair was bleached and sprayed to a point it clattered in dry chunks atop her head, and her face so plastic, she could pass as a Tupperware container. Not to mention, there was a medieval witch somewhere who wanted her dreadful dress back.

"Oh, my, now I know why you are so familiar! You were leading a charity, too, weren't you, darling? Back in Europe. France, if I'm not mistaken?" She clicked her fork against her champagne glass, making a grand, idiotic announcement of some sort.

I was about to snort out a dismissal. Nemesis only cared about her horses, garden, and Angelo Bandini. Not necessarily in that order. My plus one's ears pinked immediately, and she set her utensils on her half-full plate.

"Switzerland." She dabbed at the corner of her mouth with her napkin for nonexistent crumbs of food.

I stopped listening to Bryan gushing about the secretary of state and turned my attention to the ladies' conversation. Francesca looked down, and a hint of her cleavage caught my eye. Her milky tits were pressed together in a tight bra. Looking away was not in my near future. Dying of blue balls—might be.

"Fascinating charity, it was. I remember there was some gardening involved? You gave us a tour a few years back. I couldn't stop blabbing for months afterward about the sweet American girl who showed us the gardens," Galia hooted loudly. My eyes dragged from my wife's chest to her face. Her blush deepened; her face so fresh and youthful even under the minimal makeup she applied. She didn't want me to know. I could see no reason she'd withhold the information from me, other than fearing that I'd actually take a liking to her if I knew that she was philanthropic.

No trouble there, darling.

"Did you know your wife is also a patron?" Bryan raised his thick gray eyebrows at me when he realized I wasn't paying attention to his words. I did now. And although she possessed admirable first lady qualities, including her beauty, wits, and ability to entertain women as thick as Galia, who could drive a monkey into alcoholism, I found myself thoroughly aggravated. Francesca had officially proven to have too much personality than necessary. It was time to clip her black-inked Nemesis wings.

"Naturally." I threw my napkin on the table, signaling the four servants standing against each of the walls of my dining room to clear out our plates ahead of dessert. Francesca avoided my gaze, somehow sensing how irritated I was. She could read me fairly well by now. Another thing to add to the never-ending list of things I disliked about her. When her foot found mine under the table and the sharp pointy heel kicked my loafers in warning, I realized that I wanted a refund on my deal with Arthur Rossi.

His daughter wasn't a toy or a weapon.

She was a liability.

"We grew self-sustaining vegetable gardens in poor parts of the country, mainly those areas that employed refugees and immigrants who lived in severe circumstances," Nem provided, sitting back and running her long, thin fingers over her neck, avoiding my gaze. Her heel traveled up to my knee, and then toward my inner thigh. I dragged my chair back before she had the chance to smash my balls with her stilettos.

Two can play this game.

"Is everything okay?" Galia asked Francesca with a concerned smile as my fiancée's hand flew to her lips. At the same time, I raised my leg under the table, pressing my heel between her thighs. It was a knee-jerk reaction on her part, as if she forgot something *on* those lips, and I had a knee-jerk reaction of my own when my cock stood at attention at the gesture as if saying, *Yes, Nemesis, I'm the thing that's missing from your mouth.*

That kiss on the museum's stairs felt like a first kiss. But after she'd bragged about sleeping with Angelo plenty of times, and probably rode half The Outfit, I concluded that my future wife was simply a very convincing kisser. If I could see the same disgust on her face again after putting my lips on hers, I'd remember the cold bitch who reminded me so much of her asshole father.

"I could use a cigarette." Francesca smiled apologetically, pushing her chair back and relieving her groin from my hard-pressed foot, which no doubt put pressure on her clit.

"Such a pretty girl, such a filthy habit." Galia scrunched her nose, not missing a chance to patronize her younger, prettier companion.

I happen to like my fiancée filthy, I wanted to bite out, but of course, I kept the unwarranted reaction to myself. Smoking was a vice, and vices were weaknesses. I didn't allow for any of them in my life. I drank very casually with strict control over the amount, quality, and frequency of my drinks. Other than that, I did not consume junk food, did not bet, smoke, do drugs, or even play *Best Fiends* and *Candy Crush*.

Zero addictions. Other than Arthur Rossi's misery, of course.

I couldn't get enough of that shit.

"May I be excused?" Francesca cleared her throat.

I waved her off impatiently. "Make it fast."

After dessert, which Bryan and I didn't touch yet Galia consumed it in its entirety and even asked for a second serving, I noticed that Francesca took two bites of her own before declaring it was sinfully good, but she was too full (that boarding school was worth every penny). Afterward, we retired with our drinks to the salon to listen to my bride-to-be play the piano. Since

Nem was nineteen, practically a baby in the world I operated in, it was of essence to show that she was well-bred, soft-spoken, and destined to become American royalty. The three of us sat on the upholstered sofas overlooking the piano as Francesca took a seat. The entire round room had shelves stacked with books for walls. It was my final touch when entertaining colleagues and peers, but having a wife who could play the instrument was even more impressive.

Francesca arranged her dress on her seat with admirable precision, her back straight as an arrow, her neck long and delicate, begging to be bruised. Her fingers floated over the keys—flirting, barely touching them. She took her time admiring the piece I'd inherited from my parents. The late Keatons were big on classical music. They'd been begging for me to learn up until the day they died.

Bryan and Galia held their breaths, staring at what I had no choice but to look at myself. My fiancée—so painfully beautiful in her black velvet dress, her hair secured in a French twist, as she gazed adoringly at an antique piano, caressing it with her fingers while wearing an enchanted smile on her face. She was, to my utter displeasure, much more than an ivory pawn, expensive and striking, but useless and still. She was a living thing with a pulse you could feel from across the room, and for the first time since I took her from her father, I truly wished I hadn't. Not only because of the picture, but because she was not going to be easy to tame. And difficult, I'd decided from a very young age, was a flavor I found distasteful.

She began to play Chopin. Her fingers moved with grace, but it was the look on her face that betrayed her. The intense pleasure music brought to her both mesmerized and enraged me. She looked like she was coming, her head thrown back, her eyes closed, her lips humming silently to the music. She was chasing the notes with her lips.

I shifted on the couch, looking to my left at the Hatch's

as the room grew smaller and hotter with the dramatic music bouncing on the walls. Galia was smiling and nodding, unaware of the fact that her husband was sporting a hard-on the size of her arm. Up until now, I had no issue with Bryan Hatch. In fact, I quite liked him, despite his incompetence to take care of a goldfish, let alone occupy a seat in the Cabinet. This, however, changed my view of him.

My things were mine.

Not to be admired.

Not to be desired.

Not to be touched.

Suddenly, the need to ruin the moment for my young bride-to-be was overwhelming, almost violent. My provocative fiancée, who had the guts to fuck another man on the night I'd presented her to my colleagues and peers after having put an engagement ring on her finger that cost more than some people's houses, would most definitely pay.

Dispassionately, and oh-so-smugly, I raised my tumbler of whiskey to my lips, standing up and sauntering to Francesca. Since I was positioned behind her back, she wouldn't see me even if she opened her eyes. But she didn't, caught in a trance of art and desire. She was dripping lust on the floor for our guests to see, and they gulped every drop of it—so much so that I had to make a point, both to them and to her.

With every step I took, the tune under her fingers became louder and more dramatic. The piece reached its peak just as I planted the first, soft kiss on her shoulder blade from behind, causing her eyes to snap open and her body to jerk with surprise. She kept her fingers on the piano, still playing, but the rest of her body shuddered as my lips dragged along her soft, warm neck, sinking to the spot behind her ear for another seductive kiss.

"Play away, Nemesis. You're giving us quite a show, coming all over my antique piano. Are you ready to try to measure up to Emily?"

I could feel her skin blossoming with heat, quivering with passion as my lips moved again, over her shoulder, biting into her inviting flesh, dipping my teeth to her soft skin in front of our guests and exhibiting terrible lack of self-control that made me want to punch myself in the face.

Francesca messed up her notes, her fingers fumbling on the keys without direction. I took pleasure in the fact I threw her off balance. I started to pull away and straighten. Withdrawing from the sweet mist of her body, I assumed she'd stop playing, but she repositioned her fingers on the piano, took a deep, calming breath, and started playing "Take Me to Church" by Hozier. I knew instantly that this was an invite for more kissing.

I looked down. She looked up. Our eyes met. If this was how she responded to chaste kisses on the neck, what kind of reaction did she have in bed?

Stop thinking about her in bed, you tool.

I sank right back, brushing my thumb along her neck as I nuzzled my nose into the crook of it.

"They can see how wet you are for me. It turns them on."

"Jesus," she hissed between closed lips. She was beginning to screw up the notes again. I liked the song better under her fingertips. Less perfect. More of what I craved—her failure.

"It turns me on, too."

"Don't do this," she breathed, her labored panting making her chest move up and down quickly. Yet she didn't do one, simple thing—she didn't tell me to stop.

"They can watch if they want. You're not the only exhibitionist in this household, Nem," I taunted.

"*Wolfe*," she warned. It was the first time she said my name. To me, anyway. Another wall fell between us. I wanted to raise it back up, but not as much as I wanted to hurt her for exceeding my expectations.

"Please don't come on my piano. It would leave a terrible

impression in front of our guests. Not to mention, you'd have to lick the seat clean with your tongue."

She slammed her fingers over the keys just as our guests darted up behind us on cue. I made it uncomfortable enough for everyone in the room, and the message hit home. They were to retire to their room and stop drooling over my fiancée. Secretary Hatch, with his wood, and Mrs. Hatch, with her unfortunate choices of charity names and unnaturally stiff hair, bid us adieu for the evening.

"This was quite an evening," Galia sniffed behind me, arranging her plump figure inside her multi-layered dress. I spared her husband the humiliation of turning around and catching his erection through his pants. Francesca wasn't worth tarnishing my work relationship with him.

"A lovely evening." He cleared his throat, the lust still thick in his voice.

"Darling, say good night to our guests," I said, still staring down at my future wife with my back to them.

"Good night," Francesca murmured, not turning around either as my face was still buried in her shoulder. As soon as the door shut behind them, she jumped up from her seat. I made my way to the door at the same time, disinterested in another third-grade bickering session with a mouthy teenager.

"West wing," I clipped, my back to her.

"I hate you so much." She raised her voice behind me, but it remained steady and defiant. She didn't kick anything or try to push me like Kristen did. She cut all my clothes without crying about it like a little pussy.

I closed the door on her and walked away. She wasn't worth a response.

Ten minutes later, I was in my room, undoing my tie. I'd already had my daily quota of alcohol, so I resorted to sipping water, watching the main street out of my window. I heard my fiancée's heels sauntering across the hallway behind my closed doors. Shortly after, the scent of cigarette smoke crawled into my nostrils. She was trying to tell me she was not going to abide the house rules, but by lighting up a cigarette, she was playing with a much bigger fire. Did she think we were equals? She was about to be served with a huge piece of humble pie. And unlike her dessert—I'd force-feed her every bite of that dish until the message was clear.

I was about to enter my walk-in closet and change when my door flung open.

"How could you!" she hissed, her eyes so narrow you could barely make out their unique color. There was a lit cigarette between her fingers. She galloped toward me, but every step was measured and catwalk-worthy. "You had no right to touch me. No right to say those things about my body."

I rolled my eyes. Testing boundaries was very Terrible Twos of her. But I didn't do liars, and she made it sound like she was a virginal saint who didn't try to touch my cock with her heels and almost came when I kissed her shoulder not so long ago.

"Unless you're here to suck my cock, please see yourself out of my room. I'd hate to call security and have you removed to a temporary hotel, but I will."

"Wolfe!" She pushed my chest, losing her footing. I was already riled up about the picture, and the loss of the only materialistic thing that I cared about. I didn't respond. She pushed me again, harder.

Teenager, I thought bitterly. *Out of all the women in Chicago, you are marrying a teenager.*

I fished my phone from my pocket and punched the extension of my bodyguard. Her eyes widened, and she tried to snatch the phone from my hand. I clamped my hand over her wrist and pushed her away.

"What the hell!" she yelled.

"I said I'd throw you out. I meant it."

"Why?"

"Because you're confused, and horny, and getting on my nerves. The only reason you're in my bedroom is because you'd like to have sex. Only you'd hate to have it with me. And since I'm not in the business of forcing myself upon women, I am not interested in watching you having a meltdown for half an hour before you figure it out."

She growled but said nothing. More blushing. More sucking on her cigarette. Her lips were made to torture grown men. I was sure of it.

"Out," I said.

"Whose picture was it?" she asked out of nowhere.

"None of your business. Did you see who cleaned my room?" I'd hired a professional company three times a week. They weren't in the habit of throwing things away, but the photo was probably buried between mountains of clothes. *Another thing she ruined.* Of course, Francesca never bothered to clean her shit up. She had the upbringing of a monarch. Cleaning her own mess wasn't a concept she was familiar with.

"No," she said, biting on the corner of her thumbnail and looking down. She put out the cigarette in my glass of water (I was going to kill her) and looked straight at me. "And I do know why I'm here."

"You do?" I arched an eyebrow, feigning interest.

"I came here to tell you to never touch me again."

"Coincidentally, you came here breaking the news while wearing a nightgown that barely covers your tits and shows off every inch of your legs." I looked outside my window again, finding the sight of her unbearable all of a sudden.

I caught her in my periphery looking down, surprised by the fact that she was already in her pale blue nightgown. She was such a fucking mess. I'd met a variety of women in my life, but I'd yet to meet a woman who was so hell-bent on seducing me, only to freak out whenever I showed faint signs of interest.

"Fine." I ran my thumb over my lips, watching the manicured neighborhood with indifference.

"Fine?"

"Yes. You seem like a particularly boring lay as it is."

"I'd take being boring over being a psycho any day of the week."

"Humiliation looks good on you, Nemesis. Now, go," I ordered drily, sliding my tie from my neck.

I watched her reflection in my window as she started to walk toward the doors, stopping with her hand on one of the handles and turning around to face me again. I turned around to meet her eyes.

"You know how I knew you weren't Angelo when we kissed? Not because of your height or your scent. It was because you tasted like ash. Like betrayal. You, Senator Keaton, taste bitter and cold, like poison. *You taste like a villain.*"

That did it. I stalked over to her, too fast to make her second-guess her next move, buried a hand in her hair, my mouth coming down on hers to shut her up. I wrapped my tie around the back of her neck with my other hand, tugging her toward me and binding us together.

It was a long, violent kiss. Our teeth clashed, her tongue chasing mine first while I plastered her little body against my doors, grinning into her mouth at the fact that her back hit the round handles. Her lips moving against mine confirmed that she was a liar, and her groin bucking against my own cemented the fact she wanted to be fucked badly—she just didn't like idea of yielding to me. I tightened my grip on the back of her skull, deepening our kiss. She was dazed, and I knew it by the way her hands slid up my chest, cupping my cheeks and drawing me closer to her. It was the same thing she did with Angelo at the wedding. That was how I caught them when I left the restroom. Her hands on his cheeks. In one move, she switched her touch from passionate to intimate. She pulled the tie between us, moaning helplessly into my mouth. I drew back instantly.

Ours is not a love story.

"Leave," I barked.

"But…" She blinked.

"Leave!" I threw the door open, waiting for her to run away. "I made my point. You made yours. I won. Tuck your tail between your legs and get the hell out, Francesca."

"Why?" Her eyes widened. She was more embarrassed than hurt, judging by the way she hugged her chest to cover her puckered nipples under her nightgown. She'd never been rejected. But it was her pride, not feelings, which had been wounded.

Because you love another man and are trying to pretend that I am him.

I flashed her a sardonic smile, smacked her butt, and gave her a little push out my door. "You said I taste like a villain, but you taste like the victim. Now, save whatever's left of your self-worth and leave."

I slammed the door in her face.

Turned around.

Grabbed the glass of water with the cigarette butt swimming in it.

And threw it out the window.

CHAPTER SEVEN

Francesca

MY PARENTS WERE NOT GOING TO FIGHT FOR MY freedom.

The realization should have struck me sooner, but I clung to that hope like the edge of a cliff. Helplessly, foolishly, humiliatingly.

I called my mother the morning after Wolfe threw me out of his room, telling her about the text messages I'd received from Angelo and about last night's events. Blush hit my face and neck in uneven patches. Terrible shame gnawed at my gut for acting so carelessly last night. True, we were engaged to be married, but we weren't a couple. Not really. Technically, it was just a kiss. But I was there, and there was much more to it. More touching. More grinding. More devouring. More feelings I couldn't pinpoint—far away from love, yet shockingly close to affection.

When my mother heard about Angelo's texts, she berated me for contemplating answering them. *"You're an engaged woman, Francesca. Please start acting like one."* When my face was so hot with shame I was about to explode, she connected my father to the other line. Together, they informed me, rather tactfully, that Angelo was to attend an upcoming wedding with

Emily as his plus one, with my father adding that they'd made a beautiful couple at the Bishop's wedding. It was in that moment of clarity when I realized that not only was my father not going to claim me, but that perhaps I didn't want to be claimed by him. The only difference between the monster who currently housed me and the one I'd been born to was that the former made no empty promises or brought me to believe he cared.

They say the devil you know is better than the one that you don't, but I didn't feel as though I truly knew my father anymore. His affection apparently depended on the circumstances, and I was to meet each one of his expectations.

Last night's humiliation, paired with the fact that my mother changed her tune overnight and my father was eager for me to please Wolfe, made me want to rebel.

"I'm sure they look lovely together, Papa. I'm also glad I'll see Angelo around and hear all about his relationship with Emily directly from him." I inspected my muddy nails casually as if my parents could see me. I paced around the garden, taking a break from potting and fertilizing my radishes. Ms. Sterling was pretending to read in the pavilion next to me, her nose stuck in a historical book as thick as her glasses, but I knew she was eavesdropping. In fact, I figured she'd been snooping every time anyone opened their mouths in the house—cleaners, gardeners, and UPS deliverymen included. I'd be shocked to discover she hadn't heard our kiss, then our fight when Wolfe shooed me away.

My cheeks heated just thinking about last night. Senator Keaton had yet to leave his room this morning since returning from escorting his guests to his private jet while I was asleep. I'd be content not to see him the remainder of the weekend, month, and the span of my lifetime.

"How do you mean?" my father demanded.

"Why, Papa, I have the best news. My new groom has decided to send me off to college. Northwestern, no less. I've already taken a tour, and I'm filling out an application today. He was *so* supportive of that decision," I uttered, noticing with satisfaction the thin smile tugging at Ms. Sterling's lips as her eyes remained on the same page for long minutes. I was sure my father was well aware of the fact that Angelo, too, applied for a masters at Northwestern. He was good at connecting the dots.

A few days ago, I'd sighed and complained to the garden around me that I needed more pots and a new watering can. The day after, new ones were waiting for me in the shed. She could be nosy, but she was definitely not as bad as my husband-to-be. "He even expressed his support to my pursuing a career. Now I just need to figure out what I want to do. I'm thinking a lawyer or maybe a cop." That last touch was laying it on thick. My father hated lawyers and cops more than he hated child molesters and atheists. With illogic rage that burned in his blood.

I'd been my parents' puppet for so long, clipping the strings felt scary and forbidden. I wore long skirts and dresses I absolutely detested because they liked them. Attended Sunday mass regularly even though other church girls usually disliked me for having better clothes and nicer shoes. I even refrained from kissing boys to appease my strict folks. And what good did it do to me? My father sold me off to a senator. And my mother, despite her deep pain and disappointment, was helpless against him. But that did not stop her from discouraging me to pursue the same route as her.

She didn't want me to study and get a job.

She wanted me to be as stranded as she was.

"Is this a joke?" My father choked on his drink on the other line. "No daughter of mine will *work*," he spat.

"Your future son-in-law doesn't seem to share the sentiment," I singsonged, momentarily putting my hatred toward Wolfe aside.

"Francesca, you have the breeding, the beauty, and the wealth. You were not born to work, Vita Mia. You're rich in your own right and more so since you're marrying a *Keaton*," Mama cried out. I didn't even know the Keatons were a thing before all this. I'd never bothered to ask anyone, least of all my future husband, since money was the last thing on my mind.

"I'm going to college. Unless…" It was a crazy idea, but it made sense. A cunning smile touched my lips, and my eyes met Ms. Sterling's from across the garden. She gave me a barely noticeable nod.

"What?" my father snarled.

"Unless you tell me why you gave Wolfe my hand. Then I'd consider not going." Mainly because then I'd have the full picture. I very much doubted I could change my fate at this point, but I wanted to know what he'd gotten me into to see if I could dig my way out.

My father snorted, his glacial tenor stabbing at my nerves. "I do not discuss my business with women, much less my own daughter."

"What's wrong with being a woman, Papa?"

You sure acted like a pussy the day you gave me to Wolfe Keaton.

"We play different roles," he clipped.

"And mine is to make babies and look pretty?"

"Yours is to continue the legacy of your family and leave the hardworking jobs to people who need them."

"This sounds a lot like you don't respect me as an equal," I hissed, holding the phone between my ear and shoulder and stabbing the trowel in the mud and wiping my forehead simultaneously.

"That's because you're not my equal, my dear Frankie."

The line went dead on the other side.

I planted twenty pots of flowers that day. Then went to my room, took a shower, and started filling out my application to Northwestern. Political Science and Legal Studies, I decided, would be my major. In all fairness, I always thought gardening was my calling, but since my father infuriated me to no end, sticking my major in his face was worth going through years and years of studying something I doubted would interest me much. I was Petty McPetson, but I was gaining an education, and it felt good.

I hunched over my oak desk when something in the air changed. I didn't have to lift my head to know what it was.

My fiancé was here to check on his prisoner bride.

"You have your first dress fitting tomorrow. Go to bed."

From my peripheral, I could see he was not wearing a suit. A white V-neck shirt that highlighted his tan, lean but muscled body and dark denim that clung low on his narrow hips. He looked nothing like a senator, acted nothing like a politician, and the fact I couldn't box him this way or the other unsettled me.

"I'm filling out my application to Northwestern," I replied, feeling heat coating my face and neck again. Why did it feel like he dipped me in liquid fire every time his eyes were on me? And how could I make it stop?

"You're wasting your time."

My head snapped up, and I granted him the eye contact he'd been looking for.

"You promised," I growled.

"And I shall deliver." He pushed off my doorframe and stepped into my room, sauntering toward me. "You don't need to fill out an application. My people have already taken care of that. You're about to become a Keaton."

"Are Keatons too precious to fill out their own college applications?" I could barely keep myself from snapping at him.

He plucked the documents from my desk, balled and slam-dunked them in the trash can by my desk. "It means you could've drawn dicks in all shapes and sizes on the document, and you'd still get in."

I shot up from my chair, putting some much-needed

distance between us. I couldn't risk another kiss. My lips still stung every time I thought of his rejection.

"How dare you!" I thundered.

"You seem to be asking this question a lot. Care to change your tune a little?" He shoved one hand into the front pocket of his jeans and picked up my cell phone on my desk, scrolling through it with his thumb with easy monotony. My parents forbade me from having a passcode. When my mom gave me back my phone, protecting my privacy was low on my to-do list, seeing as the majority of it had already been taken anyway.

"What are you doing?" My voice turned eerily calm and shocked at the same time.

His eyes were still on my phone. "Go ahead. Ask again. How dare I, right?"

I was too stunned to form words. The man was a savage in a suit. He taunted and aggravated me at every turn. My father was a stubborn jerk, but this guy…*this* guy was the devil who returned to my nightmares every night. He was hell wrapped in a heavenly rugged mask. He was fire. Gorgeous to the eye, lethal to the touch.

"Give me my phone right now." I threw my open palm in his direction. He waved a dismissive hand my way, still reading my text messages. *Angelo's* text messages.

"You can't do that." I launched at him, raising my arms to reach the phone. He raised his arm, grabbed me by the waist with his other hand, capturing both my wrists and plastering my hands to his lower stomach over his shirt.

"Move, and you'll see what your anger does to me. A friendly hint: it thrills me and in more ways than you'd like to know."

A part of me wanted to defy him so he *would* push my hands down. I'd never touched a man down there before, and the idea of it excited me. My life was already in shambles. My morals were the last things I'd clung to, and frankly, my fingers were tired from holding them.

I moved on principle, and he smirked, scrolling down my texts and tightening his hold on my wrists. He didn't make good on his promise to put my hands on his manhood.

"Are you going to answer lover-boy?" he asked conversationally.

"None of your business."

"You're about to become my wife. Everything about you is my business. Especially boys with blue eyes and smiles I don't trust."

He dropped my hands, pocketed my phone, and cocked his head, scanning me through his scorn. I wanted to cry. After yesterday's humiliation, not only did he not apologize, but he also taunted me twice today—both by throwing my application in the trash and by reading through my messages.

He confiscated my phone as though I was his daughter.

"My phone, Wolfe. Give it." I took a step back. I wanted to hurt him so bad, it hurt to breathe. He stared me down, calm and quiet.

"Only if you delete Bandini from your contacts."

"He's a childhood friend."

"Out of curiosity, do you fuck all your childhood friends?"

I flashed him a sugary smile, "Afraid I'll run off and have sex with Angelo again?"

The tip of his tongue darted out to lick his lower lip sinisterly, "Me? No. But he should be. Unless, of course, he wants his dick cut off."

"You sound like a mobster, not a future president." I jutted my chin out.

"Both are positions of extreme power executed differently. You'd be surprised how many things they have in common."

"Stop justifying your actions," I said.

"Stop fighting your fate. You're not doing your father any favors. Even he wants you to submit."

"How do you know that?"

"One of his Magnificent Mile properties caught fire this morning. Fifty kilograms of cocaine straight from Europe—*poof!* Gone. He can't contact the insurance until he cleans up the evidence, and by then, they'll figure out he tampered with the scene. He just lost millions."

"You did that," I accused, narrowing my eyes at him. He shrugged.

"Drugs kill."

"You did that so they'd tell me off," I said.

He laughed. "Sweetheart, you're a nuisance at best and entirely not worth the risk."

Before I slapped him—or worse—I stormed outside, my anger following me like a shadow. I couldn't leave the house since I didn't have a car or anywhere to go, but I wanted to disappear. I ran out to the pavilion, where I broke down, falling to my knees and bawling my eyes out.

I couldn't take it anymore. The combination of my father being a tyrant and Wolfe trying to ruin my family's and my life was too much. I rested my head against the cool white wood of the bench, wailing softly as I felt the fight leaving my body.

A calming hand caressing my back. I was afraid to turn around even though I knew in my gut that Wolfe would never seek me out and try to make things better.

"Do you need your gloves?" It was Ms. Sterling, her voice soft like cotton. I shook my head between my arms.

"You know, he is just as confused and disoriented by your situation. Only difference is he's had years of perfecting how to hide his emotions."

I appreciated her trying to humanize my fiancé in my eyes, but it hardly worked.

"I had the pleasure of raising Wolfe. He was always a clever boy. He always wore his anger on his sleeve." Her voice rang like bells as she drew lazy circles on my back, like my mom used to do when I was young. I kept quiet. I didn't care that Wolfe had his own baggage. I'd done nothing to deserve his treatment.

"You need to weather the storm, my dear. I think you'll find, after your adjustment period, that you two are so explosive together because you finally met your challenges in one another." She sat on the bench above me, removing traces of my hair from my face. I looked up and blinked at her.

"I don't think anything can scare Senator Keaton."

"Oh, you'd be surprised. I think you give him a healthy dose of things to worry about. He did not expect you to be so...*you*."

"What does that mean?"

Her face wrinkled as she considered her next words. Seeing as Wolfe had obviously hired her because he felt attached to her after raising him, I at least had the hope in believing that one day, he'd warm up to me, too.

She offered me her hands, and when I took them, she surprised me by pulling me up and standing up at the same time, drawing me in for a hug. We were both the same height—tiny— and she was even scrawnier than me. She spoke against my hair.

"I think your love story started off on the wrong foot, but it will be magnificent precisely because of that. Wolfe Keaton has walls, but you're already starting to break them. He is fighting it, and you. Would you like the secret to disarming Wolfe Keaton, my dear girl?"

I wasn't sure how to answer that. Because a part of me sincerely feared that I would tear him to shreds given the opportunity. And I wouldn't be able to live with myself knowing I'd hurt someone so profoundly.

"Yes," I heard myself say.

"*Love* him. He will be defenseless against your love."

With that, I felt her body disconnecting from mine, and she retreated to the glass doors, the vast mansion swallowing her figure. I took a deep breath.

The man had just destroyed a building in which my father

processed drugs. And half-admitted it to me. That was more information than my father ever offered or admitted to. He also let me go to school. He also allowed me to leave whenever I pleased.

I glanced at my wrist watch. It was two in the morning. Somehow, I'd spent two hours in the garden. Two hours Wolfe must've spent reading through every message I'd ever received.

The late-night chill was seeping into my bones. Dejected, I turned to head back into the house. When I'd made my way back inside, I spotted Wolfe standing on the threshold of the open door. He had one arm propped against its frame, blocking me from getting in. I took measured steps toward him.

I stopped when I was a foot away.

"Give me my phone back," I said. To my surprise, he reached into his back pocket and tossed it into my hands. I clutched it in my fist, still reeling from our latest fight but also oddly touched by the fact he stayed awake and waited for me. He started his days at five in the morning, after all.

"You're in my way." I rustled, trying to keep my teeth from chattering.

He stared at me blankly.

"Push me away. Fight for what you want, Francesca."

"I thought that's what made us enemies." A vicious smile found my lips. "Because I want to break free from you."

It was his turn to smirk.

"Wanting and fighting are two different things. One is passive, the other active. Are we enemies, Nemesis?"

"What else can we be?"

"Allies. I'll scratch your back. You'll scratch mine."

"I'm all for not touching you ever again after last night."

He shrugged. "You might've been more believable if you hadn't grinded on me before I kicked you out of my bedroom. At any rate, you're welcome to come in. But I won't be making it easy for you, unless you give me your word Bandini is deleted from your phone *and* your life."

I got why he did that. He could have done it himself, but he wanted it to come from me. He didn't want another battle—he wanted my complete surrender.

"Angelo will always be in my life. We grew up together, and just because you bought me doesn't mean you own me," I said evenly even though really, I had no intention of responding to Angelo's texts. More so since I'd heard that he was going on a second date with the vile Emily.

"Then I'm afraid you'll have to show some of your temper and fight me."

"Can I ask you something?" I rubbed my forehead tiredly.

"Certainly. Whether I'll answer or not is a completely different story." His smirk grew more smug and mocking.

"What's your leverage over my father? He obviously hates your guts, yet he won't claim me back, even after I told him I'm going to college. That'd put a huge strain on his reputation as people will know that I am going against his wish. It must be quite substantial, then, if he'd rather have me in your bed than have *you* dish out the goods on him."

I scanned his face, expecting him to rebuke and belittle me as my father had done earlier that day.

Wolfe surprised me again.

"Whatever I have on him could take away everything he's worked for, not to mention throw him in jail for the rest of his miserable life. But your father didn't throw you to the dogs. He trusts me not to hurt you."

"Is that foolish of him?" I looked up.

Wolfe's muscular arm flexed under his shirt. A barely visible movement.

"I'm not a monster."

"Could've fooled me. Just tell me why?" I whispered, the air rattling in my lungs. "Why do you hate him so much?"

"That's two questions. Go to bed."

"Move out of the way."

"Accomplishments are so much more rewarding when obstacles are in the way. *Fight me, darling.*"

I snuck under his arm, ducking into the house and launching for the staircase. He caught me by the waist in one swift movement, pulling me into his arms and plastering me against his strong chest. His knuckles trailed down the length of my spine, and goose bumps burst all over my skin. His lips found my ear, hot and soft in contrast to the harsh man they belonged to, his breath tickling my hair. "Maybe I am the monster. After all, I come out to play at night. But so do you, little one. You're out in the darkness, too."

CHAPTER EIGHT

Wolfe

BLOWING UP ARTHUR'S PROPERTY SLASH METH LAB—AND the coke with it—was just another Tuesday. The work of saints was done through others, and mine had definitely been taken care of.

The next four days were spent bending White's and Bishop's arms until they snapped and agreed to assign over five hundred additional cops to be on duty at any given time to protect the streets of Chicago from the mess I'd created. It was going to blow up the bill to the sky, but it wasn't the state of Illinois that was going to shell out the money. The money was sitting firmly in White's and Bishop's pockets.

Money given by my future father-in-law.

Who, by the way, changed his tune from trying to coax his daughter into warming up to me and decided to repay me by throwing hundreds of pounds of trash in parks across Chicago. He couldn't do much more than that, considering all the juice I had on him. I was a power player. Touching what was mine—even scratching my car—came with a hefty price tag and would award him more unneeded attention from the FBI.

I had the trash picked up by volunteers and thrown into his

garden. That was when the phone calls began to pour in. Dozens of them. Like a needy, drunk ex-girlfriend on Valentine's Day. I didn't pick up. I was a senator. He was a highly connected mobster. I could marry his daughter, but I wouldn't listen to what he had to say. My job was to clean the streets he soiled with drugs, guns, and blood.

I made a point to be at home as little as possible, which wasn't very hard between flying out to Springfield and DC frequently.

Francesca was still adamant about having her dinners in her room (not that I cared). She did, however, fulfill her commitments as far as cake-tasting, trying on dresses, and doing all the other bullshit wedding planning I'd dumped on her (*not* that I minded if she showed up in a goddamn oversized napkin). I didn't care for my fiancée's affection. As far as I was concerned, with the exception of amending the no-fucking-other-people clause before my balls fell off, she could live on her side of the house—or better yet, across town—until her last breath.

On the fifth day, after dinner, I buried myself in paperwork in my office when Sterling summoned me to the kitchen. It was well past eleven o'clock, and Sterling knew better than to interrupt me in general, so I figured it was of critical importance.

Last thing I needed was hearing that Nemesis was planning an escape. It seemed like Francesca had finally realized she didn't have an out from this arrangement.

I descended the stairs. When I reached the landing, the smell of sugar, baked dough, and chocolate wafted from the kitchen. Sweet, sticky, and nostalgic in a way that sliced through your body like a knife. I stopped at the threshold and examined tiny, fierce Sterling as she served a simple chocolate cake with forty-six candles on the long dining table. Her hands were shaking. She wiped them on her stained apron the minute I walked in, refusing eye contact.

We both knew why.

"Romeo's birthday," she mumbled under her breath, hurrying to the sink to wash her hands.

I ambled in, dragged over a chair, and sank into it, watching the cake as if it was my opponent. I wasn't particularly sentimental and exceptionally bad with remembering dates, which was just as well as all my family members were dead. Their death dates, however, I remembered.

I also remembered the cause of their deaths.

Sterling handed me a plate on which she'd piled enough cake to clog a toilet bowl. I was torn between thanking her for paying her respects to the person I loved the most and yelling at her for reminding me that my heart had a hole the size of Arthur Rossi's fist. I settled for stuffing my mouth with the cake without tasting it. Sugar consumption was not a habit of mine, but it seemed excessively spiteful not to take a bite after she went through so much trouble.

"He would have been proud of you if he were alive." She lowered herself onto the seat in front of mine, wrapping her hands around a steamy cup of herbal tea. My back was to the kitchen door. She faced it—and me. I stabbed a fork into my cake, unfolding the layers of the chocolate and sugar like they were a human gut, digging harder with each motion.

"Wolfe, look at me."

I dragged my eyes to her face, pacifying her for a reason beyond my grasp. It was not in my nature to be nice and cordial. But something in that demanded an emotion from me that wasn't disdain. Her eyes widened, dotted sky-blue. She was trying to tell me something.

"Be gentle with her, Wolfe."

"That would give her false hope that what we have is real, and that's entirely too cruel, even by my standards," I drawled, pushing the cake across the table.

"She's lonely. She's young, isolated, and frightened to the bone. You're treating her like an enemy before she even lets you down. All she knows about you is that you're a powerful man, you hate her family, and don't want anything to do with her. Yet you made it clear that you'll never let her go.

"She is a prisoner," she finished simply. "For a crime she did not commit."

"It's called collateral." I laced my fingers behind my head and sat back. "And it's not very different from the life she would have led with anyone else. With the exception that unlike the majority of Made Men, I'd spare her the lies when I cheated on her."

Sterling winced as though I'd struck her across the face. She then leaned across the table and took my hand in hers. It took everything in me not to withdraw. I hated touching people in any capacity in which my cock wasn't in one of their holes, and Sterling was the last person on the entire planet I'd fuck. Not to mention, I particularly disliked it when she exhibited her feelings openly. It was inappropriate and way out of her job description.

"Choosing something doomed and being forced into it are two very different things. Showing her mercy will not weaken you. If anything, it will assure her you're confident in your power."

She sounded like Oprah.

"What do you have in mind?" I sneered. If I could throw money at Francesca and send her off on a shopping spree in Europe to spend some time with her cousin Andrea and get her out of my hair, I would do it in a heartbeat. At this point, I even considered Cabo as an option. It was still on the same continent, but far enough away from here.

"Take her to her parents."

"Have you been drinking?" I stared at her blankly. I hoped not. Sterling and alcohol were a lethal combination.

"Why not?"

"Because the reason I'm celebrating Romeo's birthday *without* Romeo's presence is due to her father."

"She is *not* her father!" Sterling darted up to her feet. Her palm crashed on the table, producing an explosive sound I didn't know she was capable of. The fork on my plate rattled and flew across the table.

"His blood is running through her veins. That's contaminated enough for me," I said drily.

"But not enough to prevent you from wanting to touch her," she taunted.

I smiled. "Tainting what's his would be a nice bonus."

I stood. A vase fell to the ground behind me, no doubt knocked down by my future wife. Bare feet jogged across the dark wooden floors, *pitter-pattering* as they slapped the stairs on her way back to her wing. I left Sterling in the kitchen to stew in her anger and followed my bride-to-be up with deliberate leisure. I stopped on the cleft between the west and the east wing when I reached the top floor, before deciding to retire back to my office. No point in trying to pacify her.

At three in the morning, after answering every email personally, including replying to concerned citizens about the state of Illinois' tomatoes, I decided to check on Nemesis. I hated that she was a night owl since I had to wake up every day at four, but she seemed to like getting out of the coop at nighttime. Knowing my quirky bride-to-be, it was not out of question for her to try to escape her cage. She certainly made a habit of rattling the bars. I strolled to her room and pushed the door open without knocking. The room was empty.

Rage began to course inside my veins, and I bit down on a curse. I moved to her window, and sure enough, she was downstairs, a cigarette dangling from the corner of her pink, pouty mouth, weeding a vegetable garden that wasn't there before I threw her in the east wing and left her to her own devices.

"With a little bit of hope, and a lot of love, you will make it to winter," she told the…radishes? And was she talking about herself or them? Her conversing with vegetables was a new and disturbing twist in her already awkward personality.

"Be good for me, okay? Because he won't."

You hardly make the cut for fiancée of the year either, Nem.

"Do you think he'd ever tell me whose birthday it was?" She crouched down, fingering the lettuce heads.

No, he won't.

"Yeah, I don't think so, either." She sighed. "But, anyway, you drink some water. I'll come check on you tomorrow morning. For lack of anything better to do." She chuckled, rising up and putting her cigarette out against a wooden passageway.

Nem had been sending Smithy to buy her a pack a day. I made a mental note to tell her the wife of a senator was not allowed to puff like a chimney in public.

I waited a few moments, then made my way to the corridor, expecting the balcony doors to slide open and to catch her going up the stairs. After waiting for long minutes—something I despised doing with every bone in my body—I descended the stairs, making my way to the terrace. Her disappearing act was grating on my nerves. First, she broke Romeo's picture, and now, she snooped around and talked to her future salad. I pushed the balcony doors open, ready to roar at her to go to bed, when I found her at the far end of the garden. She was in the open, second shed where we kept our trash cans. Great. She was talking to garbage, now, too.

I made my way to her, noticing that leaves were no longer crunching under my loafers. The garden was in much better shape. She had her back to me, bending into one of the green recycling cans, surrounded by garbage. There was no way to sugarcoat what I was seeing here. She was going through the trash.

I walked in the open door, leaning against it with my hands stuffed inside my front pockets. I watched as she sorted through bags of trash, then cleared my throat, making myself known. She jumped, gasping.

"Looking for a snack?"

She placed a palm on her chest over her heart and shook her head.

"I just…Ms. Sterling said that the clothes that I…uh…"

"Ruined?" I offered.

"Yeah, they're still here. Some of them, anyway." She gestured to the heaps of clothes at her feet. "They're going to send them to charity tomorrow. Most of the items are salvageable. So, I figured, if the clothes are still here, then maybe…"

The picture was still here.

She was trying to save Romeo's picture without knowing who he was, after seeing Sterling and me celebrating his birthday. She didn't know that she wouldn't find it—I asked Sterling, who confirmed that the batch with the picture had been already taken away. I raked a hand over my face. I wanted to kick something. Surprisingly—she wasn't that something. Heartache and regret etched her face as she turned around and looked at me with eyes raw with emotion. She understood she not only ripped fabric—*fuck* the fabric—but also something deep inside me. Tears hung on her eyelashes. It struck me as ironic that I'd spent my entire adult life choosing cold-blooded, unsentimental women for my flings, only to get married to a complete wuss.

"Leave it alone." I waved her off. "I don't need your pity, Nemesis."

"I'm not trying to give you pity, Villain. I'm trying to give you comfort."

"I don't want that, either. I don't want anything from you, other than your obedience, and maybe, down the road, your pussy."

"Why must you be so crass?" Tears made her eyes shimmer. She was a crier, too. Could we be any less compatible? I didn't think so.

"Why must you be such an emotional train wreck?" I responded curtly, pushing off the door and getting ready to leave. "We are who we are."

"We are who we choose to be," she corrected, throwing a piece of clothing at her feet. "And unlike you, I choose to *feel*."

"Go to bed, Francesca. We're going to visit your parents tomorrow, and I'd appreciate you hanging on my arm without looking like shit."

"We are?" Her mouth hung open.

"We are."

My version of accepting her apology.

My version of letting her know I wasn't a monster.

Not that night, anyway.

The night that marked the birthday of the man who taught me how to be good, and as a homage, I allowed this one small crack in my shield, giving her a hint of warmth.

My dead brother was a good man.

But me? I was a great villain.

CHAPTER NINE

Francesca

"**J**UST TELL ME WHO IT WAS. AN EX-GIRLFRIEND? A missing cousin? Who? *Who!*" I probed Ms. Sterling the next day between tending to my vegetable garden, chain-smoking, and looking through the trash for the broken picture—the one thing my future husband cared about, and I somehow managed to ruin.

I was met with stern, snippy answers. She explained, between huffs and phone calls, barking at the cleaning company once again, that if I wanted to learn more about Wolfe's life, I needed to earn his trust.

"Earn his trust? I can't even earn a smile from him."

"Have you actually tried making him smile?" She squinted, checking my face for lies.

"Should I have? He practically kidnapped me."

"He also saved you from your parents."

"I didn't want to be saved!"

"Two things people should be grateful for without asking— love and to be saved. You are offered both. Yet, my dear, you seem quite ungracious."

Ms. Sterling, I deduced, was senile to the bone. She sounded so different from the woman who persuaded my future husband to show me mercy yesterday when I eavesdropped on them. I saw through her game. Trying to defrost us toward one another while always playing the devil's advocate.

I thought she was wasting her time. On both ends.

Still, bickering with Ms. Sterling was the best part of my day. She showed more passion and involvement in my life than Wolfe and my father combined.

My fiancé and I were to arrive at my parents' house at six o'clock for dinner. Our first dinner as an engaged couple. Ms. Sterling said that showing my folks I was happy and taken care of was of the essence. She aided me with the preparations, helping me slide into a yellow maxi summer chiffon dress and matching Jimmy Choo sandaled heels. When she fixed my hair in front of the mirror, it dawned on me that our light banter about the weather, my love for horses, and her love for romance books reminded me a lot of my connection with Clara. Something that felt a lot like hope started blooming in my chest. Having a friend would make living here so much more bearable. My new beau, of course, must've sensed my cautious optimism because he decided to crush and burn it by sending me a text message:

Will be late. Meet you there. No pulling tricks, Nem.

He couldn't even show up on time to our first dinner with my parents. And, of course, he still thought I'd try to run away somehow.

Heat bubbled in my veins throughout the drive. The black Escalade pulled up to my parents' curb, and Mama and Clara hurried outside, showering me with hugs and kisses as if I'd just returned from a warzone. My father was standing at the doorway in his sharp suit, frowning at my nearing figure as I laced my arms with the women of my former household as we walked in. I daren't meet his eyes. When I took the four steps up to our entrance door, he merely moved aside to let me pass, not offering me a hug, a kiss, or even a pleasantry.

I looked the other way. Our shoulders brushed, and it felt like his sliced mine with its rigid, icy stance.

"You look beautiful, Vita Mia," Mama breathed behind me, pulling at the hem of my dress.

"Freedom agrees with me," I bit out bitterly, my back to Papa as I went to the dining room and poured myself a glass of wine before Wolfe arrived.

The next hour was spent making idle conversation with my mother while my father nursed a glass of brandy and stared me down from across the room. Clara came and went out of the salon, providing refreshments and zeppole to curb our hunger.

"Something smells." I scrunched my nose.

"That would be your fiancé," my father said, sitting back in his executive chair. My mother laughed off his words.

"We had a bit of an incident in the backyard. It's fine now."

Another hour vanished, washed away by a stream of words as my mother brought my father and me up to date with all the latest gossip regarding the desperate housewives of The Outfit. Who got married and who got divorced. Who was cheating and who was being cheated on. Angelo's little brother wanted to propose to his girlfriend, but Mike Bandini, his father, thought it to be a problematic announcement, especially as Angelo didn't have any prospects to marry anyone anytime soon. *Thanks to me.*

Mom bit her lower lip when she realized it sounded a lot like an accusation, fiddling with the hem of her sleeve. She did that a lot. I chucked it to her low self-esteem after years of being married to my father.

"Of course, Angelo will move on." She swatted the air.

"Think before you speak, Sofia. It would serve you well," he advised.

When the grandfather clock chimed for the second time that evening—announcing it was eight o'clock—we moved to the dining room and began to eat our starters. I did not make any excuses for Wolfe since all my text messages to him went unanswered. My heart was soggy with shame and drenched with disappointment at the humiliation of being stood up by the man who ripped me from my family.

The three of us ate with our heads bowed down. The clinking of the salt and pepper shakers and utensils unbearably loud against the silence in the room. My mind drifted back to the notes in the wooden box. I had decided that this was all a mistake. Senator Keaton couldn't be the love of my life.

The hate of my life? Absolutely.

Anything more than that was a stretch.

When Clara served us the reheated entrees shortly before the doorbell rang, instead of feeling relieved, more dread poured into me, heavy like lead. The three of us put our forks down and exchanged glances. *What now?*

"Well, then! That's a pleasant surprise." Mama clapped her hands once.

"No more than cancer." My father patted the sides of his mouth with a napkin.

Wolfe came in a short minute later in a tailored suit, black raven hair tousled to a fault, and a purposeful expression that flirted with menace.

"Senator Keaton," Papa sneered, not looking up from his dish of homemade lasagna. "I see you finally decided to grace us with your presence."

Wolfe dropped a casual kiss on the crown of my head, and I hated the way silken satin wrapped around my heart and squeezed it with delight. I despised him for being so late and careless and myself for foolishly melting just because of the way his lips felt on my hair. My father watched the scene from the corner of his eye, one side of his mouth upturned in amused satisfaction.

You're miserable, Francesca, aren't you? His eyes taunted.

Yes, Papa. Yes, I am. Good job.

"What took you so long?" I whisper-shouted, bumping

Wolfe's hard thigh with my own underneath the table as he took a seat.

"Business," he clipped, flapping his napkin over his lap in a whip-sharp movement and taking a generous sip of his wine.

"So, not only do you work all day," my father launched into the conversation in full swing, sitting back and knotting his fingers together on the table, "but you're sending off my daughter to college now. Are you planning on providing us with grandchildren anytime this decade?" he inquired flatly, not giving a damn this way or the other. I saw through my father's behavior and knew without a shadow of a doubt this was not only about my college education.

In the time that passed between my leaving the house and now, he'd had the chance to process everything.

Wolfe Keaton's future children, no matter how much of the Rossi blood ran in their veins, would never inherit Papa's business. Senator Keaton would not let it happen. And so, my marriage to Wolfe not only killed his dream of a perfect little daughter raising beautiful, well-behaved, ruthless children, but it also killed his legacy. My father was slowly beginning to disconnect from me emotionally to protect his own heart from hurting, yet he was breaking mine to pieces in the process.

My gaze darted to Wolfe, who glanced at his Cartier, visibly waiting for dinner to be over.

"Ask your daughter. She's in charge of her school schedule. *And* her womb."

"Quite true, to my utter disappointment. Women need *real* men to tell them what they want. Left to their own devices, they are bound to make reckless mistakes."

"*Real* men don't shit bricks when their wives gain higher education and the basic power to survive without them, pardon my language." Wolfe chewed a mouthful of lasagna, signaling me with his hand to pass him the pepper. He was in hostile territory, looking as cool as a cucumber.

"Alrighty, now," Mama chortled, tapping my father's hand from across the table. "Has anyone heard the latest gossip about the governor's wife's latest facelift? Word around town is she looks permanently surprised and not by his tax scandal."

"What will you be studying, Francesca?" Papa turned his attention to me, cutting into Mama's speech. "Surely, you don't actually believe you can become a lawyer."

I accidentally dropped my fork onto my lasagna. Small splashes of tomato flew on my yellow dress. I dabbed at the stains with a napkin, swallowing a pool of saliva that gathered in my mouth.

"You can't even eat a damn meal without making a mess," my father pointed out, stabbing his lasagna with unabashed violence.

"That's because my father is belittling me in front of my fiancé and mother." I squared my shoulders. "Not because I'm incapable."

"You are of average IQ, Francesca. You can become a lawyer but probably not a good one. And you haven't worked a day in your life. You would make a lazy intern and get fired. Wasting everyone's time and resources, including your own. Not to mention, the opportunity you'd receive being Senator Keaton's wife could go to someone who actually deserves the job. Nepotism is America's number-one disease."

"I thought that was organized crime," Wolfe commented, taking another sip of his wine.

"And you." My father looked at my future husband with an expression that would have stapled me to the wall had it been directed at me, yet my husband stayed aloof as ever. "I would strongly advise that you stop your antics. You got what you wanted. May I remind you that I came from nothing? I'm not going to sit around and watch you ruin all I have. I'm a very resourceful man."

"Threat noted." Wolfe chuckled.

"So I should just stay at home and pop out babies?" I pushed my plate away, fed up with the food, conversation, and company. My mother's gaze ping-ponged among everyone, her eyes wide as saucers. It was all a big mess, and I was in the middle of it.

My father threw his napkin over his plate to signal to the servants that he was done. Two of them rushed over to clear his plate, nodding and nodding and nodding.

Scared.

"That'd be a good start. Although, with a husband like yours, God knows."

"A husband *you* chose." I speared something with my fork, imagining it was his heart.

"Before I knew he was going to make you go out and work like some kind of…"

"Twenty-first century woman?" I finished for him, my eyebrows jumping to my hairline. Wolfe chuckled into his wine glass next to me, his quaking shoulder brushing mine.

My father knocked down his drink, then followed it by topping his glass to the hilt. His nose grew redder and rounder, his cheeks pinking under the yellow hues of the chandelier light. My father always drank responsibly. He didn't tonight.

"Your boarding school was an expensive, elaborate daycare for the rich and connected. Your doing well in Switzerland is no indication you can survive the real world."

"That's because you sheltered me from the real world."

"No, that's because you can't *handle* the real world." He grabbed his full glass of wine and tossed it across the room. The glass broke into tiny pieces as it hit the wall, the red wine spreading on the carpets and wallpaper like blood.

Wolfe stood, braced his hands over the table, and leaned forward, staring Papa in the eye. The world ceased to spin, and everyone in the room seemed to appear significantly smaller, holding their breath and staring at my fiancé. The air fluttered behind my lungs.

"This is the last time you raise your voice to my fiancée, not to mention throw things around like a poorly trained circus monkey. Nobody—and I do mean no person on this planet—talks to the future Mrs. Keaton like this. Any wrath she is to endure is mine. The only person she answers to is me. The only man to put her in her place—if and when needed—would. Be. Me. You will be respectful, agreeable, and polite to her. Tell me if I'm not understood, and I'll make sure to make my point by destroying everything you care about."

The air felt thick and heavy with the threat, and I was no longer sure where my loyalty lay. I hated both of them but had to root for one of them. It was my future on the line, after all.

"Mario!" My father called out his security. Was he throwing us out? I didn't want to be there when it happened. Couldn't face the humiliation of being thrown out of my own house. I stared at my father's eyes. The same eyes that glittered with pride and respect not too long ago every time I entered the room as he ricocheted dreams of my marrying into a good, Italian Outfit family and filling this house with happy, privileged grandchildren.

They were empty.

I shot up from my seat, my legs padding across the carpets. I had no direction. Tears blurred my vision as my feet carried me to the drawing room on the first floor, on the other side of the house where the grand piano sat.

I wiped my face quickly, tucking myself behind the piano, gathering the tulle of my summer dress to make sure I wasn't visible to anyone walking into the room. It was a childish thing to do, but I didn't want to be found. I wrapped my hands around my legs and buried my face between my knees. My whole body trembled as I sobbed into my thighs.

Minutes passed before I felt someone else enter the room. It was pointless to look up. Whomever it was—they were an unwelcome company.

"Lift your head."

God. My pulse jumped at his voice. *Why him?*

I remained motionless. His footsteps carried across the room, becoming louder as he made his way toward me. When I finally peeked from behind my knees, I found my fiancé crouching down in front of me with a grave look on his face.

He'd found me.

I didn't know how, but he did.

Not my mother. Not my father. Not Clara. *Him.*

"What took you so long?" I lashed out at him, dragging the pads of my fingers across my cheeks. I felt childish seeking his alliance, but he was the only one who could. Mama and Clara meant well but lacked any sort of power over my father.

"Work."

"Work could've waited until tomorrow."

"It could have until your father got into the picture." His jaw clenched. "I had a meeting at a bar called Murphy's. I left my briefcase there. It disappeared from my side, then a mysterious fire started in the kitchen, spreading to the rest of the pub soon after. Take a wild guess what happened."

I blinked at him. "The Italian and the Irish have had rivalry dated back to the early twenties in this town."

He arched an eyebrow. "Your father had my briefcase stolen and burned. He wanted to destroy the evidence I have on him."

"Did he succeed?"

"What kind of idiot keeps his most valuable possession in one place without any spare copies and walks around with it in broad daylight?"

The kind of people my father messes with.

"Are you going to tell him?" I sniffed.

"I'd rather keep him guessing. It's thoroughly entertaining."

"He's not going to stop, then."

"Good. Neither will I."

I knew he spoke the truth. I also knew that it was more truth than I could ever squeeze out of my father.

The pieces of the puzzle fell into place. Papa orchestrated this evening to be a disaster. He wanted to destroy whatever Wolfe had on him, and the fact I was left waiting while Wolfe had to extinguish another potential PR disaster was a nice, fat bonus.

"I hate him." I stared at the floor, the words exploding from my mouth bitterly. I meant it with every bone and ounce of blood in my body.

"I know." Wolfe settled in front of me, crossing his long, muscular legs at the ankles. I glanced at the cut of his dress pants. No hint of socks. Tailor-made to his exact height and frame just like everything else about him. A man so calculated, I decided, was going to hit back harder once he decided to punish my father.

And my father wouldn't stop until he dismantled him. One of them was going to kill the other, and I was the poor idiot stuck right in the middle of their war.

I closed my eyes, trying to muster the mental strength to walk out of this room and face my parents. Everything was such a mess.

I am an unwanted puppy, running from door to door in the pouring rain, looking for shelter.

Slowly, and despite my better judgment, I crawled into my future husband's lap. I knew that by doing that, I was raising a white flag. Surrendering to him. Seeking his protection, both from my father and from my own internal turmoil. I flew directly into my cage, asking him to lock me inside. Because the beautiful lie was far more desirable than the awful truth. The cage was warm and safe. No harm could find me. I wrapped my arms around his neck, burying my head in his steel chest and holding my breath to prevent the next sob.

He stiffened, his body rigid with our sudden proximity.

I thought about what Ms. Sterling said about killing him with kindness. Defeating him with love.

Break. Crack. Feel me. Accept me.

I felt his arms slowly enveloping my body as he acknowl-
edged my surrender, opened the gates, and let my army skulk
into his kingdom, wounded and famished. He lowered his head
and cupped both my cheeks, tilting my head up. Our eyes locked.
We were so close, I could see the unique, silvery shade of his
irises. Pale and frightening like the planet Mercury, with icy,
blue speckles inside the craters. I knew instantly that there was
a chink in his indifferent mask, and that it was my job to worm
my way through the crack and plant my seeds there. Grow them
like my vegetable garden and hope like hell they could bloom.

He tipped his head forward, molding our mouths together, our lips meeting like they already knew each other. I realized—and not to my discomfort—that they did. It was a discreet,
bolstering kiss. For long minutes, we explored each other with
cautious strokes. The only audible noise was our lips and tongue,
licking wounds more than skin-deep. When we disconnected, my heart twisted in my chest. I was afraid he was going to
leave the room angrily like he did the last time we'd kissed. But
he just brushed his thumb over my cheek and scanned my face
with a dark frown.

"Have you had enough of your father for the week, Nem?"

I took a shuddering breath. "I think I've had my fill for the
year."

"Good. Because I'm beginning to think I haven't had enough
of my fiancée, and I'd like to rectify that."

During the drive back home, Wolfe slid his fingers through mine,
clasping my palm and pressing it down on his muscular thigh.
I looked out the window, the small smile on my lips a telltale
I chose to ignore. After we left my parents' piano room, my
mother apologized profusely for the disastrous dinner. My father was nowhere in sight; his driver pulled up to the curb while

she was making excuses, and he probably went someplace where he could plot against my future husband. Not that said fiancé looked particularly bothered by the situation.

I hugged Mama and told her that I loved her. I meant it even though I recognized that my entire perception of her had changed. Growing up, I truly believed that my mother could protect me from anything. Even death. I did not think so anymore. In fact, a small, frightened part of me speculated that the day where I'd have to protect her was near. I vowed to never do this to my own child.

When I had a daughter, I would protect her from anyone, even from her father.

Even from our legacy.

Even from wooden boxes with decades of tradition.

Wolfe helped me into my casual wool jacket and pierced my mother with a look she didn't deserve.

Now, in the vehicle, his hand covering mine, he dragged my palm deeper into his inner thigh, much too near to his groin. My own thighs clenched together, but I didn't pull back. There was one thing I could neither deny, nor did I care to at this point: my future husband stirred a physical reaction in me.

With Angelo, I felt warm and fuzzy. Under a rich blanket of security. With Wolfe, I felt as if I was on fire. As though he could end me at any given moment, and all I could do was hope for his mercy. I felt safe, but not secure. Desired, but unwanted. Admired, but unloved.

When we got to the house, Ms. Sterling was sitting in the kitchen, reading a historical romance. I walked in to get a glass of water, with Wolfe following me. As soon as her eyes snapped up from the yellowed pages, she angled her reading glasses down the bridge of her nose and grinned.

"How was your evening?" She batted her lashes, feigning innocence. "Pleasant, I take it?"

The fact that we entered a room together for the first time since we'd known each other probably gave our truce away.

"Get out," Wolfe ordered, no menace or manners in his voice. Ms. Sterling hopped out, giggling to herself, as I poured myself a glass of water, refusing to spare him a look. We'd come here because he wanted to spend more time with me. I had no doubt it was neither my wit nor conversation he was after. The finality of what was going to happen between us hit me somewhere between the heart and the womb, sending waves of passion and panic through my body.

"Care for some water?" My voice pitched high. My back was still to him.

Wolfe covered my body with his from behind, running his fingers from the side of my thigh to my midriff. He cupped my small breast, making me gasp in shock and unexplained pleasure. His warm lips were on my shoulder, and I felt him stiffening behind me, his erection pressing against my butt. My heart fluttered behind my ribcage like a butterfly. *Oh, my God*. He was firm and hot everywhere, and the sensation of being shielded by him made me feel both helpless and invincible.

I drank my water in measured gulps, biding my time, as his fingers pinched one of my nipples through my dress and bra. I groaned, my back arching involuntarily, and I had to put the glass down on the counter before it slipped between my fingers. He chuckled, his hand sliding down my leg again and snaking through the side slit of my dress. His fingertips brushed the hem of my cotton underwear and he grumbled into my ear, making my skin break into violent goose bumps. Instead of running for my life—something every bone in my body screamed at me to do—I found myself wanting to dissolve in his arms. I was the idiot who told him I wasn't a virgin. Now I had to deal with the consequences of my stupid lie.

"Water?" I muttered again, horrified when I felt my panties sticking to my skin from the dampness. My body felt rebellious and adventurous under his fingertips, but my mind told me we were still rivals.

He thrust his penis between my butt cheeks through my dress, and I moaned, my hip bones slamming against the counter. The pain of the hit was laced with delight I couldn't understand. Part of me wanted him to do it again.

"The only thing I'm in the mood for right now is my bride-to-be."

"Huh." I looked at the ceiling, racking my brain for something to say. Was he going to take me from behind like some kind of animal? Sex was a foreign land I had yet to set foot on. I had plenty of time to surf the internet and read all about my future husband. He was a womanizer and had more than his fair share of girlfriends and flings. They were always well-educated, leggy socialites with shiny hair and an envious family tree. They always hung on his arms in the tabloids, staring at his face as though it was a rare gift he'd offered just for them. But among the squeaky-clean items about him, I'd also found a lot of headlines that flirted with a scandal. Hotel rooms with a trash can full of used condoms, a restroom incident at a gala thrown by his political party, and he'd even been locked in a car with a European princess for two hours, much to her family and country's disdain.

"We need to take this slow. I don't know you yet." My hand trembled its way to his shoulder, pushing him awkwardly with no real force in my touch. I was still with my back to him.

"Getting in bed together will help rectify that," he pointed out. I wished I'd stopped to think before I taunted him about sleeping with Angelo. But the lie got bigger and more important the more time passed.

He spun me around so I faced him and shoved me flush against the counter. I was both amazed and disturbed by how easily he manhandled me.

"Slow," I repeated, my voice quivering around the word.

"Slow," he echoed, hoisting me up on the counter. He stepped between my legs as if he'd done it a thousand times before—and he had. Just not with me. My dress rode up, and if he looked down—which he did, of course, he did—he could see my matching yellow panties and the unmistakable stain of lust where the slit was. He cupped my behind in a punishing grip, slamming our groins together, and my breath hitched at the thing that met my damp panties.

My *very* damp panties.

I was soaked. Embarrassed to the bone. I hoped he wasn't going to touch me down there because that would only prove to him how much I craved him.

My eyelids lowered, heavy under the weight of my desire for him. He put his lips on mine and kissed me long and hard, plunging into my mouth in a rhythm that made a ball of something warm and brilliant swell in my womb. He crushed his body against mine and rubbed his swollen cock against my center, and I dragged my fingers over his back like I'd seen women do in the movies, enjoying the power of touching him however I liked. It felt good, and I didn't want to think about anything else. Like how we were a lie. Or how the lie felt better than the truth—the reality of my life. I pushed aside my feelings for my father, and my missing Angelo, and the worry for Mama.

It was just the two of us tucked in a bubble I knew was bound to burst.

Wolfe snaked one hand between us and rubbed my slit through the fabric of my panties. I was so wet, an apology for reacting this way to his body was dancing on the tip of my tongue. He continued kissing me, chuckling into my mouth every time I squirmed and moaned.

"You're so responsive," he muttered in what I thought could be actual awe between kisses that became dirtier, longer, and wetter, rubbing me faster down there. Was being responsive a good or a bad thing? As a good girl, that was another thing to worry about. I found myself opening my legs wider for him, inviting him to do more of this magic. Some girls touched themselves, but I preferred not to. Not that I thought it wasn't okay, I just knew that I couldn't risk losing my virginity accidentally. It was priceless. But he was my husband-to-be, and it seemed to please him.

And me.

I knew that the first time was supposed to hurt, but a part of me was happy it was going to be in the experienced arms of Wolfe. Everything tingled inside me, and I felt like I was about to burst. On the tip of something monumental. His mouth moved against mine more angrily, but I knew it wasn't the same anger as the day he threw me out of his room.

"So wet," he growled, pushing his thumb halfway into my opening through my panties. I arched my back and closed my eyes, my body bursting with a thousand different sensations. My fingers fluttered against his groin through his pants. Huge and hard and even warmer than the rest of him. A terrible thought crossed my mind. I wanted him in my mouth.

What was I thinking? Why would I want it there? This was definitely not something I was going to share with Clara or Mama. Not even Ms. Sterling.

Jesus, Francesca. The mouth. You pervert.

He grabbed me by the back of my thighs and wrapped my legs around his waist, kissing me as he made his way to the stairs, my arms still draped across his neck. I realized he was taking me to a bedroom—his or mine—and that I couldn't go there. I had to tell him I was a virgin. That in my world, we had rules. And one of mine was no sex until marriage. But that was entirely too awkward in this particular situation. I needed to choose the time and the place to come clean.

"Put me down," I slurred between drunken kisses.

"I don't give oral on principle, but you're wet enough to fit a fucking shovel in."

What? Fright gripped my throat, tightening its claws on my neck from the inside. He was half-ready to maul me right there on the floor. We were already upstairs when I began to push him off me, untangling my legs from his waist. He let go of me immediately, watching as I stumbled out of his embrace, my back hitting the wall.

"Nemesis?" He frowned, tilting his chin down. He looked more confused than angry. For all his shortcomings, Wolfe had never forced me to do anything physical with him.

"I said I'm not ready!"

"You also said it as though I personally escorted you to Hell's gates. What's the matter?"

I was embarrassed by my behavior. Embarrassed by both my lie of being experienced and my virginity. Last but not least, I was ashamed of wanting it so badly. Was that all it took for me to forget Angelo? The hard length of Wolfe against my softness?

"Are you a virgin?" His mouth nearly blossomed into a smile. So rare was laughter on my fiancé's face, I was beginning to think he was incapable of true joy.

"Of course, I'm not a virgin." I slapped my thigh, turning away toward my room. He grabbed my arm and pulled me back to his embrace. I melted against his body like butter on a fry pan. "I just need a little time. You're still more experienced than I am."

"It's not a competition."

"I've seen the papers." I narrowed my eyes accusingly. "You're a Casanova."

"Casanova." His chest danced against mine as he rumbled with a chuckle at my choice of words. "Shall I escort you to the nearest portal to take you back to the sixteenth century?" He faked a theatrical English accent.

I knew I sounded like a prude. Worse—I knew I was raised to be one, and shaking off the chains of my dated scruples would be difficult. But I wasn't nineteen. Not really. I had the manners of a fifty-year-old and the life experience of a goddamn toddler.

"Forget it."

He sucked his teeth in, smirking. "Fine. No fucking. We can fool around. Senior-year style. A blast from the past."

That sounded equally as dangerous as going all the way. The mere idea of being with him in the same room with the door closed felt scandalous, somehow.

"In your room?"

He hitched one shoulder up. "Your call. One of us will have to leave after it's over. I don't share a bed with women."

"And men?" I slid back into my element, glad we were back in friendly territory.

"Watch your mouth, Miss Rossi, unless you want to find it wrapped around my something long and hard that'd make your jaw snap."

I knew he was kidding this time, and even had to cover a grin, ducking my head down.

"Is sleeping alone a principle, too?"

"Yes."

So he did not share a bed with his partners, did not perform oral sex, and was not interested in forming a relationship with a woman. I didn't know much about the world of dating, but I was pretty certain my future husband wasn't a great catch.

"I feel like there's a Francesca question coming my way." He scanned me, and I realized I'd been munching on my lower lip contemplatively.

"Why do you not give oral?" I asked, pinking again. It didn't help that we were having the conversation in the middle of the foyer where Ms. Sterling could hear us through the thin door of her room.

Wolfe, of course, seemed anything but embarrassed, placing his shoulder on the wall and watching me through lazy eyes.

"I actually quite enjoy the taste of pussy. It's the bowing down part I have severe dislike to."

"You think it's degrading?"

"I will never kneel for anyone. Don't take it personally."

"Surely, there are plenty of positions that would not require that of you."

What was I saying?

He smirked. "In all of them, the person giving the pleasure looks like the peasant."

"And how come you never share a bed with anyone?"

"People leave. Getting used to them is pointless."

"A husband and a wife are not supposed to leave each other."

"Yet you would be more than willing to turn your back on this, would you not, my dear fiancée?"

I said nothing. He pushed off the wall and took a step toward me, tilting my chin up with his thumb. Wolfe was wrong. Or at least, not completely right. I was no longer hell-bent on running away from him. Not since I realized my parents weren't going to fight for me. Angelo said we'd be together this lifetime, but I hadn't heard from him since. With every day that passed, breathing without feeling as if a knife had been shoved into my lungs became easier.

But I didn't confess that to Wolfe. I didn't utter aloud what my body spoke to him in my parents' piano room.

I stepped out of his embrace, telling him everything there was to say.

I'm not ready yet.

"Good night, Villain." I ambled to my bedroom.

The jagged edge of his voice ran like fingers over my back behind me, but he relented. Accepted my reluctance to be with him like that.

"Sleep tight, Nemesis."

CHAPTER TEN

Wolfe

I WATCHED FROM THE BACK OF MY CADILLAC AS THE PRIVATE investigator I'd hired slammed his car door shut and walked over to knock on the Rossi's door. Francesca's mother answered, and he handed her the brown manila file and turned around without a word, just as I had instructed him to.

Arthur Rossi tried to destroy the evidence against him.

I was going to destroy *him*.

I'd filled Chicago's streets with more cops and moles. For the past three decades, he'd been ruling those streets with an iron fist. And now, in only a short few weeks, I'd managed to eliminate a lot of his power.

The investigator I'd hired reported back that Arthur had been drinking more, sleeping less, and raised his hand to two of his most trustworthy soldiers. For the first time in three decades, he was spotted leaving his own strip clubs, smelling not only like cigars and alcohol but also other women's pussies. Two of the women, out-of-towners, were stupid enough to allow the investigator to take pictures of them with Arthur.

I'd created more of a mess for him, and it seemed as though his Keaton problem wasn't going to go away.

I watched Francesca's mother's face crumpling as she slid the pictures out of the envelope. I simultaneously clutched a letter in my own hand. It was addressed to me from her husband. Containing anthrax, I was sure, if it weren't too incriminating against him.

Francesca's mother started after the investigator's white Hyundai, but he already took off before she could question him further about the things he showed her.

I tore open the letter and skimmed over it.

It was an invitation to throw his daughter and me an engagement party.

It was suspicious, but a part of me gave him the benefit of the doubt. I figured he wanted to put on a show and make people think our marriage had his blessing in order to try and assert more power over the situation. Furthermore, staging the fire at Murphy's didn't serve him well. My briefcase (which didn't contain the evidence against him, as he'd been tipped) was gone, but now he reopened a front with the Irish, who saw the fire as a direct attack on them.

Saying Francesca and her parents ended their last encounter on a bad note with me would be the understatement of the goddamn century, and this could give them a chance to patch things up. Not that I had any plans to play *The Brady Bunch* with a mobster, but the last thing I wanted was a scandal-filled wedding with a tearful bride. And the future Mrs. Keaton, much to my disdain, excelled at turning on that Buckingham Fountain and crying her eyes out every time things didn't work according to her Instagram-perfect ideas.

Francesca was at church again. She'd been spending a lot of time at church, because on top of being a prude and a crier, she was also—you guessed it—a closeted nun. On the bright side, it couldn't hurt my chances of gaining more supporters. Everyone loved a good Christian family. They didn't have to know the groom's bride was more interested in banging the family's friend.

Today, Francesca had previewed the decorations for our upcoming nuptials. Since we'd agreed there was no need for a rehearsal dinner, we decided on a speedy event in the house of God, followed by a modest party at her parents'.

Arthur also asked in the letter if we'd do the Rossi couple the honor of staying the night at their house and attend a celebratory breakfast afterward.

It was a good opportunity to finally sit him down and lay it all out for him, play by play. How I was going to take away everything he'd ever worked for. Then break the news that none of the money, property, and reputation he'd gained over the years mattered and make him realize that none of it would help him one bit in his dire situation.

Francesca and I weren't going to give him any grandchildren.

It wouldn't hurt that my bride would get the chance to spend time with her mother. A reward for her sensible behavior.

"Back to the house," I told Smithy.

"You have the pep rally at six o'clock," one of my Executive Protection Agents (fancy name for a bodyguard, just as well—as there was zero chance of my remembering his real name) pointed out from the passenger's seat. Usually, it was my PA's job to remind me about social obligations. However, he was down with his fifth stomach bug for the summer and texted Smithy and my bodyguards relentlessly to keep me on schedule.

I waved my hand. "Make it quick."

As we zipped by the Sears Tower, deep dish pizza parlors with cheap neon signs, and buskers performing their own version of Billboard's current hits, I thought about my fiancée. Francesca had been growing on me like fingernails. Slowly, determinedly, and completely without my attention or encouragement.

She waited for me every evening in her vegetable garden, an oddly attractive scent of mud, cigarettes, clean soap clinging on her body, and not wearing much more than a barely there long camisole that cleaved to her body with sweat and mist. She was always surprised and delighted when I lowered her on the wet soil, still fully clad in my suit, pressed my knee between her legs and devoured her sweet mouth until our lips were cracked and our mouths were dry. She always gasped when I rubbed her hand over my cock through my dress pants, and she even chanced a squeeze in the pavilion, somewhere exposed enough for her to feel safe but hidden enough for us not to have an audience. Her eyes flared in awe and joy when I flicked her clit through her panties not-so-accidentally. Every time I gave her a chance to pull away, she stapled her body to mine, making us one entity.

I kept my word and didn't initiate sex with her. Figured the day we'd sleep together was drawing close with our pending nuptials. She was receptive, syrupy and...*fascinated*. Long gone were the days of the jaded, experienced Kristens. Francesca, despite the fact she'd slept with men before, was raw. I was going to teach her all the dirty tricks the Bandini kid couldn't and have fun doing so.

I'd visited her room a few times when I knew she wasn't there, always watching out for two things. The third note—she hadn't opened the box yet. I knew because the tiny golden key was positioned precisely in the same place, not moving an inch between the cracks of her expensive, ancient wooden floors. The floor was due to be replaced before her arrival, but now that I knew where she kept her secrets, I decided to keep the cracks intact. The other was to check her phone for traces of Angelo. There were none. His messages were left unanswered, though she did not delete him from her contacts.

"We're here," Smithy said as he parked by Lincoln Brooks High School. The place had produced more gang members than literate citizens, and it was my job to smile, wave, and pretend that things would be okay for the students. They were going to be—once I'd clean their streets of Francesca's father's employees.

Protocol demanded one executive protection agent should

open my door while the other positioned himself behind me at all time, so that was what we did.

I walked across the yellow, uneven lawn toward the low, gray, depressingly square building, passing metal barricades with excited students and their parents who came to see an alumni rapper who was going to perform there later that evening. The kid had more ink on his face than a *Harry Potter* book and some questionable scars. I waltzed toward the principal of the school, a shapely woman with a cheap suit and an '80's haircut. She ran toward me, her heels stubbing the dry ground beneath us.

"Senator Keaton! We're beyond excited…" she started, just as gunfire cracked through the air. One of my bodyguards jumped over my body instinctively, throwing me to the floor. My stomach plastered to the ground, I twisted my head to the side, watching the barricaded crowd.

People started running in every direction, parents tugging their children, babies crying, and teachers yelling hysterically at the students to calm down. The principal slid down to the grass and began to scream in my face, covering her head with her hands.

Thanks for the help, lady.

Another bullet sliced through the air. Then another. Then *another*, each of them getting closer to me.

"Get off me," I growled to the EPA on top of me.

"But protocol says…"

"Protocol can go fuck itself in the ass," I snapped, the remainder of my previous, less-than-delightful life creeping into my language. "Call 911 and let me deal with this."

He disconnected his heavy body from mine reluctantly, and I sprang up to my feet and started running for the kid with the gun. I doubted he had more bullets in that thing. Even if he had, he proved to be a shit aim. He couldn't put a bullet in me if I literally hugged him. I raced right toward him, knowing that I wasn't brave as much as I was vindictive and stupid but not giving much damn.

You took it too far, Arthur, I thought. *Further than I gave you credit for.*

He played nice and sent me an invitation to an engagement party and suggested we stay at his place. He was building an alibi. I bet he was sitting somewhere in public right now. Maybe even pouring bowls of soup in a fucking charity basement.

By the time I put a good dent on the distance between me and my pimply assassin, the crowd had evaporated, and he was exposed. He turned around and started running. I was faster. I caught the hem of his white tee from behind, yanking him back to me.

"Who sent you?"

"I don't know what you're talking about!" he shouted, kicking the air as I dragged him back, but not before prying the gun from his hand and kicking it to the side. Not ten seconds later, ten police vehicles were surrounding us from every direction, and armed and shielded, special unit officers came out, officially arresting him. I cursed under my breath. I needed a few more minutes with him. I knew, without a shadow of the doubt, that he wasn't going to throw Arthur under the bus. But my EPAs and driver already escorted me to the other side of the building with two detectives and four officers tailing behind us.

"What you did today is a very admirable thing, Senator Keaton. School shootings are a real issue these days, and I…" the principal started.

God, woman, just shut up.

"Any injuries?" I cut her words.

"Not so far," one of the officers said as we made our way to my vehicle. "But you will be the talk of the town for the next couple of days. That was heroic."

"Thank you." I hated compliments. They made you lax and unguarded.

"Zion says you'll need to make some media appearances today," my EPA—the one who shielded me from the bullets—stared at his phone.

"Fine."

I took out my phone and texted Arthur's number in an instant. The first text message I had ever sent my future father-in-law.

Thank you for the invitation. My fiancée and I gladly accept.

Tucking the phone back into the breast pocket of my jacket, I smirked.

Arthur Rossi tried to kill me.

He was about to find out that he was a pussy, and I was a cat.

With nine lives.

Two down, seven to go.

The next few days were all about talking to the media, raising awareness about school shootings, and milking every second of the incident. Nobody suspected it was an attempt to assassinate me. The kid—an Italian school alumni and a Marine on vacation who got cold feet and forgot how to aim—was in custody now, and insisted that it was video games that made him do it.

The day of the engagement party, Nem and I were to meet downstairs at seven o'clock. I took a shower and got dressed at the office but made it home in a timely manner. Leaving Francesca as prey for Arthur was no longer an option. Arthur was beginning to feel a lot like a loose cannon, and I didn't want it anywhere near the smoothly operating machine called my life.

When I arrived on time, Francesca was waiting for me in a tight white gown that made my cock jump in a standing ovation. God, she was beautiful. And God, I was going to fuck her tonight. Even if I had to give her the foreplay she loved so much until my tongue fell off. The woman was delicious and ripe. And *mine*.

And *mine*.

And *mine*.

If I repeated these words in my head enough times, I could make it true.

I walked over to my bride-to-be, yanked her by the waist, and kissed her openly in front of Sterling, who was fretting with the hem of Francesca's gown. The old woman nearly swooned when our lips touched. She'd known me my entire life, and had never seen me kiss a woman, in public or otherwise. Sterling twirled to the kitchen with a spring in her step, giving us privacy.

Francesca and I cocked our eyebrows in unison. Our bodies were mimicking one another, too.

"How are you feeling?"

She'd been asking me this a lot since the rally incident. I wished she wouldn't. It served as a constant reminder that she was the spawn of the person responsible for it, yet she had no idea of her father's indiscretions.

"Stop asking. The answer will always be the same—I'm fine."

"To be honest, it's not me who is worried at this point. Did you know Ms. Sterling eavesdrops on everything we do and say?" Nem scrunched her button-y nose.

I flicked her chin playfully. I found out about Sterling's fascination with other people's business the hard way. After masturbating in the room next door to Sterling at thirteen and a half, I found a box of Kleenex on my nightstand and a Practice Safe Sex brochure the next day. To Sterling's credit, I would say I read the motherfucker twice and had never in my thirty years of miserable existence on this planet had sex without a condom.

"I wonder how she'd react when we do more than kissing," my bride-to-be reddened, looking down between us.

Might want to reconsider that, darling. I have an erection the size of a salami and any audience be damned.

"I suggest we find out tonight."

"How curious of you. You'd make a wonderful investigator." She bit on a smile.

"The only mystery I intend to unfold is how deep I can bury myself inside you."

"I can't believe you're a senator…" she mumbled to herself.

Me neither.

On that high note, we left, arm in arm.

The evening took a nosedive from the moment we set foot in Francesca's parents' manor. Not unexpected, but unsatisfactory all the same.

For one thing, as soon as we reached the Rossi estate, I'd noticed news vans swarming the neighborhood, barricading the main street, and causing a commotion of bystanders. Arthur had invited journalists and local news channels, and they, of course, came running to his doorstep.

A senator marrying the daughter of a mobster. It had more juice than a Big Gulp.

Determined not to allow Arthur to fuck up my life more than he already had, I opened the door for Francesca and escorted her into her former house, ignoring the catcalls from the reporters and the flash of the cameras from the photographers by their side. Once we got inside, Francesca clung to me like I was her lifeline, and I realized with dread instead of glee that, in a way, I was. Nemesis no longer saw this house as her home. I was her home now. And I was haunted beyond belief, ready to exorcise my need for her.

Her parents approached us, keeping a safe distance from one another. Her mother looked like she hadn't slept in approximately two months, wearing too much makeup to hide the effects of her mental state, and Arthur looked an inch or two shorter. Since I had zero illusions about Sofia Rossi leaving her cheating husband, I had to deduce that I'd done just what I came here to—rocked his boat a little more and shattered another facet of his life.

We did the customary kisses and hugs charade, "Salute!" glasses of Bellini, then they introduced us to their circle of friends.

I noticed three things immediately and simultaneously:

1. Arthur Rossi had invited a very leggy, very blonde, very *demoted,* and therefore very vindictive reporter who was intimately acquainted with my cock—Kristen Rhys.

2. He also invited some of the most fishy and ill-reputable people in the country, including ex-cons, gang leaders, and the likes of which I normally stayed far away from. He hoped this would contaminate my reputation—which, I had no doubt it would, since Kristen was there to take notes.

3. Without even really needing to look, I instantly found Angelo standing there, nursing a glass of wine, making lazy conversation with other guests.

This wasn't an attempt to appease me and show that the Rossi's were on board with our upcoming nuptials. This was a setup.

"We have quite the audience tonight; think you can handle our flavor of guests?" Arthur swirled his drink, shooting me a menacing smile. We hadn't spoken since I RSVPed his invitation, after which I hadn't filled in the authorities about what really happened. More leverage for me—one more secret I could use against him. Of course, that meant this place was swarming with security, thanks to my future father-in-law.

Good thing we only had a few more weeks of pretending. Francesca and I would soon be married, and then my plan would be executed. I was going to throw him in jail and make sure he rotted there while I fucked his daughter and left his wife to accept the Keaton couple's very charitable hospitality. I was not generous enough to pay for the grand mansion in Little Italy, though. Francesca's mother was welcome to move to one of the multiple properties I owned across Chicago.

The ultimatum was going to be clear—if the mother and daughter wanted my protection, and my money, and my mercy, they were to turn their back on Arthur—and I'd found the poetic justice almost perfect. After all, there was only one thing worse than losing a close, loved relative to an unexpected death—losing their love and affection while they were still alive.

"I can handle anything you throw at me, Arthur. Including, but not limited to, your spawn, who *is*, in fact, handled quite nicely behind closed doors." I yawned, ignoring the look of surprise and hurt Francesca flashed me.

It was not in my nature to kiss and tell, but in that case, there really was nothing to tell. We did nothing but heavy petting. It wasn't my intention to humiliate Nemesis, but it was necessary in order to humiliate her father. And choosing between her anguish and his pride, I'd run over my future wife to get a kick out of Arthur any day.

Rossi's nostrils flared, his eyes zooming in on me like two barrels of a gun.

He shook it off quickly, turning his head to his daughter.

"Angelo Bandini and his family are here. Shame it didn't work out with him and Emily after all," Arthur *tsked*, studying Francesca's expression through the rim of his glass, which was tilted up again—no surprises there. Nemesis was still staring at me, bewildered. It took everything for her to drag her eyes to her father and address him. If I were half-decent, I'd apologize. As it happened, I was not only a bastard but also keen on her forming this opinion of me prior to us having sex. It would help me set boundaries for what we were and weren't.

"Oh?" She smiled politely as though they were complete strangers. Either my future wife was a very good actress, or she really was over her silly fixation with the Italian stud. "I'm sorry to hear." She moved her gaze back to me, demanding an explanation.

Your father is a cunt. Good enough for you?

"Don't say that to him, you fool. Say that to him." Arthur shoved Francesca in the other direction toward Bandini. I was about to escort my betrothed to her fuck buddy when Arthur placed a firm hand on my shoulder. His smile was full of teeth and menace, and he reeked of alcohol. His eyes were red and small but laser-focused on me.

"Senator Keaton, I would love to introduce you to my friend, Charles Burton."

As in the same congressman who had just resigned to avoid an ethics investigation after groping his employees. Might as well stick my cock in the nearest squirrel's ass. It would make less of an embarrassing headline and wouldn't put my morals in question.

"I'm sure you would, but I have something to attend to," I gritted out, taking a side step, my shoulder brushing his.

"Nonsense." He clasped my arm, pulling me back. The only reason I relented was because I didn't want to cause a scene in front of Kristen and give her something else to write about tomorrow morning. "Didn't you donate to his campaign?"

I did. Before he tried to put his dick in everything in his office, pencil sharpener included. Of course, Burton was already next to me, hugging and congratulating me, as my bride drifted like a magnet to Angelo, who was already racing toward her, his hurried, barely contained steps making my eyelid twitch. They met halfway, then stopped abruptly, their arms dangled beside their bodies. Their awkwardness told me that nothing had changed. They still didn't know how to act un-in-love. My eyes followed them religiously as Burton began to talk my ear off, shooting excuses about why he had to step down. The notion that I cared nearly disturbed me. At this point, he could murder an entire strip club, and I would still be more interested in the way my bride-to-be—*my* fucking bride-to-be, thank you very much—flushed at something Angelo had told her, lowering her gaze to the floor and tucking a stray strand of hair behind her ear. They knew I was looking, so they kept a respectable distance, but everything in their body language screamed intimacy.

The place was full of people, and I had to remind myself that this was not Bishop's son's wedding. They couldn't sneak into the bathroom and fuck. On the other hand, I did just throw her under the bus to get a rise out of her father, so my defiant fiancée had every motivation to poke me back with the one thing she knew drove me mad—her ex-whatever (I didn't know or care what they labeled each other).

"...and then I told them that I will not, under any circumstances, take a lie detector test." Burton continued blabbing, clasping my shoulder. "The audacity to even ask—"

"Hey, Charles?" I cut him off.

"Yeah?"

"I don't give a single flying fuck why you stepped down or about the rest of your nonexistent career. Have a nice life. Or don't. I regretfully do not care either way."

With that, I shook his touch off, plucking a glass of champagne from a silver tray that floated around the busy room by one of the penguin-looking waiters as I dashed toward my bride-to-be. I was a few feet away from them when a shoulder sliced through the crowd, blocking my way. My eyes met the top of a gray head, hair sleeked back and carefully trimmed. *Bishop*.

He shook his head, his shit-eating grin wider than his face. Finally, and after weeks of my dangling his future over his head since I'd found out he and White were bribed by Arthur, he was in a position to shit over my plans.

"Nineteen, huh? She must be tight as our goddamn budget." He chuckled, swirling his whiskey in his tumbler.

"How would you know anything about tightness? Everything about you is loose, your morals included." I smirked back. I was, for all intents and purposes, a perfect gentleman and a polite conversationalist when in social circles. But Bishop and White were no longer people I needed to impress. I'd known that since before the masquerade, which was why I had allowed myself to piss off Francesca there in the first place.

"I don't remember you leaving a lasting impression on the Rossi girl the first time you met. Suffice to say, I'm not the only one with questionable ethics in this room," Preston replied, throwing smiles and waves to everyone around us.

"Whatever you're implying, you can go ahead and say it," I hissed.

"You're already blackmailing Arthur for his daughter. That much is clear. The girl is not yours." He tipped his chin toward Angelo and Francesca. He said something that made her cup her mouth and duck her head down. *Smitten.* "What I'm trying to figure out is—does that mean that White and I are in the clear?"

Thank fuck for arrogant idiots like Bishop who had their lives handed to them on a silver platter. He actually thought my end game was young pussy as opposed to taking down the biggest mobster in Chicago since Al Capone. That, of course, worked to my advantage. If Bishop and White were under the impression that I'd already got what I was looking for, they'd keep their guards down.

And so, even though separating Francesca and Angelo was of the essence, settling this matter took priority now.

"I have what I need." I smiled easily.

Bishop nodded, smiling and tapping my shoulder. He leaned toward me and whispered, "How is she in the sack? A lamb or a lioness? She is spectacular, Keaton."

I was glad it was not possible to strangle a person through an expression alone because if it were, Preston Bishop would be dead, and I would be escorted to the nearest police station. I neither knew nor cared why it bothered me so much that the governor spoke of my future wife as if she were a racehorse I'd purchased. I downed my champagne glass and tipped my chin up.

"How's your wife in the sack?" I asked.

He blinked. "Excuse me?"

"Actually, I don't think I will, Preston. Miss Rossi's age does not give you the permission to talk about her like she's a piece of meat."

"But…"

"Enjoy the rest of the party."

I sauntered past him, inwardly cursing Arthur for being an asshole, Angelo for existing, and myself for ever wanting to lay a hand on the beautiful siren dressed as Nemesis. The decision to marry her was supposed to chain Arthur further to my plan and clean up my reputation. Instead, it made everything a thousand times more difficult and complex. When I slanted my gaze sideways to look for Nem in the throng of partygoers, I found Kristen instead, cradling her drink and raising it in my direction with a cunning smile.

It was an invitation I declined by ignoring the gesture, roaming the room with my eyes for long minutes only to find that Francesca and Angelo were not in the room anymore. I climbed up to the second floor, checking her room, and every single other bedroom in the house, then the bathrooms, before I remembered that my fiancée was fond of gardens. I figured if Angelo and Francesca were going to fuck, they'd go somewhere private. But I forgot one little thing. Nemesis claimed to have *loved* Angelo. A few stolen kisses and rushed promises under the pink sunset were just as rewarding to them as a rendezvous between the sheets.

I descended the garden's stairs to find them sitting on a stone fountain, their knees angled toward one another. He caressed her cheek, and she let him.

He tucked a curl behind her ear, and she let him.

He plastered his forehead against hers, and she let him do

that, too. Their breaths were heavy, their chests falling and rising in harmony.

And I stood there, watching, simmering, fire coursing through me, I regretted humiliating her in front of her father. For I learned, for the first time, that my actions toward her had consequences.

I compromised her honor, so she was compromising mine.

The only difference was, I did it to spite someone else. She truly loved another.

Bandini leaned toward her face, brushing his thumb along her lips. Her eyes drifted to her thighs again, drunk on a moment they both knew they couldn't prolong. There was pain and sadness in his touch, confusion in her expression, and I knew, without a shadow of a doubt, that I stepped into something bigger than I'd anticipated. This wasn't puppy love. This was the real thing.

She looked up and said something, taking his hands in hers and bringing them to her chest. She was begging for something.

What the hell can this boy give you that I can't? But the answer was obvious. Love. He could give her real love, something she would never receive in the Keaton mansion. Not from me and not from her vegetables.

He nodded, getting up and walking toward the balcony's double doors. I was surprised and disturbed by the relief I felt before hardening again. She probably noticed me and told him to run off before I killed him with my bare hands. I took a step toward the garden, ready to reclaim her and make sure she did not leave my sight again the rest of the evening. But as soon as Angelo walked away, she looked left then right and approached a group of middle-aged women. Making polite, disinterested conversation, she kept her eyes stuck on the second floor of the house the entire time, and after no longer than five minutes, she disappeared inside the house.

I followed her steps again, convinced they were going to the same place, when a feminine hand clasped my forearm, making me turn around.

"Do you at least go down on her?" Kristen smirked, her freshly applied red lipstick and precisely pinned blond updo showing she'd freshened up before hunting me down. I shook her off, laser-focused on going upstairs and finding my fiancée, but she blocked my way to the staircase, which was already teeming with people as it was. I had no particular objection to shoving her out of my way, but considering the amount of security, media, and the fact that she, herself, was a journalist, it wasn't the best idea of the century. Yet again, I had to face the question that seemed to be eternal since Francesca had walked into my life—my career and reputation, or catching her little cheating ass red-handed?

Good news? I still had logic on my side.

Bad news? *For now.*

"I dug around." Kristen snapped her fruity gum in my face, batting her lashes.

"Did you find a bone, or someone to bone you, for that matter?"

It irritated me that my internal thoughts bled outside my mouth. I usually prided myself in an admirable dose of self-control. But knowing my fiancée was probably fucking another guy upstairs made me want to rip the walls off with my own fingernails. Whereas I was quite content letting Francesca scratch her Angelo itch a few weeks ago, now was a completely different matter.

"Are you not interested to hear what I found out?"

"Not really." I elbowed her aside gently, starting up the stairs. She chased me, grabbing the hem of my blazer and tugging. *Not a chance, sweetheart.* I was at the curve of the stairway when her words made me stop.

"I know why you did this to Rossi. He was responsible for

that explosion. The one that killed your parents when you were at Harvard."

I turned around, observing her—really looking, not just skimming her features—for the first time. Kristen was not a bad journalist, and under any other circumstances, I would respect her. But since it was me she was trying to fuck over, I had no choice but to fuck her harder, all puns intended.

"Do you have a point to your hearsay?"

"Rossi made you an orphan, so you took his daughter as retribution. An eye for an eye. I'd say it's a pretty good lead." She tipped her champagne glass back, taking a sip. I smirked, assessing her coldly.

"I took Francesca Rossi as a bride because I liked her. True, I have no kind words to say about her father, but it won't be him warming my bed at night."

"She doesn't even share your bed yet. How interesting." Kristen slow-clapped at my restraint at putting up with such behavior. Since she finally let go of my blazer, I turned around to complete my journey to the second floor just as Angelo slipped out of a guestroom, squeezing past my shoulder in the narrow hallway. I took one sniff at him and knew that he had just had sex. His lips were swollen, and his hair was disheveled and damp with sweat. Kristen's eyes lit up at the look of him making his grand escape. Glee oozed from her big fat smile. I grabbed his arm, turning him around to face me. This night was going down in the books as my worst night as a public figure and possibly as a human being. Angelo stared at me, heaving.

Frantic. Breathless. *Guilty.*

"Leave before I ruin your life," I spat out at Kristen. "And this time, you won't get a third warning."

She laughed. "Seems like you two have a lot to talk about."

My former mistress scurried away, her laughter carrying in my ears long seconds after she was gone. I plastered Angelo to the wall, grabbing him by the collar.

I knew it looked bad.

I knew I had to explain it tomorrow morning.

I simply no longer cared.

"Who was with you in that room?" I demanded.

"I'd strongly advise you stop acting like a thug unless you'd like to be treated like one."

I strongly advise you to stay away from my future wife before I really do kill you.

"You've had sex," I countered.

"Thanks, Captain Obvious. I was there." He laughed, regaining some of his composure, which infuriated me even more.

"Who with?" I pulled at his collar, almost to the point of choking. That sure wiped the smile off his face. I knew I had to calm down before people started noticing the little scene I'd created. But I couldn't, for the life of me, gather my wits.

"See, my first answer to you. None. Of. Your. Business, Keaton."

"Senator Keaton."

"Nah. You sure as hell don't represent me."

"Any particular reason why you insist on getting on my bad side?"

"You're on my future father-in-law's bad side," he said, unflinching. I had to hand it to him—he had balls the size of cantaloupes. "And the race to Francesca's heart is one I'm going to beat you at."

"I very much doubt you're capable of beating me to anything other than pre-ejaculation, kid."

"I'm fully prepared to test that theory. Heads up—I told Francesca I would gladly marry her without dowry, and that I am more than happy for my family to shell out whatever money is needed to untangle her from her Keaton situation. Might want to find another bride to fit that dress you bought."

I was about to punch him in the middle of my engagement party when my fiancée slipped out of the second floor, too. She looked like a barely contained mess. Her smeared makeup was carefully wiped from her face, her eyes were wild with realization. Paired with Bandini's frank admission that he'd slept with her, I saw very clearly what everyone else at the party were about to see, too.

Yet again, Francesca Rossi had been fucked by a man who was not her fiancé.

At her own engagement party.

Minutes after she was on my arm, no less.

I pushed Angelo down the stairs, pulling my future wife by the arm. She shrieked when I touched her, her eyes darting up in hysteria before softening when she saw it was me. Then she saw what was written on my face. If she could read me—which she could by now—she knew she was in deep trouble.

"What do you want?" she seethed.

A loyal fiancée.

A fucking shotgun.

For this nightmare of a sham relationship to be over.

"You just broke our verbal contract, Nemesis. Not a good thing to do with a lawyer."

She frowned but didn't try to defend herself.

There was a guillotine inside me, and I wanted to snap her pretty head off her body.

Tonight.

Francesca

I'd just wiped the tears from my eyes after telling my mother that I was starting to warm up to my husband. The revelation was bittersweet, if not completely crushing. Perhaps it was the nightly encounters in the vegetable garden, or the way he kissed me so openly in front of Ms. Sterling tonight when he picked me up.

"*Is it Stockholm syndrome, Mama?*"

"*I think it's just young love, Vita Mia. Love is, after all, a little mad. Otherwise, it is not love but merely infatuation.*"

"*Do you have to be mad to fall in love?*"

"*Of course, you do. Falling in love is, by definition, going crazy for someone else.*"

"*Are you crazy about Dad?*"

"*I'm afraid I am. Otherwise, I wouldn't stay even though he is cheating on me.*"

That happened, too. And it threw me off even though I should have seen it coming. It was not uncommon for the men of The Outfit to take a mistress or two.

Mom said that if it rips you apart, that means it is real.

"But shouldn't love feel good?"

"Oh, nothing is good if it doesn't have the power to feel bad, too. It's all about the quantities, Francesca."

Quantities.

The quantity of my affection toward Wolfe revealed itself when Angelo ushered me to the garden away from the throng of people. Despite my feeling completely crushed and angry at my coldhearted fiancé, I'd wanted to stay with him and brave my father together. Then Angelo sat me down and brushed a dark curl from my eyes and asked me if I was happy. I thought about it long and hard.

I wasn't happy.

I was not unhappy, either.

I'd realized that not only did I harbor unexplainable, positive feelings for the man who'd imprisoned me, but I no longer craved Angelo's touch the way I had before Wolfe bulldozed his way into my life. I still loved Angelo, but only as the kid who protected me from his brothers and shared smiles with me from across the dining table. Instead of his warm, familiar, soft hands, I longed for my fiancé's strong, callous, hard palms. The realization struck me like lightning, and I told Angelo that although I felt bad about him and Emily—it was over between us.

For good.

Once I saw the look on his face, I took his hand and brought it to my chest, begging for his forgiveness. And when he stood up and walked away, all I wanted to do was find my mother and tell her. I had to wait until Angelo was nowhere near me so it wouldn't look like we were going to the same place.

Angelo had disappeared inside the house shortly after. My cousin Andrea said between sipping mimosas that she saw him slipping into a guestroom upstairs with the blonde reporter Wolfe used to date.

"The one with the pretty hair? Tall? Lanky? Tan?"

I didn't need a reminder to the fact that Kristen was gorgeous.

"Right. Thanks."

Instead of feeling anger at his behavior, all I felt was strange hostility. Even that wasn't toward Angelo—it was toward my own fiancé, who had humiliated me in front of my parents when my father threw a jab at him.

Now we were in the car, staring outside our windows as we always did, watching Chicago whooshing by in its majestic, grayer-than-Wolfe's-eyes glory. I fiddled with the edges of my white dress, unsure what to say or do. Again, Wolfe arrived at the silly conclusion that I'd slept with Angelo. And again, I felt that defending myself was encouraging a pattern where I always had to make excuses for talking to a friend.

Did he really think so little of me? We had a verbal contract, and since striking it, time had passed. Time in which I kissed him and caressed him and opened my thighs for him to stroke me there through my clothes. I stroked him, too. Did that mean nothing to him? Did he really think I could do that with any man at any time?

"I will not marry a whore," Wolfe said with dry resolute,

still staring out the window. In the rearview mirror, I could see Smithy, his driver, cringing behind the wheel and shaking his head. I closed my eyes, willing myself not to cry.

"Let me go, then."

"Am I hearing an admission, Miss Rossi?"

"I will not defend myself in front of a man who does not deserve my pleas," I said, as calmly as I could.

"Is he worth my wrath?"

"You don't scare me, Senator Keaton," I lied, ignoring the tears clogging my throat. I liked him. I did. I liked that he defended me in front of my father, and that he offered me the freedom to study and work and leave the house unattended. I liked that he was at war with my family but didn't put me in the middle of it.

I even liked that he didn't want me to be his baby machine. Liked that he was agreeable whenever I decided to play nice with him. That the version of Wolfe I was going to get—the jerk or the sharp-tongued admirer—solely depended on my behavior toward him. I liked how his body enveloped mine like a shield, how his lips scorched my skin, how his tongue swirled over my needy flesh.

"*Yet,*" he corrected, his jaw as hard as granite. "You're not scared of me yet."

"You want me to be scared of you?"

"I want you to behave for once in your miserable, bratty life."

"I did not sleep with Angelo Bandini," I said for the first time that evening, and—I promised myself—also for the last time.

"Shut up, Francesca."

My heart coiled in the corner of my chest, and I swallowed the bitterness bleeding in my mouth.

When we arrived at the house, he rounded the car and opened the door for me. I stepped out and ignored him, pushing the front door open. I was so mad I wanted to scream until my vocal cords tore. He had such little faith when it came to me. Who had made him so hardened and skeptical?

Probably my father. There was no other way to explain the bad blood between them.

Behind me, I heard Wolfe instruct his bodyguards to stay out of the house, which was against protocol. He never went against protocol.

I rushed to my room, desperate to gather my thoughts and think of a way to tackle this. I didn't stop to think that running away from confrontation may look to him like an admittance. My only sin was sitting somewhere public with Angelo and telling him that he needed to stop texting me. That I wanted to give my future husband a fair chance.

"You can forget about college." Wolfe slammed his phone and wallet against the marble mantel behind me. "The deal is off."

I turned around sharply, my eyes flaring in disbelief.

"I *didn't* sleep with Angelo!" I railed for the second time. God, he frustrated me to no end. He never once asked me for an explanation or voiced his concern. He just assumed.

Wolfe stared at me, placid. I ran toward him, pushing his chest. This time, unlike the first and second time I pushed him, he moved backward, just an inch. There was heat in my touch. I wanted to hurt him, I realized, more than he had hurt me.

Quantities.

"Are you sure you're a lawyer? Because you sure suck at collecting evidence. I did not sleep with Angelo." *Third time.*

"I saw you in the garden together."

"So what?" I was so upset I couldn't even explain myself properly. I clung to his dress shirt, tugging down and twining my arms around his neck to pull his head down. I pressed my lips to his, desperate to show him that what we had was real, at least for me, and that in my kiss, there was something unique—a potion—I could never give anyone else.

He didn't move or reciprocate. For the first time since I'd

met him, he did not demolish whatever stood between us the second I gave him permission to touch me. Normally, whenever I moved an inch toward him, he crossed an ocean, drowning me with kisses and caresses. He devoured me if I let him. This time, his body felt rigid and cold under my fingertips.

I took a step back, the dull pain in my chest spreading all over my body.

"I like you, Wolfe. I don't know why, but I do, okay? You make my body feel different. It's confusing, but it's true."

And boy, was it ever. The truest thing I'd ever said. My blush was back in full force, ready to obliterate my face.

"That's very kind of you." He smiled at me sardonically, standing taller and bigger and more frightening than I'd ever seen him before. "Tell me, Nemesis, do you think allowing me to fuck him out of you would help your chances at attending Northwestern?"

"Wh…what?" I pulled back, blinking. He still didn't believe me. There was nothing I could do or say to change his mind.

He lifted his hand, stroking my cheek. Usually, I basked in his attention as though it were a glorious sunray on a December day. Tonight, his touch made me shiver and not with excitement. I was still wet because he was there, because he was present, and because his eyes were on me. But it felt all wrong. My desire for him felt dirty and desperate. Doomed, somehow.

"I'm not lying to you," I said, biting my lower lip to keep it from trembling. "Why do you always think the worst of me?"

He lowered his lips to mine, and whispered, "Because you're a Rossi."

I closed my eyes, inhaling venom, exhaling hope. I felt like I was drowning even though I was standing in the middle of the foyer in the arms of the man I was going to marry. I knew what I had to do just then to save him from hating me. I just wasn't sure if, by the end of it, I would still be able not to loathe him.

Wolfe was not going to believe me, and it was too late and too convenient to tell him that I was a virgin now.

No. He had to learn that himself.

"Take me," I whispered brokenly. "Sleep with me. Compromise me." I squeezed my eyes shut, feeling my pride leaving my body, evaporating like mist. "*Fuck* Angelo out of me."

He took a step back, and I could see the war raging inside of him.

Too proud to accept my offering, and too angry to turn it down.

"Please," I clung to the collar of his shirt, rising on my toes and plastering my body against his. His erection dug into my stomach and gave me false, stupid hope.

"I want you."

"You want Angelo more."

I shook my head fiercely, kissing his jaw, the corner of his lips, his Cupid's Bow.

"You," I breathed. "Just you."

He squeezed his eyes shut, took a deep breath, and stepped away from me. I clung harder to the fabric of his shirt, clutching him in a vise grip.

"You're turning me down? Really?" I whispered against his neck, feeling his Adam's apple bob against my lips, his stubble, and his tight muscles. Every inch of his body tried to fight it. Us.

"Get on your knees," he rasped, "and beg for me to fuck you."

I drew away from him, my eyes widening.

"What?"

"You fucked another man at our engagement party. The second time you have fucked him since we got engaged. I want you to kneel and beg for me to fuck him out of you. And I am afraid that there is no other way around it, Nemesis," he said coldly, raising a thick, dark eyebrow, his jaw locked with rage.

I was speechless.

I cupped my mouth, stifling an agonized moan that had

threatened to tear past my lips. His face remained indifferent, unaffected; I wondered how he could be so cruel to the woman he was going to promise his forever. There was no going back from what I was about to do, if, indeed, I was to do it. I wanted to turn around and walk away. But I knew, without a shadow of a doubt, that if I did that, we would be over.

He needed to know that I didn't sleep with Angelo. And, after lying to him that I had, multiple times, there was only one way to prove my innocence.

The logic behind the idea was twisted, but so was Wolfe. Our whole relationship was crazy.

With an unsteady inhale, I began to lower myself to my knees in front of him. I pressed my eyes shut, determined not to see what was on his face as I stripped off my dignity for him. Mama used to say that pride was the most exquisite jewelry a woman could wear even when you're naked. But Wolfe had just ripped it from my neck, every pearl of confidence rolling on the floor. I bowed my head down, and when my knees touched the marble, a groan of pain and self-hatred escaped my mouth.

I hate you.

I like you.

I wish I could quit you.

If I didn't show Wolfe the truth, he'd make my life hell or worse—throw me back to my parents, cancel our engagement, and make me the talk of the entire city of Chicago. He would use whatever he had against my father, and we would be poor, powerless, and defenseless without my father to protect my mama and me from poverty, the Irish, or The Outfit's cutthroat society.

I would lose everything.

The choice not to kneel was never truly mine. I couldn't afford for this wedding not to happen. And I couldn't afford for my future husband not to believe me as I knew it would make both of us miserable and hateful toward one another.

The foyer was so silent, I could hear the echo of my heartbeat ricocheting off the ceilings. I slanted my chin up and cracked my eyes open, meeting his punishing gray ones. We stared at each other for a few seconds, my fingers laced together at the small of my back. He was right. Kneeling for someone did make you feel like a peasant.

The minute you willingly lowered yourself for someone else, they would never, ever look at you the same way. In or out of bed.

"I will not take you by force." His voice was a sharp-edged knife, traveling across my nerves, nipping though not cutting all the way in.

"I offer myself willingly," I said, my head bowed down.

"Up."

I stood up.

"Come to me and kiss me the way you did Angelo tonight."

I swallowed the sour bile rising in my throat. Hatred, humiliation, excitement, dread, and hope swirled in my chest. With my knees bumping into each other, I made my way back to him, pressing my lips to his as I wrapped my arms around his neck.

My body hummed with dark energy. I wanted to devour him with rage and show him that I was innocent. That I was still untarnished, and that I was his. But I was met with such passive disinterest, I couldn't muster up the courage to do to him all the things I wanted to.

He lowered his lips to meet mine—finally—and I thought he would reciprocate, but he just grinned into my mouth. "If that's how you kiss the man you want so desperately, I can see why Angelo didn't put up a better fight to win you."

That was when I lost it.

I bit down on his lower lip, hard, raking my fingernails through his hair and tugging at the same time he tore the front of my dress by the cleavage, ruining the designer number completely. My skin burned, and my back arched. I kicked out of the dress, crushed silk mounting under my heels, pulling him to me, wrapping myself around him like a deadly octopus. I was a black widow swallowing him whole. We wrestled each other furiously, stumbling toward the staircase and bumping into a hanging picture, a console table, and a statue. He hoisted me up and carried me upstairs, drowning my moans with kisses, suffocating his own groans of pleasure by biting my chin and lips and earlobes. Bruising me with punishing lust. Marking me with his envy.

Ms. Sterling was in the hallway, watering the huge plants on the marble stands against the grand crème walls. When she saw us biting and groaning at each other, me in his arms mostly-naked, she gasped, rushing toward the west wing.

He bit my upper lip and drew it into his mouth, carrying me to my bedroom. Angelo seemed a lifetime away, out of reach and as far away as the moon. Wolfe was here, in the flesh, burning me like the sun. Deadly and infuriating and—I knew, I just *knew*, as lost as I was in his touch. I had no idea how he was going to deal with the aftermath of what was about to happen. But I did know that he was going to be humbled when this was all over.

I was not a liar.

I was not a cheater.

I was his future wife.

I tried to warn him, but he didn't believe me.

When we reached my room, he kicked the door open and threw me on the bed.

I laid there, staring at him with raised chin and what I hoped was confidence. I wanted to be arrogant and cold even as he took me. Even as I submitted to him. Even when I gave him my most precious and only possession. A possession he most assuredly did not earn tonight.

My virginity.

He stuffed his hands in the pockets of his cigar pants and regarded me with disdain, assessing me now that we were completely alone. I was wearing nothing but my white bra and matching panties. I knew he liked what he saw because he had that darkened look in his eyes. The one that made the room hotter, the air dense like fur.

"Take everything off but the heels," he demanded.

"I'm not a stripper," I hissed, narrowing my stinging eyes at him. "I'm your future wife. Strip me like you take your vows—like you mean it, Senator Keaton."

"Vows that obviously mean nothing to you," he said again, even more aloof. He barely looked at me as he did, making a point. "*Off*, Francesca."

I grinned, gathering my courage. When my arm moved to my back, unclasping my bra, I could almost see his pulse quickening on the side of his neck. His face remained cool even when I removed my underwear, remaining in nothing but my heels in my bed.

He leaned down, still fully clothed, stared into my eyes, and brought his arm between us. He pressed the heel of his palm against my private area. I felt my wetness pushed against the dusting of hair there, damp and cool on the outside but hot from within.

"I will say this one time, Francesca, then consider my conscience clean. If you don't tell me to leave right this minute, you will be devoured, wrecked, possessed, and owned for the entire night. I will fuck Angelo out of you, and then the rest of the idiots who were unfortunate enough to touch you and think there'd be a second time. I will not be considerate. I will not be compassionate. So if you're used to gentle lovers and hour-long spooning, say the word, and our verbal contract will be terminated."

"And you will still marry me?" I asked.

His nostrils flared. "I will marry you, but you'd wish I wouldn't."

He thought I'd been with other men. I told him I was someone else—and he took my word for it. Who I really was didn't matter to him. Wolfe went to extreme lengths to prove that to me. What struck me as peculiar, though, wasn't his words, but the situation. He was willing to forgive me, to honor our verbal agreement I allegedly broke, even though in his eyes, I'd slept with my former flame not once, but twice since we'd gotten engaged. He said he did not negotiate, yet he absolutely did. With me.

"Are you afraid to actually feel something if you touch me?" I taunted. "Your walls of icebergs are thawing, Senator."

"Ten seconds to decide, Nemesis."

"You already know the answer."

"Say it. Eight."

I smiled, though inside, I was crumbling. He was going to take my virginity and by force. He thought I was already compromised, and to prove how wrong he was, I needed to let him hurt me the way it hurt him to see me with another man. I knew what it looked like. Angelo did touch me. He did lean against me. He did trace my hair with his fingers. Moved his thumb across my lips. And then he snuck out of a room after having sex with someone else while I was MIA.

The evidence was there, stacked against me.

"Five."

"Try not to fall in love with me." I opened my thighs.

"*Francesca.* Three."

"It will be a terrible inconvenience, *il mio amore*. To love the wife you took in vengeance."

"One."

"*Stay,*" I snapped, loud and clear.

He advanced toward me and pulled me down by my waist so I was lying underneath him. I sucked in a breath as he put his hand on my neck and scooted up, caging me with his knees locking my thighs, still fully dressed.

"Open my zipper."

I couldn't breathe, let alone work his zipper. So I just stared at him, hoping he would not misread my shock as defiance. But he did. Of course, he did. With a growl, he unzipped himself and pushed down his pants. I didn't dare glance down and see what was waiting for me. My heart pounded so fast and hard I thought I was going to puke. I quickly assembled all the information I had on lovemaking and decided that I'd be okay. I was aroused, wet where I needed to be, and in the hands of the most desirable man in Chicago.

With his pants around his knees, he slid one finger into me, his face void of emotion.

I inhaled and tried to look calm even when the tears slammed into the back of my eyeballs again. It hurt. I wasn't sure what hurt more, the physical discomfort or the way he looked past me as though I was nothing but a body.

The same way he had stared at Kristen.

He popped his finger into his mouth and sucked on it, expressionless, then dipped his finger into me again, retrieved my arousal, and pushed it between my own lips. I was forced to taste myself. Musky and sweet. I flushed red, my nipples puckering, so sensitive I wanted to rub them against his hard chest.

"He used a condom?" He wiped the remainder of my wetness on my cheek. I wanted to cry until there was nothing left of me but held back.

He was about to find out the truth in a few short moments that I was telling the truth the first three times, so I told him what he wanted to hear.

"Yes."

"At least you had the decency to do that. I will not be using one, but a morning-after pill will be waiting on your nightstand first thing. See, having children with a leg-spreading whore is low on my to-do list. You will take the pill, no questions asked. Am I understood?"

I closed my eyes, shame dripping down my body like sweat. I was agreeing to this. To all of this. Consenting to his words, his actions, and his cruelty. I had, after all, gone down on my knees, begging for this moment to happen.

"Understood."

"I would play with you a little, but you've been prepped by another, and I'm not in a generous mood." He smirked darkly, and then, with one sudden thrust, he pressed his cock home, slamming into me with such force, my back arched, my chest meeting his, and stars exploded behind my eyelids as pain pierced through me. He tore past the natural barrier of my body and was buried so deep inside me, it felt like he was ripping me apart. The sting was so profound, I had to bite my lower lip to suppress a scream of sheer agony. My whole life, Clara and Mom warned me off tampons, bike riding, and I even had to wear thick breeches for my horse rides, to preserve that which was so sacrosanct, so holy. Only to be met with *this*.

Motionless, soundless, and tense under his body, the only clue that I was still conscious was the tears that began streaming down my face. I bit my lip hard so as not to make a sound.

I am a rusty barbwire, twisted together, knotted into a ball of fear.

"Tight as a fist," he groaned, his feral voice meeting my complete silence as he thrust so hard, so fast, and so rough, I thought he was going to slash me apart into miniscule shreds. My tears slid from my cheeks down to my pillow as he pushed deeper and deeper, and I could feel the walls of my virginity coming down and bleeding out of me. But I didn't tell him to stop, and I didn't confess my virginity.

I lay there and let him have me. He took my innocence with force, but I couldn't give him any part of my pride. Not even a small piece of it. Not after what occurred in the foyer.

After a few thrusts, I forced myself to open my eyes and blurrily watched his impassive, angry face. Something seeped between us, covering my thighs, and I knew what it was. I prayed with everything I had in me that he didn't notice it yet.

But he did. He noticed. His eyebrows snapped together, and he registered my face, my tears, my agony for the first time.

"Period?"

I didn't answer.

He pulled back from me carefully, his gaze dropping between us. There was blood on the inside of my thighs and on my white linen. I grabbed the collar of his shirt, drawing him back to me. I was desperate for his body to hide mine.

"Finish what you started," I rustled, exposing my teeth. I could feel the pulse of his heart against his chest, he was so close.

"Francesca." His voice was gruff and drenched with guilt. He brought his hand to my face to rub my cheek, but I slapped it away. I couldn't bear his new, tender tenor. I didn't want him to be gentle with me. I wanted him to treat me as his equal. With the same anger and lust and hatred I felt for him right now.

"Now do you believe me?" I smiled bitterly through the tears that just kept coming down like rain, desperate to wash away the last few minutes. His frown smoothed, and he raised himself up from me, about to draw away, but I pulled him back to my body harder.

"It's done." I looked him in the eye and saw so much misery in them. I locked my ankles behind his back, caging him inside me. "I decide how I want my first time to be. Finish this. Now."

To my horror, more tears came through, and he licked them as he lowered himself back to me. His tongue rolled from my neck to the pillows of my cheeks, catching all the tears parachuting from my eyes. "Nem," he tried reasoning with me.

"Shut up," I buried my face in his shoulder as our bodies connected, him driving into me again.

"I'm sorry," he whispered.

His thrusts were gentle now, easing into me while brushing the tips of his fingers back and forth over my outer thigh, a leisured, intimate gesture that was nothing more than a sweet lie. The heel of my foot rubbed the fabric of the pants he never bothered to remove. I knew that he wanted to try and finish to get it out of the way. I also knew that it was too late to minimize the damage.

After a few minutes of dull pain, he began to up the pace. His face grew tight and his eyes darkened, and that was when I could bear to look at his features again without feeling like he shoved a knife into my chest every time he pushed into me. He finished deep inside me, the warmth of his lust conquering every part inside me. I clung to his shoulders, feeling frayed and tattered beneath him, my lower body so wounded it almost felt numb.

He levered up so he could look at me, staring at my face without meeting my eyes.

We stayed silent for a few moments, him still on top of me. He didn't ask me why I didn't tell him I was a virgin earlier. He knew. Finally, he rolled off me. I scooted away and stood up, covering myself in a lavender satin nightgown I retrieved from the back of my desk chair.

He sat on my bed behind my back, bent forward, looking a little stunned. His face blank, his shoulders hunched. A far cry from the brash asshole, future husband I knew who always oozed of overconfidence. I didn't blame him for his silence. Words seem too insignificant for what happened here tonight.

I took my cigarette pack from my nightstand and lit one up right inside his house. It was the least he owed me.

He knew and I knew that if he tried to give me affection, I wouldn't be able to live it down.

"I have an early day tomorrow. My final dress fitting, then shopping for college," I said, taking a seat at my desk overlooking the garden I'd loved the way I'd wished I could love my future husband. Wholly and without expecting much back.

"Nem." His voice was so gentle, I couldn't bear it. I propped my chin on my knuckles. His hands were on my shoulders now as he stood behind me, lowering his forehead to meet the crown of my head. He released a rugged breath that made my hair fly everywhere on my face. The room smelled of sex and metallic blood and desperation that wasn't there before.

"Leave," I said coldly.

He kissed the top of my head.

"I will never doubt you again, Francesca."

"Leave!" I screamed, pushing off the desk. The wheels of the chair hit his feet, but he didn't seem to care about the pain. He left after that, but what happened between us stayed in my room.

When I woke up the next morning, two Advils, a morning-after pill, a bottle of water, and a warm, wet washcloth waited on my nightstand. I instantly knew that Ms. Sterling was privy to what happened during the night.

I took the Advils and the pill, drinking all the water. Then I spent the rest of the day crying in my bed.

Wolfe

I paced the east wing.

Back, forth.

Back, forth.

Walking had never been so excruciatingly maddening. I wanted to kick down the door and barge inside. I barely had it in me to send Kristen a letter from my lawyer, threatening to sue her for every penny she ever earned if she published the piece on me. I also knew I couldn't hold her back from dishing out the dirt for much longer, but again—did I care?

Not. One. Bit.

"Give her time." Sterling was shadowing my every movement like a fucking tail. As if I was going to force my way in.

Done quite enough of that for a lifetime, Sterling.

"How much time?" I barked. I was not well versed in the whole relationship gig.

I was even less familiar with the world and feelings of teenage girls. Even as a teenager myself, I opted for more mature women. They didn't take me seriously, and there were no expectations to be met.

"Until she feels well enough to leave her bedroom."

"That could take *weeks*," I spat out. Francesca already proved to be able not to eat for long periods of time. If disobedience was a competitive sport, my future wife would make it to the Olympics. And medal.

"Then that's what you'll give her," Sterling said with conviction, signaling me with her head to leave Francesca's wing and come down to the kitchen with her.

I couldn't unsee the bloodbath between her legs, or the way her thighs shook, twitched, and tensed under mine.

I'd always had a talent for reading people. That was how I'd become a star politician, impeccable prosecutor, and one of the most formidable men in Chicago. Which was at odds with the fact that I failed to notice my young, very sheltered, nervous fiancée was a virgin. I was so blinded with rage thinking she'd slept with Angelo that I didn't take her word for it. And she— the smart, sensitive, gorgeous vixen that she was—served me with a healthy slice of humble pie, making me finish every bite of what I'd started.

I should've seen it from miles away. She came from a strict Italian family and went to church every Sunday. She simply wanted me to see her as more worldly and less of a naïve little mouse. Unfortunately, it worked. Too well for her liking.

The weight of my guilt sat squarely on my shoulders. I shredded her savagely, and she met me, thrust for thrust, her eyes on mine, her tears fierce but silent. I thought she was guilty and angry with emotion. I hadn't realized I was bulldozing through walls I had no right bringing down.

Traditionally, in Italian weddings in The Outfit, the bride-groom was supposed to present the bloodied sheets to his peers. I had no doubt Arthur Rossi was going to die a slow, painful, internal death if I sent her sheets his way six days before the wedding. There was no mistaking what happened here. And there was no confounding Francesca suffered every moment of it. But somehow, and despite my worst intentions, I couldn't bring myself to do that to her.

I retired to my study, resisting the urge to check in on her. I wasn't entirely sure I should give her time, but I no longer trust-ed my instincts when it came to her. Typically a cruel and calcu-lated creature, I'd lost control several times in the past month, all of them because of my young bride-to-be. Maybe it was best to take my housekeeper's advice and let her be.

I opted to work at home that day on the off chance she'd leave her room. She'd missed her appointments, and when her mother came to pick her up to shop for her upcoming school year, Sterling sent her away, albeit with a carrot cake, explain-ing that Francesca was suffering from a terrible migraine. Mrs. Rossi looked distraught as her driver pulled away from the curb. Through the window of my study, I caught her trying desper-ately to call her daughter. Still, I didn't have it in me to feel sorry about what happened to anyone who was not my future wife.

The day passed, as bad days do, significantly slow. All the meetings I'd summoned to my house turned beneficial and pro-ductive, however. I'd even managed to squeeze in a conference call with my public relations manager and his assistant, some-thing I'd postponed for weeks. When I finally left my office, it was well past dinnertime.

I ate in the kitchen, not meeting Sterling's judgmental gaze. She sat across from me, her hands in her lap, staring at me as though I just mauled a baby. In a sense, that was exactly what I had done.

"Any more great ideas? Maybe I should send her back to

her parents?" I snarled when it became apparent she was not going to stop looking at me.

"You should definitely *not* do that." It was the first time Sterling spoke to me in that tone. Even when I was a child, she did not treat me like one. She did now.

"I'm not going to wait for her to come out any longer."

"You shouldn't have waited a *minute*," she agreed, sipping my fine scotch. Things were dire between Francesca and me if Sterling resorted to drinking. She hadn't drunk an alcoholic beverage in two decades.

"Then why did you tell me to wait?" I flipped over the plate with the prime rib, sending it flying across the kitchen. It crashed against the wall.

"I wanted you to suffer the way she did." She shrugged, standing up and walking out of the kitchen, leaving me to stew in the fact that I *did*, in fact, suffer.

I fixed myself a glass of bourbon, heavy on the rocks, and made my way to the east wing. Nem's bedroom door was closed, and I pushed it halfway open without knocking, out of habit, before thinking the better of it.

I brushed my knuckles over the oak wood of her door.

"May I come in?" My voice felt stiff and rigid.

I did not ask for permission to do anything.

And I was not fond of the idea of making it a habit.

No answer.

I pressed my head to the hard surface and closed my eyes, breathing in traces of her scent. The mandarin shampoo she used. The sweet, vanilla lotion that made her skin glow. The thought she was so sore she might have needed to go to the doctor's today flashed through my mind, accompanied by an even more unsettling idea—Francesca wouldn't tell me if she was too sore. She would cling to the remainder of her pride. The same pride I stripped off her viciously in my quest to avenge something that did not really happen.

I pushed the door open, finding my fiancée splayed on her four-poster bed, staring at nothing. I followed her line of vision. It was a blank spot on the wall that captured her attention. She did not so much as blink when I stepped in.

I made my way to her, sat on the edge of her bed, and took a sip of my bourbon, handing it over to her. She ignored both me and the drink.

"I'm sorry," I rasped.

"Go away," she groaned.

"I'm not sure that's an option," I admitted frankly. "The more you think about what happened, the more you'll hate me."

"I *should* hate you."

I took another sip of my drink. I wasn't going to argue my defense. It was inexcusable whether she told me she was a virgin or not. "That may be true, but we'd both suffer if you do. And although I deserve my fair share of suffering—" I said, and she cut through my words.

"Yes, yes, you do."

"I do," I agreed, my voice too soft for my ears to believe it was mine, "but you don't. You've done nothing wrong. And while I'm not a good man, I am not a terrible one, either."

She looked down at her hands, inspecting them as she tried not to cry. The fact that I knew how Francesca's almost-crying face looked like proved that I'd been less than an ideal fiancé to her.

"Why didn't you tell me you were a virgin?"

She chuckled, shaking her head.

"You'd already made up your mind about me before I even opened my mouth at the masquerade. And frankly, I didn't much care what you thought of me. But yesterday, I told you…no, I *repeatedly* told you I didn't sleep with Angelo. Three times. So I think the better question is—why didn't *you* believe *me*?"

I gave it some thought. "It made disliking you easier."

"What a coincidence. Your actions made me dislike you, fiercely." She crossed her arms over her chest, looking away.

"I do not dislike you any more, Nemesis."

I didn't hate her. I respected her. Even more so since she didn't let her pride get in the way yesterday. She got down on her knees to prove a point. That I was a bastard, and that she was speaking the truth. I took her purity and knew that in order to fix this, I would need to give her some of my own pride.

A price beyond anything I'd ever agreed to pay. A security deposit to make sure I could keep my fiancée, not only physically but in the same mental state from prior to our engagement party. The same fiancée who rubbed her soft, little body all over mine in her vegetable garden every evening, gasping in awe every time I "accidentally" touched her clit through the fabric of her dress.

"Put your hands above your head," I said, turning around to face her.

She arched an eyebrow, still staring at the wall.

"If you continue staring at it, I'll have to give you a good reason to."

"Such as?" I piqued her interest. That was my in.

"I'm thinking about a life-size portrait of myself."

"My idea of a nightmare," she mumbled.

"With Sterling standing above my seated figure, holding one of her novels."

She bit her lower lip, stifling a smile. "You're not funny, Senator."

"That may be, but I'll have plenty of time to find your brand of humor. Hands above your head, Nem."

She turned her head to look at me, her eyes two pools of misery. Misery I created, adding drops of it every single day I kept her here. I didn't look away. I faced the result of my sins.

"I'm still sore." She was first to break the eye contact, looking down.

"I know," I whispered. "I'm asking you to trust me."

"Why should I trust you?"

"Because if you stop trusting, you'll end up like me, and that's a miserable existence."

Hesitantly, she curled her fingers around the edge of the headboard. My heart squeezed at the implication of her obedience. She wore the same simple, pastel lilac nightgown that she'd covered herself with yesterday. It rode up her smooth, milky white thighs. I dragged my hand from my knee to her inner thigh, massaging the sensitive area for a few minutes, loosening her bundled muscles. At first, she was as stiff as a stone, but when I moved to the other thigh and she realized I wasn't going to go anywhere north without her permission, she began to relax under my hands.

"I won't hurt you," I assured her, sliding her underwear gently down her thighs, "in the bedroom," I finished.

"You did yesterday," she pointed out.

"And I apologize for that. From here on out, I'll make sure it will always be good for you."

"You said you don't care about making it good for women."

I said those words before I nearly raped you.

Not that I actually did in the eyes of the dry law. She asked for it. She *begged* for it. Got down on her knees for it. But it was to prove a point. We both knew she didn't enjoy it. We both knew I took something from her I did not deserve.

Her eyes met mine as I spread her thighs, sliding my thumbs toward her slit and rubbing circles in the sensitive area near her groin. I did not bow down to anyone, much less a Rossi. But I wasn't bowing down to Nemesis, I was merely making my own point. That sex was great, if done right, and if both participants were on the same wavelength.

"Don't move your hands," I ordered, my voice hardening with lust. I saw her chest rising and falling in a mix of anticipation and fear. I could work with that. Her legs quivered with adrenaline before I even laid my tongue on her. I slid her night-gown up and tossed it over her shoulder, exposing her pink, coin-like nipples.

Wretchedly gorgeous.

Wickedly innocent.

Irrevocably mine.

After she was completely exposed to me, I took off my shoes, socks, dress pants, blazer, and dress shirt until I remained with nothing but my black Armani briefs. Another thing I didn't do often—get naked in front of a woman. Sex wasn't indulgent. For me, it was an outlet. I rarely fucked my flings in a bed, opting for quickies, and even when I did, it usually didn't last past my climax. Nemesis stared at my hard-on through my briefs, curiosity and dread swimming in her cerulean eyes.

"Do you want to see it?"

She nodded, blushing. Something inside me burned hot.

"Would you like to see all of me? You will not have to touch me. Tonight's all about you."

She swallowed, biting the corner of her lower lip. Carefully, I took down my briefs, standing completely naked in front of her. I couldn't remember the last time that happened and tried to reason with myself that the concept of marrying someone forced you into lowering your walls, but that didn't mean they were going to be broken. There was going to be a lot of bathroom and Jacuzzi and shower and mirror sex in the years to come. It made no difference if she saw me naked today, tomorrow, or in a month. I joined her in her bed and settled between her legs, cupping her cheeks. I lowered myself down to her and kissed her, gently at first, before squeezing her jaw open, wrestling my tongue against hers, licking the corners of her mouth and sucking her lower lip the way that drove her crazy.

Her muscle memory kicked in instantly, and she remembered all the times before last night. She moaned, responding to my peace offering by removing her hands from the headboard and tracing my jaw with her fingers.

I took her wrists and placed her hands back on the headboard.

"Patience, Nem, is a virtue."

"Which I don't have." She momentarily forgot that she was mad at me, grinning like the sweet teenager she was.

"Which you'll have to learn, being the wife of a senator." I chucked her under the chin—that was my MO—then kissed her again with more abandon, and passion, and fury. She gave in to me completely, and I trailed my kisses down her neck and between her breasts, before taking one of her nipples and sucking it into my mouth. It pebbled between my teeth, and I tugged at it softly enough not to scare her, but her body still jerked in fear. I moved to the other nipple, rubbing the one I'd just sucked with my thumb, and when she braced herself for the same treatment, I licked a pattern around it, blowing cold air on the sensitive, wet skin. She shuddered against me, another groan slipping past her lips.

Francesca was a tentative woman, and I had no doubt, despite the poor introduction I'd given her to sex, she would be a fast learner.

I slid my tongue down the center of her chest, dipping it inside her navel, then began to trace wet kisses on her inner thighs and just above her slit. I knew by the patches of faded dry blood marking her thighs that she'd yet to take a shower since yesterday. It seemed fitting that I would lick her better, tasting my own semen on her skin, knowing that it was awfully unhygienic, but that I couldn't ask her to shower. Not for me. She groaned, thrusting her groin into my face, her knuckles whitening with the strain it put her under not to touch me.

"Hold still."

"Sorry." Something that sounded a lot like a giggle fell from her luscious lips.

I loved that she let me do this to her despite the bastard I'd been to her so far. I didn't find it docile. It showed that she had courage and the guts to face me in bed, after all. I also loved that she was so innocent. Neither waxed nor groomed for sex. I slid my hands to the back of her thighs and grabbed her ass cheeks, elevating her up as I started licking a shallow trace along her slit. It was red and engorged from yesterday, and I hated myself with a passion I usually reserved for her father.

"You're delicious," I said hoarsely.

"Oh," she squeaked above me, panting, "this is…wow. Yeah."

I slid my tongue between her folds. I hadn't gone down on a woman in over a decade, but if someone was worth tasting, it was my future wife. Her body coiled a little at first, then loosened as she spread her thighs wider and let me push my tongue all the way in, fighting against the tightness of her pussy. She was tense—not surprising, considering everything she went through yesterday—and still extremely small. The idea of thrusting my fat cock into her again, and soon, made my erection strain against her bloodied linen. I felt it throbbing, my pulse smashing against my balls.

After a few minutes of licking her, I flicked my tongue in and out of her. She moaned, her body rocking with pleasure as she became looser and less self-conscious. She peeked at me, cracking open one eye. Her hip met my face time after time as she chased my tongue, her nipples so hard, I couldn't help but play with them simultaneously. I put pressure on her clit, sucking and swirling my tongue around it for long minutes, prolonging her orgasm every time she was close by abandoning her clit and licking at a stain of blood on her inner thigh. After twenty minutes, I decided she could have her climax. I closed my lips on her little nub and sucked it so hard, she screamed. Francesca quaked around my face as her first orgasm shot through her, and her hands left the headboard, finding my hair and yanking at it brutally. I felt the burn in my scalp but didn't relent. Instead,

I reached for my bourbon and fished out an ice cube, sucking the alcohol out of it before sliding it between the sore lips of her pussy as I drew her clit with less ferocity now, sending her into another climax that crashed into her and made her moan so loud the windows nearly rattled.

There were two more orgasms after that.

"Can you teach me how to touch a man?" she asked when we were done, and she was propped against the headboard, me beside her, still naked and hard.

"No," I deadpanned. "I can teach you how to touch me. Touching other men in this lifetime is not looking good for you, Nem."

It was stupid to think about that kid, Angelo, at that moment. The need to make him go away hit me somewhere dark and primal. I spared her the part where he set her up and made me believe that he actually fucked her. She'd had enough of a shitty night yesterday, thanks to yours truly.

She wrapped the sheets around her body, tapping her chin, as if contemplating whether she should say the next thing.

"What you saw in the garden…" She hesitated. I wanted to tell her not to bother, but the truth was, I was interested to know what happened. Where they'd both disappeared to.

"My father pushed me to talk to Angelo. After Bishop approached you, Angelo offered to take the conversation somewhere we didn't have to shout over other people's voices. I told him I didn't hate it here. Which I guess was true until last night. He got upset and walked off. I went upstairs to my room, and on my way up, my cousin told me he slipped into a guestroom with the blonde reporter who was trying to coax Bishop into an interview."

Kristen.

The little witch set me up, and Angelo played along. I wondered if they knew how far I'd go. They were going to pay for that little stunt. Too bad the two assholes were taken with Francesca and myself. They'd make a fitting couple.

Francesca chewed on a lock of her hair. "My mom was in my room. I'd seen her from the garden, and we talked for a while."

Pause.

"My dad is cheating on her."

"I'm sorry," I said. I was. Not for her parents. Her mother let me take her daughter away. But for Francesca herself, who had to deal with the fall of her family over a period of a few short weeks.

"Thank you."

There was no trace of hostility in Francesca's voice. God, she was sweet, and she was all mine. Not just her body but also her words and her courage.

I knew, without a shadow of a doubt, that my future wife's pussy was going to be on my daily menu from this day forward. I put my glass on her nightstand and turned around to her, pressing a kiss on her forehead.

"Go eat your dinner, Nem."

"I'm not hungry." She shifted and winced. She was still sore all over, and I made a mental note to have Sterling provide her with a new warm washcloth every night for the next week.

"You can't look famished at the wedding," I retorted.

She sighed, rolling her eyes. "What's for dinner?"

I was still sitting naked next to her, ignoring the vulnerability of my position. Intimacy was too awkward for my liking.

"Prime rib and sautéed asparagus."

She scrunched her nose. "I think I'll pass."

Such a teenager.

"What do you feel like eating?"

"I don't know, waffles? I don't normally crave sweet things, but I've had the worst day."

My nostrils flared. I was such a piece of shit to her.

"Diner down the road serves them. Thick and fluffy. Come on. We could use the fresh air."

"It's eleven o'clock." She shifted her gaze to her wristwatch, her teeth sinking to her lower lip with unease.

"It's open twenty-four hours."

"Uhm. Okay. Together?"

I grazed her chin. *Again*. "Yes. Together."

"You don't strike me as a waffle-eating man."

"True, but I might eat *you* for dessert when we come back. It's been a while since I've done that, and quite frankly, pussy has never tasted as good as yours."

She reddened in an instant, looking away. "Your compliments are strange."

"I am strange."

"You are," she said, munching on her lower lip. "And that's the part of you I dislike the least."

I stood up, casually slipping into my clothes again. Much, *much* better. Less vulnerability. More barriers. Then something occurred to me.

"Tomorrow is your first day of college."

Of course, Francesca opted to start college a week before her wedding. We were both relieved not to have to plan a sham honeymoon. Back when we had our verbal deal, we could barely pretend to stand each other.

"Yeah. I'm excited." She offered me a small smile, scurrying toward her walk-in closet and slipping into one of her dresses.

"Who's driving you?"

She didn't have a driver's license, and I hated her parents for never bothering to teach her. She was almost like a tropical fish to them. Gorgeous in her fancy aquarium, but they put no effort into nurturing her.

"Smithy, of course."

Of course. My blood was still making its way from my dick back to my brain.

"Time?"

"Eight o'clock."

"I'll drive you."

"Okay."

"Okay," I repeated. I had absolutely no idea what came over me. Not about the waffles, and not about driving her there. Up until now, I offered her independence only when she asked for it, dangling a demand over her head. *If* she did this, *then* she could have that. As we made our way downstairs, I noticed Sterling sitting at the kitchen table, reading a book and smiling. I bet she was quite smug, knowing I'd gone upstairs to get back in my future wife's good graces. I wiped my mouth, then licked my lips for traces of my fiancée.

"Not a word," I warned Sterling as Francesca went to get her jacket.

She zipped her lips with her fingers.

Francesca appeared at the kitchen door. I turned around, lacing her arm in mine. We poured into the starless Chicago night.

"Villain?"

"Yes, Nemesis?"

"Do you think Smithy might be able to teach me how to drive?"

She wanted her wings back.

She had every right to them. I knew since I wanted her protected from everyone around her. Including me.

"Fuck Smithy, Nem. I'll teach you."

CHAPTER ELEVEN

Francesca

THE REMAINING WEEK BEFORE OUR WEDDING, WOLFE CAME to my bedroom every single night.

We did not have sex, but he did lick me down there until I came. Every time I reached a climax, he'd suck my lips—the ones between my legs—and laugh like the devil. Sometimes he would rub himself against my stomach through our clothes, then retire to my bathroom. When he came back to the bedroom to kiss me good night before he left, his cheeks were always tinted pink.

One of the times, he asked if he could come on me. I said yes, mainly because I wasn't entirely sure if it meant what I think it meant. He rubbed against me, and when he was ready, he took himself out and climaxed between my breasts, all over my nightgown.

A part of me wanted to sleep with him to show him that I forgave him because as much as I hated to admit it—and despite myself—I *did* forgive him. But another part of me was terrified of having sex again. I was still sore from the incident, and every time he rubbed against me, I remembered the awful night he drove into me in one go. But then I'd push the memory aside and force myself to think happy thoughts.

As much as our relationship had improved after our engagement party night, we still weren't a real couple. We slept in separate wings of the house, something he'd warn would happen for the rest of our days. He limited his attention toward me to only the nighttime. We would have dinner together, then retire back to our designated rooms. Then, a short hour after I showered and slipped into a sexy nightgown, he would knock on my door, and I'd be ready for him, with my thighs open and the thing between them aching for his touch and tongue and mouth.

I felt dirty for what we did. I'd been taught that sex was a way to get pregnant and please your husband, not something you should desire to do so frequently. Yet having Wolfe lick me there was *all* I wanted to do, all day, every day. Even now, when I went to college and made a conscious effort to meet new people and get a grip on my class schedule, the only thing I could think about was his nose and mouth buried deep inside me as he mumbled filthy, degrading things about my body that made more and more wetness leak from me.

I didn't make an effort to make friends, or to open up, or to form a life of my own. I wanted to do my homework, attend all my lectures, and have the Big, Bad Wolfe eat me out.

The day before our wedding, Wolfe was in his home office and I was gardening outside when I heard the doorbell ring. Since I knew Ms. Sterling was upstairs, reading one of her less-than-innocent books (I was no longer in a position to judge her, though), I took off my gardening gloves, rose to my feet, and made my way into the house. Through the peephole, I saw it was my father and his bodyguards. My pulse quickened. Was he trying to make amends?

I flung the front door open and was pushed to the side. My back slammed against the door as he stomped in.

"Where is he?" he clipped. His two bodyguards trailed

behind him. I furrowed my brows. He didn't even say hello to me. After everything he'd done at our engagement party—inviting the dodgiest people the state had to offer to try and hurt Wolfe's reputation, not to mention throwing Kristen and Angelo into the mix—he didn't even afford me an offhand pleasantry. What a jerk.

I closed the door behind them, straightening my back. I felt oddly secure in my domain. I had no illusions about Wolfe's feelings for me, but I did know that he would not have anyone disrespecting me in my own house.

"Is he expecting you?" I drawled, playing dumb. Truly, I was sick of him. Sick of him cheating on my mother and selling his daughter to the highest bidder. My father was selfish, and he allowed it to hurt his family.

My father sneered, "Get him here. Now."

"Do you or do you not have an appointment with Senator Keaton?" I braved my fear, raising my voice slightly.

I am the wind. Strong and evasive and everywhere. He can't touch me.

He scanned me head-to-toe. "Who *are* you?"

"Wolfe Keaton's future wife," I answered with faux obedience. "Who are *you*?"

"Your father. Though you seem to have forgotten that."

"You haven't been acting like a father. Maybe that's why." I folded my arms over my chest, ignoring the reddening faces of his two guards. He looked intoxicated, swaying a little, his face a shade too red for it just to be the summer weather.

He waved me off impatiently. "I'm not the one who has changed, Francesca. You're the one going off to college and talking about getting a job."

"Being independent is not a disease," I gritted out. "But that's not your issue with me. Your issue with me is that I now belong to a man who wants to ruin you, and you are no longer sure where my loyalty lies."

The cat was out of the bag, and even though I stood behind every word, it didn't make it any less painful. He took a step toward me, and we were nose to nose. We felt different at that moment. *Equal.*

"Where does your loyalty lie, mascalzone?" *Rascal.* He used to call me that when I was a kid. It always made me giggle because in Spanish it sounded like más calzones. *More underpants.*

I stared deep into his icy blue eyes, leaned forward, and whispered into his face.

"Me, Papa. My loyalty will always be with *me.*"

He sneered, brushing a lock of hair off my forehead gently. Imperial as ever, even drunk. "Tell me, figlia, does it not bother you that your future husband encourages you to get an education and a job? Do you not think perhaps he doesn't want to keep you long enough to take care of you, so he makes sure you can take care of yourself?"

I opened my mouth, then clamped it shut. When I wanted to marry Angelo, I also knew that my father would always have this power over him. He couldn't divorce me, toss me aside, or wrong me. Wolfe, however, did not answer to Arthur Rossi. He did not answer to anyone.

"That's what I thought." My father laughed. "Take me to see him."

"I will not…" I started, then stopped when I heard the sound of heavy feet behind me.

"Arthur Rossi. What an unpleasant surprise," my fiancé said from behind me. I turned around, hating the butterflies that took flight in my chest when he arrived. Hating that the first thing I saw was how much taller and more impressive he was than Papa. And absolutely despising how my thighs clenched and my panties dampened at the sight of him.

Wolfe descended the stairs in leisured steps, passing me by without acknowledging my existence as he came face to face with my father. They stared each other in the eye. I instantly knew that something else had happened. Something much bigger than the stunt my father pulled at the engagement party.

"You raided the pier," my father hissed, getting in his face. It was the first time I saw my father lose control over his voice. It was brittle around the edges, like a wrinkly piece of paper. His face was so swollen and red, he was barely recognizable. The last few weeks had obviously been eventful between them, but it only showed on one of them. "You sent cops when you knew we'd be there. Thirteen of my men are in jail."

Wolfe smiled, plucking the handkerchief from my father's blazer's pocket and using it to dispose of the gum in his mouth, tucking it back in neatly and patting the pocket. "That's where they should be. Francesca, leave," he ordered me, his tone steel. He was a different man from the one who visited my bedroom every night. Not even related to the man who took me to eat waffles in the middle of the night, then came back to lick me again and again until my thighs squeezed his face.

"But…" I started. My father turned around from Wolfe to snap at me.

"I sent you an obedient, well-mannered girl, and look at her now. She's wild, talks back, and doesn't even follow your orders. You think you can crush me? You can't even handle my teenage daughter."

Wolfe was still staring at him, smirking and not paying any attention to me, when I shook my head and, deflated, made my way outside to the garden. I put my gardening gloves back on, then lit a cigarette. As I crouched down, internally cursing my father and my fiancé for treating me like a dumb kid for the millionth time, I noticed something peculiar peeking from the edge of the vegetable garden. A rusty door leading to what I assumed was the mansion's pantry. It was laced with ivy, but I could tell that it was recently used since the ivy was torn around the edges. I stood back up and sauntered toward it, yanking the handle. It opened easily. I took a step in, realizing that it did not lead to the pantry, but to the laundry room right next to the foyer. My father and Wolfe no longer had the privacy of the double-glazed balcony doors. I could hear them through the thin, wooden door of the laundry room. I wasn't supposed to eavesdrop, but I figured they deserved it for keeping so many secrets from me in the first place. I pressed my ear against the door.

"Where I come from, Senator Keaton, words have meanings, and deals are honored," my father hissed. "I gave you Francesca, yet you seem adamant about ruining what's mine."

"We seem to be in the same boat. I have a briefcase missing with your fingerprints all over it." Wolfe chuckled darkly.

"Not my doing."

"Aren't men in the Chicago Outfit supposed to pride themselves in never stabbing a man in the back and always telling the truth?"

"I've never stabbed anyone in the back," my father said cautiously, "and Murphy's was an unfortunate incident, which I am sure the Irish will benefit from once the insurance kicks in."

"Let's talk about the pep rally," Wolfe continued. The one where there were shootings? I heard about it briefly in the news but knew that nobody got hurt. A deranged kid who played too many violent video games, they said. It was on the same day the stock market fell, and no one made a fuss of it.

"What about it?" My father crushed his teeth together. I could hear it clearly even past the door.

"You're lucky you're still out and about, and not locked up with the shooter," Wolfe said.

"I'm out and about because you have no proof."

"Neither do you that I had anything to do with the pier. But the cherry on the shit cake wasn't my attempted assassination. No. That was half-baked and completely amateur. It was the engagement party."

I choked on my own saliva. My father tried to assassinate

my husband. And my husband didn't even tell me. He *hid* it from the world, essentially protecting my father. Why?

"Are you seriously comparing sending off my frivolous daughter to flirt with her childhood crush at a party to locking up thirteen of my men?" Arthur Rossi spat out. It was the second time his voice rose. Real rivalry did change him and not for the best.

"Your daughter is neither frivolous, nor is she a flirt. She is, however, my soon-to-be wife, and I'm growing tired of you disrespecting her. I will also not have you push her into anyone's arms, much less someone she was fond of when she was younger. In fact, for every time you act up concerning Francesca, or put my reputation in jeopardy as you did during the engagement party, I will kill one of your businesses. The pier. A restaurant. Perhaps a poker joint. The list is endless, and I have the means and the time. Get this past that thick skull of yours—she is mine now. I decide if she works, where she studies, and in what positions I want to fuck her. Furthermore, eliminating me from the equation will not work. Not only did I spread the evidence on you in different places, secured by different people, but I also have written letters instructing my trustees what to do in case of my untimely death."

He talked as though he was going to do terrible things to me. But I didn't believe him. Not anymore. This past week, he had put my physical needs before his own. He obviously said these words to piss my father off, but I no longer cared why he'd said them. If he truly cared about my pride, he would stop flaunting our sex life like that in front of my father. I heard something smash—a vase or a glass—and Wolfe chuckling enigmatically.

"What makes you think Bishop and White will let you get away with it?"

"The fact that they *are* letting me get away with it. I have the upper hand in this game of cards. You will play by my rules or lose your hand. There is no other option."

"I will take Francesca away," my father threatened, his voice lacking that same icy authority that usually laced his speech. I swallowed back a scream. Now he wanted to take me back? I wasn't a toy. I was a human being who had grown oddly attached to my future husband. Besides, no one in The Outfit was going to want to have me now, especially after Wolfe had taken my virginity.

Only, my father didn't know that.

Even if he suspected it—he obviously didn't care.

Wolfe did. Wolfe had the potential to ruin my life now. He got what he wanted. My virginity and reputation. He could end this today. It would be enough humiliation for my father. Sweat clung to the back of my neck at the thought. It took forever for Wolfe to speak again.

"You will not."

"How are you so sure?"

"You love The Outfit more than you love your daughter," he said simply. An arrow of venom pierced my heart. *This is why humans invented lies*, I thought. No other animal in nature lies. The truth is ruthless. It cuts you open, shoving your face into the mud. It forces you to look reality in the eye and deal with it. To feel the real weight of the world that you live in.

"And you?" Papa asked. "How do you feel about my daughter?"

"I feel positive she will be a delight to fuck and decent arm candy, which I can quietly replace when her expiry date arrives," Wolfe said good-naturedly. I wanted to throw up. I could feel the acid bubbling in my stomach, making its way to my throat. I was about to open the door and confront them both. How dare they talk about me like this? But the second my hand grasped the door handle, I felt someone clasping my shoulder from behind. I turned around in the darkened room. It was Ms. Sterling. She shook her head, her eyes almost bulging out of their sockets.

"He is aggravating your father," she enunciated every word, slating her chin down and forcing me into eye contact.

There was a commotion outside the door. My father was shouting, cursing in Italian, as Wolfe laughed, the provocative, throaty tilt of his voice dancing on the walls and ceiling. I heard the screeching of my father's shoes dragging along the marble floor and knew that his bodyguards pulled him out before he embarrassed himself any further. It was loud enough outside for me to confront Ms. Sterling without them hearing us.

"How do you know that?" I asked, wiping away angry, hot tears from my eyes. I was crying again. I could count on one hand the number of days I hadn't cried since Wolfe walked into my life.

"Because I know how he feels about your father, and right now, his hatred toward your father trumps his affection for you. But things are shifting, my dear. All the time."

Ms. Sterling had to drag me back outside, closing the secret door with precise, careful movements so Wolfe wouldn't hear us. She glanced around to make sure the coast was clear, before grabbing my wrist and ushering me to the pavilion. She parked her wrinkly, bluish hands on her hips, sitting me down in front of her. For the second time that day, I felt like a punished kid.

"How can Wolfe even like me when he hates my family with such passion?" I dragged a hand through my hair, wishing I had a cigarette.

Ms. Sterling looked down, momentarily speechless. I made a good point. Her sheer white bob danced here and there as she scratched her head.

"He is halfway in love, Francesca."

"He is in hate with my father and in lust with me."

There was a beat of silence before she spoke again.

"My last name is not Sterling, and I am not who I seem to

be. I actually grew up not too many blocks from you in Little Italy."

I looked up, frowning. Ms. Sterling was Italian? She was strikingly pale. Then again, so was I. So was my father. My mother was darker, but I inherited my father's looks. Another reason I feared Wolfe hated me. I kept quiet, listening to her.

"Something I did when I was young and confused made me start over. I was to pick a last name, any last name, and I picked Sterling after Wolfe's eyes. I'm not proud of some of the things I did to young Wolfe Keaton when he was too defenseless to stand up for himself, but he still forgave me. His heart is not as black as you think it is. It beats fiercely for the ones he loves. It just so happens that…" Ms. Sterling blinked, choking on her words, "all the people he loves are dead."

I began to pace in the pavilion overlooking the garden. The summer flowers burst in purples and pinks. My vegetable garden grew nicely, too. I injected life into this little land, and I hoped—perhaps even foolishly believed—that I could do the same with my future husband. I stopped, kicking a little stone.

"My point is, Francesca, his heart has taken quite a few hits. He is calloused and mean, especially to those who have wronged him, but he is not a monster."

"Do you think he can love again?" I asked quietly.

"Do you think *you* can?" Ms. Sterling retorted with a tired smile. I groaned. Of course, I could. But I was also a forlorn dreamer with a lousy reputation of a person who insisted on seeing the good in almost everyone. My father called it naiveté. I called it hope.

"Yes," I admitted. "My heart has room for him. He just needs to claim it." My honesty rattled me. I didn't know why I opened up to Ms. Sterling like this. Maybe because she did the same to me, offering me a clandestine peek into her own life.

"Then, my dear girl"—she cupped my cheeks with her

cold, veiny hands—"to answer your question, Wolfe is capable of feeling whatever you feel toward him but much, much stronger. More resilient and more powerful. For everything he does, he does thoroughly and brilliantly. Most of all, love."

I'd asked Ms. Sterling to tell Wolfe not to come to my bed that night, and he hadn't. Since it was the night before the wedding, he chalked the fact that I stayed in my room for dinner up to nerves. He did insist that Ms. Sterling bring me my dinner upstairs and made sure that I ate it.

There were waffles drowning in maple syrup and peanut butter straight from the diner down the road. He obviously did not care for a swooning bride tomorrow morning.

I didn't sleep a wink.

At five in the morning, Ms. Sterling walked into my room, bristling and singing with a herd of stylists at her heels. Clara, Mama, and Andrea also came along, whisking me off the bed like Cinderella waking up with the help of tiny furry creatures and canaries. I decided to push aside the fact that my father was a bastard and my fiancé was a heartless man, determined to enjoy the day. As far as I could tell, I only had one wedding to celebrate in this lifetime. Might as well make the best out of it.

I wore a rose-gold Vera Wang wedding dress with floral lace appliqués and a pleated tulle skirt. My hair flowed down in luscious waves all the way to the small of my back, complete with a Swarovski tiara. My bouquet was simple and contained only white roses. When I arrived at the Little Italy church where we were to get married—honoring my family's tradition—the place was already swarming with media vans and dozens of local journalists. My heart accelerated. I didn't even talk to my husband the night before our wedding. Didn't have the chance to confront him about the horrid things he once again said about me to my father. According to him, he was going to toss me away when I got old. The reality of my situation sank in at that moment.

We hadn't gone on one date (the diner was an apology, not a date, and the entire time I shoveled food into my mouth, he worked on his phone). We hadn't texted regularly. We never slept in each other's bed. We never talked for the sake of talking.

No matter how I tried to spin it, my relationship with Wolfe Keaton was doomed.

I walked down the aisle to find my seamlessly dressed, clean-shaven fiancé waiting for me by the priest with a solemn look on his face. Next to him stood Preston Bishop and Bryan Hatch. It did not escape me that Wolfe Keaton had no real friends. Only work friends he could benefit from. *I* didn't have any real friends, either. Clara and Ms. Sterling were triple my age. Andrea, my cousin, was twenty-four, but she was mostly there for me out of pity. She worked in a salon and dated Made Men regularly, though she always said she wouldn't let them touch her, not even a kiss. My mother was twice my age. This left both Wolfe and me in vulnerable positions. We were both lonely and guarded. Wounded and distrusting.

The ceremony went off without a hitch, and once we were pronounced husband and wife, Wolfe offered me a chaste peck on the lips. He was more concerned about the cameras flashing in front of us, and making sure we looked nice and proper, than our first kiss as a married couple. We still hadn't spoken one word to each other the entire day, and it was nearly noon.

We drove in silence from the church to my parents' house. I wasn't sure this would not escalate into a fight had I confronted him about what I'd heard yesterday, and I didn't want to kill the already-charged mood. After the engagement incident, Wolfe had sent out a list of demands which were to be met if my father had wanted us to set foot in his house. Sure enough, the house was filled with people who were pre-approved by my husband. Unsurprisingly, Angelo was not there, but his parents arrived, congratulated me curtly, dropped off their gifts, and shot straight for the door. People were talking, laughing, and congratulating us before the grand dinner when I turned to my husband and spoke the first words since we tied the knot and made it official.

"Have you done something to Angelo?"

There was significance in this exchange. Our first conversation was about another man. Another man I'd lusted after not too long ago. He continued shaking hands, nodding and smiling brightly, the public figure that he was.

"I told you I will not be so tolerant toward Angelo should a third incident occur. Though I profoundly apologize for jumping to conclusions about what *you* did with him, there's no denying that *he* tried to cross the line and coax an engaged woman."

"What did you do?"

He grinned, turning to look at me fully now from the guests fighting for his attention.

"He's currently under investigation for his involvement in his father's business. No need to worry, darling. I'm sure he's found a good lawyer by now. Maybe Kristen hired the same one. I just got her fired from her job for crossing approximately five-hundred red lines and losing all her credibility."

"You snitched on a family from The Outfit?" I balled my fists, barely containing my rage. He blinked at me as though he had no idea who I was or why I was talking to him.

"I gave them what they deserved to make sure they never get near what's mine again."

Me. I was his.

"What will happen to him?" I sucked in a breath.

He shrugged. "They'll probably scare him to death and let him go. As for Kristen, her career is officially over. Not that you should care."

"You are despicable."

"You are *delicious*," he whispered under his breath, dismissing my rage, if not enjoying it a little. Ms. Sterling was somewhere in the crowd, probably taking pictures, and I wished she was here to referee the situation and explain his behavior now. "And officially now my wife. You do know we need to soil our sheets with blood, right?"

I shuddered at his words. I was counting on Wolfe to never agree to participate in this tradition, being a senator and all. But I forgot how much joy he'd had torturing my father—and what was more awful than proof he'd slept with his daughter?

"I think I'm all out of blood after the last time." I smiled against the rim of my wine glass in which I drank orange juice. He didn't have to know that it was spiked with enough vodka to drown a poodle. *Thank you, Clara.*

"It's not in your nature to pledge defeat, my darling wife. I assure you, we can produce blood if we try hard."

"I want a divorce," I groaned, not really taking him seriously, but not completely joking, either.

He chuckled. "I'm afraid you're stuck with me till my last breath."

Or until you replace me with a newer model.

"Then let's both hope it will occur soon."

Two hours into the celebration, Wolfe and I finally parted ways. I went to the bathroom, taking my time with the voluminous tulle as I attempted to pee. I managed it, though it took me a good fifteen minutes to complete the task unscathed. I washed my hands, opened the door and padded outside, back toward the party, when I heard something crashing in the room next door. I stopped in my tracks, turning my head toward one of the guest rooms on the ground floor. Scowling, I made my way to the source of the noise. If someone was drunk and vandalizing my parents' house, I sure was going to give them a piece of my mind. I stopped in front of the open door of the room, my eyes widening in disbelief as the scene in front of me trickled into my conscience.

My mother was lying on the bed, my father standing above

her, roaring at her, flecks of his saliva raining down on her face. Underneath them was a shattered glass of brandy. He stomped on it, thick glass flying under his Oxfords across the carpet.

"What kind of example are you setting for her? Getting her ready for her big day when she *neglected* her father and talked back to me yesterday? In front of that devil! She made me look like a fool, and you? You make me look like an idiot for marrying you."

She spat on his face. "Cheater."

He raised his arm, the back of his hand ready to smack her across the face. I didn't think. I jumped to Mama's defense, yelling "No!" as I came between them. I had intended to push my father away, but I wasn't quick or strong enough. He ended up slapping me across the face, hard. I staggered down, falling next to my mother, elbowing her rib in the process. My cheek burned, and my eyes stung. The pain spread from my neck to my eye, and I felt like my entire face was in flames. I blinked and swayed, righting myself and leaning against the mattress, shaking my head. God, it hurt. How many times had he hit her? Before and after he handed me to Wolfe? Before or after she found out that he was cheating and confronted him?

"Great timing, Francesca." He chuckled bitterly, kicking a shard of glass my way. "Just in time to see all the mess you've created."

My mother burst into tears on the bed, covering her face in her hands with shame.

She didn't want to deal with the messy situation, so she disappeared inside herself, tucked under the layers of her sorrow and her grief. After years of playing the dutiful, perfect wife, she finally crumpled. I had to face Arthur myself. Brave whatever he became as a result of Wolfe's blackmail.

I looked up, my back rod-straight.

"How many times have you hit her?" I felt my nostrils flaring, my mouth thinning with disgust.

"Not enough to teach her to behave properly." He flashed me a sickening smirk, swaying lightly in place. He was drunk. Hammered, more like. I picked up a large shard of glass for protection, taking a step back and raising it between us to use as a weapon. I knew for a fact that one of the things Wolfe had insisted on before we'd agreed to celebrate our marriage here was absolutely no weapons. There was even a metal detector at the front gate. Even if my father hid a gun somewhere around here, it wasn't on him.

"Is that true, Mama?" I spoke to her but kept staring at him. She sniffed a weak denial from the bed.

"Leave it, Vita Mia. He is just upset about the wedding, is all."

"I couldn't care less if he sold her on the black market after the utter disrespect she exhibited to me since he took her in. The only thing I care about is saving face and making sure the two of them don't do anything embarrassing." My father rolled up his sleeves as though he was ready to disarm me.

I knew he spoke the truth.

I pointed the shard at him. "Let Mama go. Let's settle this alone."

"There's nothing to settle, and you are not my peer. I will not discuss my matters with you."

"You will not raise your hand to my mother," I said, my voice barely shaking. I wanted to add a request for him to try not to kill my lawful husband, too, but let's admit it—it wasn't my job to take care of Wolfe. He made it perfectly clear that he couldn't care less about me.

"Or…what? You'll go running to your husband? I've eaten bigger, more powerful men than him for breakfast, so don't think you can talk back to me now. Have you given him the goods, Francesca? Before marriage?" Papa took another menacing step in my direction. I shrank into myself but didn't cower, waving the glass in his face in warning.

"Did you suck Wolfe Keaton's cock just as all the other stupid girls in Chicago who were dumb enough to think they were different did? It wouldn't surprise me in the least. You were always too silly for your own good. Pretty, but silly."

"Papa!" I yelled, swallowing back a lump of tears. How could he say things like that? And how come it still hurt when he said those things even though I knew he did not deserve my love or regard?

"You're drunk." I wasn't sure if I pointed it out to myself or to him. My cheek was still on fire. I wanted to erase the last fifteen minutes from my mind permanently. "And pathetic."

"I am fed up and on the verge of ruining your lives," he countered.

"Mama, come," I urged her.

"I think I'll stay here and take a nap." She curled up higher on the bed into a fetal position, still in her pearls and deep green silk dress.

A nap. Right. My mother was still insistent on not defying her husband even after everything he'd done. I shook my head, turned around, and left the room, squeezing the glass so hard inside my hand, I felt the trickle of blood running over my dress. I stopped in the bathroom again, cleaning myself up and making sure there were no visible stains on my dress, then returned to the party, knowing that the combination of my parents and myself both going MIA at the same time was a recipe for gossip disaster. I stumbled into guests, disoriented and woozy, and ignored the worried glances and spearing gazes. I found Ms. Sterling at the bar, trying appetizers. I threw myself between her arms, ignoring the small platter of food she was holding. It dropped, crab cakes and deviled-egg rolls spilling on the floor.

"Can we go upstairs?" I heaved. "I need help reapplying my makeup."

She opened her mouth when a firm hand grabbed my shoulder and turned me around. I came face to face with my new husband, who stared me down through dark lashes and furrowed brows.

I'd never seen him so angry in my entire life.

"What happened to your face?" he demanded. I immediately brought my hand to my cheek, rubbing it and laughing off the embarrassment. Luckily, his tone was controlled enough that we didn't have an audience.

"Nothing. Just an accident."

"Francesca…" His voice softened, and he took me by the hand—not my elbow, which was an improvement—and pulled me under an alcove between the sunroom and the drawing room. I looked down at my huge dress, determined not to cry. I wondered when I would survive an entire twenty-four hours without bawling.

"Did he hit you?" he asked quietly, bending his knees to get on my level. He stared right into my eyes, looking for that something other than the pattern of my father's hand on my cheek to give him the okay to do what he wanted to do.

"He didn't mean to. He wanted to slap my mother. I stopped it and got in his way."

"Jesus." He shook his head.

I looked sideways, blinking. "Why does it matter, Wolfe? You're not much better than him. True, you don't hit me, but you say mean things about me all the time. I heard you telling him that you're with me just so we can f…have sex, and that you plan to discard me the minute I won't look so good on your arm."

From my periphery, I saw him straightening up to his full height, his jaw clenching in annoyance.

"You weren't supposed to hear that."

"You weren't supposed to say it. You say a lot of hurtful things about me to him."

"I was baiting him."

"Good job. He got so pissed, he tried to hit my mom. This is partly your doing. My father is a madman, and anyone affiliated with him is a potential victim."

"I'd never let him lay a hand on you."

"Never, or until I'm not pretty enough to be Mrs. Keaton?"

"*Never,*" he enunciated. "And I'd advise you cut the bullshit. You will be Mrs. Keaton until the day you die."

"It's not the point!" I shouted, turning around and grabbing a glass of champagne for liquid courage, downing it in one go. He spared me the lecture. I looked around. The crowd was thinning. I'd lost track of time since the incident with my parents.

"What time is it?"

"Time for everyone to leave so we can sort out this mess," Wolfe replied.

"And in practice?" I huffed. He twisted his wrist and pushed the sleeve of his blazer up, checking his Cartier.

"Eleven o'clock. You know they won't leave until they escort us to the bedroom."

I sighed. That was the tradition. He offered me his arm, and I took it. Not because I particularly wanted to spend the night with him, but because I wanted everything to be over.

Five minutes later, Senator Keaton announced that we were retiring to our bedroom. People whistled, clapped, and cupped their mouths with delighted chuckles. He helped me up the stairs to my old bedroom, which my parents had prepared for my wedding night. People followed, throwing candy and singing drunkenly, their voices high pitched and slurred. Wolfe threw his arm over my shoulder protectively, hiding the side of my face that was still red and swelling from my father's offense earlier that evening. I twisted my head and caught a glimpse of my parents following the crowd. They were clapping along, ducking their heads down to listen to things people shouted in their ears. My mom had a wide smile on her face, and my father had that smirk that suggested he still had the world at his feet. It broke something deep inside me to know that it was all an act.

An act I must've bought as a child.

The summer vacations, the beautiful Christmases, their public displays of affection during social functions.

Lies, lies, and more lies.

Wolfe closed the door behind us, locking it twice for good measure. We both looked around the room. There was pristine white linen over the king-size bed that'd been put here, replacing my twin bed especially for the occasion. I wanted to throw up. Not only because we didn't have anything to show them—I was not going to bleed on my wedding night—but also because the idea that everyone knew we were going to have sex tonight was unsettling. I took a seat on the edge of the bed, my hands tucked under my butt, staring down at my dress.

"Do we have to?" I whispered.

"We don't have to do anything." He unscrewed a bottle of water and took a sip, sitting next to me. He handed me the bottle. I put it to my mouth.

"Good. Because I'm still on my period. I started it a day after I took the Plan B." I didn't know why I was telling him this. Only I did. And it was time I asked it.

"Why did you make me take it?"

"Are you ready for children?"

"No, but you didn't know that. And, frankly, many would have guessed the baby was conceived after the wedding. Why did you care so much?"

"I don't want children, Francesca." He sighed, rubbing his face. "And I mean…ever."

"What?" I whispered. I'd been told that big, strong families were what dreams were made of and always wanted one for myself. He stood up and turned me around so my back was to him and began unzipping my dress.

"I didn't have the best childhood. My birth parents were shitty. My brother practically raised me, but he died when I was thirteen. My adoptive parents died when I was at Harvard. Relationships, as I view them, are messy and redundant. I try my best to avoid them unless they are professional, in which case, I do not have much choice. Kids, by definition, are the messiest,

and therefore the lowest on my wish list. However, I do understand your need to reproduce, and I will not stop you if you wish
to have children. You will just have to take into consideration
two things. One—they will not be mine. You can get pregnant
through a sperm donor. And two—I will not play a role in their
lives. If you choose to have kids, I will make sure to provide for
you and them, and house you somewhere nice and safe. But if
you choose to be with me—*really* be with me—we will never
have children, Francesca."

I bit down on my lower lip. I didn't know how many heart-
breaks I could endure in one day, let alone one *month*. I still
hadn't opened the wooden box and took out the last note, and
I knew exactly why. Every note so far indicated that he was the
man for me. But his actions proved he wasn't. The truth was, I
didn't want to know whether he was the love of my life or not,
simply because my heart was undecided, too.

When I said nothing for a while, he walked over to my girly
pink closet, returning with a nightgown and a robe. He gave them
to me, and I realized in my drunken haze that while I was deep
inside my head, pondering our relationship, he had undressed
me completely. I was naked, save for my panties.

"I'll be back in five minutes. Be decent."

I did as I was told. A part of me—a small part of me—didn't
care anymore. Perhaps not having kids was the right thing to
do. We sure didn't love or respect one another enough to reproduce. He wasn't going to come to my OB-GYN appointments.
He wasn't going to care if it was a boy or a girl, or pick out furniture for the nursery, or kiss my swollen belly every night like
I'd dreamed of Angelo doing.

Angelo.

Nostalgia prickled my heart. Angelo would have given me
all those things and more. He came from a huge family and
wanted one of his own. We talked about it when I was seven-
teen with our legs dangling from the dock. I said I wanted four

children, and he answered that the lucky man I'd marry would have fun making them with me. Then we both laughed, and I swatted his shoulder. God, why did the notes point to Wolfe? Angelo was the man for me. Always had been.

I decided, as I wrapped my silky robe around my waist, that I would visit the clinic first thing next week and get on the pill. I would adopt Wolfe's way of life. At least for the time being. Study, and have a career. Go out and work every day, the entire day.

Or maybe we would decide to divorce, and I'd be free. Free to marry Angelo, or anyone else.

I snapped out of my reverie when the door opened, and Wolfe walked in with none other than my father. I lowered myself to the bed, sitting on its edge as I took in the scene. Arthur's lower lip shook, and he swayed from side to side when he walked. Wolfe held his elbow firmly as though he was a punished child.

"Say it," my husband spat out, throwing my father to the floor underneath me. He fell on all fours, scrambling up quickly. I sucked in a breath. I'd never seen my father like this. Vulnerable. It was hard to decipher what was happening.

It was even harder to believe what left his mouth.

"Figlia mia, it was never my intention to hurt your pretty face."

He sounded surprisingly genuine, and what was even more sickening was the way my heart thawed to his voice for the first few seconds. Then I remembered what he did today. How he'd acted the entire month. I stood up and walked over to my window, giving them my back.

"Now let me go or by God…" My father snapped at Wolfe behind me. I heard them shuffling behind my back and smiled grimly to myself. My father stood no chance against my husband. Neither did I.

"Before you go, there's one matter that needs to be settled," Wolfe said as I produced a pack of cigarettes from a drawer, flicking my Zippo and inhaling deeply. I cracked the window open, allowing the black night to swallow the blue smoke.

"Save me the riddles," Dad barked.

"The matter of the bloodied sheets," Wolfe finished.

"Of course." My father snorted behind my back. I didn't have it in me to turn around and watch what was written on his face. "I figured you milked the cow before you bought it."

I heard a sharp slap and twisted on my heel. My father tumbled backward, holding his cheek, his back hitting my closet. My eyes widened, and my mouth went slack.

"Francesca is not ready yet," Wolfe announced in his metallic tenor, his brooding, calm movements a sharp contrast to what he just did. He took one step toward him, erasing all the space between them, and yanked him up by his dress shirt. "And, unlike others, I will not touch a woman against her will even if she has my ring on her finger. Which really leaves us with no choice, does it, Arthur?"

My father narrowed his eyes at him, spitting a lump of blood on Wolfe's loafers. He was a tough man, Arthur Rossi. I'd seen him in some stressful situations but never as out of sorts as he was now. It soothed me to know that I wasn't the only one helpless against my husband, but it also frightened me that he had that kind of hold on people.

Wolfe strode to a black duffel bag near the foot of the bed and unzipped it, producing a small Swiss knife. He turned around. Papa stood tall and proud despite his dire situation and being completely wasted and in desperate need to support himself. He leaned against my old closet, his nostrils flaring.

"You're dead. Both of you."

"Open your hand." Wolfe ignored the threat, flipping the knife open and producing a sharp edge.

"Are you going to cut me?" my father taunted, his lips twisting in revulsion.

"Unless my bride will do me the honor." Wolfe turned his

head around to look at me. I blinked, puffing off my cigarette to buy time. Perhaps it was true that I no longer felt despair and anger toward these two men. They'd ruined my life, each of them, in his own unique way. And they succeeded in such a way that I had felt positively damaged. Enough to sway my hips nonchalantly on my way to them. Whereas my father looked content with Wolfe cutting him open, when he saw me nearing him, his teeth slammed together and his jaw locked.

"She wouldn't dare."

I arched an eyebrow. "The girl you gave away wouldn't. Me? I might."

Wolfe handed me the knife, leaning back on the wall as I stood in front of the man who created me holding a weapon in my hand. Could I do it? I stared at my father's open palm, outreached and staring back at me. The same palm he'd used earlier this evening to slap me in the face. The same palm that was directed at my mother.

But also the same palm that braided my hair during bedtime after Clara washed it. The same hand who patted my own not too long ago at the masquerade, belonging to a man who stared at me as though I was the brightest star in the sky.

I held the Swiss knife with quivering fingers. It nearly slipped from between them. *Dammit.* I couldn't do it. I wanted to, but I couldn't.

I shook my head, handing Wolfe the Swiss knife.

My father clucked his tongue in satisfaction.

"You will always be the Francesca I raised. A spineless little lamb."

Ignoring him and the churning in my stomach, I took a step back.

Wolfe took the knife from my hand, his face placid, grabbed my father's hand, and sliced it open vertically, cutting shallow and wide. Blood gushed out, and I winced, looking away. Papa stood there, staring at the blood pouring from his open palm, oddly tranquil. Wolfe turned around and pulled the linen from my bed, then threw it into my father's hands. His blood soiled the sheets as he clutched them.

"*Bastardo*," my father mouthed. "You were born a bastard, and no matter your shoes and suits—you will die one, too." He stared at my husband with sheer hate in his eyes.

"You were the original bastard." Wolfe grinned. "Before you became a Made Man."

Whoa. My eyes ping-ponged between them, shooting to my father.

Instead of gracing the accusation with an answer, my father had told me that his own parents died in a car crash when he was eighteen, but I'd never seen any pictures of them. He pinned me with his narrow, indigo eyes.

"Vendicare me."

Avenge me.

"Take the sheets and get the hell out. Tomorrow morning, you may present them to your very close family members. No friends. No Made Men. And if this leaks to the media, I will make sure to personally put that knife to your neck…and twist hard," Wolfe said, unbuttoning the first buttons of his dress shirt.

My father turned his back on us and stalked out of the room, slamming the door in his wake.

The thud of the door banging still rang in my ears when I registered my new reality—married to a man who did not love me but enjoyed my body frequently. Betrothed to a man who did not want to have kids and hated my father with passion.

"I'll take the couch," Wolfe said, grabbing a pillow from the bed and throwing it over on a settee by my window. He wasn't going to share a bed with me. Even on our wedding night.

I scurried into bed and turned off the light.

Neither of us said good night.

We both knew it was just another lie.

CHAPTER TWELVE

Francesca

A WEEK TICKED BY AND WOLFE AND I EASED BACK INTO our usual nighttime routine.

There was plenty of kissing, touching galore, licking and moaning and taunting each other with our mouths and fingers alone. But every time he went there—really there—I recoiled and asked him to leave the room. He always did. The pain I endured my first time left me scarred and scared. Not just physically, either. The way he hadn't believed served as a reminder that we didn't share much more than physical attraction. There was no trust. No love.

We were going to have sex, and probably soon—but only on my terms. Only when I felt comfortable.

Life crawled on. The days were busy and cluttered with things to do and places to go, yet nothing of significance happened.

My husband was growing frustrated with my refusal to sleep with him. Ms. Sterling was growing frustrated with how we shared lust but nothing else, and my father had stopped talking to me altogether, though my mother continued to call me every day.

Seven days after the wedding, I walked out of college, heading for Smithy's waiting car. When I reached the black Cadillac, I found Smithy leaning against the passenger door with his cheap suit and black Ray-Bans. He rolled a lollipop in his mouth from side to side, offering me a nod.

"Your turn to drive."

"Huh?"

"Big man's order. He said it's cool since there are no highways on the way home."

I'd only had two lessons with Wolfe since he'd promised to teach me—my husband didn't have much time outside of his work life—but I knew I could do it. Wolfe said I was a natural, and he wasn't loose in the compliments department. Besides, Smithy was right—the way back to the house was urban and busy. It was perfect for practice.

"All right." I bit down a giddy smile. Smithy threw the keys in the air, and I caught them. He pushed off the car and signaled to the coffee shop on the other side of the street.

"Nature's calling."

"Feel free to pick up."

He came back after five minutes, all smiles.

"If your husband ever asks, please don't tell him I even mentioned that I'm capable of peeing. He just might cut off my dick for reminding you that it is there." He surprised me with the banter, and I shook my head, smiling.

"Wolfe's not like that."

"You're kidding, right? Wolfe cares about everything you do or are exposed to, including annoying radio commercials and that street you hate because there's a stray cat living there."

"We need to find it a home," I pointed out, sliding into the driver's seat and dragging it forward to adjust it to my small frame. I fixed the mirrors, then sighed and turned on the keyless ignition. The vehicle purred to life. I wrapped my fingers around the wheel just as Smithy slid into the seat next to me.

"Ready?"

"As I'll ever be."

He gestured with his freckled hand toward the horizon. He had a mane of red-orange hair and matching eyelashes.

"Take us home, Frankie."

It was the first time he'd called me Frankie, and for some reason, it made my heart flutter. My mother called me Vita Mia, my father hadn't called me anything at all recently, and Wolfe referred to me as Nemesis or Francesca. Angelo referred to me as goddess, and I missed it. I missed him.

I hadn't seen or spoken to him in a lifetime. I contemplated texting him to check if he was fine, but I didn't want to enrage my husband. Instead, I asked Mama if he was doing okay during our daily chats. She said that Angelo's father, Mike, was livid and complaining to Papa about my husband's unfair behavior toward his son, which only put more strain on their already problematic relationship since my sudden marriage. Things didn't look too good for the men of The Outfit these days.

I slid out of the parking space and started for Wolfe's mansion. *Our* mansion, I guessed. I rounded the corner, my heart slowing down from the sudden rush of adrenaline of sitting behind the wheel, when Smithy groaned.

"That Volvo behind us is tailgating the fuck out of our ass." His Irish accent came out when he was upset. It unsettled me to be in a car with an Irishman from Chicago even though I knew Smithy had no affiliation with the underworld and had probably been thoroughly checked before he accepted the job as Senator Keaton's driver.

I glanced in the rearview mirror and noticed two people I immediately recognized. Two Made Men who worked for the Bandini family. Meaty, six-foot-five type of beasts who were usually sent to handle business that required less conversation and more muscle. The one behind the wheel flashed me a rancid, rotten-toothed smirk.

Shoot.

"Speed up," Smithy ordered.

"The street is crowded. We could get someone killed." My eyes danced frantically, and I gripped the wheel tighter. Smithy shifted in his seat, glancing backward, no doubt regretting the moment he'd offered to let me drive.

"They're about to bump into us. No, cancel that—crash into us. Hard."

"What do I do?"

"Take a left. Now."

"What?"

"*Now*, Francesca."

Without thinking, I took a sharp left, heading out of the busy neighborhood we'd been driving in and galloping west. The road was clearer, and I could gain more speed, though I was still scared to push the gas pedal all the way down. I understood what Smithy tried to do. He was hoping to lose them. But he didn't know these men chased people for a living.

"Get on the highway," he shouted.

"Smithy!" I yelped at the same time he took his phone out of his pocket and wiped his forehead.

"Focus, Francesca."

"Okay. Okay."

I took another sharp turn, rolling onto the highway and checking my rearview mirror every few seconds to see if I was creating a gap between the two vehicles. My heart was bursting with fear. My entire body pricked with goosebumps. What were they doing? Why were they after me? But the reason was crystal clear to me. I'd shamed their family by getting engaged to Wolfe when I was supposed to get married to Angelo. On top of this, my husband just put Angelo in jail for a night or two over his affiliation with The Outfit (and with Mike Bandini's accounting firm, which, I assumed, was now under investigation by the IRS).

The sound of metal scratching metal deafened my ears, and

the Cadillac lurched forward as they hit us from behind. Heat rose from the doors, and the scent of burnt rubber leaked into my nostrils.

"Foot on the accelerator, sweetheart. Put some distance between us," Smithy screamed, spit flying out of his mouth as he scrolled through his phone with shaky fingers.

"I'm trying." I gripped the wheel harder, hyperventilating. My chest rattled, and my hands shook so bad I felt the car zigzagging between the lanes. The road was relatively clear, but cars were honking and sliding to the shoulder of the road as I tried to lose Bandini's soldiers.

"What is it?" Wolfe's voice boomed inside the car. Smithy connected him to the Bluetooth. I let out a sharp exhale. It was good to hear his voice. Even though he wasn't there, I immediately felt a bit more in control.

"We're being chased," Smithy said.

"By who?"

My relief was immediately replaced with dread. Maybe he would be happy to get rid of me. He'd achieve the same level of revenge over my father without having to endure my presence.

"I don't know," Smithy said.

"Bandini's soldiers," I shouted over the car's noise.

There was a pause as Wolfe digested the information.

"Angelo's father?" he asked.

Another crashing sound exploded in the air, and our vehicle flew three feet forward as they smashed into us again. My head hit the steering wheel. I let out a breathless groan.

"Francesca, where are you?" Wolfe's voice grew tighter. I looked around, trying to find signs.

"I-190," Smithy said, snatching my schoolbag from under his feet and looking for my phone. "I'm going to call the police."

"Don't call the police," Wolfe shot out.

"What?" Smithy and I yelled in unison. Bandini's guys were getting close to us again. The Cadillac coughed and made a terrible sound. The bumper was scratching over the road, dragging over the concrete. It reminded me of the noise vehicles on the videogame *Grand Theft Auto* made before they burst into flames. Angelo and his brothers used to play that game all the time during our summers in Italy.

Angelo always won.

"I'm coming for you. Take the Lawrence Avenue exit." I heard Wolfe picking up his keys. I didn't remember ever seeing him drive. Ever. Either he was driven, or he sat next to me as I drove around the neighborhood.

"I'm not a good driver." I tried to keep my emotions under control, reminding him that he shouldn't be as sure as he was of my abilities to get us out of this in one piece. My eyes looked for the exit he was talking about, my eyeballs running maniacally in their sockets.

"You're an excellent fucking driver," Wolfe said, and I heard him zipping through traffic, breaking approximately two thousand laws based on the honking and yelling in the background. "Besides, if something happens to you, I will blow up the entire Outfit and put every Made Men in Chicago behind bars the rest of their lives, and they know it."

"I think it's because I married you," I muttered, blinking away the tears so I could spot Lawrence Avenue better. Smithy shook his head in my periphery. It wasn't the time or the place to discuss this.

"It's not your fault," Wolfe said. "I threw his son in jail for the night, and his firm is under IRS investigation. He wants to get back at me through you."

"Is it working?" My voice shook. I heard the engine of Wolfe's Jaguar straining against the speed. He didn't answer me. Another bump to our car. I held back a sob.

"They're running us off the road," Smithy yelled, slapping the dashboard. "Can I draw a weapon?"

"Don't you dare," Wolfe barked. "If a hair on Francesca's head accidentally moves…"

Just as he said that, the loudest crash of all rang in my ears at the same time that the air bag shot out, knocking our heads backward against the headrest. White powder floated in the air like confetti. The Cadillac screeched and rolled to the side of the road, and I felt something hissing underneath us. I couldn't move. I couldn't open my mouth. I couldn't even groan. My nose felt like it'd been pushed to the back of my head. I wondered if I broke it. I pondered if now, that my face was all jacked, my husband would finally lose interest in me.

That was the last thought I had before I passed out.

"Francesca? Nem? Talk to me," Wolfe demanded in the background. A dark screen spilled over my eyes as my eyelids gave in. I wanted to answer him but couldn't. I heard him slap his wheel. "Damn it all to fucking hell. I'm on my way."

I dragged my eyes to Smithy with whatever energy I had left. His head began to bob as the airbag shrank back, and he groaned in pain.

"She's fine," Smithy croaked. "Bleeding from her mouth and nose. Her eye doesn't look too good, either."

"Fuck!" Wolfe yelled.

Smithy unbuckled himself and reached across, unbuckling me, too.

"Should I…?" Smithy started at the same time Wolfe barked, "Yes. Draw your weapon. And if they get close to her, by God, kill the bastards before I do. Because I would be much less humane."

I passed out after that. It felt like a thick blanket of nightmares covered me, suffocating and scorching hot. I was there but not really. I didn't know how much time had passed. The first thing I remembered were the blue and red police lights shimmering behind my closed eyelids, and Smithy explaining to the police officers that we didn't see them, and that they took off without getting out of their vehicle. Their license plate was missing, of course, but they were probably just punk kids who wanted to vandalize an expensive new car. Then I felt Wolfe's arms wrapping around me and carrying me, bridal-style, to an ambulance. He tucked me in a gurney and barked when someone else tried to touch me.

"Sir," a male paramedic snapped, "we need to put a brace on her neck and strap her to a backboard to stabilize her in case of spinal injuries."

"Fine. Be gentle," he snapped. When I opened my eyes, I noticed that Wolfe wasn't alone. A chubby man in a fancy suit with a black mane stood next to him.

A paramedic shined a penlight into my eyes, patting my body and looking for any visible injuries. My forehead was bruised, and my entire face felt swollen and sore.

"If she lands in the ER, we'll need to issue a statement," the guy next to Wolfe was texting on his phone, still staring at it. "It's going to look bad."

"I don't care what it looks like," my husband retorted.

"When an airbag goes off, you have to go to the hospital. If you don't, you have to sign an Against Medical Advice form. I would strongly suggest we just take her and get her checked." I heard a soft female paramedic's voice and blinked my eyes open. She was an attractive woman in her late twenties, and I wondered, briefly, if my Lothario husband was going to put his schmuck in her, too. Suddenly, I despised her, to a point I wanted to tell her I was feeling fine, just as long as she left us alone.

"Darling?" Wolfe probed, his fingers skimming my face gently. Too gently for me to even believe they were actually his. "We're going to take you to the hospital."

"No hospital," I groaned into the palm of his hand. "Just… home. Please."

"Francesca…"

"It's fine. The airbags went off but didn't touch us," Smithy interfered.

"She's going to the hospital," Wolfe argued.

"Sir…" the man beside Wolfe tried to argue.

I wondered if he was like that because there were people around us. Because he ought to be nice and gentle to me in public. The thought scared me to death because something deep inside me wanted to cling to this new side of my husband and never let him go.

"Please. I just want my bed." My voice broke midsentence as I tried hard not to cry. I had a split lip I was pretty sure was going to reopen if I did. The gorgeous paramedic tapped his shoulder, and I almost mustered the strength to bite her head off, but then he shook out of her touch casually.

"It's just shallow bruises," I croaked.

"Get a private doctor to my place in an hour," Wolfe snapped his fingers in the suited man's direction, then turned back to me.

"Home," I told him.

"Yes. Home." Wolfe brushed hair from my face.

"Thank God," the suit next to him muttered under his breath, already making the call.

"Shut up, Zion."

"Yes, sir."

I woke up in my bed some hours later after a doctor's visit that stretched for almost two hours. Wolfe was sitting on the couch in front of my bed, working on his laptop. The minute I cracked an eye open, he placed the laptop on the couch, stood up, and made his way to me. I curled under my sheets, too sore to be touched, but he just sat next to me and kept his hands in his lap.

"How is Smithy?" I asked. He blinked at me as though the

question itself was ridiculous. Was I speaking in English? Pretty sure I was. Then a smile hung on his beautiful face, like the moon, and I knew—with a good portion of melancholy—that I was in love with this cruel beast of a husband. That for another one of those glowing, genuine smiles, I would butt horns with my father, slay dragons, and hand him my pride on a silver platter. It was depressing to admit, even to myself, that I was under his thumb.

"That's the first thing you ask after being chased off the roads by mobsters? How the help is doing?" He brushed his thumb across my cheek.

"He is not the help. He is a driver and our friend."

"Oh, Nemesis." He shook his head, his smile widening as he pressed a gentle kiss to my forehead. The gesture was so touching I was on the verge of bursting into a sob. Without asking if I'd like water, he brought the glass on my nightstand to my cracked lips, helping me take a few sips.

"Sterling is worried like crazy. She went to the diner down the road and got you enough waffles to build a Hansel and Gretel candy house."

"I'm not hungry." I shifted in bed. Somehow, everything hurt even more after a few hours. It wasn't actually bruises, but the impact of the adrenaline on my body as it wore off.

"Shocking." My husband rolled his eyes. Senator Wolfe Keaton rolling his eyes exasperatedly was a sight I never thought I'd see.

"But I would love a cigarette." I licked my lips, tasting the salty flavor of my dry blood. He walked over to my desk and took out a thin Vogue cigarette from its pack, sitting by my side and sliding it between my lips. He lit it for me with my Zippo, like in an old black-and-white film. I smiled around my cigarette.

"Are you going to make it a habit?" he asked.

"Make what a habit?"

"Scaring me to death."

"Depends on how much you piss me off. You forgot to tell me you almost got assassinated. By my father, no less."

"He sent a shit aim," he responded, some of the metal returning to his voice. "He was only half serious about killing me. I do, after all, hold his daughter hostage."

To that, I said nothing.

He got up from my bed, his lithe body no longer tensed. "I'm glad you're okay."

He was going to leave, I realized. My eyes glanced at my wristwatch. It was three in the morning. He needed to be up early for his flight to Springfield. But I couldn't bear the idea of him leaving me today after he showed me affection. I didn't want to lose it. Didn't want us to go back to what we were a few hours ago, before my life was on the line. Two strangers who enjoyed dry-humping each other and shared a dinner table every once in a while.

I knew, without a shadow of a doubt, that he wanted to go back to the previous state. And that if he left—we would.

"No," I croaked when he was at the door. He turned around slowly, scanning me. It was all in his expression. The dread of knowing what I was about to ask. To him, I was an asset. Now that he knew that I was okay, he could go about his day. Or rather, night.

"I don't want to stay alone tonight. Could you…only for tonight?" I blinked, hating the desperation in my voice. He peeked at the door again, almost longingly.

"I have an early morning."

"My captor has given me quite the comfy bed," I patted it, blushing under my bruises. He shifted from foot to foot.

"I need to let Sterling know that you're okay."

"Of course." I tried to make my voice sound chirp, blinking back the tears. "Yes. She's probably super worried. Forget what I said. Besides, I'm tired. I think I'll fall asleep before you close the door."

He nodded, leaving the door ajar.

I was too tired to mourn my unfulfilled request. I fell asleep a minute after he left my room with the half-smoked cigarette swimming inside my water glass, a habit that made Wolfe cuss under his breath as he collected the glasses after me.

When I woke up the next day, the clock hit seven. I tried to stir myself awake, but felt massive weight pressing against my body. God. How badly was I hurt? I could barely move an inch. When I tried to wiggle my right arm, reaching to the alarm clock to slam the button and stop its chirp, I realized that it wasn't soreness that stopped me from moving.

My husband was sleeping behind me, his stomach pressed against my back. Still in his suit, his breaths were deep and silent. I could feel his penis digging into my butt through our clothes. He had morning wood. I felt myself blushing, biting down a smile.

He returned to my room. He spent the night in my bed. I asked for something—something he had told me explicitly would never happen—and he gave it to me.

I put my hand over his arm, which circled my midriff, his nose and mouth pushed alongside my shoulder blade. I prayed for one thing that morning—that this wasn't a sweet lie, but a forbidden truth.

Lies, I couldn't deal with.

But finding a truth and digging that vein until it gushed out? I was up for that challenge.

CHAPTER THIRTEEN

Wolfe

LONG BEFORE I REALIZED THAT FRANCESCA ROSSI WAS IN
existence, I'd studied her father's workday closely. Seeking
revenge was a full-time job, and the more you knew, the more
thoroughly you could ruin. I looked for weakness in his business,
and loopholes in his contracts, when actually, his daughter was
his most-valued possession. Both more fatal and more personal
than any strip club I could shut down. The problem occurred
when I realized that Arthur no longer treasured his daughter.
As far as he could tell, she was no longer his ally. And to make
matters worse, she married a man who was determined to kill
his business, not inherit it.

The game had changed.

Arthur allowed Mike Bandini to target his daughter.

Because his daughter was also my wife.

And my wife, I foolishly proved to him, was important to me.

My Jaguar stopped in front of Mama's Pizza restaurant in
Little Italy. It was a quaint place that smelled of freshly baked
sourdough and tomato soup and my goddamn *sorrow*. The business lost mountains of money every month but made for a great
money-laundering venue. It was where The Outfit had their daily

meetings. Whatever dark feelings I harbored toward Mama's Pizza weren't enough to keep me from making my point to those idiots.

Smithy got out of the vehicle and opened the back door for me. I waltzed into the restaurant, ignoring the plump, disoriented lady behind the counter, and went through the door behind her. Stepping into the dim room, I found ten men sitting around a round table. It was the old checked white and red Italian BS, complete with a yellow, half-burned, unlit candle. Behind it sat my father-in-law.

Round tables broke hierarchy.

Last time I'd been to Mama's Pizza—the table was square, and Arthur Rossi was at the head of it.

And behind him hung a glassed window covering shotguns. Picture-effin-esque.

I sauntered toward him, the annoying woman behind me yelling and apologizing in one breath, and flipped the table with all its contents—beer, wine, water, orange juice, and breadsticks—over the laps of the men in front of it. They sat there, mouths slacked, watching me through a curtain of shock and anger. I was standing in front of Rossi, his dress pants soiled with the wine he'd been drinking. Next to him sat Mike Bandini, Angelo's father, who slowly began to rise from his chair, no doubt about to either run or point a gun at me. I grasped his shoulder, digging my fingers in until I met his bones through his skin, then pushed him back into his chair, and kicked it across the room. The chair's wooden legs skated a foot back from the force. I glimpsed at Arthur, pleased to see that his palm was still wrapped up from the night he stained the white sheets with his own blood.

"How's your face today, Bandini?" I smiled good-naturedly at Angelo's father. He sucked his teeth in, smirking at me.

"In one piece." His eyes looked left and right, trying to assess everyone else's reaction to my surprise visit. They were pale as ghosts and crapping their pants. I wasn't the police. Them—they could deal with. I was the man who had the power to get

White fired, and worse—plant Bishop and Rossi in such deep shit they'd never climb out of it. But getting rid of me didn't work, either. And now, it was out of the question. I had my driver and two security men parked up front.

"That's good to hear because my wife's face isn't. In fact, her nose is still bleeding." I threw a fist to his nose without warning, making all the men around us stand in unison, only to have Arthur motion for them to sit down with his hand, his lips thinning into a fine line. Mike's head reared back, his chair flying backward and falling to the ground, him inside it. I took two steps and swallowed the distance between us.

"Her ribs are sore, too," I added, kicking Mike in the ribs. Everyone around us sucked their teeth in, furious with the vulnerability of their situation. I took a handkerchief out of my breast pocket and wiped my hands, sighing theatrically. "Last but not least, her lips are sore. I'm going to let you choose—fist or foot?" I glanced down at him, cocking my head. Waking up in my wife's bed was an unpleasant surprise. But feeling her ass digging into my erection with little finesse as she tried to please me was definitely something I could get used to after what seemed like a lifetime without actual sex. I knew she was too sore, but still couldn't resist the urge to dry-fuck her under the sheets. So I did just that; I unbuckled my dress pants and pressed my shaft against her ass cheeks. After I came on her nightgown, I left her room, ordering Ms. Sterling to make sure that she drank, ate, and didn't do any heavy lifting. Right before I picked up the phone and had Zion hire a bodyguard for her.

"Fist." Mike grinned, his teeth covered in blood. A mobster, after all.

"Foot it is, then. I don't take any orders from you." I smashed my Oxford-clad foot right into his face and heard a crack as his nose smashed to pieces. Stepping back, I strolled around the room. I, too, had better things to do with my day than spend it with men who ruined my hard work for a living.

"I'm feeling charitable today. Maybe it's the bliss of being a newlywed. I've always been a hopeless romantic." I scanned Arthur's twisted face and the soldiers around him, who sat with the kind of electric defiance that rolled off their red-blooded bodies. Fists balled, chins high, feet tapping over the floor. They were dying to beat the hell out of me but knew I was depressingly untouchable.

I wasn't always like this, though. And Arthur Rossi was the sole reason for my weaknesses.

"So I'm going to spare the bastards' lives who did this to Francesca. But I thought a gentle reminder—and trust me, this is my idea of gentle—was more than necessary. I have the power and the means to shut you down completely and kill every part of your business. I could make sure all your recycling and sanitation projects are terminated. I have the power to purchase all the competing restaurants and bars to yours, throw money at them, and watch as they put yours out of business. I could make sure your families don't have a breadcrumb to eat for dinner, and that your medical bills are unpaid. I could send the FBI to your underground gambling joints and whorehouses. I could reopen cases that have been dormant for years and hire enough investigators to populate your streets"—I took a deep breath—"and I could bleed you dry of every dime you own. But I'm not doing that. Not yet, at least, so don't give me a reason."

Arthur frowned. Up until now, he stayed silent. "Are you implying that I harmed my daughter, you slimy little shit?"

"Bandini's muscle did." I pointed at his friend, who was standing up from the floor and wiping his face of blood. Arthur turned to Bandini sharply. Oh, brother. He didn't even know. His empire was falling apart. His power diminishing by the minute. It wasn't necessarily a good thing for me. A weak king is a mad one.

"Is that true?" Arthur spat out.

"He put my son in jail the day of their wedding." Mike spat

blood into a trash can. I walked over to Mike, balling his collar in my fist and tugging it so he looked up at me.

"Get anywhere near my wife again, and I shall consider it an act of war. A war I am more than equipped to finish, and in record time," I warned. "Understood?"

He averted his gaze from me, unwilling to see the determination in my eyes. "Fine, *stronzo*, fine!"

"Same goes for your son. I catch him near her, and he'll be sorry your wife was drunk enough to permit his conception."

"Angelo can do whatever he wants," he gobbed, waving his fist in the air. "Leave him out of this."

"We'll see about that. Rossi," I said, turning from Mike. Arthur was already standing up, refusing to go down without a fight. I'd dreamed of this moment for many years. Holding such power over his head. And now, when I finally had it, I felt nothing but disdain and wariness. Coming here was an uncalculated risk. These men had no moral compass, and if Francesca ended up six feet under, I'd never be able to forgive myself. I was the one who got her into this mess in the first place.

"Put your soldiers and associates on a shorter leash," I ordered, pointing at his face.

"You mean, like your wife does to you?" He patted his pocket and produced a cigar, sticking it between his lips. "She seems to have taken over your better judgment. You'd have never showed up here months ago, and you wanted my head even back then," Arthur said.

"I have your head."

"You're playing with your food, Senator Keaton, instead of going in for the kill. You're enamored by a teenager, and that wasn't in your plan."

"Give me your word," I repeated, feeling a tick of annoyance flickering behind my eyelid.

Arthur waved his hand. "I will not hurt my own daughter

and will make sure no one in this room does either. She is, after all, my flesh and blood."

"Don't fucking remind me."

On the way home, I put Bishop and White on a conference call. I knew two things: they weren't going to turn the conference call down, aware that I had too much ammo on them, and that they didn't want me to leak anything over the phone—for exactly the same reason. The problem was that I was sick and tired of corrupt assholes getting their way. Especially when innocent people were being hurt in the process.

Especially when one of those people was the woman who had my ring on her finger.

"I heard that you paid quite a visit to our friend." Bishop was golfing by the sounds of carts and sunshine laughter on the other line. White remained silent.

"How are you doing, Preston?" I asked, getting comfortable in the back seat as Smithy zigzagged through the busy Chicago traffic. I did not acknowledge Preston's remark about my visit to Arthur because, as far as I was concerned, I'd never been there. I took one of Francesca's Zippos out of my pocket, flicking it on and off absentmindedly. Something—hell if I know why—possessed me to take it with me when I left her room this morning.

"I'm fine. Is there a particular reason why you're asking?" Preston grated into the phone with audible annoyance. White took a labored breath, waiting for my answer. It sucked when the only person holding the cards in the conversation was a green politician with a vindictive streak.

"Just wanted to check on how you're gearing up for the elections next year." I stared through the window. It was nicer to sit in the car with Nemesis around. Not because we shared pleasant conversation—that was rarely the case—but because she always smiled at Chicago like it was beautiful and fascinating and busy especially for her. She appreciated the small things in life.

"I'm fairly sure I am doing way beyond my wildest expectations. At least according to the polls." Bishop clucked his tongue, and I heard him mounting his golf clubs to his cart. No wonder Rossi did business with him. The hedonist asshole didn't have the term work in his dictionary.

"Nothing a few bad press releases can't ruin, I assume," I quipped, getting to my point. It was hardly a social call, after all.

"What are you insinuating?" White barked, and I could practically see the spit flying out of his mouth. God, he was an awful-looking creature. I hated him a little extra for being a corrupted cop. A dishonest politician, I could handle. All politicians were corrupt, but some of them were still good. Being a corrupted cop made you a piece of shit. End of story. White represented the Chicago Police Department, something my late brother was a part of. I'd hate to think how Romeo would feel had he known White was the commander and chief of operations nowadays.

"I'm insinuating that you're still not doing your job to my satisfaction. My wife was in a car chase yesterday. Bandini's people."

"How is she doing?" Bishop asked, not even a little interested.

"Save me the pleasantries. Life's too short to pretend we give a damn about each other."

"A: do not threaten my campaign under any circumstances, and B: give me direct instructions and I'll pass them through to the source you need help with," Bishop offered.

"I don't think you get to talk to me about circumstances," I snapped. The Jaguar rolled into the gates of my mansion. Today, I'd done something I hadn't done in my entire career, not since I graduated from college. I took a day off.

I wanted to make sure that Francesca was feeling well and didn't need to pay a visit to the hospital. Smithy opened the door for me. I stepped out.

"Right now, to soothe my growing anger with your *client*,"

I highlighted, "I'd kindly demand that you tell him to keep his associates and himself far away from my wife. It's in everyone's benefit, yours included."

"Fine," White bit out.

Bishop stayed silent.

"You, too, Tiger Woods."

"I heard you," he clipped. "Are you going to hang this over our heads for a while now, Keaton? Because you're starting to make enemies everywhere. First with you-know-who and his crew and now with us. Do you have any friends left at all?" He wondered.

"I don't need friends," I said. "I have something much more powerful. The truth."

I found my wife in her vegetable garden, sucking on a thin cigarette and tending to her plants. She wore a long blue skirt and a white dress shirt. There was something strong and determined about her choice to follow her parents' rules, even after they'd disowned her completely.

When I first met her, I thought she was a puppet. A shiny, pretty toy designed by Arthur Rossi that I could break. The more I got to know her, the more I realized how wrong I was. She was humble, modest, resilient, innocent, and well-cultured. The night of the masquerade, I ridiculed her for excelling in what her parents wanted her to become, completely disregarding the fact that being proper and well-behaved was much more daunting than being another defiant, rebellious, twenty-first century kid who wore short skirts and fucked everything that moved.

I mocked her for being rotten before finding out that she was a compassionate, good-willed woman.

Francesca wiped the sweat and soil from her forehead, turning around and walking to the shed to retrieve a bag of fertilizer. She stopped and rubbed her forehead, wincing. The bruise there was shallow but nasty and green. I stepped toward the shed, reaching behind her back and taking the heavy bag from her.

"Why are you so stubborn?" I accused as I carried it toward her vegetable garden. She followed me in her little boots and little everything, really. She was so pocket-sized, I often rehashed the night I was inside her, relishing how sweet and tight she'd felt. Not because of her virginity, but simply because she was her tiny self.

"Why are you always so…you?" She followed me, a bounce to her step. I stopped in front of the vegetables, realizing for the very first time how spectacular she'd made this garden. She grew actual things. Tomatoes and radishes and peppermint and basil. Flowers spilled from fresh pots, and there were rows upon rows of flowerbeds framing her little garden. It wasn't my style. Too busy and colorful, a mishmash of too many species, sights, and scents. But it was the one thing about this place that truly made her happy other than Ms. Sterling.

"Who else would I be?" I answered, setting the bag next to her plants, careful not to squash them. I stood up straight and wiped my hands.

"Someone else," she teased.

"Like who? Angelo?" Only an idiot would utter his name aloud at a time like this. But I made it perfectly clear that I could be a real jackass where my wife was concerned.

"I actually quite like you being you," she said, hitching one shoulder up. I rubbed the back of my neck, feeling abnormally raw.

"You need to slow down."

"I am. I took it easy today. Did my homework and only came out here a half hour ago. I'm getting ready to harvest the first round of veggies and send them off to the school down the road. It's all organic." She turned to face me for the first time, and my heart squeezed at the sight of her black eye and cut lip. I chucked her under the chin.

"That's not slowing down. That's speeding up. Don't make me do something crazy."

"Like what?"

"Like abduct you."

She chuckled, looking down at her legs, her cheeks flushing. "You treat me like a kid."

"Please. If I did to kids what I want to do to you, I'd spend the rest of my life in a secluded cellar, and for damn good reason."

She crouched down, fingering the flowerbeds for dead leaves she collected, then threw away. I stuffed my fists into the pockets of my dress pants, watching her back. Nemesis had Dimples of Venus on her lower back, and the need to sink my thumbs into them as I ate her out from behind smashed into me. I cleared my throat.

"Pack a bag and some snacks. We're leaving."

"Huh?" She still gardened, not even bothering to look up.

"We're going to my cabin on Lake Michigan tomorrow for the weekend. Getting some rest is clearly not on your agenda, so I'm making it."

She twisted her head to watch me, squinting at the sun and using one of her hands as a visor from it. "It's no trouble. I'm not hurt, Wolfe."

"You look like you've been beaten up, and people are especially good at speculating. I need to get you out of town." It was only partly true. Having my new wife parade her banged-up face in public was less than ideal, sure. But I didn't want any company other than her, either. Sterling was always sniffing around us, and Smithy was a general pain in the ass. In addition, Bishop wasn't wrong. I did not, in fact, have any friends. Distancing myself from my enemies for a couple days wasn't the worst idea I'd had. I needed a breather, and, quite frankly, Nem was the only person I could somehow tolerate right now.

"I have a lot of homework," she said.

"Take it with you."

"I'd hate to leave Ms. Sterling alone."

"She'll have security stay with her. We're leaving alone."

"That's against protocol."

"Fuck protocol."

There was silence. She was chewing her lip, which meant she was trying to come up with another obstacle.

"You can drive a portion of the way to the cabin," I offered, sweetening her deal. She perked just as I knew she would. Her experience with Bandini's assholes did not deter her from learning. It was part of the reason why I couldn't hate her. Not even if I tried. She was driven, and the best part was that she didn't even know it about herself.

"Really?" Her eyes shimmered with excitement. Clear blue like the summer sky. "Even after what happened?"

"Especially after what happened. You aced it. How's your forehead?"

"It looks worse than it feels."

It looks beautiful.

Of course, uttering those words wasn't an option. I turned around toward the balcony, retreating from the garden and my wife. When I reached the glass doors, I stopped, stealing one last glance at her again. She was crouching back down, resuming her work.

"You won't have to worry about them anymore," I said.

"Them?" She blinked. The list was growing by the second. First, her father, then the Bandinis.

"Every asshole who ever had the faintest idea to hurt you."

I went into my office and locked myself there for the rest of the night, not trusting myself to go to her room for my nightly feast on her without sleeping next to her. As it was, I had a control issue.

I lacked it.

She had all of it.

CHAPTER FOURTEEN

Francesca

I T TOOK ME AN ENTIRE HOUR TO UNWIND BEHIND THE WHEEL. Not only did I worry about ruining Wolfe's precious Jaguar—the flashbacks from Bandini's guys slamming into the Cadillac from behind as they chased me—but I also didn't feel overly comfortable around my husband. After spending the night with me, he hadn't come to my room last night. We were going to his lake house. Was he planning on sleeping in different rooms there, too? Frankly, I wouldn't put it past him. I had no one to advise me about our situation. *Cosmo* and *Marie Claire*, my only sources of relationship advice, didn't exactly cover the subject of an arranged marriage with cruel, severely emotionally stunted senators in the twenty-first century.

Ms. Sterling was biased. She'd tell me anything I wanted to hear to ensure that I was happy with my husband. My mother was too busy trying to save her own marriage, and Clara was the closest thing to a grandmother I'd ever had, so, yeah, gross.

I could call Andrea, but I feared becoming a charity case at this point.

Always disoriented. Forever clueless.

That left me to stew in my thoughts all the way to the cabin on Lake Michigan. When Wolfe called it a cabin, I thought he meant somewhere quaint and modest. In practice, it was a luxurious estate, crafted from rock and glass, boasting an outdoor hot tub, a direct view of the lake, elevated, wooden balconies, and an architecturally mesmerizing rustic charm. It was tucked among cherry trees and lush, green hills, far enough from civilization without having that eerie air. My heart swelled at the prospects of spending time with my husband so far away from everyone. But mixed with the excitement was a dash of fear.

"I feel another string of Nemesis questions coming my way." Wolfe was sitting cross-legged on the passenger seat, flipping my Zippo between his strong fingers. I munched on my lower lip, tapping my thumbs against the wheel.

"Have you ever been in love?"

"What kind of question is that?"

"One I'd like an answer to."

He paused. "No. I've never been in love. Have you?"

I thought about Angelo. Then I thought about all the things I'd gone through because of my love for Angelo. I didn't know how I felt about him anymore, but I knew that lying to my husband out of fear was going to put me squarely in the same place my mother was struggling with right now.

"Yes."

"Hurts like hell, doesn't it?" He smiled to the view outside his window.

"Yes," I agreed.

"That's why I refrain from the feeling," he said.

"But it also felt good when it was requited."

He turned around to face me. "No love is fully requited. No love is equal. No love is fair. There is always one side that loves more. And you better not be that side—because it suffers."

Silence stretched until we parked the car outside of the so-called cabin.

"But you"—he turned to me, smirking—"you're smarter than to yield to your love."

I don't love Angelo anymore, you fool, I wanted to scream. *I love you.*

"Which is why I respect you," he added.

"You respect me?"

He got out, rounded the car, and opened my door for me. "If you're into milking things, I'd love for it to be my cock and not simply for compliments. You know I respect you, Nem."

The fridge in the cabin had been stocked with everything good and tasty. Freshly baked French buns sat on the counter. I wolfed down two, with local strawberry jam and chunky peanut butter. Wolfe hopped into the shower, and I did the same after him. Then he stuffed a six-pack of beer and a handful of individually wrapped brownies into my backpack and ordered me to join him for a walk. My forehead was still sore, my lip kept on opening every time I smiled, and I found out that my ribs must've bruised when I was put on the gurney, but I complied nonetheless.

I began to second-guess our mutual decision not to take a honeymoon together when he threw my girly bag over his shoulder and led me to a paved, concrete path surrounded by wild grass that whooshed in the cool breeze of the evening. The wind and the lake provided a sound more pleasurable than any symphony, and the view was a spectacular shade of purple and pink sunset diving into rolling hills. We walked for twenty minutes before I noticed another wooden cabin up the hill from where we were.

"What's there?" I pointed at the cabin.

He moved a hand over his thick, dark hair. "Do I look like a tour guide?"

"You look like a sour man, Senator," I taunted. He laughed.

"We could check."

"Could we? I don't want to trespass."

"Such a law-abiding citizen. If only your father would share the virtue."

"Hey." I frowned. He flicked me under the chin lightly. The gesture was growing on me. Especially paired with the fact that I no longer believed that Wolfe didn't have feelings for me. Not after the way he held me the day of the car chase.

"Sterling keeps telling me to stop doing that. Bunching you and your father together, I mean. It's hard."

"Do you do it often?" I winced as he took my hand and tugged me up the hill.

"Not lately."

"And why is that?" I asked.

"Because you're polar opposites."

As we went uphill, my breathing became more ragged. I was determined to make conversation to avert my thoughts from the fact I was definitely not in shape. I neglected my horse-riding sessions in favor of school. Plus, I did have a question burning on the tip of my tongue.

"Are you willing to tell me why you hate my father so much now?"

"No. You can feel free to stop asking right now because the day I'll be ready to share this with you is never."

"You're so unfair." I allowed myself a sulk.

"I never claimed to be. At any rate, the answer isn't something you'd like to know."

"But maybe I do. Maybe it'd give me peace with the fact that he disowned me."

He stopped in front of what wasn't a cabin but a red and white barn. "The fact that he gave up his precious gem just because I touched it is enough reason as to why he doesn't deserve you."

"And you do?" I asked.

"But, my darling, that's the difference between me and your father. I never pretended to deserve you. I simply took you."

I threw an arm over the barn's wooden gate, shaking my head. "That's definitely trespassing, Wolfe. I'm not going in."

He jumped over the fence, making his way inside the barn without looking back. There was fresh hay scattered by the doors, and by the scent of moist soil and what my riding instructor liked to call road apples (horse poop) floating in the air, I knew livestock were inside.

I heard Wolfe whistling from the depth of the open barn, clucking his tongue.

"She's a beauty."

"It's been two seconds since you left my side, and you're already flirting," I called out. The smile on my face hurt my cheeks. The sound of his throaty, gruff laughter filled the air. I pressed my thighs together, something empty inside me aching to finally let him in. I could have sex with him tonight. God, I *wanted* to have sex with him tonight. For the first time since our engagement party, I felt fully prepared for my husband physically. More than prepared. *Needy*. And even though Wolfe was next to impossible to read, I did know this about him—he wanted me, too.

"C'mere," he called, sounding surprisingly—perhaps even shockingly—like a young Italian boy from the variety I grew up with. It was the way the word rolled off his tongue that gave me pause, but I shook my head, laughing to myself. Wolfe Keaton was as well-bred as they came. His late father was a hotelier and his late mother was a Supreme Court judge.

"What if we get caught?" My grin threatened to slice my face in half. I heard more whistling of admiration from the inside. He whistled like a street kid but waltzed like an aristocrat. I could never pin him down.

"We're good for bail," he drawled. "Get your cute butt over here, Nem."

I looked left and right, ducked my head under the fence

and tiptoed my way inside the barn. When I got in, he grabbed my hand and pulled me close. Wolfe enveloped me from behind in a hug, jerking his chin to one of the four stalls, the only one that was occupied. A gorgeous Arabian horse, completely black, save for her stark white mane and tail, stared back at me. Wolfe wasn't exaggerating. She was breathtaking. And she blinked at me with her beautiful, tiny, and dense eyelashes. I pressed my palm to my heart, feeling it pitter-pattering in my chest. I'd never seen a horse so beautiful. Her eyes were calm and kind, and she bowed her head down, accepting the sheer admiration that must've shone in my eyes.

"Hey, girl." I made my way to her, watching my pace, allowing her time to get used to me or change her mind. I put my hand to her muzzle.

"What are you doing here all alone?" I whispered.

"She looks in good health to me," Wolfe said behind me, leaning against the opposite wall of the barn. I could feel him staring at me even with my back to him.

I nodded.

"That may be, but we need to figure out who this barn belongs to."

"Do you like her?" he asked.

"Like her? I love her. She's sweet and tender. Not to mention gorgeous." I moved my hand to her forehead, dragging it to her ears and poll. She let me as if she'd known me her whole lifetime.

"Reminds me of someone."

"Please don't tell me you're comparing me to livestock now." I laughed, surprised to find out that I had mist in my eyes. I imagined she belonged to a young girl. She looked young herself. Maybe they'd grow up together.

"What should I compare you to, then?" He pushed off the wall, striding to me, my back still to him. I heard the hay crunching under his feet. I took a deep breath, closing my eyes and savoring his touch as his arms wrapped around my midriff from behind.

"People," I whispered.

"I can't compare you to people. There aren't any people like you," he said simply, his mouth on my neck now. Heat gathered in my belly, and I felt myself shuddering with pleasure that broke on my skull and rushed all the way down to my toes.

"It's yours," he snarled in my ear, his teeth grazing my lobe.

"What?"

"The horse. It's yours. This barn is mine. All this land, three miles each way from the cabin, belongs to us. The previous owner had a barn. Took his horses with him when he sold it to my parents." His *dead* parents. There was so much I didn't know about him yet. So much he kept from me. "Before I married you, I didn't want to give you a wedding gift. But after I married you, I realized you deserve much more than diamonds."

I turned around, blinking at him. I knew I should thank him. Hug him. Kiss him. Love him even harder for his effort, which, I knew by now, did not come naturally to him. The idea of loving him so openly was startling. He held all the knowledge about every piece of my life, yet I knew nothing about him. Perhaps you don't need to know a person in order to love them. You only need to know their heart, and Wolfe's heart was far bigger than I'd previously imagined.

He stared at me, waiting for a response. When I opened my mouth, the most unexpected words came out.

"We can't keep her here. She'll be lonely."

For a moment, he didn't say anything, before closing his eyes and plastering his forehead to mine, his lips locking on my own. He sighed, warm breath skating between my lips.

"How are you so compassionate?" He mumbled into my mouth.

I clutched the collar of his jacket and drew him to me, kissing the corner of his lips.

"We'll take her somewhere on the outskirts of Chicago where you can visit her weekly. Somewhere with lots of horses. And hay. And ranchers who'll take care of her. And stay firmly away from you. Ugly ranchers," he added. "With no teeth."

I laughed. "Thank you."

"What do you want to call her?" he asked.

"Artemis," I answered, somehow knowing what her name was before I even really thought about it.

"The goddess of wildlife. Quite fitting." He kissed my nose extra carefully, then my forehead, then my lips.

We drank our beers, and I ate brownies next to Artemis, sitting on the hay. I'd eaten in the last few days more than I had in the month before. My appetite was returning, and that was a good sign.

"I've wanted to become a lawyer since I was thirteen years old," he said, and I stopped breathing altogether. He was confiding in me. Opening up. This was huge. This was *everything*. "The world is an unfair place. It does not reward you for being good, or decent, or moral. But for being talented, driven, and cunning. Those things are not necessarily positive. And none of them—not even talent—is a virtue. I wanted to protect those who needed protection, but the more I worked on cases, the more I realized that the system was corrupted. Becoming a lawyer in hopes to bring justice is like cleaning a ketchup stain on a bloodied shirt of a man who just got stabbed fifty times. So I went higher."

"Why are you so obsessed with justice?"

"Because your father robbed me out of mine. I understand that your childhood has been sheltered. I can even respect your father for sending you to boarding school and distancing you from the mess he's created in Chicago. But this mess? I grew up in it. I had to survive in it. It left me scarred and wronged."

"What are you going to do with my father?"

"I'm going to ruin him."

I swallowed. "And with me? What are you going to do with me?"

"Save you."

After a while, I became drowsy from the beer and sugar. I propped my head against his chest and closed my eyes. He took out his phone and let me nap atop of him, very unlike my husband. Since he had no reception, I didn't know what he was going to do with his phone, but part of me wanted to test the limit of his patience. To see when he was going to shake me gently and tell me it was time to get going.

I woke up an hour later in a tiny pool of my drool on his shirt. He was still messing with his phone. I glanced at his screen, trying not to move. He was reading an article offline. Probably a document he'd downloaded in advance. I stirred lightly to let him know that I was awake.

"We should head back."

I took one glance at Artemis, who was sleeping peacefully in her stall, and yawned.

"We should," I agreed. "But I love it too much here." Then, without thinking, I tilted my head up and pressed a kiss to his lips. He dropped his phone, taking me in his arms and positioning me with careful precision on his lap to straddle him. I felt immediately more powerful and awake than I had been in weeks, linking my arms around his neck and deepening our kiss. I began to grind against his erection, without even thinking about what I was doing. I wasn't on the pill yet—never got the chance to book that appointment—and I knew, now more than ever, that our first time was an angry fluke. Wolfe didn't want children, and I certainly didn't want to have them without his wishes. Especially not at nineteen. I'd just started school.

"I'm…" I said between kisses, "I…we need a condom. I'm not protected."

"I'll pull out." He kissed his way down my cleavage, opening the buttons of my navy blue polka dot dress. I pulled away, cupping his face, still in awe that I could do so.

"Even *I* know that's not a valid form of contraception."

He grinned, his teeth a row of straight pearly whites. He was excruciatingly beautiful. I didn't know how I was going to survive it if he took another Emily to his bed in this lifetime. We were no longer two strangers sharing a roof. We were entwined and entangled, connected with invisible strings, each of us trying to pull away, only to create more knots that made us closer. And he was so sophisticated and quick-witted, I didn't know how I could keep him, even if I wanted to. Dearly.

"Francesca, you're not going to get pregnant from one time."

"That's a myth, and one we can't believe right now," I persisted.

It's not that I didn't want to become a mother. It's that I didn't want to become a mother to an unwanted baby. I still held on to some foolish hope he'd change his mind with time when he realized that we could be happy together. Plus, there was something so horribly degrading about taking that Plan B pill that he had left for me. I felt like he had rejected me and what my body had to offer.

"When's your period?" he asked. I blinked.

"On the first week of the month."

"Then you're fine. You shouldn't even be ovulating right now."

"How do you know this?" I laughed, raking my fingers over his chest, frantic for some reason.

"My brother's wife…" He stopped, a mask of icy difference sliding over his face. He was not supposed to say that. I was not supposed to know that he had a brother, and that the brother had a wife. I blinked at him, desperate for him to continue. He swallowed, put me down carefully, then stood up, offering me his hand.

"You're right. Let's go, Nem."

I took it, knowing we had quite the problem.

He didn't want to let me in.

And I could no longer purge him out.

In the cabin, Wolfe threw logs into the fireplace while I speared marshmallows onto sticks. I showed him how to make a s'mores train, which is basically a huge, ongoing sandwich of s'mores still on the stick. I taught all my friends in Switzerland how to do it, and some of the parents were livid, sending angry letters to the school's administrator. They said their daughters gained a lot of weight since I showed them the trick, and that they had to have their fireplaces cleaned on a weekly basis.

"A rebel, then." He grinned at me. "Could've fooled me with your hint of British boarding school accent and impeccable manners."

"Oh, I was never a rebel," I said seriously, pushing back the nagging worry that he chose me because I made a well-bred potential first lady. "I mostly stayed out of trouble, though. It was just this incident, and when I accidentally set a teacher's toupee on fire." I laughed in Wolfe's arms, feeling more relaxed and happy than I ever had before. He drew me close to him and kissed me again, a serious kiss, from the variety that told me that the conversational portion of the night was officially over.

He flattened me on my back in front of the fireplace as the fire danced in orange and yellow, giving the room a cozy and romantic air even though it was extravagantly luxurious. The rustic furniture, top-notch appliances, and rich leather, deep brown sofas with the huge, wool throws were a perfect setting to what I so badly wanted to happen. We were on the wooden floor, lying over a knitted rug with Wolfe on top of me. He growled into my mouth and slid his hand into the hem of my panties under my dress, his fingers teasing my opening, and any trace of logic flew out the window. I found myself bucking my groin toward his hand, asking for more as he devoured my neck. Bracing himself on his knees, he opened the front buttons of my dress with his free hand while he still played with my arousal. When he got to the last button, he slid the dress off me, his eyes raking over my body, stripping me from my inhibitions.

"You're beautiful," he whispered. "Worthy of every single compliment and flattery I've heard about you before the masquerade. I said I wanted to see for myself, but I never mentioned—you smashed every single fucking expectation I've ever had."

I blinked away the tears, touching his face everywhere, claiming him somehow by doing so. "Please make love to me."

Not sex.

Not fuck.

Not screw.

Love, love, *love*.

Make love to me, my heart silently begged. He kissed my lips, moving his mouth to my nipples and suckling on one of them, applying gradual pressure with his teeth and tongue.

He teased and sucked on my tits, then traced my folds with his fingers, borrowing my wetness and using it to circle my nub in delicious rounds of pleasure.

"Just, please, do it already," I whimpered, my fingers running through his dark hair as he kissed and leisurely licked the inside of my thighs and the sensitive place between them. "I need you inside me."

"Why?"

"I can't explain."

"Yes, you can. You're just afraid to."

Wolfe Keaton was a kiss thief, but it wasn't only a kiss that he stole. He stole my heart, too. Ripped it from my chest and put it in his pocket. I did what he promised me I would do, and willingly—I spread my legs and begged him, once again, this time meaning every word. "Because you were right. You said I'd come to your bed willingly—and I am. So, take me."

He kissed me dirty, biting down on my tender lower lip, that was still sore from the accident. "Still not the entire truth, but this'll do."

He rose on his forearms, reaching for his wallet and taking out a condom. I swallowed down my disappointment. He pulled back, scanning my face.

"What's wrong?"

"Nothing."

He was about to chuck my chin, before thinking the better of it and running his thumb along my jawline. "We're past the point of lying to each other. Spill."

My eyes drifted to the condom. "I just…I thought the first time—our *real* first time—would be more personal." My face heated as I said that because I realized that I berated him for suggesting the exact same thing mere hours ago.

"Can you…?"

"I'll finish out." He shut me up with a kiss. "We won't make a habit until you're on the pill. Deal?"

I nodded.

He tossed the condom on the carpet, his eyes staring deep into mine as he eased into me. I involuntarily tensed, before he lowered himself to kiss my mouth.

"Relax for me."

I took a deep breath, doing as I was told. Halfway through the penetration, it started to hurt, but in a very different way than last time. This time, it was a delicious pain as he stretched me from within, allowing me the time to accommodate his girth by kissing me in between. He showered me with words that gave me courage and strength. Words I believed with every piece of my soul.

"You're as graceful as rain."

"Beautiful as the starless Chicago sky on a sad, masquerade night."

"You feel so good, Nemesis. I would drown in you and die if you don't stop me."

It was oceans away from the last time he commented about my tightness, which felt dirty and degrading. I clutched his shoulders, moaning softly and cradling him, my body slowly mirroring his until the discomfort was replaced by lusty, jerky rolls of my hips. I purred into his ear as he drove faster into me, bracing himself on his hands, determined not to touch my ribs and forehead. Not to hurt me. Then his thrusts became so deep and feral, I knew he was close. I sank my nails into the flesh of his back, feeling the climax rising within my belly, too. It was different than all the times he licked me. Deeper, more profound.

"Gonna come now, Nem."

He was about to pull out when I clung to him for a fierce kiss, and I felt him emptying inside me. The warm, sticky, thick liquid filling me from the inside. We held onto each other for a long moment before he rolled off me. This time, there was no shame and distress. I didn't look away. He didn't cradle his face and wish he could crawl into a crack in the floor and die. Our heads were tilted toward one another, both of us on the carpet by the fire.

He chucked me under the chin.

"You finished inside." I licked my lips.

He yawned and stretched at the same time, not looking particularly worried, and *that* worried me.

"I'm not taking another pill," I said, shaking my head as I held my dress to my chest. "It's not healthy."

"Sweetheart." His eyes crinkled as he looked at me. "As I said before, the dates don't add up."

"Screw the dates."

"Can I screw you instead?"

I laughed. "Fine. I'm taking your word for it."

"As you should." He chucked my chin again.

"Stop doing that, Wolfe. I told you. It makes me feel like a kid."

He stood up, completely naked, and hoisted me over his shoulder, careful not to touch my ribs, then carried me to the master bedroom, planting a teasing slap on my butt cheek, before biting on it softly.

"What are you doing?" I laughed breathlessly.

"Some very grown-up things to you."

We spent the night in the same bed, going through three condoms. The morning after, we checked on Artemis again. She was happy to see us, and I took her for a quick ride, surprised with the minimal discomfort having sex four times last night had caused me. We gave her food and water and sat by her side in the barn. That morning, in the barn with Artemis as our audience, Wolfe taught me how to perform oral sex on a man. He lowered me to my knees, stood up, unzipped his dark Diesels, and took himself out. At first, he taught me how to stroke it, then how to squeeze it. When I felt comfortable enough, he asked if I wanted to put it in my mouth.

"Yes." I looked down at the hay, swallowing down my shame.

"Look at me, Francesca."

I looked up, blinking at his gray eyes.

"There's nothing wrong with what you're about to do. You know that, right?"

I nodded, but I didn't actually believe it. I was pretty certain every single person I went to church with, including my own parents, would have a heart attack if they knew what we were doing.

"What if people find out?"

He laughed. The bastard full-blown laughed.

"Everyone you know older than eighteen has had oral sex, Francesca."

"I didn't."

"And thank fuck for that."

Surely, he was just telling me what I wanted to hear. Wolfe probably read the doubt on my face because he stroked the side of my cheek and sighed.

"Do you think I'm a pervert?" he asked.

"What?" I felt my face heating. "No, of course not."

"Good. Because I eat your pussy every day. Have been for weeks, now. And plan to do so for the rest of my life. You giving your husband pleasure is nothing to be ashamed of."

"But you said oral sex is degrading." I licked my lips, tossing his words from when we were engaged to the air between us.

"It's degrading to kneel, in general. It is not degrading to kneel for someone who is worth your pride."

I knew Wolfe was not one to talk lightly about pride. He was, after all, the Narcissus to my Nemesis. Whatever made him clutch to his pride like this had scarred him thoroughly. I wrapped my lips around his engorged head, feeling his hand guiding mine around the base of his shaft, before he put his hand over the back of my head and slowly dragged my mouth along his girth, until his crown touched the back of my throat. I wanted to gag but held back.

"Now suck on it." He sank his fingers into my hair and clutched my roots, hard.

I was surprised by how much I enjoyed sucking his cock. I not only enjoyed the act and the velvety, warm skin, but also his unique, manly scent and the way he responded to it, jerking in my mouth and letting out desperate groans. My jaw and lips hurt by the time he held my hair and pulled out of me, tilting my head up and making me look deep into his eyes.

"You know I respect you," he said gruffly.

"I know," I murmured, my lips swollen and sensitive.

"Good. Because for the next five seconds, it's going to look like I don't." He squeezed his length and shot his cum all over my face and breasts.

The warm liquid slithered down my cheek. It was thick and slimy but oddly enough, not degrading. All I could feel was more lust, and my womb clenching against nothing, begging for *something* that my husband had.

I licked the cum from the corner of my lips and looked back up to him, smiling.

He smiled back.

"I think we're going to get along fine, my dear wife."

CHAPTER FIFTEEN

Francesca

I woke up with the same, terrible craving. A sweet tooth that wouldn't go away.

I feel like a strawberry milkshake.

No. I need one. Bad.

I rolled from my side of the bed and bumped into hard abs, groaning as I cracked one eye open. Five weeks after our retreat to Lake Michigan, and I'd found out some interesting facts about my new life with Senator Wolfe Keaton. For one thing, I very much enjoyed waking my husband up with a blow job. For another, he thoroughly enjoyed my new role as his human alarm. I kissed my way down his stomach, following the happy trail of dark hair, and lowered his gray sweatpants with his college name on them. Once I had him in my mouth, he stirred awake, but unlike the other times, he flung the blankets off of us and pulled me by my hair, gentle, but firm.

"Not gonna cut it today I'm afraid." He threw me back on the mattress so I was on all fours, retrieving a condom from the nightstand. I still wasn't on the pill. I was supposed to book an appointment as soon as we got back from Lake Michigan, but I was embarrassed to go by myself, knowing I'd get checked down there. I didn't want to go with Ms. Sterling, and knew that Mama and Clara did not believe in contraception, in general. I called Andrea three times, and she said that she'd have loved to come with me, but my father would kill her if she was seen with me in public.

"It's not personal, Frankie. You know that, right?"

I did. I knew that. Hell, I couldn't even blame her. I feared my father just as much at some point.

This left me with asking my husband to come with. When I heavily hinted at appreciating his company over dinner that week, he dismissed me and said I could go on my own.

"What if it hurts?" I asked him. He shrugged.

"My being there won't take away the pain." It was BS, and he knew it.

The next day, he came back from work with a huge package of condoms and a receipt from Costco.

Wolfe threw the no-sleeping together rule out the window. We still had our clothes and belongings in separate wings of the house, but we always spent the entire night together. Most nights, he came to my room, holding me close after making love to me. But sometimes, especially on days he worked very late, I entered his domain and served him in his bed. We began to attend galas and charity events together. We became *that* couple. The couple I always thought Angelo and I would be. People watched us with open fascination as we flirted with each other at our dinner table. Wolfe would always have his hand on mine, press a kiss to my lips, and behave like the perfect gentleman that he was—a far cry from the sarcastic, taunting bastard who dragged me to Bishop's son's wedding.

I even began to lower my guard when it came to other women. In fact, Senator Keaton showed no interest in any of them even though the offers kept pouring in, including, but not limited to, panties I'd found in our mailbox (Ms. Sterling was outraged and disgusted; she waved the pair of thongs all the way to the trash bin), and endless business cards Wolfe and I found ourselves emptying from his pocket at the end of every night.

Life with Wolfe was good.

Between school, horseback riding with Artemis, my garden, and the piano lessons I resumed, I had very little time to sit and ponder over my father's next chess move. Mama came over every week, and we gossiped, drank tea, and flipped through fashion magazines, something she enjoyed and I couldn't stand, but I humored her. My husband never showed any opposition to having Mama or Clara over. In fact, he often invited them to stay longer, and Ms. Sterling and Clara really seemed to hit it off, sharing their love for daytime soap operas and even sneakily trading romance books with each other.

I bumped into Angelo a few times at school after Lake Michigan. He was taking classes, too, though we didn't have any together. I was pretty sure that could never happen. Not when my husband was so acutely aware of his presence at Northwestern. I felt the need to apologize for what happened the day of my wedding, and he waved it off and told me that it wasn't my fault. Which might've been true but that didn't make me feel any less guilty. At the same time, I could understand why Wolfe didn't want Angelo and me to maintain our friendship, seeing as I was silly in love with him when we'd first met. Angelo, however, wasn't a fan of my husband's opinion. Every time we met at the cafeteria or local coffee shop, he'd strike up lengthy conversations with me and fill me in on every little detail from my old neighborhood.

I snickered when he told me who got married, who got divorced, and that Emily—"*our* Emily"—was seeing a Bostonian mobster from New York, Irish, no less.

"Good Lord!" I made a scandalized face. He laughed.

"Thought you should know, in case you were still wondering about me and her, goddess."

Goddess.

My husband was stoic, powerful, and ruthless. Angelo was sweet and confident and forgiving. They were night and day. Summer and winter. And I was beginning to realize I knew where I belonged—in the storm with Wolfe.

One conscious decision I took in order to maintain my blissful life with my husband was not to open the wooden box. Technically, I needed to do that a long time ago. Right after my wedding to Wolfe. But I only had one note left, and Wolfe turned out to be the rightful owner of my heart with both previous notes. I didn't want to ruin his perfect strike. Not when I was so close to happiness, I could almost feel it at my fingertips.

Now I was feeling woozy and drowsy, still craving the milkshake, but also dangling my butt in my husband's face, wanting him to satisfy my other need. Wolfe entered me from behind, sheathed and fully erect.

"My sweet poison, my gorgeous rival." He kissed the back of my neck as he drove into me from behind. I purred. When he finished inside me, he took off his condom, tied it up and strolled to the bathroom, completely naked. I collapsed on his bed facedown, a heap of warm flesh and lust.

He emerged ten minutes later, freshly shaven, showered, and already getting dressed in a full suit. By the time I rolled on my back to take a look at him, he had a tie on.

"I want a strawberry milkshake." I pouted.

He frowned, flipping his tie and tying it without even looking at a mirror. "You don't normally have a sweet tooth."

"I'm about to get my period." It was, in fact, a little overdue.

"I'll have Smithy get you one before I go to work. You good for school? Need a ride?"

I was due to take my driver's test next week.

"I don't want Smithy to get me a milkshake. I want you to get me one," I rose on my knees, walking on them across the bed and toward him. "He always screws my orders up."

"What's to screw up in ordering a strawberry milkshake?"

Wolfe returned to his bathroom to put some of the delicious-smelling product in his hair. One day, I was going to have a heart attack with how attractive he was and how tantalizing he smelled.

"You'd be surprised," I lied. Smithy was great. I just had an irrational need to have my husband do something nice for me. Since Artemis, he was careful not to show any signs of romantic gestures.

"I'll get you your milkshake," he said in no particular tone, leaving the room.

"Thank you!" I called out.

A moment later, Ms. Sterling, the number-one eavesdropper in North America, popped her head into the room.

"You two are the thickest smart people I know." She shook her head. I was still lying on the bed, staring at the ceiling, basking in my post-orgasm bliss. The sheets were wrapped around my body, but I wasn't particularly worried about what she saw. She must've heard us hundreds of time by now doing what married couples did.

"What do you mean?" I stretched lazily, stifling a yawn.

"You're pregnant, my sweet, foolish child!"

No.

It's not happening.
It can't happen.
Only it can. It must. And it makes so much sense.

The words looped in my head when I paid for my pregnancy test at Walgreens before I went to school. I devoured the strawberry milkshake as if my life depended on it, only to feel terribly nauseous afterwards, and I had a bad feeling, even before I crouched down and peed on the stick in the restrooms of my school, that Ms. Sterling was right. I swore under my breath. I could use Andrea right now. Someone to hold me when it was time to flip that stick and check the results. But Andrea was scared of my dad, and it was time to find and make new friends, outside of The Outfit.

Putting the cap back on the test and setting my phone to count down the minutes, I pressed my forehead against the door. I knew two things for certain:

1. I didn't want to be pregnant.
2. I didn't want to not be pregnant.

If I were pregnant, I'd have a huge problem on my hands. My husband did not want kids. He told me so himself. Quite a few times, actually. He even went so far as suggesting I'd live in a different place and get a sperm donor if I cared so much for children. Bringing an unwanted baby into the world was immoral, if not completely deranged, considering our circumstances.

But then, oddly, not being with child was also going to leave me disappointed. Because there was excitement and anticipation in finding out that I was carrying Wolfe's baby. My mind took me to insane places. Places I had no business visiting. What eye color would our child have? They would have dark hair. Slim build, like both of us. But—gray or blue? Tall or short? And would they have his wit and my talent with the piano? Would they be ivory and snow, like my pale skin? Or would they have his rather tan complexion? I wanted to know everything. I resisted the urge to drag my palm over my stomach, imagining it getting swollen and round and perfect, carrying the fruit of our love.

The fruit of *my* love.

No one ever said that he loved me. No one even suggested that. Not even Ms. Sterling.

My phone beeped, and I jumped, my heart stuttering in my chest. No matter the result, I wanted to get it over with. I flipped the pregnancy test over and blinked back.

Two lines. Blue. Sharp. Prominent. Strong.

I was pregnant.

I broke into tears.

I couldn't believe it was happening to me. Wolfe asked—*no*, he strictly *stated*—he didn't want any children, and now, not even six months after our wedding, when we finally hit our stride, I was going to tell him that I was with child. A part of me pointed out, quite reasonably, that this wasn't entirely my fault. He was to blame, too. In fact, *he* was the one who tried to coax me into having unprotected sex in the first place, with the nonsense about pulling out (great job with that one), and calculating the dates and telling me I wasn't ovulating.

Only both of us didn't take into consideration the fact that my period had changed the minute I took the Plan B pill.

Then again, *I* was the one who drew him close when he came inside me, preventing him—albeit by accident—from pulling out. I knew that there was no other occasion in which this might have happened. Save for the weekend at the cabin, we always used condoms.

Shoulders sagging, I got out of the bathroom, dragging myself down the corridor, out of the college, and into the unassuming autumn day. I needed to confide in Ms. Sterling. She'd know what to do.

I was heading toward Smithy's car when Angelo tackled me to the grass out of nowhere. I yelped. The first thing I thought about was the baby. I pushed him off, watching as he laughed breathlessly, trying to tickle me.

"Angelo…" Hysteria bubbled in my chest. Wasn't the first trimester the most crucial one? I couldn't afford to roll on the ground. "Get off!"

He scrambled to his feet, rubbing his dark blond hair and staring me down. Where was it coming from? Angelo was always reserved and respectful. He was always nice to me, true, but he never touched me like this in the weeks after I got married.

"Jesus, goddess, sorry." He offered me his hand, and I took it. I hated that he still called me goddess, but I guessed there were no laws against idle flirtation. Even though maybe there ought to be. That way women wouldn't be able to proposition my husband every time he left the house.

That way you'd also live in an oppressive country.

I stood up and looked around, not really sure what I was looking for. I cleaned my dress and cardigan free of grass blades.

"It looked like you were having a bad day. I just wanted to make you laugh," Angelo explained. How could I tell my sweet friend that he was absolutely right? I was having both the worst and the best day combined. I brushed a blade of grass from his shoulder, smiling.

"It's not your fault. I'm sorry I was snippy. I was just surprised."

"Your driver is waiting for you on the other side of the lot. So are your executive protection agents, who, by the way, are doing a crappy job, seeing as they're not with you right now." Angelo wiggled his brows, digging his finger into my shoulder muscles in a soothing massage. Wolfe insisted I have bodyguards with me after the car chase. It was only this week that I had finally managed to convince him to break protocol and have the bodyguards stay in the car and leave me alone on school grounds. We hadn't heard from my father or Mike Bandini in a while. Apparently, they were busy trying to keep The Outfit afloat and from Wolfe's iron fist. And if I ever wanted to make friends at school, I couldn't have two men the size of elephants shadowing my every step.

I didn't tell Angelo about what his father did. Unlike Wolfe, I was good with making the separation between father and offspring. Maybe because I knew too well what it felt like to be embarrassed by your parents' actions.

"Thanks." I threw my bag over my shoulder, standing in front of him, awkward and guilt-stricken. He was making an effort, trying to rebuild that bridge that had burned between us, and I was standing on the other end with a match, ready to destroy it once again. But there was a delicacy in keeping my loyalty to my husband and patching things up with a boy who'd meant the world to me. A tightrope I was too clumsy to walk.

"I need to make a confession." He messed with his tousled, beautiful hair. It hurt my heart to recognize what I refused to see in the beginning of my engagement to Wolfe. That one day, Angelo would make an amazing husband to someone, but that someone wasn't going to be me.

"Go on." I rubbed my eyes. I never felt so tired in my life, and it's not like I missed an hour of sleep. He looked down now, shuffling from foot to foot. No longer confident and cocky.

"The night of your engagement party, something happened…something that shouldn't have happened." He swallowed, his gaze becoming hooded. He took a deep breath. "The blonde chick from the masquerade was there. You just shut me down after I had this whole speech in my head about how the evening was going to play out. I fucked up and couldn't find my words, and you kept looking for your fiancé. I felt like my world was collapsing, one wall at a time." He rubbed his cheek now as though he'd been slapped with the truth. "I made a mistake. A huge one. I slept with the reporter. Actually, that was only a small error. Not the terrible one. The terrible one occurred afterward when I met your husband on the stairs."

I looked up, searching his face. To my shock, I found Angelo blinking back tears. Actual tears. Tears I absolutely hated seeing there even though I knew what he was about to tell me was nothing short of awful. That it ruined me in a lot of ways. Whatever Wolfe and I were today, he could never erase the night he took my innocence by force.

"You told him we slept together?" My voice trembled.

He shook his head. "No. No. I wouldn't do that. I just…I didn't exactly tell him it *didn't* happen, either. I was busy trying to get back at him instead of clearing up what looked like a misunderstanding. I was so mad, Frankie. And a part of me still hoped that you guys were going to break up over it. I wanted to give fate a little push. I wasn't planning on ruining it for both of you. I mean, I was, but only because I thought you were on board. I thought you wanted to try giving him a chance because your parents pressured you. Not because, well…"

"Because I love him?" I finished, my voice hoarse. I squeezed his shoulder. He looked down at my hand and sniffed.

"Yeah."

"I do," I said, letting out an exasperated sigh. "God, Angelo, I'm so sorry, but I do. I never planned on falling for him. It just happened. But that's the thing about love, isn't it? It's like death. You know it will happen one day. You just don't know how or why or when."

"That's a rather dark view on life." He offered me a grim smile.

I couldn't be mad at Angelo. Not really. And especially when Wolfe and I had overcome what he and Kristen threw at us. Some would even call it the pivotal moment of our entire relationship.

"Still." Angelo grinned, his boyish dimples on full display. The same smile that broke my heart every time I saw it on his face, peeking under his dark lashes. "If you ever change your mind, I'm here."

"I'm compromised," I answered him with an arched brow, blushing. He sighed theatrically.

"Believe it or not, goddess, so am I."

"Get out." I slapped his chest, feeling the tension evaporating from my bones. "When was your first time? With who?" The question sat on the tip of my tongue for years, but up until now, I never had the chance to ask. We were trying the whole friendship thing now. Well, sort of.

Angelo let out a sharp exhale.

"Junior year. Cheryl Evans, after calc class."

"Was she little Miss Popular?" I grinned.

"Guess you could say that. She was the teacher," he deadpanned.

"What?" I choked on my laughter. "You lost your virginity to your teacher?"

"She was, like, twenty-three. No other girl that age would put out without a serious relationship, and I was getting antsy. I was also saving the whole real thing for you," he admitted. It made me sad and happy at the same time. That life took us in a different direction, but that Angelo whom I loved not too long ago was on the same wavelength as I was.

"Welp." He gave me two thumbs down. "Maybe in the next lifetime."

Last time he said it would happen in this one. I grinned.

"Almost definitely."

We hugged, and I hurried across the lawn toward the line of double-parked vehicles full of college students bumming rides from one another, scanning the landscape for Smithy's shielded, brand-new Cadillac. This time, Wolfe went above and beyond with all the accessories to make sure it was bulletproof. I spotted Smithy in the car, messing with his phone, and smiled to myself. Everything was going to be okay. Wolfe might not respond to the news with enthusiasm, but I hoped he wouldn't be crushed, either. I was almost at the car when Kristen, the journalist, appeared out of thin air, jumping in front of me, looking haggard. Her hair was frizzy and the bags under her eyes purplish from what I assumed was lack of sleep.

My two executive protection agents got out of the car simultaneously, hurrying toward us. I raised my arm and waved them away.

"It's okay."

"Mrs. Keaton."

"It's *fine*," I insisted. "Take a step back, please."

Kristen didn't even notice them. She zigzagged in place.

"Francescaaaa," she slurred, pointing her finger in my general direction. She was too drunk to point it at me. I tried to remember where we left things off with her. Last I heard, Wolfe said he got her fired. She was obviously feeling vindictive. But it'd been weeks.

"Where have you been?" I asked, trying not to scan her tattered shirt and dirty jeans. She waved a hand around, hiccupping.

"Oh, here and there. Everywhere, really. Crashed at my parents' in Ohio. Came back here to try and look for a job. Called your husband hundreds of time to try and get me un-blacklisted. And then…crap, why am I telling you this anyway?" She laughed, flipping her greasy hair aside. I looked behind me to see if Angelo was around. She read my mind.

"Relax. I just fucked your friend so Wolfe would get mad at you. He's too young for me anyway."

And too good for you, I thought to myself.

Pregnancy obviously messed with my logic because I felt the urge to rub her arm or buy her a cup of coffee. I knew damn well that she tried to ruin my life to save hers, and that she wanted my husband for herself (at least before he got her fired). But the thing about compassion was that it wasn't given to people who necessarily deserved it, but needed it nonetheless.

"Obviously, my plan failed miserably." She dragged her chipped fingernails over her cheeks, scanning my pristine white cardigan over my knee-length black dress.

"You look like a fucking church girl."

"I am a church girl."

She snorted out a laugh.

"He's a kinky bastard."

"Or maybe he just likes me." I dug in an imaginary knife into her chest. She did, after all, try to make my husband believe that

I cheated on him. No matter how dire her situation was, there was no need to be mean to me. I hadn't done anything to her.

"Good one. Wolfe just likes fucking something that belongs to Arthur Rossi. You know, because Arthur fucked with *his* family. Poetic justice, and all that."

"Excuse me?" I took a step back, assessing her fully now. I'd had my fill of surprises today. Between the pregnancy test, Angelo's confession, and now this, I realized that the universe was trying to tell me something. Hopefully not that my fairy tale, which hadn't begun just yet, was ending abruptly.

One of my bodyguards took a step forward, and I spun on him.

"Stay away. Let her talk."

"He didn't tell you?" Kristen threw her head back and laughed, pointing at me. *Ridiculing* me. "Did you ever wonder why he took you from your father? What he had on him?"

I did. All the time. Hell, I asked Wolfe about it on a daily basis.

But of course, admitting this to her was giving her more power than she deserved.

Kristen leaned her elbow over a huge oak tree, whistling. "Where do I begin? This is all confirmed, by the way, so you can cross-examine your husband the minute you get back home. Wolfe Keaton wasn't really born Wolfe Keaton. He was born Fabio Nucci, a poor, bastard Italian kid who lived not too far from your block. Same zip code but trust me—very different houses. His momma was a drunk, neglectful excuse for a human being, and his father was out of the picture before he was even born. His older—much older brother, Romeo—raised him. Romeo became a cop. He was doing a fine job until he was caught in the wrong place at the wrong time. Namely—Mama's Pizza, the little parlor three blocks down from you. Romeo went to get Wolfe some pizza. They walked into a gun fight. Romeo, still clad in his uniform, burst through the back of the parlor to break things off. They had to kill him, or he'd have outed all of them. Your father killed Romeo in front of your husband despite his desperate pleas."

I never beg.

I never kneel.

I have my pride.

Wolfe's words came back to haunt me, making my skin dampen and chill. That was why he was so adamant on not negotiating or showing remorse or mercy. My father didn't spare him any of those things when he needed them the most. I stared at Kristen, knowing there was more. Knowing that was the tip of a very thick, very lethal iceberg.

She continued.

"After that happened, he was adopted by the Keatons, a rich family from the *right* side of the tracks. The same house you live in right now, in fact. The Keatons were Chicago's finest. A high-profiled couple who never had any children and had the world to give to him. They changed his name to separate him from the mess that was his early life. Things were looking up for little Wolfey for a minute there. He even managed to overcome the severe trauma of seeing your father putting a bullet between his brother's eyes."

"Why didn't my father deal with Wolfe? Since he watched, too?" I hated that I was asking her questions. But unlike my husband, my pride was not as vital for my survival.

Kristen huffed. "Wolfe was just a kid back then. He didn't know the key players and didn't have an open beef with The Outfit like his brother. Not to mention, no one was going to believe him. Plus, I guess even your father has some morals," she scanned me with disgust. My jaw tensed, but I said nothing, too afraid she'd stop talking.

"Anyway," she singsonged, "can you guess what happened next?"

"No," I gritted out. "But I bet you'll be happy to tell me."

I knew that she was telling the truth. Not because Kristen wasn't capable of lying, but because she was having too much fun delivering the news for it not to be accurate.

"Wolfe goes off to college. Makes friends. Lives his best life, so to speak. Second year at Harvard, he's about to come back for summer vacation when the ballroom where his parents are attending a charity gala explodes with a ton of politicians and high-end diplomats inside. Any guesses who's responsible for it?"

My father, of course.

I remembered that incident. One summer when I was eight, we didn't go to Italy. My father was arrested for the ballroom incident and released shortly after for lack of evidence. My mother was crying all the time, and her friends were always around. When Dad got out, they started fighting. A lot. Maybe that was the moment my mother realized she didn't marry a good man.

In the end, they decided that the best course of action would be to send me to boarding school. I knew they were protecting me from my father's reputation here in Chicago and giving me my best shot.

Kristen whistled again, shaking her head. "Suffice it to say, your husband did not return from *that* trauma. The problem was, officially, and on paper, the blowout was the result of a gas leak. The entire hotel chain shut down soon after. Your father's arrest was a farce. They couldn't even send him to trial even though everyone knew he got back at Wolfe's mother, a Supreme Court judge, for ruling against one of his best friends."

Lorenzo Florence. He was still in prison. He smuggled over five-hundred kilograms of heroin into the US, working for my father.

I stumbled back, collapsing to the grass. My bodyguards had had enough. They both started in my direction. Kristen pushed off the tree, squatting to my eye level, and smiling brightly. "So now Wolfe really wants to get back at your father and gather ammo against him. He's been doing that ever since he graduated, actually. Through private investigators and endless resources, he managed to find something on your father. Whatever it is, he is hanging it over his head. You know the end game was always to kill your father, right?"

I couldn't answer. They dragged me toward the car while I kicked and screamed. I wanted to stay and listen. I wanted to run away.

"He'll be the heir to The Outfit…" Kristen yelled, running after us. One of the bodyguards pushed her, but she was having too much fun.

"He doesn't want The Outfit," I screamed back to her.

"He'll discard you just as he's always planned. Have you ever wondered why he never bothered to have you sign a pre-nup? Don't be so sure you'll get out of this in one piece. It's not like anyone from Wolfe's family did…"

"No, you're wrong." I felt my lower lip trembling. They ducked me into the back seat of the vehicle and slammed the door behind me. I felt dizzy and nauseous. I was too physically weak and emotionally shocked to cope with these revelations.

Kristen appeared at the window and signaled for me to roll it down. One of the EPAs nearly beat her off from inside the car, but I rolled the window down, anyway. She pushed her head into the car.

"He'll throw you out by the end of the year, sweetheart. Once he's had enough of fucking you. I've seen it happen a thousand times before. Wolfe Keaton doesn't do love, sweetie."

"Maybe not with you," I bit back. She frowned, looking wounded.

"You're delusional," she said.

"And you're desperate. How did you find out this information?"

She shrugged, a bitter smile spreading on her face like margarine. Easy but toxic.

I didn't have to ask again. I knew.

My father.

That night, when Wolfe arrived at my bed to bring me the dinner I'd missed, I turned him away. I wasn't ready to face him, and I definitely wasn't ready to tell him about the pregnancy. I knew deep down that Kristen was at least partly right. This was Wolfe's plan all along. To ruin my family and discard me somewhere along the way. Whether the plan was still in motion or not was beside the point. Not that I had the greenest clue what his plan was nowadays.

All I knew was that the odds were against us.

"Everything okay?" he asked, brushing my hair away from my face.

I couldn't look him in the eye. I flipped through pages in a book I didn't really read. I was pretty sure I was holding it upside down, too, but couldn't tell, since my eyes could barely register the shape of the book, let alone its contents.

"Sure. I just got my period," I lied.

"I could still stay," he suggested, his hand sliding from my cheek, his thumb tilting my chin up to face him. "I'm not coming here just for the sex."

"Well, I'm not in the mood to give you a blow job, either."

"*Francesca*," he growled, and my eyes darted up to meet his. I hated the fact that I loved him so much. He was right. Love, by definition, was unrequited. One party always loved more.

"Should I be worried?" he demanded.

"What about?" I flipped another page.

"Your ability to read, for one thing. You're holding it upside down," he snapped. I closed the book. "You. Us. *This*." He motioned between us with his hand.

"No."

Silence fell between us, but he still wouldn't leave. I became agitated. It was weird how we started the morning unassumingly, with a strawberry milkshake and a quickie, and how fast we could turn into enemies again.

"Let's go outside. You can suck on a cancer stick and bring me up to speed about what crawled up your ass." He stood up and snatched my cigarette pack from my desk.

"No, thank you." I forgot to throw away the cigarettes when I got back home tonight, but they were definitely not on the menu for me in the foreseeable future.

"Nothing you want to say to me?" He scanned my face again, his jaw tense, his eyes dark and feral.

"No." I reopened the book, this time in the right direction.

"Do you want me to come with you to the OB-GYN?"

My pulse jumped, hammering against my throat.

"Nice of you to offer months later, but the answer is still no. Can I be left alone, please? I think I outdid my duty as a trophy wife and a warm hole at night this week."

He narrowed his eyes, taking a step back. My words hurt him—the man who was steel and metal. He turned around and dashed away before we exploded on one another.

I fell to my pillow and cried as soon as the door shut behind him, making up my mind.

Tomorrow, I was going to open the box and retrieve the very last note.

The one that would determine if Wolfe really was the love of my life.

CHAPTER SIXTEEN

Francesca

I HELD THE NOTE CLOSE TO MY CHEST AS I MADE MY WAY OUT
of the cafeteria, blazing right onto the lush, wet grass at the
entrance. The first rain of autumn knocked softly on my face,
making me blink as the world shifted in and out of focus.

The first rain of the season. A sign.

Most cities were the most romantic during springtime, but
Chicago thrived in the fall. When the leaves were orange and yellow and the sky as gray as my husband's eyes. The note was wet
between my fingers. It was probably ruined, but I still clutched
it with a death grip. I stood in the middle of the turf overlooking the road, under the open sky, and let the drops pound over
my face and body.

Come rescue me, Wolfe.

I prayed, even despite my bitter knowledge and everything
Kristen had told me, that he would fulfill the last note and be
my knight in shining armor.

The love of your life will shelter you from the storm.

I inwardly begged, and pleaded, and sobbed.

Please, please, *please* shelter me.

I wanted a promise that he would not discard me after he was done with my father.

That despite hating my family—and for good reason—he *loved* me.

This morning, after I read the last note, I tucked it in my bra, just like I did the night of the masquerade. Smithy drove me to school. On our way there, rain started dancing across the windshield.

"Goddammit," Smithy mumbled, flicking the wipers on.

"Don't pick me up today." It was the first and last order I gave Smithy.

"Huh?" He popped his gum, distracted. My EPAs shifted in their seats, exchanging looks.

"Wolfe is going to pick me up."

"He'll be in Springfield."

"Change of plan. He's staying in town."

I was only half-lying. If Wolfe was the love of my life, he would be here.

But now I was standing in the rain with no one to turn to.

"Francesca! What the hell!" I heard a voice behind me. I turned around. Angelo was standing on the stairs of the front entrance, shielded by an umbrella, squinting at me. I wanted to shake my head, but I didn't want to interfere with fate anymore.

Please, Angelo. No. Don't come here.

"It's raining!" he yelled.

"I know." I stared at the cars whizzing by, waiting for my husband to somehow show up, out of the blue, and tell me that he wanted to give me a ride. Waiting for him to come and whisk me away. Praying he would shield me, not only from the storm outside, but the one inside me, too.

"Goddess, come here."

Dropping my head, I tried to swallow the ball of tears in my throat.

"Francesca, it's pouring. What the fuck?"

I heard Angelo's feet slapping the concrete stairs as he made his way across the lawn, wanting to stop him, but knowing that I'd already messed with my destiny too much. Opening the notes when I shouldn't have. Feeling things I shouldn't feel for someone who was only after my family's misery.

I felt Angelo's embrace from behind me. It was all wrong and right. Comforting and distressing. Beautiful and ugly. And my brain kept screaming, *no, no, no.* He twisted me around. I was shivering in his arms, and he jerked me close, hugging me before bringing me to shelter within his chest. He somehow knew that my need for human warmth was stronger than the need for a roof over my head.

He cupped my cheeks, and I relented to his touch, knowing, without a shadow of a doubt now, that Wolfe had read the second note, about the chocolate, shortly after I moved into his house. And that he was also privy to the first note, as I'd told him, and ruined it for me, too.

Those notes didn't count.

They never counted.

This was true. This was real. Angelo and me, under the open sky that was crying for all the time I'd spent trying to make my husband fall in love with me.

Angelo.

Maybe it was always Angelo. "I'm pregnant," I yelped into his chest. "And I want a divorce," I added, not entirely sure that it was really what I wanted.

He shook his head, bringing his lips to my forehead. "I'll be there for you. No matter what."

"Your father hates me," I moaned, the pain inside me cutting deep.

He saved me.

Angelo saved me.

Sheltered me from the storm.

"Who cares about my father? *I* love you." He nuzzled his nose against mine. "I've loved you since the day you smiled at me—all braces—and I still wanted to kiss you."

"Angelo…"

"You're not a toy, Francesca. You're not my leverage, or my pawn, or my arm candy. You're the girl from the river. The kid who smiled at me with colorful braces. Just because your story had a few chapters where I wasn't the main lead doesn't make me any less the love of your life. And you're mine. This is it. This is us."

His lips crushed on mine, soft and firm. So determined I wanted to cry with both relief and heartbreak. Angelo was kissing me in front of the entire school. With Wolfe's rings on my finger. Both engagement and wedding band. I knew, without even looking, that people took out their phones and recorded the entire thing. I knew, without a doubt, that my life had taken the sharpest turn of all. Yet I gave in to Angelo, knowing somehow that it needed to happen.

I was cheating on my husband.

Who wanted to ruin my family.

Who didn't want our baby.

Who kept secrets from me.

I was cheating on my husband.

Who offered me everything he owned but his heart.

Who kissed me soft.

And fought me hard.

I was cheating on my husband.

After my father killed his family.

And there was no going back.

Our lips disconnected, and Angelo took my hand in his, tugging me back toward the school.

"Whatever it is, we'll make it. You know that, right?"

"I know that."

I turned my head around one last time to see if there was something I'd missed, and sure enough, there was.

While Wolfe wasn't there, Kristen sure was, tucked inside a parked car, recording the whole thing.

I cheated on my husband, Wolfe Keaton.

The end.

Wolfe

She's been fucking him the whole time.

They're in a hotel in Buffalo Grove now, FYI. Might wanna make sure she takes a shower before you dip into it tonight.

I hope you know what it looks like to the media, Senator Keaton. You're officially the joke of the state.

I'd read Kristen's text messages until my eyes nearly bled. They were accompanied by pictures. Or rather, evidence. Evidence I couldn't overlook since Twitter and Instagram burst with the same images from a hundred different angles of my wife, Mrs. Francesca Keaton, kissing her former flame and fellow student, Angelo Bandini, in the rain. It was like a fucked-up scene from *The Notebook*. The way he held her. The way she submitted to him. Kissed him back. Fiercely.

I couldn't unglue my eyes even if I wanted to. And, quite frankly, I didn't want to.

This is what you get for putting your trust in another human being, idiot.

In a fucking Rossi, no less.

I ignored Kristen's message, knowing damn well that she was not at the school by chance. She wanted me to see those pictures. Wanted me to know that Francesca had an affair with Angelo. Throughout our entire marriage, he'd been a third wheel.

A thorn in my side. Now, finally, Francesca made a proactive choice.

She kissed him in front of the world.

She. Chose. Him.

I had to hand it to my young, spitfire wife. She almost managed to crack me completely. It was that sweet pussy and smart mouth. A lethal combination if I ever met one. But this was the wake-up call that I'd needed.

I left the store I was standing in, making my way out of it and toward my car, on my way home. I'd given up my driver for my wife. I'd given up a lot for my wife.

Which reminded me—where on earth was fucking Smithy?

"Hey. Hi. Hey," Smithy greeted when I called him as I got into my car. My EPAs were at my side. Protocol dictated they couldn't drive for me. Shame. I was about to hurl all of us off the Michigan Avenue Bridge.

"Where the fuck were you this afternoon?" I demanded. By his way of answering, I knew he'd already seen the pictures on Twitter. Jesus Christ, who the hell hadn't at this point?

"She said you were going to pick her up. That you didn't fly out to Springfield today. And I didn't see your car in the garage in the morning, so I figured it was true."

It was. I had two meetings downtown today. And, strangely, I was going to surprise Francesca at her school. I ran late because my second appointment—the one in which I purchased a Yamaha C-7 Grand Piano for my unhappy wife—ran late. It was supposed to be a surprise. Of course, my lovely wife beat me to it this round.

My phone buzzed in my hand. For a second, I thought it'd be Francesca, calling to tell me that it wasn't what it looked like. I glanced at the caller ID. No. It was just Preston Bishop, eager for some blood sport.

Damn it, Francesca.

I sent the call to voicemail, along with the dozen other calls from Bishop, White, and Arthur Rossi, who were all keen to offer their two pennies about the situation, no doubt. I'd been humiliated beyond my worst nightmares after I'd sworn to never be put in this position again. Not after I got down on my knees to Rossi.

The only person who did not try and reach me—other than my cheating wife, of course—was Sterling, who wasn't connected to social media and wasn't privy to what her darling girl had done.

When I got home, I told Sterling to leave for the nearest hotel and gave her ten minutes to pack a bag while I called an Uber for her. I didn't want her there when I faced Francesca. She did not deserve to see that ugly side of me.

"For how long?" Sterling grinned, flinging dresses and stockings into the open suitcase on her bed. As far as she was concerned, everything was still dandy between me and my wife. She probably thought we were planning a fuck-fest over every surface of the house. I glanced at my Rolex.

Two, maybe three years.

"A couple of days. I'll call you when I'm done."

Whenever my lawful wife takes her head out of her ass.

"Wonderful! You have fun, lovebirds."

"Count on it."

Calling her when she was with her lover in a hotel room would be redundant. And hysterical. No. I sat on my wife's bed the remainder of the afternoon, replaying last night in my head. Aunt Flo my ass. She didn't get her period. She didn't want my dick inside her body, probably because she was too busy nurturing an affair with her college buddy.

I was consumed by guilt and self-hatred after the night I'd taken her here, on this bed, thinking that she'd spread her legs to Angelo. But really, my only error was chronological. Because she might have been a virgin when I took her that first time, but that public kiss she had shared with him? It was as real as ours, if not more.

She cheated on me with the man she'd loved since she was in diapers.

And I was the idiot who kept on taking her after all their discriminating evidence.

The Bishop's wedding.

The engagement party.

The kiss.

No more.

I heard the door downstairs open some hours after I arrived. My wife always took off her shoes and arranged them neatly by the door before taking a glass of water from the kitchen and going upstairs. Today was no different. With the exception that when she climbed up the stairs and got into her bedroom, she found me sitting on her bed, holding my phone in my hand, the screen lit and showcasing her kissing Angelo.

Her glass slipped from between her fingers, hitting the floor. She turned around, about to run away. I stood up.

"I wouldn't do that if I were you, Nemesis." My voice dripped ice and menace.

She stopped in her tracks, her back to me, her shoulders sagging, but her head was still high.

"Do what?" she asked.

"Turn your back on me when I'm in my current state."

"And why is that? Are you going to stab me?" She twisted on her heel, her azure eyes shimmering with unshed tears. She was brave, but she was emotional. I mistook all her tears for weakness. No more. Francesca was definitely in the habit of going for what she wanted in life.

I cocked my head to the side. "Why must you Rossis always turn to violence? There are plenty of things I can do to hurt you beyond belief without laying a finger on your beautiful body."

"Enlighten me."

"I think I will, Nemesis. Tonight, in fact."

Her throat bobbed. Her false façade was collapsing inch by

inch with each ragged breath and shiver. She scanned her sur-
roundings. Nothing was different about the room. Other than
my invisible pride, shattered on her floor, with her footmarks
all over it.

"Where is Ms. Sterling?" Her eyes slid to the window, then
to the door. She wanted to escape me.

Too late, darling.

"I sent her on a mini vacation for a few days to freshen up.
She doesn't need to be here for this."

"For what?"

"For when I break you like you broke me. Humiliate you
in the way you humiliated me. Punish you the exact same way
you punished me."

"You've read the notes." She pointed at the wooden box on
her nightstand. I smiled, sliding my wedding band from my finger with slow precision, watching her eyes drink in my movement. I placed it by the box on her nightstand.

"Why else would I send you chocolate when I couldn't even
stand your face?"

The truth felt like ash in my mouth. But the truth was also
a weapon I'd used to wound her little soul. I couldn't breathe
without feeling my chest tightening, and I wanted to slice her
open in the same way she cut me. Bone-deep.

"Well"—a bitter smile fluttered across her face—"I suppose
you know what the last note said."

"I do."

"Angelo sheltered me from the storm."

This made me grab the box and slam it against the opposite wall, not many inches from where she was. The lid broke
off, both pieces rolling on the floor. She cupped her mouth but
stayed silent.

"Because he kissed you in the rain? Are you fucking kidding me? *I* sheltered you." I stabbed a finger to my chest, ad-
vancing toward her and losing the remainder of my self-control.

My anger was a red cloud surrounding both of us, and I could hardly see her through it anymore. I grabbed her shoulders, plastering her to the wall, forcing her to look at me. "I sheltered you from your father and Mike Bandini and Kristen Rhys. From every asshole who looked at you the wrong way because of your age or your lineage or your last name. I put my reputation, and career, and fucking sanity on the line to make sure that you were safe, and accomplished, and happy. I broke my rules. All of them. Demolished my own resolutions—for you. I gave you everything I could within reason, and you *shit* all over it."

I paced her room, the words burning on the tip of my tongue, pleading to be said.

I want a divorce.

But I didn't want a fucking divorce.

And that was a problem.

She loved Angelo, much to my disdain and fury, but that didn't change what I felt for her. I still longed for her warm body next to mine. Her sweet mouth and quirky thoughts and that vegetable garden she talked to and piano sessions, stretched over lazy weekends, where I'd read the papers while she played a mishmash of classics and The Cure.

Besides, wasn't that far more cruel than letting her go to Angelo? Watching as she stayed and wilted here, her heart blackening and hardening next to mine? She could fake her affection for me, sure, but our desire? That was real. And consensual. Wouldn't it be far more grueling to have her suck my cock and cream my face while she pined for another?

Wasn't revenge a good enough reason to keep her?

"I'm going to the Bernard's gala tonight," I announced, kicking a part of the wooden box aside on my way to her closet. I picked out a scarlet, skin-tight dress she particularly loved.

"I don't remember seeing it in our calendar." She rubbed her face tiredly, fleetingly forgetting that our calendar no longer meant shit because our charade was formally over. I'd hand her one thing—she was a good actress. I was an idiot enough to buy into it.

"I originally turned it down."

"What made you change your mind?" She took the bait.

"I secured myself a date."

"Wolfe." She pushed herself past me, blocking my way. I stopped. "What are you talking about, a date?"

"Her name is Karolina Ivanova. She's a Russian ballerina. Fuck hot, and damn *responsive*." I'd used the same word to describe Francesca when we first started to explore each other's bodies.

She threw her head back, growling in frustration.

"You're a cheater now on top of everything else. Nice touch."

"Not exactly. We're obviously in an open marriage." I swiped the touch screen of my phone in her face. Her kiss with Angelo flashed, taunting her back. "Remember our verbal contract, Nem? You said both of us needed to be loyal. Well, that ship has fucking sailed."

It's somewhere in the Atlantic Ocean, hitting an iceberg that would split the Titanic in half.

"Thanks for the memo. Does that mean I can invite Angelo over?" She smiled sweetly.

I didn't know what had made her such a bitch overnight. I just knew it wasn't warranted on my part.

"Not if he wants to make it out of here with his dick intact."

"Explain the logic behind your words, Senator Keaton."

"Gladly, Mrs. Keaton: I plan to fuck my way through the better half of Chicago until I've had enough of what it has to offer me. Then, and only then, and *only* if by the time I'm done fucking everything that breathes, you and Angelo will be done with one another, I'd consider letting you suck my cock again. We'll start small. A couple times a week. Then take it from there. That is, *if* I'll ever get bored from the variety," I added.

"And the dress?" She knotted her arms over her chest, pointing her chin to the dark blue number.

"Would look ravishing on Ivanova's tight little bod," I provided.

"Walk out this door tonight, Wolfe, and you won't have a wife to return to." she stood at the doorway now, tall and proud.

She took a deep breath. "Whatever happened this evening will need to be discussed between us. But we will never have a chance to do that if you don't stay. If you leave to spend the night with another woman, I will not be here come morning."

I smiled sardonically, leaning down, our mouths nearly touching. Her breath hitched, and her eyes glazed over. I dragged my lips across her cheek to her ear.

"Don't let the door hit your ass on your way out, Nemesis."

Francesca

I shivered under my covers, hitting refresh on all the local media Twitter accounts, checking their websites for live updates. It was about as constructive to my mental state as watching videos of puppies drowning, but I couldn't help it.

Three hours after he'd left the house, my husband was seen with a gorgeous brunette on his arm. She was wearing my favorite Valentino dress and a proud smile.

Screw you, Wolfe.

Her eyes were bigger and bluer and deeper. They saw and knew things I could hardly even imagine. She was taller and considerably more beautiful. She pressed her cheek to his shoulder, smiling dreamily as their photo was taken, staring directly to the camera. Flirting with it. Loving it back. And, as my husband looked down at her, his cold mercury eyes darkening with lust, I knew what I had to do even before I'd read the caption under their image.

Senator Wolfe Keaton (30) and prima ballerina Karolina Ivanova (28) were seen spending time together at a local gala. Keaton, who was married to Francesca Rossi (19) this summer, is currently in the midst of a scandal after his young wife was seen kissing a childhood friend on the grounds of Northwestern University earlier this afternoon.

Frantic, I checked for more pictures. More items. More tweets about my husband and his lady friend. The entire world saw them together now. We were officially over. Only it was never my intention to humiliate him. I understood how bad it looked, but it was just one kiss. A moment of weakness.

Not that it mattered.

It was no longer about me, and I knew it.

Wolfe was a loose cannon. Angry and vindictive and full of hate. And I had my baby to think about. I packed up a suitcase and called my mother, informing Smithy in a text message that he needed to take me back home to Little Italy.

I saw him texting Wolfe frantically in the car as I pushed my bags out the door, braving the drizzle and the chilly, autumn night.

By the way he banged his head against the headrest, his messages were left unanswered.

CHAPTER SEVENTEEN

Wolfe

I SAT ON THE EDGE OF THE KING-SIZED BED OF THE HOTEL room and took another sip of whiskey. I wasn't hungover, simply because I never stopped drinking throughout the night. I was still blissfully drunk, though the dull heartache had been replaced with a persistent headache that pressed against my eyes and nose.

This was the first time in a decade I'd drank more than the customary two tumblers in one evening.

The moan behind me reminded me that I wasn't alone. Karolina stretched along the bed on a yawn, allowing the sun-rays drifting through the tall French windows to cast a natural light that complemented the soft curves of her face.

"Feeling better?" she murmured, hugging the pillow to her chest, her eyelids still heavy with sleep. I stood up and sauntered across the room toward my phone and wallet on the dresser, still fully dressed. As I checked their contents—and her bag, to make sure she didn't put a recorder in there or took any pictures she shouldn't have been taking—I pondered the question, why the hell couldn't I bring myself to fuck Karolina last night?

The opportunity was there, and she was willing to jump into

my bed. I could not, however, get myself to be with her, though not because of my feelings toward my wife, God forbid, but simply because I lacked the basic need to *want* to fuck Karolina.

As lovely and gorgeous as she was, and as happy as I was to spend the night in her hotel room and not drag myself back home, I had no interest in touching her.

The woman I wanted to be inside was my wife. My wife, who could not, for the life of her, get rid of her fixation with Angelo fucking Bandini.

I tucked my wallet and phone into my pocket and left the room without saying goodbye. It was better that way. Ms. Ivanova shouldn't seek me out again. There wasn't going to be a second time to this. I was not at all opposed to parading mistresses on my arm until my wife died of jealousy and fury—at this point, I cared very little about what it'd do to my name—but touching them, really touching them, was not in the cards for me, apparently.

No matter. Francesca would still warm up my nights. She couldn't deny this attraction, not with the way she hoovered my cock into her mouth every morning and chased my shaft every time I slammed into her from behind. She wanted this as much as I did. She was going to get more of it, all right. Sans the part where I let my guard down.

I arrived at the house at around ten in the morning and immediately went to her room, but it was empty. I glanced at the garden outside her window. Empty, too. Going through every room in the house, I mentally checked all the boxes. Kitchen? No. Master bedroom? No. Piano room? No. I dialed Sterling's number, barking at her to come back home. She needed to help me look for my missing bride, though there weren't many places she could go.

I checked my phone again. Two messages from Smithy.

Smithy: Your wife asked to go back home.

Smithy: She's technically my boss. I have to take her. I'm sorry.

After summoning my housekeeper, I went upstairs, back to Francesca's room, tearing it apart. Now that she was gone, I needed to see for myself if she meant business or not. The closet was missing all her favorite items, and her toothbrush and photo albums and horse-riding gear were gone, too. The wooden box, which I'd destroyed yesterday, was nowhere to be found.

She wasn't going to come back anytime soon.

All the things she valued were missing.

She left just as she said she would. I hadn't given her enough credit. Figured she was going to brave the night and talk to me the next morning. It was, after all, understandable that I'd avenged her fierce kiss on Northwestern's lawn—followed by hours of her being MIA and in a hotel with Angelo—with the same token of humiliation. Of course, my wife was anything but obedient. Instead of snapping, she grew more of a backbone.

And, of course, she'd actually kissed Angelo. I hadn't even touched Karolina, save for ushering her into the ballroom on my arm.

I opened every drawer and emptied them onto the floor, looking for a hint to Francesca's long-term infidelity. Kristen claimed that this had been going on for a while, but I chose not to believe it. Thinking clearer now, the evidence was stacked in my wife's favor. She was a virgin when I'd met her. And as much as I adored her, she was—outside of the bedroom, at least—a bit of a prude. Not one to conduct illicit, long-term affairs. Francesca also pointed out that she'd broken things off with Angelo, and by the way her phone was Angelo-free for many, many weeks, I had no reason not to believe her.

This left me to consider that the kiss was a one-off. A moment of passion and weakness. If Francesca really was conducting an affair, she would not be cheating on me so openly. No. She would be more calculated than that.

When I was done emptying the drawers, I ripped off her linen and pillowcases. Something fell out of one of the pillows, rolling under the bed. I crouched down to the floor to retrieve it, examining it in my hand.

A pregnancy test.

A positive pregnancy test.

I plopped on the edge of the bed, clutching it in my fist. Francesca was pregnant. We'd only slept together without protection in Lake Michigan.

Francesca was pregnant with my baby.

Jesus Christ.

I heard the door pushing open downstairs, and Sterling humming to herself.

"Lovebirds? Are you around?" Her voice echoed in the vast foyer. I dropped my head, trying to keep my jaw from snapping out of my mouth, I clenched it so hard. Sterling appeared at the doorway to Francesca's room a couple minutes later, scrunching her nose and looking at the havoc I'd caused.

"It looks like this place has been raided by the FBI."

No, but close.

I lifted the positive pregnancy test in my hand, still sitting down and staring at the floor.

"Did you know about this?"

In my periphery, I saw her eyes widening, her throat bobbing with a swallow. She looked older than ever. Like the scene she'd walked into had aged her.

"I had a feeling, yes." She walked over to me, placing a hand on my shoulder and sitting down beside me. "Did you really have no idea? The girl developed a sweet tooth overnight, clung onto you every time you walked through the door, and has been frightened to go to the OB-GYN. She knows you don't want any children, doesn't she?"

I looked out the window, dragging my hand across my face. She did. She knew.

"Is that why she left?" Sterling gasped. "Please don't tell me that you kicked her out because you found out…"

"No." I cut into her words, standing up and pacing the room again. A room I was beginning to hate and love at the very same time. It still held her scent and personality, but too many bad things had happened between these walls.

"Francesca cheated on me."

"I don't believe it." Sterling tilted her chin high, locking her jaw to prevent it from quivering. "She's in love with you."

"She kissed Angelo." They probably did a lot more in the hotel room.

I felt like a teenager confiding in his mother for the first time about a crush. It was the first time I'd showed vulnerability since the age of thirteen. Even at my parents' funeral, I didn't shed a tear.

"You hurt her," Sterling whispered, standing up and walking over to me. She pressed her hand to my arm in a maternal gesture and squeezed. "You hurt her all the time, and she is highly emotional right now. Her hormones are running wild. You're unwilling to admit your feelings for her, not even allowing her to bring her clothes into your room, let alone tell her why she's here. Why you took her from her parents and ripped her out of her life."

"There's nothing to admit. I'm not in love with her."

"Really?" She folded her arms over her chest. "Can you live without her?"

"Yes."

"Then why didn't you all those years before she came along?" she wondered, a thin white eyebrow curving high on her forehead. "Why did you merely exist until she walked into this house?"

"I haven't changed." I shook my head, running my fingers through my hair. Figured. The minute I said anything remotely emotional, Sterling went full-blown *Dawson's Creek* on my ass.

"In that case, stay here, and give her the time she obviously needs. Do not try and chase her around."

"Is this one of those times you tell me not to do something just to see me do it and prove to me that I care?" I barely stopped myself from rolling my eyes.

She shrugged.

"Yes."

"Then prepare to be underwhelmed, Sterling. If Francesca is carrying my child, I will be there for both of them, but I will not beg for forgiveness."

"Good." Sterling patted my arm. "Because frankly, I'm not sure she'll give it to you."

Francesca

Three days had passed since I packed my bags and left.

I didn't leave my room at my parents' house, not even to go to school, dreading the moment I'd come face to face with Angelo, not to mention my father.

When Angelo and I went to a hotel together, it was mainly to do what we needed to do all those months ago and never had the chance—talked about what we were and weren't.

He tried to persuade me to take off and leave.

"We could raise the baby together. I've got savings."

"Angelo, I'm not going to mess up your life so you can save mine."

"You're not messing up anything. We will have children of our own. We'll create a life for ourselves."

"If I run away with you, both Wolfe and The Outfit will look for us. They will find us. And while Wolfe might be happy to divorce and discard me, my father would never let us live it down."

"I can get us fake passports."

"Angelo, I want to stay."

And it was true. I needed to stay here, despite everything, and perhaps even *because* of everything. My marriage was a sham, my father had disowned me, and my mother didn't even have a say about what china we'd dine with, let alone the ability to help me.

Angelo had called several times and even showed up at my door once to see how I was doing, but Clara shooed him away. My father took two business trips and stayed at Mama's Pizza for the majority of my visit so far, which surprised no one at all.

Mama and Clara were my near-constant companions. They fed and bathed me and told me that my husband would come to his senses and seek me out.

They said that the minute he learned I was pregnant, he would drop everything and beg for my forgiveness. But I knew Wolfe did not want to become a father. And coming forward and telling him about the pregnancy would mean crawling back to him. I had allowed him to stomp on my pride one too many times.

This time, he would have to come to me.

Not to get a kick out of it—but because I genuinely needed to know that he cared.

Three days after I left Wolfe's mansion, Clara opened the door to my room and announced, "You have a visitor, little one."

I jumped out of bed, feeling woozy, hopeful, and excited all at the same time. So he was here, after all. And he wanted to talk. That was a good sign, right? Unless he wanted to serve me with divorce papers. But, knowing Wolfe, he was the type to send someone else over to hand them to me. Once he truly cut you out of his life, he wouldn't bother making the trip. Clara saw the light flicking on behind my eyes as I rushed toward the vanity mirror, slapping my cheeks to make myself look livelier and flushed, then applying a generous layer of lip gloss. She lowered her head, fiddling with her thumbs.

"It's Ms. Sterling."

"Oh." I blinked, tossing the lip gloss aside and wiping my hands over my thighs. "How nice of her to stop by. Thank you, Clara."

In the salon, Clara served us tea and pandoro. Ms. Sterling sat with her back straight, her pinky lifted in the air over her tea cup, and her lips pursed with barely restrained fury. I stared into my cup of tea, wishing she'd both talk and never open her mouth at the same time. What if she came to tell me Wolfe and I were over? She certainly didn't look pleased.

"Why are you looking at me like that?" I finally asked her when it became apparent that we could sit like this for long, soundless minutes.

"Because you're a fool, and he is a complete idiot. Together, you make the perfect couple. Which begs the question—why are you here and he is there?" She slammed her tea cup on the table, causing the hot liquid to swoosh from side to side.

"Well, the obvious answer is because he hates me." I picked invisible lint from my pajama pants. "And the secondary one is because he married me so he could ruin my father and everything he cares about."

"I can't sit and listen to this nonsense any longer. How could you be so dense?" She threw her arms in the air.

"How do you mean?"

"Wolfe never entertained himself with the idea of marriage and a wife. Not until he saw you for the first time. You were never in his plan. He never spoke of you. Barely even knew about your existence until he saw you. Which leads me to believe that his spontaneous decision had less to do about your father and more to do with the fact that he simply wanted you for himself and knew that courting you was out of the question. Since he had leverage on your father, he thought it would be a win-win scenario. But it wasn't." She shook her head. "You made things harder for him. Messier. He could have had your father locked in prison for life if it wasn't for you. The minute you stepped into the picture—he wanted something of your father's, and they both had things to bargain. You didn't help Wolfe's plan. You sabotaged it."

"Wolfe is doing the best he can to ruin my father's business."

"But he is still out and about, is he not? Your father tried to *assassinate* him, and Wolfe still held his wedding in this house. The boy has had it bad for you from the moment he saw your face."

I didn't know whether I should laugh or cry. I'd seen Ms. Sterling going to extreme measures to try and patch things up between Wolfe and me, but this was stretching it, even by her standards.

"What kind of leverage does he have on my father?" I changed the subject before my eyes decided to spontaneously leak again.

Ms. Sterling raised her tea cup to her mouth, glancing at me from behind the rim.

I didn't think she'd actually answer, much less that she would know what was going on, but she surprised me on both matters.

"Your father is paying off the governor, Preston Bishop, and Felix White, the man in charge of Chicago's Police Department, a handsome monthly fee in exchange for their silence and full cooperation. Wolfe's investigators found out about this not too many months ago. Since Senator Keaton was always in the habit of playing with his food, he decided to torture your father a little before airing his dirty laundry. Have you ever wondered why he never hit a home run?"

I munched on my lower lip. My father had murdered Wolfe's brother and then his adoptive parents. He then tried to assassinate him right after burning down an entire pub just to get rid of Wolfe's briefcase.

Yet Wolfe never striked back.

And it wasn't as if he was incapable of ruining my father.

"I'm guessing the answer is me," I said. She was relentless.

Ms. Sterling smiled, leaning forward. I thought she was

going to pat my thigh as she often did, but no. She clutched onto my cheek, forcing me to look into her eyes.

"You took a hammer and broke down his walls, brick by brick. I watched as they collapsed, how he scrambled to try and rebuild them every time he left your room. Your love story was no fairy tale. More like a witch tale. Wicked and real and painful. I swooned when he began to seek you out in the house. When I noticed he was spending less time in his office and more time in the garden. I was thrilled when he gave you gifts, took you places, and showed you off, barely able to contain his joy every time you entered his vicinity. And I must admit, I was relieved to see him breaking down in your room, devastated and guilt-stricken, when he found your pregnancy test in your pillowcase."

My head reared back, and I shot her a helpless glance.

"How are you feeling, sweetheart?" Her eyes crinkled with naked joy.

He knew. They both knew. Yet Wolfe still hadn't come for me. Contradicting, fierce emotions of excitement, dread, and fear stunned me into silence.

"Francesca?" Ms. Sterling probed, nudging my hand. I ducked my head down, not daring to see what was on her face.

"It doesn't matter. Too many things have happened. I cheated on him, and he cheated on me."

"Love is stronger than hate."

"How can he love me after all the bad blood between our families?" My head shot up, tears clinging to my lower lashes. "He can't."

"He can," Ms. Sterling insisted. "Forgiving is one of his more beautiful virtues."

"Right." I snorted out a laugh. "Tell that to my father."

"Your father never asked for forgiveness. But I did. And Wolfe? He forgave me."

She put her tea down and straightened her spine, delivering the information with a schooled chin and a steady voice.

"I'm Wolfe Keaton's biological mother. A recovering alcoholic who was too busy drinking herself to death to fix my son dinner on the night he watched his brother, Romeo, get shot to death by your father. After that happened, the Keatons took him. I couldn't fight the system, and Romeo's death shook me out of my addiction. I went to rehab, and after I completed my time in the facility, I trickled back into Wolfe's life—his real name is Fabio, by the way. Fabio Nucci." She smiled, looking down. "At first, he wanted nothing to do with me. He was blind with anger about my alcoholism, getting thrown into the system, and about how I couldn't bring myself to fix him dinner so he dragged his brother to Mama's Pizza. But as time passed, he allowed me back into his life. His adoptive parents hired me as his live-in nanny even though he was a pre-teen. They just wanted us to be together. After they were killed in that explosion…" She sucked in a breath. Tears glittered in her eyes when she spoke of her late employers. "It was two years after I completed my work at the Keatons. When Wolfe turned eighteen. I was working at Sam's Club when he rehired me to run his mansion. He is taking care of me more than I'm taking care of him after I betrayed him in the worst possible way. I wasn't able to protect him and his brother from the cruel neighborhood they grew up in."

I sat back, digesting.

Ms. Sterling was Wolfe's mother. *Biological* mother.

That was why she loved him so dearly.

That was why she begged me to be patient with him.

That was why she drove us into each other's arms. She wanted her son to have the happy ending his brother never got.

"His brother was married." I sucked in a breath, collecting all the pieces, fitting them into the screwed-up puzzle my father had created. "He had a wife."

"Yes. Lori. They were having fertility issues." Ms. Sterling nodded. "Went through several IVF treatments. Then she finally got pregnant. She lost the baby when she was six months in, the day after they delivered the news that her husband had died."

That was why Wolfe didn't want any children.

It was also why he knew so much about ovulation and when to have sex. He didn't want the heartache, though heartache was all he knew. He'd lost the people he cared about the most, one by one, and all by the same man. It felt like someone ripped my chest open with a knife and watched as my organs poured out of me.

I plastered a hand over my mouth, willing my pulse to slow down. It was neither good for me nor for the baby. But the truth was scandalizing and too harsh to digest. That was why Wolfe didn't want me to know—he knew I'd hate myself for the rest of my life for what my father did. Hell, I wanted to throw up right now.

"Thank you for sharing this with me," I said.

Ms. Sterling nodded. "Give him a chance. He is far from perfect. But who is?"

"Ms. Sterling…" I hesitated, glancing around us. "I'm devastated over your revelations, but I don't think Wolfe wants a second chance. He knows that I'm here and that I'm pregnant, and he still hasn't showed up. He hasn't even called."

Every time I thought about this fact, I wanted to crawl into a ball and die.

By the way Ms. Sterling winced, I knew that it didn't look good for me. I escorted her back to her car. We hugged for long minutes.

"Always remember, Francesca—you're worth more than the sums of your mistakes."

As she drove away, I realized she was right. I didn't need Wolfe to save me, or for Angelo to come to my rescue, or even for my mother to grow a backbone or my father to start acting like he had one.

The only person I needed was me.

CHAPTER EIGHTEEN

Wolfe

THE NEXT FEW DAYS WERE PURE, UNADULTERATED TORTURE. The stuff we should bottle up, write down, and use on convicted child molesters.

Three days in, I caved and picked up the phone to call Arthur. Now *he* was playing hard to get. The tables had turned. The only person I wanted to speak to—my wife—was tucked in Arthur's kingdom, and the place was gated and guarded more heavily than the Buckingham Palace.

I arrived at my wife's parents' house every single day, at six o'clock sharp, before boarding my flight, then again at eight o'clock at night, to try and talk to her.

I was always stopped at the gate by one of Rossi's muscle, and they were beefier and stupider than his usual variety of Made Men, and showed no signs of stopping, even when my own bodyguards flexed their biceps.

Calling, or texting her was ball-less and inappropriate altogether. Especially since Sterling admitted to spilling the beans about all the things that happened between our families. Considering Francesca was under the impression that my original plan consisted of tossing her in a dark tower and killing her father slowly by stripping him and his wife of everything they owned, I knew I needed a little more than a fucking "Sorry" GIF. The conversation was too important not to be conducted face to face. There was much I needed to tell her. Much I'd found out in the days since she departed.

I was in love with her.

I was dreadfully in love with her.

Ruthlessly, tragically mad about the teenager with big blue eyes who talked to her vegetables.

I needed to tell her that I wanted this baby no less than she did. Not because I wanted children, but because I wanted everything she had to offer. And the things she didn't offer—I wanted them, too. Not to own necessarily, but to simply admire.

The realization that I was in love didn't happen in one glorious, Hallmark-worthy moment. It spread across the week we spent apart. With every failed attempt to reach out to her, I realized how important it was for me to see her.

Each time I got turned down, I looked up at the window of her room, willing her to materialize behind the white-laced curtain. She never did.

And that was why I avoided connections, in general. That whole climbing-the-walls thing? It wasn't for me. But climbing, I did. Kicking things. Breaking things. Rehearsing words and speeches I would say. Avoiding suits who called and called, telling me that I needed to make a statement about my current family situation.

It was my issue. My life. My wife.

No one else mattered.

Not even my country.

A week into the delight called heartbreak, I decided to bend the rules and rush fate. She was going to hate me for it—but frankly, she had enough reason to want to spit in my face even before my next stunt.

On the seventh day of separation, I dragged Felix White in

all his sweaty, shiny-faced glory to accompany me to Arthur's house, carrying an urgent search warrant.

The thing missing? *My fucking wife.*

White had no real grounds to issue a warrant, other than he didn't want me to dish out the dirt on him. Forever the double agent, he texted Arthur hours before, so the mobster actually dragged himself back home to be there when I came over.

Anyway, that was the story of how I came knocking on Francesca's door with the chief of CPD, a warrant, and two cops.

And they said romance was dead.

When Rossi opened the door, his forehead was so creased, he looked like a bulldog. He slid his head between the cracked doors and tapered his eyes into slits.

"Senator, to what do I owe the pleasure?" He completely disregarded White, knowing damn well why the letter compromised him.

"Now's not the time to play games." I smiled coolly. "Unless you really want to lose. Let me in or send her out. Either way, I'm seeing her tonight."

"I don't think so. Not after you paraded that Russian whore in front of the entire city, leaving your pregnant wife at home."

"I didn't know." Why I was explaining myself to him was beyond me. If he was the moral police, Michael Moore was a goddamn health guru.

"At any rate, I've been trying to reach her for seven days, and I have it on good authority that you want to open up before I do something you'll regret."

"You will never do it. Not with your pregnant wife in the picture." Arthur had the audacity to flash me a taunting grin.

White coughed from beside me.

"Mr. Rossi, if you don't let us in, I'll have to arrest you. I have a court order to search your house."

It was apparent that one person on the threshold believed I'd throw my father-in-law to the wolves.

Slowly, Arthur pushed the door open and allowed me to walk in. White remained behind me, shifting his weight from foot to foot like a teenager wondering how to ask a girl for a prom date. The man possessed the charisma of a can of soda.

"S-should I wait here?" White stuttered. I waved him off.

"Go back to pretending you're good at what you're doing."

"You sure?" He wiped the sweat off his forehead, the blue vein in his neck still pulsing.

"You're wasting my precious time and what's leftovers of my patience. Go."

Arthur led me to his office, giving me his back. Last time I'd been in his office, I demanded his daughter's hand. As I walked up the staircase, the memories flooded in. It was on the landing where we shared one of our earlier banters. At the top of the stairs, I recalled how I clasped her delicate wrist in my hand and tugged her down forcefully after I thought she'd cheated on me.

Fucking idiot. Going around labelling White and Bishop as stupid when you've proven to be a clown more than one time in the span of your short marriage.

I knew Francesca was somewhere in the house, and I longed to see her pink smile and hear her throaty laughter that did not match the softness of her being.

"Give me one good reason why we're heading into your office and not into my wife's old room," I said when my mouth cleared from the fog of everything my wife.

"Despite our differences, my daughter cares very much for my approval, and my giving it to you would help your chances when you talk to her. Now, Senator Keaton, we both know it's long overdue that we settle the score." He stopped by the door to his office and motioned for me to walk in. Two of his muscle guys stood on each side of the door.

"Get rid of them," I said, still staring at him. He didn't break our gaze as he snapped his fingers, making both of them descend the stairs silently.

We got into his office, and he closed the door halfway, obviously not trusting me not to throttle him with my bare hands. I understood him perfectly. Even I had difficulty predicting how I'd react, depending on the outcome of this visit.

He leaned against his desk while I took a seat on the couch in front of him, spreading my arms over the headrest and making myself comfortable. I knew two things with certainty:

1. Today was the day my love for my wife was going to be tested.
2. I was going to pass with flying fucking colors.

Francesca

Like a moth to a flame, my feet dragged me out of my room and to the hallway the minute I heard my husband's gruff tenor. His voice was a poem, and I drank every word as if my life depended on it.

I caught his back, his broad shoulders and tailored suit as he glided through the corridor, ushered by my father into his study. I counted one, two, three, five, eight...*ten* seconds before I tiptoed my way to the study. Weeks of watching how Ms. Sterling eavesdropped had taught me some invaluable tricks. My barefooted figure was pressed against the wall, and I took shallow, measured breaths.

My father lit a cigar. The aroma of burnt leaves and tobacco hit my nostrils, and nausea washed over my gut. God, I felt sick every time someone breathed in my direction. I peeked into the room, fighting the bile bubbling in my throat. My father leaned against his desk, my husband on the red velvet settee in front of him, looking relaxed and nonchalant as ever.

My husband, metal and steel.

Formidable and untouchable.

With a stone-carved heart I'd do anything to soften.

"I suppose you think that you can walk into her room and claim her back. Hang White and Bishop over my head again as leverage," my father said, puffing on his cigar, his legs crossed at the ankles. He had yet to acknowledge my existence since I'd moved back into the house, but he didn't let that deter him from blackmailing my husband. With every fiber of my body, I wanted to burst through the door and set the record straight. But I was too humiliated and hurt to risk another rejection. Wolfe might've come here to let me go, and I was done begging.

"How is she doing?" Wolfe ignored his question.

"She doesn't want to see you," my father replied curtly, sending another waft of smoke into the air and ignoring the question at hand.

"Have you taken her to the doctor?"

"She hasn't left the house."

"What the hell are you waiting for?" Wolfe spat.

"As far as I can remember, Francesca was old enough to get pregnant. She is therefore old enough to book an appointment with an OB-GYN. Not to mention, if anyone should help her, it should be the man responsible for her dire situation."

Dire situation? My nostrils flared, hot air coming down from them like fire.

It was the moment in which it dawned on me that my father was completely irredeemable. He didn't care for me or the baby. The only thing he cared about—ever—was The Outfit. He loved and adored me when I was his puppet. And at the first sign of defiance, he discarded me and shook off any responsibility toward me. He sold me. Then lost his interest in me when he could no longer marry me off to another strong Italian family. Wolfe, however, stuck around through thick and thin. Even when we antagonized each other. Even when he thought I'd slept with Angelo and saw me kissing him, and when I defied him again and again and again. The word divorce never left his mouth. Failure wasn't an option.

He showed me more loyalty than my father did.

"Good point." Wolfe stood up. "I'll take her to the doctor right away."

"You will do no such thing. In fact, you will not be seeing her tonight, at all," my father retorted.

Wolfe strolled toward him unflappably, stopping a few feet from my father and towering over his head. "Is that her request or yours?"

"Her *demand*. Why do you think you haven't heard from her yet?" My father put his cigar in an ashtray, sending a plume of smoke in Wolfe's face as he spoke. "She requested I make sure that you grovel properly."

"Let me guess—you have plenty of ideas."

"I do." My father unknotted his ankles, pushing off the desk so he was nose to nose with Wolfe. I wished I could see my husband's face at that moment. My father was lying to him, and he was too smart not to see that. Then again, love was like a drug. You didn't think clearly under the influence.

"I'll let you see Francesca if you comply."

"And if I don't?"

"White can personally come and arrest me today, and you can burst through Francesca's bedroom door armed with police force. I'm sure she'd appreciate it. Especially in her current state."

Wolfe was silent for a moment.

"Do you realize she misses you?" he asked my father.

My heart clenched painfully. God, Wolfe.

"Do *you* realize that I'm a businessman?" my father retorted. "She's a damaged asset. We all have a price tag, Fabio Nucci." He laughed in my husband's face. "I was born on the streets and left at the steps of a church door to almost die. My mother was a prostitute, and my father? Who knows who he was. Everything I have, every square foot in this house, every piece of furniture, every fucking pen, I've worked for. Francesca had one job—to be obedient. And she failed."

"Because I set her up for failure." Wolfe raised his voice, spitting in my father's face.

"That may be, but her only value to me right now is to be a pawn against you. You see, I've made the mistake of under-valuing a person once in my life. When I decided to foolishly let you live."

Something dropped between them, and it thudded against the silence of the room. Jesus. He actually said it. My father regretted not killing my husband.

"Why didn't you?" Wolfe seethed. "Why did you let me live?"

"You were frightened, Nucci, but you were also strong. You didn't cry. You didn't piss your pants. You even tried to snatch one of my men's weapons. You reminded me of my young self when I ran on the streets barefoot, stealing food, pickpocketing, and working my way up. Hustling to the core and making ties with The Outfit. I knew you had a chance to survive this part of the neighborhood. More than that—I knew you were a savage. Wolfe Keaton plays nice with the law, but let's admit it—Fabio Nucci is inside you, and he is out for blood."

"I will never be your ally."

"Good. You make a fascinating enemy."

"Whatever you need me to do, get it over with," Wolfe barked.

My father leaned back, clucking his tongue and tapping a fist over his lip.

"If you truly love my daughter, Senator Keaton, if you sincerely care for her, you will strip from the one thing you never part ways with—your pride."

"What are you asking?" I could practically envision Wolfe's jaw as it locked in anger.

"Beg for her, son. *Kneel.*" Papa lifted his chin, somehow

looking down at Wolfe despite my husband being several inches taller. "Beg like you made me beg for her when you took her from me."

My dad begged for me?

"I do not beg," Wolfe said, and I knew he meant it. Even my father knew better than to ask for something like this. He set Wolfe up for failure and doomed my marriage by asking that. Wolfe never bowed to anyone, much less my own father. I was going to burst in the door and set the record straight when I heard Papa speak again.

"Then you don't love my daughter, Senator Keaton. You merely want your possession back. Because as far as I recall, she did a lot of begging and groveling when you took her from this house as your prisoner."

I bit down on my lip, resting my forehead against the door-frame. It hurt me to see Wolfe hurting, but it pained me even more that I understood why he couldn't do it. Why he couldn't beg the man who had ruined his life. It wasn't just about his pride and dignity. It was also about his morals and everything he stood for. About his family.

My father had stripped him from his pride once in front of his brother. He was not going to do it again.

"You're not doing this because of her; you're doing this because of *you*," Wolfe accused, point-blank. My dad braced the edges of his desk behind him as he stared at the ceiling, contemplating this.

"Why I'm doing this shouldn't matter to you. If you want her, you will stop at nothing, much less the floor."

Tears prickled my eyes once again. My father was humiliating him, and as much as I wanted to step inside and order them both to stop this, I couldn't. Because my father wasn't wrong about one thing—Wolfe always held the power in my relationship with him, and if he couldn't let go, even once, was this really a marriage, or was it a captive and master, glorified under the flattering light of lust?

Slowly, I watched to my utter shock as Wolfe began to lower himself down to his knees. I choked on my breath, unable to tear my eyes from the scene unfolding in front of me. My husband, the proud, take-no-bullshit, arrogant bastard was kneeling, begging for me. What's more, he didn't look an inch less superior than he did walking into this room. He tilted his face up, allowing me an angle from which I could see him clearly. He was the picture of conceited, his regal features sharp and open. His eyes were determined, his eyebrows arched in mockery, and his entire composure was unimpeachable. Based on their faces alone, you couldn't tell which one of them was bowing down to the other.

"Arthur," his voice boomed in the room, "I beg you, please let me talk to your daughter. My wife is, and always will be, the most important thing in my life."

My heart burst in my chest at his words, and I quivered, feeling the heat of a thousand suns warming me from the inside.

"You will never make her happy for as long as you hang *my* sins over *her* head," my father warned. My husband was still on his knees, and I couldn't stop the tears anymore. They rushed down in the form of a sob. I slapped a hand over my mouth, afraid they'd hear me.

Wolfe smirked, his eyes flashing with determination.

"I do not intend to do that anymore, Arthur."

"Does that mean you will stop messing with my business?"

"That means I will make an effort to play nice for *her*."

"What about White and Bishop?" my father asked.

"I'll do whatever I see fit with them."

"I can take Francesca awa—"

"No, you can't," Wolfe interfered, cutting him sharply. "The only person who is in a position to take Francesca away from me is Francesca herself. It's her choice who she wants to be with— not mine. Definitely not yours. You've killed my brother, then my parents. My wife is where I draw the line. You cannot take her. I will unleash hell if you do."

I closed my eyes, feeling my body swaying from side to side. I hadn't eaten all day, and the scent of the cigar made me want to throw up.

"Go to her," my father said brokenly.

My husband got up on his feet.

Then, for the second time in my life, I swooned.

CHAPTER NINETEEN

Francesca

I WOKE UP COCOONED IN MY HUSBAND'S ARMS.

He sat on the king-sized bed, my head resting on him in the exact same position we were curled in when we were in the barn, when he showed me Artemis. His spicy cologne and distinctive male scent engulfed me in comfort, and I pretended to be asleep a little longer, prolonging the uncomfortable conversation that waited at the end of my slumber.

He dragged the tip of his fingers over my back through my shirt, pressing a kiss to my hairline. I visited the memory of him kneeling in front of my father, telling him that I was the most important thing to him. Warm honey coated my heart.

"I know you're awake," I heard my husband murmur to my temple. I groaned, shifting in his arms. The thought that these arms were wrapped around Karolina Ivanova a week ago made me want to throw up all over again. I propped myself on my forearms, shooting him a tired look.

"You're pregnant." He looked down at my stomach as if he was expecting to see a bump. Seeing his face again was the greatest gift I'd ever been given. It was absurd to think I dreaded said face the morning after the masquerade. Shortly after, he became my favorite thing about myself. I became his reminder that there was something more than vengeance and justice in this world. We were co-dependent, and we had to co-exist. One without the other was a dormant being.

To be alive and not really living was a terrible curse.

"It's yours." I put my hand on his for emphasis.

"I know." He ran the tip of his nose along mine, gathering me in his arms as though I was something great and precious and hugging me close.

"Does that make you unhappy?" I sniffed.

"Becoming a father? I always thought it would. I was sure life ended when parenthood began. But that was before I found someone worthy to start a family with. I'm still not entirely sure about my abilities when it comes to parenthood. Luckily, I know my wife will be the best mother this planet has to offer."

Silently, my eyes raked the room. There was so much I wanted to say, but I knew that it could break something that was not yet even glued.

"What about you, Nem? Are you happy being pregnant?"

I straightened, swallowing my fear and letting the words rip from my throat before I lost my courage.

"I'm…unsure. We're constantly fighting. We set a world record in miscommunications. And you just slept with someone else a week ago to get back at me—and not for the first time. I kissed Angelo last week, furious with the truth about you and my father, but I didn't take it any further. We're volatile and unfaithful. We don't live in the same wing…"

"We will," he cut me off. "If that's what you want."

"We need some time to think."

I needed some time apart from him. Not because I didn't love him, but because I loved him too much to make a conscious, healthy decision for our baby.

"There's nothing to think about. I didn't sleep with Karolina. I couldn't do it. I wanted to—God, Nemesis, I wanted to fuck you out of my life for good—but there could never be anyone else. It is you that I love. It is you whom I want. It is you whom makes living a spectacular thing I want to experience, rather than participate in reluctantly, every day."

I felt the tears sliding down my cheeks, fat and salty. We were so good at hurting each other. This had to stop.

"I kissed another," I whispered. "I cheated on you."

"I forgive you." He cupped my cheeks in his big hands. "Forgive yourself, and let's move on. Come back home, Nem."

"Nothing happened in that hotel room."

"I don't give a *fuck* what happened between then and there. I believe you, but it makes no difference. I want to start this over. The right way."

"I need time." The words broke me. Maybe because they were brutally honest.

I needed time to digest everything that was happening. To make sure this was not just another grand gesture he was going to offer and forget about the next morning. We fell in love fast and slow. Hard and soft. With everything we had in us, yet we both refused to give anything away. We didn't have time to digest what was happening. We clashed into each other's lives with our walls still up. We needed to start over. We needed to flirt. We needed to distribute the power between us, this time more equally. We needed to learn to fight without wounding each other. Without running into other people's arms. Without dragging and tossing each other into rooms like wild beasts.

"It should be my choice to be with you. You understand that, right?"

Wolfe nodded, standing up before he changed his mind. I could tell it took a tremendous effort for him not to demand from me what he used to think he deserved. He made his way to the door, and I wanted to take the words back and go with him. But I couldn't. I had to be better for the person inside me.

A person I was going to be able to save, like my mother couldn't.

Wolfe stopped at the threshold, his back still to me.

"Can I call you?"

"Yes." I let out a breath. "Can I text you?"

"You may. Can I book you an appointment with an OB-GYN?"

"Yes." I laughed through the tears, wiping them quickly. He still didn't turn around to look at me. Wolfe Keaton wasn't much of a negotiator, but for me—he broke his rules.

"May I join you?" His voice was grave.

"You better."

His shoulders quaked in a soft chuckle, and he finally turned around to face me.

"Go on a date with me, Mrs. Keaton? Not a gala. Not a charity event. Not an official outing. A date."

God.

Oh, yes.

"I would love that very much."

"Good," he said, looking down and chuckling to himself. I had to remind myself that this was the same cruel man from the masquerade. The one I swore to hate for the rest of my life. He looked up, his face still tilted down, with a shy yet devastated gaze.

"Will I get lucky on that date?"

I threw myself on my pillow, covering my face with my arm, the sound of my laughter drowning the *click* of the door as it closed.

Two days later, we paid our first visit to my new OB-GYN. Barbara was in her fifties with cropped blond hair, kind eyes, and thick glasses. She did an ultrasound and showed us the peanut swimming in my womb. Its little pulse pitter-pattered like tiny bare feet down the stairs on Christmas morning.

Wolfe held my hand and stared at the screen as though we had just discovered a new planet.

We went to lunch after that. Our first public unofficial outing as a couple. He invited me over to our house. I politely declined, explaining I made plans with Sher and Tricia from my study group. I tried to bite down my smile when I broke the news to him. I hadn't had friends my age ever since I moved back from Switzerland.

"Nemesis." He arched an eyebrow when he drove me back to my house. "Next thing I know, you'll be attending frat parties."

"Don't hold your breath." Parties weren't my scene. Besides, the ones I was used to were fancy and demanded a dress code my pregnant self wasn't eager to follow. Even in my first trimester, I opted for loose, comfortable attire.

"I think everyone needs to go to at least one frat party to see what all the fuss is about."

"Would it bother you?" I asked. I wanted to put across that he didn't have this kind of power over me anymore.

"Not at all. Unless Angelo is your date."

That was a fair request, which I could no longer deny it. I took out my phone from my bag and tossed it into his hands.

"Check this."

"What am I checking, exactly?"

"I deleted his number."

He stopped the car in front of my house and killed the engine. He handed me back my phone. "I'll take your word for it. What changed your mind?"

I rolled my eyes. "I'm in love with this guy, and he has this idea in his head that I will run away with my childhood sweetheart."

Wolfe shot me a dirty look. "He is tragically in love with

you, too, and I don't blame him for being adamant about keeping you."

There were many more dates between Wolfe and me after that day.

We went to the movies and to restaurants and even to hotel bars, in which we both didn't drink—me because of my age and pregnancy, him out of solidarity.

We shared a bowl of french fries and played pool and argued about books. I found out that my husband was a Stephen King fanatic. I was more of a Nora Roberts fan myself. We stopped at a bookstore and purchased each other books to read. We laughed when Wolfe told me he nearly kicked the Hatch's out of our house that time they visited us because Bryan had an erection as impressive as a baseball bat while I played the piano.

Andrea, my cousin, called. She said that she'd been thinking, and she reached the conclusion she could no longer not speak to me just because my father didn't approve of the husband he himself chose for me. She asked for my forgiveness.

"I wasn't being a good Christian about it, doll." She snapped her gum in my ear. "Come to think about it, I wasn't even a good manicurist about it. I bet you bit into those nails like nobody's business without me reminding you to stop chewing on them."

I told her the truth—forgiveness cost me nothing, and more than that, it enriched my soul. We met for a cappuccino the following day, and I bombarded her with all the twenty-first century questions that sat on my tongue.

Some days later, Wolfe announced that we were taking a weekend-long trip to visit Artemis. I wasn't in a condition to ride her, but I enjoyed taking care of her and making sure she was doing okay.

A month ticked by. A month in which my husband called every morning to wake me up and every night to tell me good night. A month in which we didn't fight, or cuss, or slam doors. A month in which he did not withhold any information from me, and I did not refuse his every request, simply because he'd made it. I let the EPAs escort me to school, didn't break protocol, and still managed to make a handful of friends. Wolfe worked hard but always made sure to put me first.

I still wasn't wearing my engagement and wedding rings—I left them at his house the night he went to the black-tie gala with Karolina Ivanova. But I never felt as if I belonged to someone else in my entire life more than now, ring or not.

We fell back in lust just as you do into a rabbit hole—fast and frantic. Wolfe, I found out, was quite fond of having sex in unusual places. We had sex in his office and in a restroom at a wedding, on the bed in my old room when my parents weren't home and against his bedroom window, watching over the pristine street.

He fingered me under the table during an official black-tie dinner and thrust himself into me without warning when I bent down after a shower to open the bottom drawer in the bathroom and retrieve my blow dryer.

I loved every second of us in bed because no one ever needed to wonder when it was time to retreat back to their spot, their wing, or their house. We always fell asleep together and woke up together, insulated in this new, exciting thing called us.

The morning I woke up with a small, visible bump in my lower belly—it felt hard and tough and exciting—my mother walked into my room and sat down on the edge of my bed.

"I'm divorcing your father."

I had a thousand things I wanted to tell her. From *thank God* to *what took you so long?* but I settled for a simple nod, squeezing her hand in mine to give her strength. I couldn't be more proud of her if I tried. She had a lot to lose. But she was willing to lose it, anyway, if it meant winning back her freedom and voice.

"I think I deserve more. I think I deserved more all along, I just didn't know that it could be possible. I know that now, through you, Vita Mia. Your happy ending inspired mine." She wiped away a tear, forcing a smile on her face.

"My story hasn't ended just yet." I laughed.

"Not yet," she agreed with a wink, "but I see where the plot is going."

"Mama." I clutched her palm, tears brewing in my eyes. "The best part of your story is yet to be written. You're doing the right thing."

Clara and I helped Mama pack her bags. Clara suggested she should book a hotel. I shook my head. It was time for me to go back to where I belonged. And it was time for Wolfe to play nice with both of our mothers—his and mine. I picked up the phone and called my husband. He answered on the first ring.

"I'm ready to come home."

"Thank *fuck*," he breathed. "What took you so long?"

"I needed to see that you meant it. That my freedom was really mine."

"It is yours," he said gravely. "It has always been yours."

"Can Mama and Clara come stay with us for a while?"

"You can bring an entire hostile army into the house and I'd still welcome them with open arms."

That evening, Wolfe threw all our suitcases into the back of his car with Smithy's help. My father stood at the doorway and watched us with a glass of something strong. He did not say one thing. It didn't matter that Wolfe bowed down to him for ten seconds weeks ago. Senator Keaton was still the person who had won everything in the grand scheme of things.

My father had lost, and the game was over.

Once we got to the house, Ms. Sterling (I insisted on calling her Patricia now that I knew she was my mother-in-law), led my mother and Clara to the east wing to get settled. Wolfe and I climbed up the stairs behind them. When we made it to the second floor, I turned toward my room.

"Is this real?" I asked him.

"It is real."

For the first time, it felt that way, too.

We walked hand in hand to the west wing. We passed by his bedroom, entering the guestroom next to it, where I'd slept the night we entertained the Hatch's. My breath fluttered behind my ribcage when I realized what I was looking at when he opened the door.

A nursery. All white and crème and soft yellows. Bright and big and fully furnished. I cupped my mouth to stop myself from bawling. His acceptance of this baby somehow tore me apart. It was much more than his acceptance of his child. It was his acceptance of *me*.

"Everything is changeable," he said. "Well, other than the fact that we're having a baby."

"It's perfect," I breathed. "Thank you."

"You were right. You're my wife. We'll sleep together. We'll live together." There was a dramatic pause. "We'll even share a walk-in closet. I used some of the free space you so charitably made for me to accommodate your garments."

I laughed through my tears. This. Right here. This was everything. Beyond my wildest dreams. A man who loved me without asking for anything back. A man who suffered quietly as I was in love with another man and creeped on me, feeling by feeling, second by second, day by day. He was patient and determined. Callous and overbearing. He watched me kiss and grind Angelo all with his ring on my finger. He went down on his knees to beg the man who'd killed his family to bring me back to him. He did not think he could be a good father, but I knew—I wholeheartedly knew—that he would be the greatest dad in the entire world.

I rose on my toes, pressing a kiss to my husband's delicious mouth.

He tugged at my long hair.

"Only you," he said.

"Only you," I replied.

Senator Wolfe Keaton bent down on one knee and produced the engagement ring I'd left on my pillow weeks ago.

"Be my wife, Nemesis. But know one thing—if you ever wish to leave, I will not clip your wings."

It was the easiest answer to the toughest question I'd ever been asked. I jerked my husband up by the collar, knowing damn well how much he hated the position in which he was lowered on the ground.

"My wings are not meant to fly," I whispered. "They're meant to shield our family."

EPILOGUE

Francesca

Four Years After.

"I NOW BAPTIZE YOU IN THE NAME OF THE FATHER, AND of the Son, and of the Holy Spirit for the forgiveness of your sins and the gifts of the Holy Spirits."

Our second child, Joshua Romeo Keaton, was baptized in St. Raphael's church in Little Italy in front of our friends and family just days after I received my undergraduate degree in law. I held Josh when the priest trickled holy water on his forehead, looking to my left at my husband, who cradled our very sleepy three-year-old daughter, Emmaline.

As I scanned the long wooden pews to look for the people who made my heart sing, I realized how incredibly blessed I was. I found my mother and her new beau, Charles 'Charlie' Stephens, whom she'd been dating for the past six months. He held her hand in his and whispered softly in her ear. She pointed at sleepy Joshua in my arms, and they shared a chuckle. Next to them, Clara and Patricia (or Sterling, as my husband still insisted on calling her) were shedding happy tears, dabbing their faces with tissue. Andrea sat there with her new boyfriend—a Made

Man named Mateo and I knew, by the way they held hands, that this was the one guy she would let kiss her—next to some of my school friends and the new governor, Austin Berger. Missing in action, and not by accident, were the people who had loaded obstacles on Wolfe's and my happily ever after. The people who pushed us together yet tore us apart each in their own way.

My father was in prison, serving a twenty-five-year sentence for attempted murder. Shortly after Mama came to live with us, he tried to take her life. He went mad after he realized her filing for divorce wasn't just a phase. Naturally, he blamed me and Wolfe for her decision to better her life and leave her abusive husband, who'd left countless purple welts all over her body through their past few years together before I came back from Switzerland. Since Papa had paid some serious money to White under the table, and the latter had tried dragging his feet with collecting evidence against him when my mother's car blew up to the sky in front of Wolfe's and my house, an internal, quiet investigation against White and Bishop took place, and the police chief and former governor were now on trial for receiving bribery and illegal campaign contributions from the infamous Arthur Rossi.

During the media coverage of the high-profile case, the person who kept coming up in the news as an example for good morals was my husband, who married into The Outfit yet made sure not to have anything to do with my father or his business.

I felt my husband's thumb swiping across my upper cheek as he wiped away a tear of joy from my eye. He chucked me under the chin, then grinned. He'd made his way over to me without my even noticing. I was too wrapped up in how fortunate we were. Joshua fussed in my arms, and the priest took a step back and smoothed back his thin and velvety dark hair.

"He was made with God's love," Father Spina commented.

My husband scoffed beside me. He wasn't big on God. Or people. He was big on me and our family. The priest stepped away, and my husband plastered his lips to my ear. "While you did call me god, he was not present during the conception."

I chuckled, holding Josh to my chest and breathing in his pure scent of new life, shuddering with intense joy coursing through my veins.

"Are you ready to take the little ones home? I think they need their sleep." My husband put a hand on my shoulder, our daughter fast asleep in the crook of his other arm. We decided to refrain from a big party after the baptism, seeing as our family was constantly in the news because of the trial.

"They're not the only ones. *I* could use some sleep, too," I murmured into my son's temple.

"Sterling and Clara can take care of Emmie and Josh while I ruin what's left of your innocence."

"I think you did a thorough job the first week we met." I wiggled my brows, and he burst out laughing, something he'd learned how to do slowly after we got back together. "Besides, don't you need to fly out to DC this evening?"

"Cancelled it."

"How come?"

"I'm in the mood for spending time with my family."

"Your country needs you," I teased.

"And I need *you*." He drew me into a hug, kids and all.

Ms. Sterling still lived with us even though she was given strict instructions to stop eavesdropping—a rule she was surprisingly good at following. Clara lived across the city in my mother's new house, but the two often helped with babysitting the kids together. Despite the fact my father was out of my life, I'd never felt more loved and protected by the people I cared about. And Wolfe was entering an important stage in his career. His time as senator would come to an end in less than two years.

"There's somewhere I want to take you tonight. Your pump is already packed and in the car." He chucked my chin. This was my life now. From cheating and fighting and tearing each other apart, we moved to a ritual that was so domestically blissful, I was sometimes terrified of how happy I was.

I am pink cotton candy at a fair, happy and bubbly and sweet. All fluff.

"Nothing says romance more than your husband packing your breast pump for you."

"There's always the alternative if you just keep your mind open." He was referring to our last visit to a restaurant, when I was so engorged, I had to lock myself in the bathroom to pump myself manually into the toilet. He very kindly offered to drink the wasted milk. I wasn't even sure he was entirely kidding.

"Our plan sounds cryptic." I arched an eyebrow.

"Perhaps, but it's fun." He took Joshua from me, securing him in his baby seat before opening the car door for me. I got my driver's license shortly after I'd moved back in with Wolfe. He was not the happiest to have me behind the wheel, or in a vehicle at all for that matter, while pregnant and at odds with my father. Too worried about the baby and me. But he also knew I needed my freedom.

After taking a lengthy nap, I slipped into an elegant red dress. Wolfe drove us to Little Italy with Clara and Sterling staying with the kids. I wore matching matte red lipstick and a smile that didn't waver. Despite supporting my husband's ambitions, I couldn't deny my delight to hear he'd canceled his flight to DC to spend more time with us.

We stopped in front of our Italian restaurant, Pasta Bella, and I unbuckled, about to get out. My husband had purchased Mama's Pizza not too long after my father had been convicted of attempted murder. He gutted and refurbished it, liquidating the dark memories the walls and cracks inside it harbored. It was just another dinner date, then. Nice and cozy. A chance to unwind and maybe drink a glass of wine. Wolfe put a hand on my thigh.

"Confession time."

"We *just* left the church, Wolfe."

"The only person I owe an explanation to is you."

"Tell me." I smiled.

"Angelo is about to announce his engagement to a girl he met at the accounting firm he works at." Wolfe ran his fingers along my arm, cocking his head in the restaurant's direction. "He's a little tight on money, so he reached out to ask if he could have it here. I said yes. My ulterior motive? I know that you've been feeling a little guilty, so I wanted you to see that he is fine."

My lips fell open in shock.

In the months and years after I found out that I was pregnant with Emmie, I often agonized over the fact that Angelo hadn't moved on. He didn't have a girlfriend or date anyone seriously. Shortly before he got his master's degree, his father's accounting firm shut down after the IRS had found that they'd been laundering money for The Outfit in the millions. Mike Bandini was firmly tucked away in prison now, serving twenty years. Angelo was still on good terms with his parents from what my mother had told me—he certainly took care of his mama and brothers—but he had officially cut all ties with The Outfit. It had been months since I'd asked Mama about him, and I guess he'd finally found someone.

Wolfe stared at me, trying to gauge my reaction. I could tell he didn't want to upset me, but I could also tell that he really wanted me not to have an overemotional reaction one way or the other. Angelo was, and always would be, a sensitive subject in our marriage. I sliced him open by kissing Angelo in front of the entire world. He forgave, but I couldn't expect him to forget.

I cracked a smile, yanking my husband into a hug.

"Thank you. That makes me so happy for him. And for me, too."

"God, you're perfect," my husband muttered, sealing our conversation with a kiss. "I took you hoping for vengeance. I never thought I'd receive something so much more powerful. Love."

He got out, rounded the car, and opened the door for me. Together, we walked into Pasta Bella, hand in hand. The only person I hadn't thought about today, as nostalgia flooded me, was Kristen Rhys, the woman who orchestrated two of the worst days of my life. I knew we wouldn't be bumping into her. After she cornered me at school, Wolfe had finally picked up the phone and answered her. He helped her find a job in Alaska, then proceeded to make her sign a contract more restricting than a restraining order. Rhys was not to return to the state of Illinois and seek us out. She gave him her word that she was done messing with our family.

"What are you thinking about?" my husband asked as he pushed the door to the restaurant open. Buttery, liquid light enveloped us immediately, candles and red tablecloths and rich wood everywhere. The place was packed, and among the bobbing heads and laughter, I found Angelo, his arm draped over the shoulder of a beautiful girl with long black hair and slanted eyes. We walked toward them.

"I'm thinking about how happy you make me," I said, frankly.

We stopped two feet from Angelo.

He turned around and smiled at me, happiness shining from his blue, ocean eyes.

"We made it," I whispered. "Apart."

"You look beautiful, Francesca Rossi." Angelo pulled me by the collar for a slow, suffocating hug, whispering in my ear. "But not as beautiful as my future wife."

Wolfe

Six Years After

I watched my wife from what used to be her bedroom window many, many years ago, my hand caressing the wooden box where Emmeline—it was her room now—kept all her seashells. Francesca and I had agreed early into parenthood that we didn't want to continue her family tradition of the notes. Too much pressure and confusion.

My eyes followed my wife as she said goodbye to her favorite vegetable garden that she had tended to for over a decade with Josh and Emmeline hugging each of her hips and little Christian in her arms. Sterling was there, too, rubbing my wife's shoulder with a smile.

Later on tonight, we were going to board a plane that would take us to DC. I was going to start serving my country the way I'd dreamed about since I was an orphan—as the president of the United States.

We had dreams to chase, a country to serve, and a lifetime to love each other more fiercely and strongly than we did the last year. But as I looked down at her, I knew, without a shadow of a doubt, that my decision to steal her under the starless Chicago sky ten years ago was the best choice I'd made.

I loved my country ferociously.

I loved my wife more.

THE END

ACKNOWLEDGEMENTS

They say it takes a village to raise a kid and write a book. In our fast-paced indie world, it sometimes feels like it takes a whole city. Maybe even country. Finding your tribe is essential, and makes taking this journey more pleasant and less…well, frightening.

I would like to begin by thanking Becca Hensley Mysoor and Ava Harrison for the daily phone calls—I talked your ears off. Thanks for listening and making Wolfe and Francesca everything I needed them to be. And to my beta readers, Tijuana Turner (x2,000,000 times), Sarah Grim Sentz, Lana Kart, Amy Halter and Melissa Panio-Petersen. You ladies always leave a piece of your soul with my manuscripts.

At this point of the acknowledgements, I have yet to send it to my besties, Helena Hunting and Charleigh Rose, but chances are, by the time this is out, they've read it a thousand times over and listened to my freak-outs for hours on end. Thank you (and sorry).

To Elaine York and Jenny Sims for the fabulous editing: You guys are the real MVPs. Thank you for always being there when I need you. And to my fabulous, glorious, GODDESS (yes, all caps) designer, Letitia Hasser at RBA Designs. I wanted something unique and pretty and eye-catching. You delivered. In spades.

To my formatter, Stacey Blake at Champagne Formatting, who has the ability to make everything SO pretty. Also, huge thanks to my agent, Kimberly Brower at Brower Literary.

Finally, I would like to thank my husband and son and parents and brother (and my soon-to-be sister-in-law!) for loving me almost as much as I love them. And of course, to my street team, my second family (taking a deep breath to make sure I don't leave anyone out): Lin Tahel Cohen, Avivit Egev, Galit Shmaryahoo, Vanessa Villegas, Nadine (Bookaddict), Sher Mason, Kristina Lindsey, Brittany Danielle Christina, Summer Connell, Nina Delfs, Betty Lankovits, Vanessa Serrano, Yamina Kirky, Ratula Roy, Tricia Daniels, Jacquie Czech Martin, Lisa Morgan, Sophie Broughton, Leeann Van Roseburg, Luciana Grisolia, Chele Walker, Ariadna Basulto, Tanaka Kangara, Vickie Leaf, Hayfaah Sumtally, Samantha Blundell, Aurora Hale, Erica Budd Panfile, Sheena Taylor, Keri Roth, Amanda Söderlund, and I'm pretty sure I left a few people out because I always do (but never on purpose).

Oh, and to the Sassy Sparrows, my fierce reading group! How I love you, my quick-witted, supportive, good-hearted allies.

And to you, my readers, for taking a chance on my books. It would mean the world to me if you could take a few seconds of your time to leave an honest review and tell me what you thought about The Kiss Thief.

Love and kisses,

L.J. Shen

STAY CONNECTED

Contact L.J. Shen on Social Media

Facebook: facebook.com/authorljshen

Instagram: Instagram.com/authorljshen

TikTok: tiktok.com/@authorljshen

Website: authorljshen.com

He just wanted a decent book to read ...

Not too much to ask, is it? It was in 1935 when Allen Lane, Managing Director of Bodley Head Publishers, stood on a platform at Exeter railway station looking for something good to read on his journey back to London. His choice was limited to popular magazines and poor-quality paperbacks – the same choice faced every day by the vast majority of readers, few of whom could afford hardbacks. Lane's disappointment and subsequent anger at the range of books generally available led him to found a company – and change the world.

'We believed in the existence in this country of a vast reading public for intelligent books at a low price, and staked everything on it'
Sir Allen Lane, 1902–1970, founder of Penguin Books

The quality paperback had arrived – and not just in bookshops. Lane was adamant that his Penguins should appear in chain stores and tobacconists, and should cost no more than a packet of cigarettes.

Reading habits (and cigarette prices) have changed since 1935, but Penguin still believes in publishing the best books for everybody to enjoy. We still believe that good design costs no more than bad design, and we still believe that quality books published passionately and responsibly make the world a better place.

So wherever you see the little bird – whether it's on a piece of prize-winning literary fiction or a celebrity autobiography, political tour de force or historical masterpiece, a serial-killer thriller, reference book, world classic or a piece of pure escapism – you can bet that it represents the very best that the genre has to offer.

Whatever you like to read – trust Penguin.